Mysterious Origins
The Chronicles of Joshua White
Book One

JD Tennyson

Copyright © JD Tennyson 2023

First Edition

For my beautiful wife Chelsea, without whose love and encouragement this novel would not have been possible. I love you babe xx

For my mum Julie, whose help finding issues with the story was indispensable and who has constantly believed in me. Love you mum xx

Contents

Map of Antanel

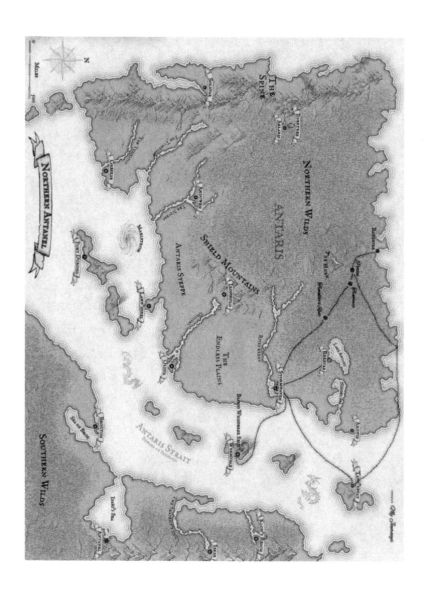

Prologue

I reached for the golf club my dad kept by the door frame, *'every caveman needs a club'*, he'd said, any excuse for a bad joke. Tiptoeing, weapon at the ready, I advanced through the hallway whilst avoiding the increasing amount of blood. I knew there was no stopping it, so instead I braced for what was to come. At first, it was just the earthy, coppery tang of blood, which wasn't particularly unpleasant. But, as I grew closer, the smell quickly changed to one so foul and cloying, that I started to retch involuntarily. Holding my nose to avoid the smell, I looked down at the bloody footprints that led from the kitchen. For the life of me, I don't think I will ever understand why I'd thought it was a good idea to go in. Nevertheless, I once again pushed open the kitchen door and fell, vomiting, to my knees.

The scene never changes; a gruesome tableau torn straight from a B-rate slasher movie. My parent's heads were sat on the breakfast bar, their bodies nailed to the wall in some gross parody of the crucifixion. The word 'Traitors' and the numerals '11' were scrawled in blood, a strange symbol carved into the wall between them. In the years since I'd tried to find what the symbol or writing meant, but despite countless online searches and even trips to local libraries, I'd never had any success. It remained a mystery, occasionally haunting my nights.

I dragged myself to my feet, closing my eyes in a futile attempt to hide from what I'd seen. Now I wish I could open them a little longer, to spot a missed detail, another clue. But

I was just a passenger, a witness to replays of the same old nightmare, I didn't look and so my eyes wouldn't open. Stumbling back into the hallway I finally opened my eyes and followed the footprints upstairs, no, Gods no! Clambering up the stairs, I burst into George's room.

The shock of seeing his small body, throat opened, with his precious games console clutched protectively to his chest, it…it still breaks me every time. I don't know how long I was curled up on the floor at that point as even the memory is fuzzy. It could have been minutes or hours as I drifted in and out of lucidity, my then ten-year-old self completely overwhelmed with shock. My mind jolted back into clarity, and I knew it was because I'd thought about my older sister, but I wouldn't get up to check. I was glued to the floor, unable to bear what I might find. I willed myself to rise with every ounce of my being, but it always ended the same, with me cursing the weakness of my younger self. I took out my phone and dialled, nine, nine, nine. I tried to talk, but I couldn't breathe. Tears blinding me, I finally choked out, "Help me, please." Then darkness claimed me.

Chapter 1

I awoke from my latest nightmare with a jolt, but the experience had become so familiar that I quickly shrugged it off and got ready for school. As usual, the Taylors had already left for work, and so whilst chowing down on some cereal, I was uninterrupted as I carried out my standard morning routine. Logging on to my laptop, I first checked for any news about my sister. Once again there was nothing, other than the original news stories. It was a relief in a way, as at least her body hadn't been found, although, I'd like to think the police would have contacted me before it ended up online anyway. I then checked her Facebook profile for any sign of activity, the last post was six years ago. No change there either. I knew it was a longshot, but you never know.

An older couple in their fifties, I had been with the Taylors for nearly two years, and it is fair to say that they literally changed my life. After that day occurred, I spent several weeks hospitalised, followed by regular visits to 'shrinks' and years bouncing between various foster families. The winning combination of grieving for my family, not knowing what happened to my big sister, and being constantly rejected by foster parents had left me depressed, angry and increasingly hard to deal with. Add to that the normal pubescent mood swings and the regular nightmares, and I was a winning package that no one could cope with for long. I was stuck in a downward spiral that I had struggled to break.

Eventually, after four long years of chaos, I was finally placed with the Taylors. They were never able to have children of their own and so instead have taken in several 'special case' foster-kids over the years. Within just a few months with them, I found myself happy for the first time in a long while, my moods started to stabilise and in turn the nightmares reduced in frequency. My life had turned a corner, I studied hard and was even predicted to achieve great grades in my GCSEs. Looking back, I guess I just needed some unconditional love and support; to know that someone cared more for me than the fostering payments.

Not wanting to be late, I quickly packed my bag with my laptop and the lunch that mum Taylor had left for me and headed out for school. It is only a fifteen-minute walk and I usually met up with my best friend Mikey on the way. However, as I turned around from locking the front door, I was intercepted by a well-dressed man who approached me from the roadside.

"I apologise that it has taken me so long to visit, my condolences for your loss, Master Joshua," he said.

"Thank you for your concern, but I'm afraid I'm not interested in giving interviews." I gave my usual reply, attempting to walk around him.

It wasn't a regular occurrence, but enough journalists or true-crime writers had tracked me down over the years that I'd gotten quite good at dealing with them, the trick was to be polite but firm.

He stepped back in front me. "Forgive me, Master Joshua! I fear I have given you the wrong impression, I'm not a journalist, my name is Felix Aldridge. I have served your family for many years, I'm here to take you home."

I started to get a little angry, as a lunatic making me late for school was just what I needed. "Served my family? I think I would have noticed you! Now, I don't want to be late, so please get out of my way."

He stepped aside. "Not your adoptive family, Master Joshua, your biological one."

I stopped dead in my tracks, confused by what he meant. "The Taylors haven't adopted me, they are just fostering me."

"Ah, I didn't mean the Taylors, Master Joshua, I was referring to the Wilkins. Awfully good people, that's why they were chosen to take you in, they raised you well and were fully aware of the risk."

My head was spinning, adopted by the Wilkins? Risk? "Firstly, I wasn't adopted, secondly, risk? Are you insinuating I was responsible for the murder of my family? I don't know what game you're fucking playing, but I'm not impressed!"

His reserved façade finally cracked, he looked tired and forlorn. "No, please forgive me, I wasn't implying you were responsible. It seems I've made rather a mess of things. But I can assure you, that you were adopted by the Wilkins. When you are ready to talk, Master Joshua, call me." He held out a business card.

The look on his face completely deflated my anger, if anything, he looked like he was suffering too. Managing a nod, I took the proffered card, then watched as he bowed and walked away.

I racked my memories for any hints that I may have been adopted but drew a blank. If he wasn't just a nutter or lying for whatever reason, then maybe mum and dad wanted to wait until I was older before telling me? Growing increasingly frustrated at yet another mystery in my life, I quickly carried on with my walk to school.

Seeing Mikey waving from the end of the road I walked over to him, and we gave our customary 'fist-bump'. At five-foot-nine, Mikey was far shorter than my height of six-foot-three, although, in all fairness, most people are shorter than me. I met Mikey on day one when I transferred to St Mary's high school, and we hit it off straight away. His West-Indian heritage on his dad's side, means he is able to wear his hair in a truly epic 'afro', and he always carries himself with an effortless swagger. Mikey is loud, confident, and everyone seems to love his combination of good looks and roguish charm, but most importantly he has a big heart and I counted myself truly lucky to have such a best friend.

It is also largely thanks to Mikey's popularity that I have had it easier at this school than in previous ones. My size and generally reserved nature had often caused boys to want to fight me. It was nothing needlessly cruel, more the typical testosterone-fuelled 'prove how manly I am by fighting the big kid' kind of way. Unfortunately, with the anger issues I was having at the time, many of them ended up in a pretty bad way and I inevitably got the blame despite just wanting to be left alone, oh well, they got what they deserved. Mikey is aware of my past, but he knows I don't like to talk about it, so being the good friend he is, he never brings it up.

We were walking in companionable silence when Mikey suddenly asked, "What's the matter bruv?"

"Nothing, why'd you ask?"

He looked at me with a smile. "If you don't want to talk about it, that's cool, you just seem quieter than normal is all."

Sometimes Mikey's easy-going nature makes me forget just how perceptive he can be. I told him all about the strange old geezer who approached me and how he suggested I was adopted.

"Whoa, that's pretty heavy, as if you need any more drama in your life! What're you going to do about it?" he asked.

I thought about it and realised that I didn't really know. "I'm not sure, it's all a bit much."

"Well, if you ever need to talk, you know I'm here."
"I know, cheers, brothers for life," I said and raised my fist for another bump.

Chapter 2

St Mary's is a massive red-brick monstrosity with over one-hundred years of history, many of those during a time when kids would have been beaten for misbehaving, or even for just writing with their left hands. The thought gave me the creeps, but all of that was quickly forgotten as I stepped through the oversized school doors and spotted Eleanor. She is super cute, and everyone adores her, myself included. Although, I'm always bewildered why she is with Damon; she is so nice to everyone and he's a jerk. That's not just me being jealous, well, maybe a little, but he is an arse and always picks on others when Eleanor isn't around to see. She caught me gazing at her and smiled at me, which made my morning. I waved and returned the smile, only then realising that Damon had noticed our interaction. From the scowl he gave me I knew there was going to be trouble.

"Damon's glaring daggers at you," Mikey said, looking a little concerned.

"Whatever, just ignore him."

Mikey laughed. "Fair enough, just don't wind him up, he's a bit of a nutter."

"I'm not scared of Damon," I said.

Mikey shook his head. "Fair enough, well, I'm off to class, see you at lunch." He waved and swaggered off down the corridor.

I smiled and waved him off, thinking how much it sucks that we didn't take the same subjects. Mikey elected for computer science and a few others, whereas I went the humanities route: history, classical civilisation, and religious studies. So, the only ones we share are the core subjects, like Maths and English.

Hustling to make it to class before the bell, I turned a corner and nearly ploughed straight into Damon, who was blocking my way past with one of his buddies.

Damon looked up at me whilst trying to be as intimidating as he could. "Who do ya think you are? Ya giant freak. I ever see you looking at my girl again and I'll fuck you up!"

I glanced at my watch; these idiots were going to make me late. "One, I can smile at whomever I want, two, you are going to make me late now get out of my way," I said, barging through them both.

"I'll be waiting for ya after school, let's see how tough you are then. Ya lanky fuck." I heard from behind me as I entered the classroom.

Like I said, the guy's a jerk.

After the morning's lessons were over, I made my way to the cafeteria to meet up with Mikey and noticed that many of the students were glancing over at me. Most likely rumours of Damon's threat had already made the school grapevine. Noticing Mikey waving at me, I walked over and sat down opposite him.

"What is wrong with you?" he hissed, looking rather agitated.

Taking out my lunch out, I started to talk whilst we ate, "I take it this is about Damon?"

He looked incredulous. "Of course it's about Damon, the whole school's talking about it, he's been telling everyone about how he is going to kick your arse in the field after school."

"It's ok, just ignore him, I am." I tried to reassure him.

"It's not ok, you know he trains in MMA? He's beat up loads of lads in the school, that is why everyone's scared of him. I know you're a big guy but." He leant in. "I've heard

8

he even went to fight kids from other schools, just to prove he's the hardest in the year."

I started laughing at Damon doing something so ridiculous and nearly choked on my sandwich. "Don't worry man, just trust me, it will be fine."

Finally, Mikey realised I genuinely wasn't worried and started to relax. "I do trust you bruv, if you say it's fine, I believe you, but you're crazy, just saying."

I looked over to the cafeteria entrance and noticed Damon and his goons making their way over to our table. Everyone sitting near us quickly picked up their stuff and moved to different tables, clearly not wanting to get caught up in the situation.

"Oh look, it's Giganticus and his boyfriend!" Damon said, loud enough for pretty much everyone to hear.

"Oh look, the pathetic little bully is making homophobic comments, no surprise there," I replied equally loud.

Damon's face turned scarlet, clearly, he wasn't used to anyone standing up to him, most bullies aren't. "Just you wait, you'll get it later, I'll be waiting for ya in the field after school, not that you'll turn up, all talk you are, I bet. Pussy!"

"You know I walk through the field on my way home, why would I avoid it? Because of you? Don't flatter yourself Damon."

"I've taken out plenty bigger than you, freak, you'll see." Damon stormed off with his cronies following him.

Mikey was looking a little pale. "That could have gone better, why'd you have to antagonise him?"

I was happy that he was so concerned for me, but I knew he'd soon find out he didn't have to be. "Because I've no time for people that hurt others for their own amusement. I'm generally an easy-going guy, you know that, but I won't be bullied, not a fucking chance."

After lunch the rest of the school day carried on as normal, but as I was leaving my final lesson of the day, I was stopped by my history teacher, Mr Bradbury, who asked if he could have a quick word with me.

"Josh, the faculty aren't ignorant to the rumours floating around. Damon's a dangerous child and unfortunately, he often gets off lightly for things because he is from an equally dangerous family, do you understand?" he said, the concern on his face evident.

"It's ok Mr Bradbury, don't worry, I'll be fine." I tried to reassure him.

"If you want, you can hang around for a bit and I could give you a lift?"

The offer was touching, as he was clearly worried about me. "That's very kind of you, sir, but I think I'm just going to walk," I said.

"Ok, but be careful, and if you need to, you run, ok?"

"Don't worry, I'm not stupid, if I find myself in danger, I have no trouble running. See you tomorrow, sir."

Outside of the school a panicked looking Mikey was waiting for me and as we came to the field, a large group of students had congregated, no doubt waiting for a spectacle. I found the whole scene depressing, as I swear no matter how civilised we think we are; it wouldn't take much for us to go all 'Lord of the Flies'.

I should probably explain why I was so calm; you see not only am I quite tall, I'm also abnormally strong and fast. I couldn't tell you why, as it's all a bit strange, but by the age of eight I was already stronger and faster than my fully-grown father. Now, at sixteen, I am so strong and fast that I don't even partake in sports for fear that I will be whisked away to some secret government lab. So, Damon was largely an annoyance rather than something to fear.

The crowd parted to allow us through, and you could feel their excitement, the bunch of savages. Finally, I saw Damon and his 'henchman' waiting ahead of us, he was arguing with Eleanor, who screamed at him and then headed towards Mikey and me.

"I thought you were a good guy Josh, it turns out you are just a thug too," she said, the disappointment plain on her face.

"Your boyfriend is a cruel and spiteful bully, Eleanor."

Ellie looked at me as if she was ashamed of me. "And the answer to that is to come and fight him? Go straight to violence?"

"Who said I came here to fight him? I'm just walking home from school with my friend, I always walk this way," I said.

"But you knew he would be here, the whole bloody school knew, you could have gone any other way." She easily picked apart my thin defence.

I knew that she was just worried about me, but Ellie would have been worried about anyone getting hurt as it was just the sort of person she was, and I needed her to understand that I wasn't the sort of person that allowed himself to be pushed around. "Why? I'm not changing my route out of fear of him, besides, the whole thing's absurd. I mean who threatens to beat someone up for just smiling at their girlfriend? I just planned on ignoring him, he's not worth my time."

Damon stalked towards me, cracking his knuckles. "You think you can just ignore me and I'll go away? I'm gonna kick your arse."

His cronies were cheering him on, urging him to do something stupid.

"Go away Damon, I'm going home, you're not qualified to be my opponent," I said and tried to walk off.

In hindsight, belittling him was stupid, and I probably should have just kept ignoring him, although I doubt it would have made a difference anyway. Obviously, my comment just inflamed him, and he stormed towards me. Squaring up to me, he attempted to push me, but I didn't budge, and he only succeeded in pushing himself backwards, the shock on his face readily apparent.

Raising one eyebrow, I looked at him disdainfully, it was getting harder to control my anger. "Are we done here?"

"I say when we're done!" He threw a left jab at my face.

I moved my head out of the way and Damon became frustrated, immediately launching into a flurry of punches. I easily swayed out of the way of most, blocking those I couldn't avoid with the palms of my hands. He did have some skill and it was obvious that he was well trained, if I wasn't so abnormal, I would have probably been in a pretty bad state. Failing to land a solid blow, eventually Damon stepped back in an attempt to catch his breath.

"Is that all you can do? Dodge? You're a pussy!" he said and attempted a takedown on me.

I grabbed his arms, spun him around and lifted him up by his biceps. Chuckling, I just held him there off the ground whilst he flailed around like an angry toddler.

Glancing around, I noticed that everyone was looking at us incredulously, and I realised I shouldn't have made it look so effortless. Some students were even filming it on their phones, so I decided it was time to call a quick end to the show and tossed him to the ground. "We are done here Damon, go home."

His friends helped him up off the ground and looked at each other. I could tell what they were thinking; should they all gang up on me? I decided to nip that idea in the bud. "Don't, it won't work, I'm not going to stand here like a punchbag, if you attack me together, I will start hitting back and it won't end well for you."

They looked unsure, but as they started to back off, it became clear they thought it wasn't worth the risk.

Damon was enraged, his face contorted in a mixture of anger and embarrassment. "This ain't over cunt, you're a dead man, a fucking dead man!" he said, as he backed his way out through the surrounding students.

Everyone started cheering as they left, but I just ignored them, I didn't need the appreciation of people who'd only come expecting to see me end up in a bloody mess. Instead, I just walked back to Mikey, who was quietly waiting at the side with Eleanor.

Eleanor looked at me as if I was a mystery she was trying to solve. "I don't know how you did that, but thanks for not beating him up, I'm sorry for calling you a thug," she said with a smile.

Smiling back, I shrugged. "It's not a big deal, I wasn't in any danger, so what would be the point in wailing on him? That'd just make me the bully. See you in school tomorrow?"

She blushed a little at my question, which I took as a great sign, then gave me a little nod and wandered off to her girlfriends.

Mikey was looking at me like I was a complete stranger. "What are you?" he asked.

"I'm me, same me I was half-an-hour ago, come on let's go." I chuckled.

Everyone else was slowly dispersing and giving me a large berth, occasionally I received friendly nods, probably from Damon's previous victims, and I so nodded back. Perhaps I had been a bit harsh about some of their motives for being there, maybe some of them just hoped to see Damon get a little of his own medicine. Admittedly, I was concerned about the videos, as they were blatantly going to end up online, but there was nothing I could do about it.

Chapter 3

The first few days after the scuffle had been weird, as the story quickly spread around the school as any notable event does and, unfortunately, the video helped it gain a lot of traction, with random groups often gathered around a phone and laughing whilst watching it. As a result, I had seen a sharp increase in both my popularity and the number of wary looks I received. A situation that wasn't helped by the fact that Damon was a massive prick and lots of the other students had loved seeing him embarrassed, in fact, it had been nearly a week and Damon still hadn't shown his face!

Luckily, the combination of keeping my head down and the addition of a newer story to the endless drama of the high school grapevine, and I was allowed to fade once again into relative obscurity. Although, perhaps not so lucky for the group of year tens who were caught smoking pot behind the bike-sheds, taking my place as the talk of the school.

Waiting for Mikey at our usual spot, I tried messaging him once again. When a few minutes passed and I still hadn't received a reply, I began to worry a little as he hadn't told me he was going to be late or off school, plus Mikey had always replied quickly to messages. But it was already quarter-past-eight, and I didn't want to be late, so, reluctantly, I headed off to school, hoping to catch up with him there.

Eleanor was stood outside the gates when I arrived and I assumed she was waiting for me, as we had been

14

spending a lot of time together following the incident with Damon and our friendship was gradually blossoming into something more.

As I got closer to Ellie, I realised that she looked fairly agitated, and I sped up a little to see what was wrong.

"Wh—" I attempted to ask.

"Damon's back at school," she said, interrupting me.

I'm not sure whether it was the news about Damon making me keen to establish where we stood, or simply because she was just so beautiful, but I found myself reaching out and taking her hands in mine. Ellie looked unsure at first but quickly smiled and relaxed as I pulled her into my arms. Looking down at her, I was filled with the overwhelming desire to kiss her and as she slowly tilted her head back and closed her eyes, it became obvious that she wanted it too and I gently pressed my lips to hers. Her lips were soft, with just a hint of cherry lip balm.

"Well, that's possibly the best start to a school day I've ever had," I said, breaking off from the kiss.

Ellie mock glared at me. "I'm serious Josh, you distracted me." She gently hit me on the chest. "Damon's back, what should we do?"

"Was he being a dick?"

Ellie shook her head. "No, not at all, he didn't really say much, just apologised and left."

"Weird," I said, unsure about his out of character behaviour. "So, are we together now?"

Ellie pressed herself against me and kissed me firmly on the lips. "Does that answer your question?"

I think the big dopey grin on my face was all the answer she needed.

I pretty much floated through the morning, caught up in the joy of our budding relationship, but when lunch time came around and I still hadn't seen Mikey, I was hit with a sudden surge of guilt. I had been so lost in the joy of my new relationship, that I had completely neglected to worry about my best friend.

"I'm worried about Mikey, he's not responded to any of my messages, it's not like him," I said to Ellie.

"Maybe you could ask at the office, see if the school knows anything?"

"Yeah, that's…" I said, before stopping in shock as Damon appeared at our table and sat down opposite us.

"Don't mind me," he mumbled over a mouthful of food.

"What do you want, Damon?" I asked.

"Just enjoying ma lunch, I see ya didn't waste any time enjoying my used goods." He gestured at Ellie with his fork.

I started to clench my fist, I didn't mind him insulting me, but there was no fucking way I would tolerate him talking about Ellie like that.

Ellie placed her hand on my thigh, gently squeezing it. "Just ignore him, Josh, he's not worth it," she said, her words quickly diffusing my growing rage.

"Yeah, you're right." I smiled at her. "Fuck off and bother someone else Damon."

"Fair enough," he said, rising to his feet.

Ellie and I looked at each other, and I could see she was just as confused as I was about his sudden change in attitude.

"Weird though ain't it? Seeing ya without ya shadow, I hope he's okay." He grinned savagely at us before strolling off whilst whistling.

He knew something, he fucking knew something! If it wasn't for Ellie tightening her grip on my leg, I would have probably leapt over the table and shook the information out of him. Instead, I found myself almost hyper-ventilating with the effort of controlling myself.

"Leave it Josh," Ellie said, pulling my face around to look at her. "Let's go to the office and see if they know anything."

"Less than a day and I already don't know what I'd do without you." I rested my forehead against hers.

"Probably something stupid, but you're a boy, so it's not entirely your fault." Ellie laughed. "Now let's go see what we can find out about Mikey."

Mrs Gumbel, the school receptionist was happily typing away on her computer when we approached.

"Two secs, Joshua," she said, tap-tapping away until she reached a convenient place to stop. "Sorry about that, didn't want to lose my chain of thought, how are you holding up?"

"It's fine." I waved off her apology. "I'm pretty good, I just wondered if you could do me a small favour?"

Mrs Gumbel looked at me strangely. "I thought that, well, never mind, I guess we all process things differently. What do you need?"

I was starting to get a horrible feeling in the pit of my stomach. "I haven't been able to reach Mikey all day and I'm a bit worried about him, I don't suppose you know why he's not at school?" I asked, already dreading the answer.

"Oh, deary me! Has no one told you?" she gasped. "I'm so sorry you have to find out like this sweetie, but Mikey was in an accident. He's currently in the ICU at East Surrey hospital."

Even though I'd been expecting the worse, I still felt the colour drain from my face. "Is he okay?" I managed to croak out, using her desk to steady myself.

Mrs Gumbel patted my hand sympathetically. "I'm sorry sweetie, but that's all I know."

"I need to go and check on him," I said.

"Just go, I will let your teachers know why you are absent."

I smiled at her. "Thank you, Mrs Gumbel."

"Would you like me to come too?" Ellie asked.

Looking at Ellie made me feel so guilty, I had been floating around like a lovestruck puppy whilst my best friend had been potentially fighting for his life. "No, it's fine, I'll call you as soon as I know what's happening," I said, knowing full well that my guilt wasn't Ellie's fault, but still needing some time on my own to process things.

"You don't have to go through this alone, I'm here for you," Ellie said, stroking my face.

"I know, I'll call you later." I gave her a quick kiss goodbye and made my way out of the school.

*****

According to Google maps, East Surrey hospital is only a couple of miles from St Mary's, easily a distance I could run without any issue, so run I did, at a pace that would put an Olympic sprinter to shame, only stopping for the occasional glance at my phone to ensure I remained heading in the right direction. When I got within a mile, I switched to following the road signs that had appeared and all things considered, I'm pretty sure I couldn't have made it to the hospital much quicker in a car.

East Surrey hospital itself is a series of relatively modern buildings, but when I arrived outside the main entrance, I couldn't help noticing how much it resembled a petrol station forecourt. Entering the building, I quickly located a map upon the wall, and, rather oddly, found the sections were assigned colours rather than names, but I found the ICU easily enough, purple, first floor, bingo!

Unfortunately, when I arrived at the ICU, I found out that visiting hours were between two and seven pm, and I had an hour to kill before they would let me in. Left to my own devices whilst I waited, I found myself wondering how Damon knew about Mikey, as from his suggestive comments, I was pretty-much fucking certain that he did, in fact I bet the only reason he returned to school was to see my face when I found out about Mikey. That would definitely explain his out of character behaviour; he was enjoying himself. Ultimately though, I couldn't really hold that against him as I had embarrassed him pretty badly and anyone would want a little revenge for that. However, if I find out he had anything to do with causing Mikey's injuries, neither gods nor men would save him from my retribution.

Once again, I could feel an almost uncontrollable rage growing and I swear I was growing physically hotter, with rivulets of sweat running all down me. I was now sure something was wrong with me, I'm never so quick to anger, and this rage didn't feel like regular anger, it was more raw, primal. Taking deep breaths to try and centre myself, I felt the rage slowly subsiding and used my sleeve to dry my sweaty face.

I realised I had something in my hand, it was the card Felix had given me, at some point I must have started twiddling with it. Strange.

"Joshua Wilkins." I suddenly heard, pulling my attention.

Looking over to the source of the voice, I saw one of the ICU nurses was staring at me concernedly. "Are you okay? You look a little peaky. We can't have you entering the ward if you're sick."

"Yeah, sorry, I'm good, just worn out from the run to the hospital," I said.

"You ran here?" she asked, the surprise evident on her face.

"Yeah, I found out about Mikey at school and wanted to get here as quick as I could, he's my best friend."

"Well, I have some good news for you, Mikey is stable and has been moved to high dependency, you are more than welcome to go and see him, he's awake."

I jumped straight to my feet. "Thank you so much, ma'am."

"Just try not to wear him out too much, he is stable, but it will still be a fair while until he is fully recovered, likely many months."

"I understand, thank you."

Mikey looked like shit! And was inclined on a bed with casts on his left arm and both legs. His face was swollen, with bruising around his cheeks and eyes, but I had no doubt they would look worse in the coming days as they fully developed. Fuck!

"Took you long enough," Mikey said as I entered.

"What happened?" I asked, happy that he couldn't be too badly injured if he was awake and talking.

"I got hit by a car."

"Did you forget the green cross code?" I couldn't help but joke, trying to lighten the mood a little.

"You're such a prick!" Mikey said, grunting as he chuckled. "No making me laugh, it hurts too much."

"Sorry," I said, grimacing at his obvious discomfort. "So, how did a car hit you?"

"That's the thing, I didn't even step into the road, I was waiting to cross and, wham! A black SUV just swerved into me on the pavement, it was crazy!"

"That's either some serious negligence, or…" I began.

"Or they did it on purpose," Mikey finished.

"Have you spoken to the police yet?"

"Nah, didn't wake up long ago, but they'll probably turn up at some point." He shrugged.

"What about your parents?"

"The hospital's tried to reach them, but they're on some Christian retreat with no phones, so it may take a while."

"Ah, fair enough. What did the driver look like?" I asked.

"Fuck me! What is this? Twenty questions? Are you the po-po now?" He smiled.

"Sorry bruv, I'm just curious and, well, fucking angry, the prick could have killed you!" I said.

"Okay, Okay. I dunno, he was white and had dark hair, that's about all I saw, it all happened so quickly."

"I'm sure Damon knew you were in here," I said.

"How?" he asked, clearly shocked.

"I don't know, and I'm fucking positive he had something to do with it." I argued.

Mikey looked at me sceptically. "It's a bit much though isn't it, like, I'm not denying the guy's a bell-end, but attempted murder seems a bit excessive, and over what, that fight? Nah, it's a bit far-fetched."

Mikey was right, and I even started to doubt it myself, maybe I was just projecting the whole thing onto him out of dislike. No! He fucking knew, that smarmy arse smile, he definitely knew somehow, and if he was actually responsible, I'd find out.

"Looks like I lost you there for a second bruv, you okay?"

"Asks the guy with nearly his whole body in a cast," I said, shaking my head incredulously.

"Yeah, well, not like I'm going anywhere, so go on, unload your burdens to me my child," he said in a mock priestly fashion.

It was funny, but it worked and so I did, that's one of the special things about Mikey, talking to him was just...easy. I told him everything, all about how I had finally gotten together with Ellie, which made him grin from ear-to-ear, how I was struggling with sudden bursts of rage and even how I couldn't stop thinking about the fact I was potentially adopted.

"Do you think maybe your anger is because you're scared? Like you want to know, but you're worried he's just a nutter and it'll all blow up in your face?"

I found myself smiling at his words, was it really that simple? Just fear of exposing myself to more heartbreak?

"Yeah, maybe you're right." I was forced to admit.

"Well, what are you going to do about it?"

"Dunno, I think I'll probably give him a call at some point, I guess I should find out if it's all nonsense or not."

"Sounds like you have a plan then."

"Yeah, thanks bruv, what would I do without you?"

"Probably just skulk around, being all broody and shit. Like some wannabe edgelord."

"You fucking twat!" I said but couldn't help but laugh with him. "Well, I better go, places to be, things to do and all that." I reached down and gave him the gentlest hug I could manage.

"Josh," Mikey called out as I was walking out of the room.

"Yeah?"

"Maybe leave the investigation to the police though, okay?"

"Sure." I smiled

"I'm serious Josh, please, promise me?" he said with a yawn, clearly still tired.

"Fine, I promise," I said, a little shocked about the seriousness of his tone. "Try and get some sleep, Bruv."

Mikey's eyes were shutting before I even left the room.

Chapter 4

Sitting on the park bench, I spun the business card between my fingers whilst staring at the screen of my phone. Fuck it, I refused to be a coward and punched in the number, waiting with bated breath as the phone began to ring.

"Hello, Felix Aldridge speaking."

"Ermm, hi, this is Josh, Josh Wilkins," I said, still a little unsure of whether I was doing the right thing or not.

The brief silence that followed seemed to last for aeons.

"Forgive me, Master Joshua, I am afraid you have caught me at a rather un-opportune time."

His voice sounded strained, and I swear I could hear an odd whooshing sound, followed by an explosion that, if it was loud to me, must have been horrendous for Felix.

"I can call at another time if it's inconvenient."

"No, not to worry, it's all taken care of now, Master Joshua," he said, but I swear I could hear him panting slightly.

"What was all that noise?"

"Just dealing with a rather troublesome pest infestation, spiders, nasty little things."

I was at a loss as to what sort of pest control could possibly result in those sorts of noises; it sounded like heavy artillery!

"I wanted to ask if you were serious? About me being adopted."

"I assure you, Master Joshua, I would never lie about such a thing."

"I…" I wasn't sure what else to say and started to feel a little awkward, perhaps I should have planned it out a little better.

"Would you perhaps like to meet? I would be happy to answer any questions you have to the best of my ability," Felix said, rescuing me from my tied tongue.

"Err, yeah, please, that would be great. I'm currently at Grange Park, do you know it?"

"Quite well, Master Joshua, allow me to briefly freshen up and I shall be with you in, let's say, hmm, twenty minutes should suffice. Is this acceptable?"

"Yeah, that sounds great, see you soon then."

"Jolly good, be with you soon."

Hanging up the phone, I was a mixture of roiling emotions, excitement and nervousness warring chief amongst them. Had I done the right thing? Or was I just playing into the hands of some posh nutjob? Fuck it, I wanted to find out either way, and he hadn't really given me any reason to worry. Well, unless he had actually been using a bazooka to kill off some spiders. I found myself laughing at the ludicrous notion, some of the tension finally leaving me as I did.

It was a pleasant day and so, whilst I waited for Felix to arrive, I took to watching some of the people in the park, it wasn't very busy, just a few joggers out for an afternoon run and the occasional mother with a pushchair. The sound of shrill laughter drew my attention to a small child, she was hurling monkey nuts onto the floor and clapping with glee whenever one of the braver squirrels ran off with one. The pure joy on the child's face over something so simple was amazing.

Unfortunately, her fun didn't last, interrupted as it was by a large Pit bull running out from behind a bush that started chasing the squirrels. As the squirrels fled up to sanctuary within the surrounding trees, the little girl turned her attention to the dog, wagging her finger and screeching,

"Bad doggy, bad, bad doggy." It was adorable, but when the dog realised that all its prey had disappeared, it turned its attention to the child.

Now, I know that contrary to popular belief, Pit bulls can be really good with children, but nevertheless, I quickly looked around to see if the dog's owner would make an appearance; no one was in sight. The child's mother also seemed completely fucking oblivious to the situation, lost as she was in a telephone conversation whilst gazing out over the ponds. I started to have a really bad feeling about the situation, quickly rising to my feet.

As I sped up towards them, the dog sunk down on its haunches, lips drawn back in a vicious snarl and I could instantly tell that the child had replaced the squirrels as its prey. Great waves of rage once again started to rise from within me, as I sprinted towards them, whilst the mother finally off her phone, turned at the dog's growl, the horror clear on her face.

Dog, mother, and me, all of us running for the same wide-eyed child, who stood frozen in terror as the dog bounded towards her. As it got nearer, I could feel greater strength welling up in me in as I desperately willed myself on, my feet sinking into the soft, muddy grass. Faster, faster, I had to be faster. I wasn't quick enough.

The dog launched itself onto the little girl, a whirlwind of snapping teeth and claws, latching on to the arm she had raised in a meagre attempt to protect herself. Everything seemed to slow down as the beast began to savagely shake its head, dragging the bawling girl to the ground. Until finally, as the animal let go of the girls arm to go for her face, I was there, hands grabbing the jaws of the dog as my momentum carried us both clear of the little girl.

The dog tried desperately to break free of my death grip, gnashing its teeth as it shook its head, its front paws tearing long strips out of my school uniform, but my rage had become all consuming. How dare a lowly dog, a filthy mutt, bare its teeth at me, attack me! I roared in outrage at such disrespect from the creature, my fingers sinking deep into its face. The dog's snarls turned into whimpers, but I didn't care, as lost in the crimson fugue, I revelled in its whines, and crushing its muzzle, tore its lower jaw clean off its face.

Dropping the now twitching dog to the floor, I roared my dominance to the sky, slowly coming out of the haze that had clouded my thoughts and poisoned my mind. Disoriented, I looked down at the corpse of the broken dog, and my blood-soaked hands, my god, what had I done? The girl! How is the girl?

Looking over, I saw the mother trying desperately to staunch the bleeding arm of the little girl who had grown deathly pale, clearly the dog had severed something important, likely an artery. Fuck! How to stop the bleeding? I remembered once watching a documentary about surviving in the wild, they had shown how to make splints and tourniquets out of plant fibres and sticks, but I didn't have time to fuck about stripping plants! I was however wearing a belt, so hoping it would be strong enough, I tore it off and rushed over.

"I need to tourniquet her arm; she's going to bleed out otherwise," I said to the panicking mother.

"Okay, please help her." She nodded desperately.

"This is probably going to hurt her, like really fucking hurt her," I said, "but if we don't do it, she may die."

Gritting her teeth, the woman nodded as she squeezed the girl tight in her arms. Looping the belt on her tiny arm, just above her elbow, I started to cinch it tight, grimacing at the girl's pain-filled wails. Finally, blood stopped leaking from her forearm, and I tied off the belt, thankful the girl had passed out, sparing her from further pain. I tore my jumper into strips, wrapping her arm to protect it as best I could and checked her pulse, it was steady, if a little weak.

Falling back onto my arse as the adrenaline started to leave my body, I looked at the mother. "We need to call an ambulance," I said, fumbling my phone out in my blood-soaked hands.

The mother didn't even acknowledge what I said, she just slowly rocked and stroked the little girl, and I worried she was going into shock. Wiping the blood from my fingers so I could use the touchscreen, I was about to start dialling, when a hand gently squeezed my shoulder! Looking around quickly in alarm, I instantly relaxed when I saw Felix's face.

"I would hold off on calling an ambulance, Master Joshua," he said, smiling reassuringly.

"But the little girl?" I asked, "She needs blood, surgery, and I'm pretty sure the mum is in shock." I started to panic; we didn't have time for this nonsense.

"Leave them to me," he said and stepped over to the mother and child.

Kneeling in front of them both, the mother glanced up at him, but Felix waved a hand past her face, and she instantly fell unconscious. Catching the mother as she toppled over, he gently lowered them both to the floor, before passing something onto the mouth of the sleeping child. Almost instantly, colour began to return to the child's face and she gave a few pained whimpers. Taking care not to wake her, he started to delicately remove the tourniquet I had just applied.

"She'll bleed out!" I whispered.

"No! She won't, Master Joshua," he said firmly, "you'll just have to trust me."

Trust him? I barely even knew him! But pretty sure he had no intention of murdering the girl, I bit my tongue and watched as he first unwound my makeshift bandages before proceeding to release the belt. I shuffled over to get a better look and was completely gobsmacked, as where previously there had been a savage wound, only unblemished skin remained.

"Wha…how?" I mumbled.

"All in good time, all in good time." He patted my hand.

The sound of heavy footsteps interrupted my questioning, and I looked over to see a rough looking guy in grey trackies and a wife-beater run over to the mangled dog. Dropping to his knees, he looked over to us with his face contorted in anger.

"What the fuck did you to my dog?" he shouted at us.

This prick nearly let his dog maul a small child to death, and he had the audacity to shout at me! I started to feel the tell-tale rage building again, and although it wasn't nearly as strong as last time, I still found myself rising under the instinctive compulsion to tear the fucker apart. I was stopped as Felix placed a hand firmly on my shoulder, and as much as I tried, I couldn't stand up, it was like trying to lift a mountain, and I began to growl in frustration.

"That's quite enough of that, Master Joshua," Felix said, waving his free hand past my face.

Chapter 5

Opening my eyes, I found myself sprawled across the back seats of a car, and from the rumbling purr of the engine and distinct smell of old leather, probably a vintage model. I wasn't restrained in any way, so, more curious than alarmed, I pushed myself up into a seated position, and rubbed my eyes in attempt to wipe away the last vestige of sleepiness. Dropping my hands, I saw it was Felix driving, his eyes looking at me in the rear-view mirror.

"Welcome back to the land of the living, Master Joshua."

I thought back to the last thing I remembered…the dog owner, I was about to ruin his day!

"How did I get here? What happened?" I reeled off.

"I'm afraid you were about to do something rather regrettable, so I was forced to intervene."

"You put me to sleep, like the mother and child?" I ventured, more as a statement than a real question.

"I'm afraid so, Master Joshua, but I had little choice."

I got a brief flashback of what I'd wanted to do the man, damn! As much as it pained me to admit, he was probably right, I hadn't been in my right mind.

"You also healed the girl!" I suddenly remembered. "How?"

Felix chuckled at my question. "The same way I incapacitated you, magic."

"Magic he say's! That's a good one!" I laughed.

Felix wasn't laughing, his gaze was serious and almost sympathetic.

"Wait, you're being serious?" I asked incredulously.

"Deadly serious, Master Joshua. From the scene in the park, I assume you have recently had some...anger management issues?"

I thought about the rage that had overcome me, and where I could recently feel it bubbling away, waiting to erupt. There was nothing, I felt back to my usual self.

"Stop changing the subject, and for the love of fucking God, *please* call me Josh, all this Master Joshua shit, is weird."

"Out of the question, *Master Joshua*, it wouldn't be appropriate. Although I am willing to compromise, would Master Josh be more agreeable?"

I threw my hands up in surrender. "Fine, whatever. Now, what's all this nonsense about magic?"

Felix raised his empty left hand and a small bird made entirely from blue flames appeared on his palm. A small flick of his wrist and the bird fluttered towards me, causing me to flinch back into my seat as the bird flew a small loop in front of my face before finally disappearing with a 'poof'.

"Wha…" I muttered, completely tongue-tied. That had been no trick, I had even felt the heat emitting from it!

"Sorry for any alarm, Master Josh, but it is most definitely *not* nonsense, and that seemed the most expedient method to convince you."

Shrugging off my initial shock, I nodded back at him. "Okay, and where are you taking me?"

"To wherever you wish…but I'd prefer to take you to your ancestral home." He looked at me beseechingly.

Honestly, there was no need for him to try and persuade me. Between healing the little girl and manipulating the fire bird, I'd already seen too much to turn back.

"You can take me there, but you have to tell me everything," I said, wondering just how deep this magic rabbit hole would go.

"Of course, Master Josh." He smiled. "Well, as I mentioned the first time we met, the Wilkins were not in fact your birth family, you are in fact the son of the twenty-first White family patriarch."

"Up with the patriarchy, is it? Damn!" I said, attempting a joke.

"No, there have been matriarchs too actually. Now don't be facetious, Master Josh, it's unbecoming."

Suitably chastised, I forced down my snarky reply.

"The Whites are an ancient family of warriors, that keep humanity safe from supernatural threats," Felix said, continuing from where he had left off.

"That actually sounds…pretty cool." Images of warriors flying around whilst killing monsters floating through my head. "But the name White, isn't it a bit, well, ordinary?"

"What would you expect, the Flamefists, or some other trite?" Felix said with a chuckle.

I was too embarrassed to admit my teenage brain had actually been thinking of something more along those lines and smartly elected to keep my mouth shut.

"Actually, the name is in honour of the divine beast Baihu, the White Tiger, whose illustrious bloodline is borne by all of the members of the White family and provides you with heightened physical capabilities."

Finally having an explanation for my abilities, even if it was a fantastical one, actually proved to be a relief and I felt one of my deep-repressed anxieties unknotting a little.

"White, from White Tiger, seems a little…on the nose," I said with a smile.

"It is the illustrious name of a greatly lauded family, one who has made countless sacrifices to keep this world safe and you should show a little respect," Felix said, "Remember, Master Josh, levity is not always appropriate."

"Sorry, Felix, I meant no disrespect."

"Apology accepted," Felix said and then looked at me suspiciously. "You know, you are taking this all remarkably well."

"Yeah, well, between my own weird shit and what I've seen you do, I want answers, so I'm willing to give you the benefit of the doubt. And if it turns out you're just some random nutter spouting bullshit and I've been slipped some acid, then that was my own bad judgment."

Felix mouth opened and closed a few times, as if he was unsure of what to say. "I can assure you, Master Josh, it is most certainly not, *bullshit*, as you so eloquently put it." He finally settled on, sounding a little offended.

"I guess we'll see," I said.

"Right, where was I…" he muttered to himself. "Ah, yes, the Whites disappeared on one of their regular travels into other realms—"

"Wait, other realms?" I interrupted him.

"Yes, now please try to keep from interrupting me, Master Josh, or this will take all day."

Brilliant, he dropped fucking bombshell like that and acts like I'm the unreasonable one? I found myself scowling at him in irritation. Yeah, maybe it was a little immature, but I am sixteen, so I'm allowed to do the petulant teenager thing once in a while.

"As I was saying." He looked at me pointedly. "When they returned, Lord White brought a swaddled bundle with him; you. And promptly announced you as his son and heir, although he never said who your mother was, I am rather sorry to say."

Unsure of how to respond, I looked out of the window, watching the trees pass by and the occasional horse or herd of sheep milling around in the fields. I'd always loved Surrey, and other than a brief stint with an awful foster family in Sussex, I'd lived here all my life. I think it is the mixture of the beautiful countryside, whilst still being so close to London that appeals to me, and even the larger towns are still full of greenery, it is the best of both worlds. It seemed that

Felix's revelations hit me harder than I thought they would, and I was feeling a little hollow that I wouldn't be able to find out who my birth mother was, but at least I knew my father's identity and more about my roots, which was something at least.

"The bloodline you mentioned, is that why I lost it earlier? Why I was so angry?" I asked, turning back to look at Felix.

"Yes, normally the awakening is a gradual process during the later stages of puberty, but unfortunately, feelings of extreme stress or danger can drastically accelerate the process."

I thought back to how out of control I was, the savage glee I felt as I tore that animal apart and found myself looking at my blood encrusted hands. "I was like a beast, all instinct and rage."

"I understand it must be disconcerting, Master Josh, but I assure you that now your bloodline has awoken, you will not lose control again, that was just a rather unfortunate side effect of the hastened process."

The relief I felt was palpable, I never wanted to feel so out of control again, I had no desire to become a monster.

"Although, I should warn you that the physical changes are permanent."

Wait, what?! "What physical changes?" I asked, dreading the answer a little.

Felix tilted the rear-view mirror until I could see my reflection, and I was transfixed by the image that stared back at me. I ran my hands through my previously blonde hair, now largely white, except for some black and blue stripes, and prodded at my more pronounced canines with my tongue, which although not quite vampiric, were still noticeably longer. At least my eyes remained largely unchanged, if not a slightly lighter, icier, blue. What the actual fuck!

Prodding and squeezing parts of myself, which probably looked a little strange, I realised my body was different too, which I'd somehow missed, caught up as I was in all the craziness. I'd always been naturally trim and muscular, but now my muscles felt somehow denser, becoming granite hard when I tensed! I looked at Felix accusingly.

"Didn't think to start with." I gestured at myself wildly. "All of this."

Felix beamed back at me. "And ruin the surprise?"

What a massive prick! Eventually, I started laughing uncontrollably at the absurdity of it all and didn't stop until I noticed Felix looking at me concernedly.

"I'm fine." I waved away his concern. "Sorry."

"It's quite alright, Master Josh," he said, rubbing his face wearily.

"So how do you figure into this situation?" I asked.

"I am the White family…butler, would probably be the closest term."

"Hang on a minute, you spoke as if you were there, but you can't be a day over thirty. There's no way a teenager would have been a butler back when I was a baby." I suddenly realised.

"Thank you for the compliment, Master Josh, but I assure you I am a little older than thirty."

I looked at him quizzically. "How much older?"

"Well, let's just say that I recently celebrated my four-hundred and twelfth anniversary within the White household and I myself am a little older than that."

I would like to say I was shocked at his announcement, but at this point it was just another branch on the tree-of-crazy that my life was fast becoming.

"Congratulations then," I said, causing Felix to chuckle. "How long until we get to the house?"

"Not long, Master Josh, its only about fifteen minutes out of town."

"Do you think they'll like me?" I asked nervously, suddenly daunted at the idea of meeting my biological family.

"Oh my, oh my! I'm so sorry, Josh." Felix said, his usual adherence to protocol slipping in his panicked apology. "I got so caught up in explaining about your bloodline that...that I forgot to mention there is no-one there for you to meet."

"They're out of town?"

"No, I'm afraid not, Master Josh, they..." he hesitated.

"Are they dead?" I asked, a little terrified about his answer.

"I honestly don't know." Felix sighed. "Shortly after asking me to re-home you, your father led the family members into another realm, they have yet to return."

"But, if it's been so long, it's unlikely they're alive, isn't it?" I reasoned.

"Hmm...time sometimes behaves funny between realms, but after so long, I'm afraid so, Master Josh, that's part of why I took so long to contact you, I spent a long time searching for traces of them, with no luck. When I finally returned, I checked on you and found out what had happened to the Wilkins. I am truly sorry about that; they were good people. You had not long been with the Taylors at the time, and I saw you were finally starting to stabilise, to settle, and I didn't want to interfere with that, so I just kept an eye on you from a distance, making sure you were safe."

I found myself choking up at his mention of my family, he was right, they were good people, and I swore there'd be retribution for their deaths.

"What changed?" I asked, focusing back on the present.

"You did," Felix said, "I could sense from the change in the spiritual pressure you were emitting that your bloodline was about to awaken, and I knew it was time to bring you home."

I didn't really know what to say to that, I could feel he was being honest with me, and so I knew it wasn't his fault, but I couldn't help but feel a little abandoned, and bitter that

I had to languish in the foster system for so long; they weren't the greatest of years.

"So how does it work?" I asked. "Magic and all that."

"Aether."

"Aether? You are going to have to give me more than that."

"Aether is the spiritual energy that permeates the realms, it can be utilised by those sensitive to it to fuel their growth. A mage like me for instance would convert it to mana and use it to empower magic, other awakened use it in different ways," he explained.

"Huh," I said, unsure of what to say to that.

Felix seemed content to leave me to process everything, and so I sat in silence for the rest of journey, quietly watching the homes and farmsteads grow increasingly further apart. It couldn't have been more than five minutes before we finally slowed down, pulling off a small, hedged B-road onto a forest lined drive, marked: *'Private Road — No access'.*

Fifty metres or so along the drive, the way forward was blocked by a set of large iron gates, their gaudy stone posts topped with rearing alabaster tigers, of course they were! They opened automatically as we approached, and the drive continued through the trees.

"Just how long is this driveway?" I asked in surprise.

"Not too far, Master Josh, only about a quarter of a mile." He winked back at me. "The White estate is around fifteen hundred acres in total."

As more of an urbanite, I had no real frame of reference for how large that was, but I didn't want to look stupid, so I just nodded along, figuring it was safe to assume it was large, especially with a four hundred metre driveway. Ahead, I noticed we were finally about to leave the forest and a house slowly became visible through the thinning trees.

I say house, but that is wholly insufficient to describe the absolute edifice, which, surrounded by its immaculately landscaped gardens, was simply huge. Part gothic castle, part manor, it even had towers! It was the type of home you see in a BBC period drama or visit on a school trip; it screamed old money.

"Felix, not to be crass, but am I rich?"

"Master Josh, if you were to lose ninety-nine percent of your wealth, you would still be rich. The only reason the Whites don't appear on the Forbes list is because, like many families in similar positions, they wish to retain their anonymity."

Now, I'm not a greedy person, and my family, the Wilkins I mean, were never poor. However, in the years I bounced around the foster system, I had gotten used to barely receiving what I need, and even then, not always. So, I must admit, that when he said that I was now disgustingly rich, my eyes probably lit up.

As the car came to a halt in front of the palatial residence, I was hit with a pang of sadness about being unable to meet any of my biological family. "So, there will be just the two of us in this monstrosity of a house?" I asked.

Felix chuckled as we climbed the entrance steps. "Oh, dear gods no, Master Josh. The household staff numbers twenty-two people and there are another five grounds staff, this place doesn't maintain itself!"

A small part of me was disappointed, I thought that seeing as the butler could perform magic, that perhaps the house was somehow maintained by it. Although maybe that's not how magic worked? Or using it for general labour was frowned upon? I didn't really have a clue if there were any rules or conventions as far as magic was concerned. The doors opened wide as we approached; to an entrance hall with large staircases on either side, and it seemed the interior was just as impressive as the outside.

Mirroring Felix, I stopped at the threshold. Knowing that it signified more than just entering the building, and that once I crossed that line my old life would be well and truly over. I didn't need to think twice.

"You can pick any of the suites you want, Master Josh, we can catch up once you are cleaned up," Felix said, "and maybe go and check on your friend Mikey?" He winked.

Oh shit! Mikey! Why didn't I think of that? I'm such a terrible friend!

"You can heal him?" I asked, "like the little girl?"

"Certainly, Master Josh." He smiled at me. "Although, as a rule, we generally try to avoid exposing the more fantastical parts of the hidden world."

"I understand." I nodded. "You can't be instigating mass panic and hysteria!"

"Quite." He chuckled.

"Right, I'll be as quick as I can, is a tower free?" I asked, well aware I was grinning from ear to ear.

Felix clicked his fingers and a small wisp of light appeared. "A tower suite is indeed free, follow the light and it will lead you there. If you require anything just ring the bell."

The wisp of light zipped from his hand to bob in the air in front of my face, then fluttered off up the left-hand staircase, quickly leaving me behind. He could have at least controlled the pace it set! At the top of the stairs, the light zoomed off down the corridor, again leaving me in the dust, and I could see it bobbing outside the final door on the left. As I approached the door, I realised that Felix could have easily given me simple directions, and I laughed to myself as I opened the door, who was I kidding? If I could do magic, I would be showing off too!

The door led to a private sitting room, with several red chesterfield sofas arranged around a large ornate fireplace, there was also a minibar in one corner, which was clearly a far more recent addition and upon opening it, found it to be fully stocked with an assortment of soft drinks. The rooms décor was an eclectic mixture of traditional western wood panelling and wallpapers, with oriental style wall-hangings. A set of open double doors led into the tower beyond, and I quickly made my way over to check it out. The tower room was amazing! It was huge and the walls were completely covered in bookcases, the only break in them for windows and the cast iron spiral staircase on one side. Part of me wanted nothing more than to stop and explore my new personal library, but I needed to get cleaned up and get Mikey back on his feet.

Climbing the spiral staircase, the next room up was a personal study, which contained more bookcases and a large desk with a thoroughly modern flatscreen monitor, connected to a beast of a PC. The whole thing looked hugely anachronistic in such a setting, and I noticed a note addressed to me on the desk, which simply read:

Master Joshua, I had a feeling you would choose a Tower suite, I hope you enjoy the computer. Faithfully, F

Chuckling at how wily the butler was proving to be, I carried on up to the next floor, which proved to be the bedroom. It contained a huge four poster canopy bed, ensuite bathroom and walk-in wardrobe. Mounted on the wall was a large flatscreen TV that could be watched from the bed. Entering the ensuite, I peeled the blood soaked and ruined clothes from my body and climbed into the shower. As the steaming water and soap carried away the days blood and grime, I felt some of the past days trouble wash away with it and emerged feeling refreshed and eager to take on the madness of my new life.

The walk-in wardrobe held a large assortment of clothes, and I tried not to think about the fact they were all in my size. As the idea of Felix stealthily obtaining my measurements was a little creepy, even if he had the best of intentions. Most of them were far smarter than I would normally wear, but eventually I settled for some beige chinos and a blue shirt, and as I buttoned the shirt, I slowly worked through in my head what to do next.

Everything had quickly gotten crazy, and I knew that I could easily become overwhelmed, so I fell back to a tried and tested method that I had learned from one of the many shrinks I had seen. It involved breaking life down into individual problems, prioritising them and taking them on one-at-a-time, it had really helped when my problems seemed insurmountable, and I now used it as a general life tool.

First, I would check on Mikey, then visit my foster parents, after that I would start to find out what my new life would involve. Slipping on some brown leather loafers and a charcoal Blazer, I looked at myself in the mirror. For fuck's sake! I looked like a rich boy on day-release from boarding school, which was not how I usually cut about. Admittedly, the image was somewhat ruined by my new punk-rock hair, maybe I could dye it? Oh well, there was nothing I could do about it now.

I remembered Felix saying that I should ring the bell if I needed anything, but that felt a bit pretentious, so I just set off back through the house to try and track him down.

As I walked into the entrance hall, I saw him waiting for me and wondered if he was psychic too.

"Looking far more respectable, Master Josh, much more fitting for one of your status," he said as I approached.

"Cheers, I guess I do scrub up ok, shame about the hair though." I ran my fingers through it.

"Nonsense, your hair is a symbol of your noble lineage, Master Josh, and should be worn with pride."

I could tell he truly meant it, so I decided against telling him I'd considered dying it, he would probably be mortified.

"I'm just worried it will draw too much attention, and the school will definitely not allow it, as there's no way they'll believe it's natural," I said.

"Very well, I could use a little magical glamour to make it appear as your previous blonde hair to mundanes?"

I assumed by mundanes that he meant ordinary humans and thought that would be a brilliant idea. "Please, if you would."

Felix raised his hand, and after a brief gesture and a few muttered words, I felt a brief tingle on my head which quickly passed.

"All done, Master Josh, are you ready to head out?"

"Yeah, I'm excited to see Mikey back up on his feet again. Although, how we will explain his recovery to his parents is beyond me?" I said, genuinely concerned that the two devout Christians would either think it was some divine miracle, or even worse; the devil's work. I mean, they are great people, but belief can be a funny thing.

"Well, we will just have to deal with it as it comes," Felix said, "although I must warn you, Master Josh, he may end up…a little healthier than before the incident, shall we say."

I doubted Mikey would end up with tentacles or anything, so c'est la vie. "I'm sure it will be fine, as long as he recovers." I waved off his concerns.

"Very good, Master Josh." Felix smiled mysteriously.

Chapter 6

We pulled up outside the hospital and I admit I was starting to feel a little nervous, as when Mikey recovered, we still had to deal with the aftermath of his potentially miraculous improvement.

Having already visited, I didn't require directions and immediately led Felix up towards the high dependency unit, luckily it was still before seven pm, so we were still within visiting hours.

Although, even if we weren't and had to sneak in, Mikey would get the healing he needed! Besides, Felix would probably have some sort of sneaky magical ninja shit he could pull if necessary. At least I hoped so!

As we entered Mikey's room, I noticed that the other bed was still unoccupied, which was lucky as another patient would complicate matters; we didn't need any witnesses claiming to have seen miracles! Mikey was sat gazing out of the window, looking just as bad as I remembered. He noticed us approaching and his face lit up with a smile. I wondered how he'd react to what I had to say, as I knew that a day earlier, I wouldn't have believed it.

"Listen Mikey, what I'm about to tell you is going to sound nuts, so I'm asking you as your best friend, to just hear me out," I said.

"Oookay, just don't go confessing your undying love to me, you're not my type." Mikey chuckled with a pained grimace.

Smiling at his poor attempt at humour, I just launched straight into it. "Felix here, is my family butler, and I think it is safe to say, someone we can trust"

Mikey just nodded along, he looked surprised when I said I had a butler, but thankfully didn't interrupt me, just waving in greeting to Felix with his good hand.

"Well, Felix has a way to completely heal your injuries, but, and there's no easy way to say this Mikey…it's magic," I said, waiting for the expected scorn.

Mikey looked at me incredulously at first, then his eyes lit up. "I fucking knew it. Yes!" he said whilst gently fist pumping with his good arm.

I was stumped, as I'd been expecting him to accuse me of taking the piss. "I thought you'd take more convincing."

"Josh, if I'm honest, I've always felt that there was something more. Just out of reach, do you know what I mean? I've never talked about it though as I didn't want to look like a nutter."

"I wouldn't have thought you were a nutter, bruv," I said.

"Really?" he asked, looking at me pointedly.

I laughed. "Well, maybe a little bit, but I've always had that feeling too, so I wouldn't have been too mean about it."

I looked at Felix and, understanding what I wanted, he handed me a green pill bottle.

"A pill? Is that what you slipped the little girl?" I asked. "I thought…" I waved my hands about in imitation of when Felix had performed magic.

Felix rolled his eyes at my awful impression. "No, Master Josh, it was just a pill, unfortunately healing the wounded is not one of my fortes, which requires a particular skillset."

I just nodded back, like I had a clue about the different types of magic! Opening the lid on the bottle immediately released a strong minty and herbal smell, which filled the room and somehow seemed to carry whispers of new growth at Springtime, both pleasant and calming. I carefully upended the bottle over my hand and a small oval pill dropped on to my palm, which looked a bit like a green apple jellybean but with tiny golden sparkles. I held out the pill for Mikey to take.

"Are you sure this isn't dangerous?" he asked.

"Well, there may be some…side effects," Felix said, "but they won't be bad."

Mikey shrugged and popped the pill into his mouth.

"If you don't want the hospital staff to come running, I suggest you place his heart monitor onto your finger, Master Josh," Felix said, "quickly now!"

I looked at Mikey, who seemed relatively unaffected by the pill. Lifting his hand to me, he nodded for me to do as Felix said, so I unclipped the monitor from Mikey's finger and stuffed it on to my own, and not a moment too soon.

Mikey's face suddenly contorted, and he started to gasp. Arching his back, he began to thrash violently on the bed, and I began to panic that, even without the monitor, nurses would come running at the noise. But, as abruptly as the thrashing started, it stopped, with only the deep rise and fall of Mikey's chest remaining.

"What the actual fuck, Felix!" I said, "That never happened to the girl!"

"She had only flesh wounds, Master Josh, but as you can clearly see, there's nothing to worry about, Michael is fine."

I looked at Mikey's face, his eyes were closed, but there was no trace of his earlier injuries, and I was left with little doubt that the rest of his body was likewise healed. Relieved that we had done what we set out to, I was now left wondering how the fuck we would explain his rapid improvement to the hospital?

Mikey opened his eyes and looked up at me. "That hurt like an absolute bitch, but what a rush! Got any more?"

he joked as he started laughing. Which immediately set off Felix and me too.

"Seriously though, how are you feeling?" I asked.

"Better than ever, no pain and I feel...alive. Like I've spent the last sixteen years only half awake and now I've woken up. Everything is just, more...real."

Felix looked at me. "Looks like it's as I guessed, Master Josh. I'm afraid your friend is no longer a mundane, we should probably get out of here now."

I suddenly realised that some prior planning would have probably been a good idea. "What about the hospital staff? They will probably notice if a seriously injured patient miraculously recovers and just walks out. What about your parents Mikey? How are we going to explain this to them?"

"My parents still haven't been in yet, but the hospital did finally manage to reach them, they are heading here now, should still be a few hours though."

I took out my phone and gave it to Mikey. "Call them, tell them it was a mistake, someone nicked your bag with your wallet and phone inside, the hospital must have thought they were you."

I knew there would be holes picked in the story, as Mikey had clearly spoken to the hospital staff already. But fuck it, Mikey was fine and someone pretending to be him was actually far more believable than Mikey having somehow made a miraculous recovery.

Felix nodded in approval. "That's quick-thinking, Master Josh, you do that, and I'll take care of the nurse, I'll meet you both at the car."

I gave Mikey my phone and he made the call; I could tell from his expression that they were just relieved that he was okay, and after a few minutes of persuasion, he even managed to convince them to carry on with their retreat. I swear that boy's power of persuasion is borderline supernatural.

Spotting a folded wheelchair in the corner of the ward, I had an idea about how we would get to the car. A lad in a hospital gown, flashing his derriere as he walks through the hospital might raise a few eyebrows, whereas someone being pushed in a wheelchair, not so much. We wanted to make it look like no-one was ever even in the room, so Mikey tore off his various bandages. The cast on his arm didn't break so easily, but soon gave way under my prying fingertips and I stuffed it into the bin with the bandages. The drip and saline bag were next and we made sure to put the canula into the bio-waste bin. The last and only thing he hesitated over, was the catheter and bag. I couldn't help but giggle as he grunted whilst pulling the thing out.

"It's not fucking funny you prick, you keep on and I'll spray you with it." Mikey chuckled, waving it threateningly, but I could see from his wincing face that it was a less than pleasant experience.

Mikey emptied the bag in the toilet and put the last few bits in the bins. We attempted to arrange the area, so it looked like one of the adjacent empty bed-spaces, but the sheets were far too wrinkled and so we eventually gave up.

Mikey hopped into the wheelchair wearing my blazer. "Onwards to freedom!" he said, pointing to the exit.

Other than quickly bolting past whilst Felix distracted the nurse, the remainder of the journey back to the car was uneventful. It seemed that once you were off a ward, as long as you acted like you were doing nothing wrong, then no-one really pays any attention to you. I guessed if there was security, they just assumed somewhere had released him. Felix arrived back at the car only moments after us.

"Any dramas?" I asked.

"Nothing I couldn't handle, Master Josh," he grinned.

"What about the cameras?" I asked.

"What cameras?" Felix winked at me.

Fair enough, of course he took care of that too! Felix looked at Mikey's attire and cringed, and I wondered if it was because he wasn't keen on the idea of Mikey's bare arse on his upholstery. Although in all fairness, it wasn't as bad as the dog blood I had been covered in earlier and any sign of that was conspicuously absent, so I suspected once again magic was at play.

"Don't worry Felix, we can stop at Mikey's so he can grab a few bits to stay over, and he can wipe down your seat." I winked, which caused Mikey and me to break into a laughing fit.

Felix didn't look nearly as amused, but I swear I saw the brief hint of a smile as he shook his head and climbed into the car.

The drive to Mikey's didn't take long and Mikey was in and out of his house in record time. Although his mad dash into the house may have had something to do with the hospital gown, flapping open as he ran and exposing us both to a sight I hope to never witness again.

"Wow Mikey, that was quick, did you already have a bag packed and ready to go?" I joked as he climbed into the back of the car.

"No, but now that you mention it, I did feel like I was moving quicker than normal," he replied.

Felix turned to us both. "Yes, we will probably have to check you out when we arrive at White manor, to see exactly how you are awakening."

Mikey had a massive grin on his face, clearly excited about the whole thing. I, on the other hand, couldn't help but grimace at memories of my bloodline awakening only a couple of hours earlier.

Chapter 7

By the time we arrived on the driveway to White manor, the sky had started to shift into the tell-tale pink and orange hues of sunset, and I found myself taking surreptitious glances at Mikey to see his reaction to the house. He was wide eyed as we passed the gates, but his jaw literally dropped as White manor was revealed in all its early evening glory.

"Catching flies?" I asked him, even though I was positive I had a similar reaction only a few hours previous.

He closed his mouth and looked at me. "This is actually your house now?"

"Apparently so, although part of me is still waiting for someone to tell me that there's been a mix-up," I admitted.

"I'm so jealous right now bruv, seriously, I have to come and stay with you whenever possible," said Mikey, turning to Felix. "Is that okay? Me coming to stay?"

"I'm afraid it's not my decision Michael, that would be up to, Master Josh. If I were to hazard to guess though, I imagine we will be seeing a lot of you within the halls of White manor," Felix chuckled.

"Master Josh, Felix called you that earlier, I thought it was a bit weird," Mikey said.

"Yeah, I'm still trying to wrap my head around it myself," I replied.

It was only then that I realised I'd forgotten the second part of my plans, visiting the Taylors! They would be just arriving home from work and probably wondering where I was, shit! I took out my phone and gave them a call. The phone only rang a few times before Mum Taylor answered.

"Taylor residence, Mrs Taylor speaking." She was always so formal when she answered the phone, and I couldn't help but smile.

"Hi, it's Josh, I'm just calling so you don't worry about me not being home."

"Oh, hi sweetie, that's very considerate of you, is anything the matter?"

"No, I just wanted to ask if you mind if I stay at Mikey's tonight? I packed a bag earlier and forgot to leave a note." I hated lying to her, but the truth was not something to just announce over the phone and I was too tired and hungry to deal with the visit tonight.

"Well, it's not a school night, so I don't mind, just don't do anything I wouldn't do."

"I won't, and…"

"Yes sweetie?"

"I love you."

"Aww, Josh, we love you too."

"I'll see you tomorrow."

I hung up the phone, vowing to myself that no matter what, I would make sure the Taylors were taken care of. They had been there for me when I was at my lowest and I would always be there for them.

As we entered the house, Felix turned to us. "I imagine you are both rather hungry, how about I have the chef whip up some food? Any preferences?"

Once again it was if Felix had read my mind. "Errm, I'm good with burgers and fries, maybe a couple."

"Burgers sound brilliant, as long as it's not too much bother, I don't want to inconvenience anyone," Mikey said.

Felix smiled at us both. "I assure you that the chef will be more than happy to prepare some food, I will have it brought up."

As Felix left to sort the food, Mikey turned to look at me. "Well come on then, show me around."

49

I didn't really know my way around myself, so I just took him up to my suite, Mikey was clearly impressed, and we spent the next half an hour just sat on the sofas chatting. It was amazing how quickly Mikey was adjusting from his exposure to this crazy new world. I would have thought such a paradigm shift would have left him uneasy, but nope, he was like a kid in a candy shop, desperate to see what new wonders would be revealed. I guess in that manner we were rather similar, perhaps that is part of why we had become such close friends.

There was a knock at the door, and after beckoning them to come in, a maid entered pushing a trolley with two large, covered plates upon it. The maid was initially confused when I told her we would serve ourselves, but I had never been waited on and I wasn't about to start now. After I'd finally managed to convince her that it was fine for her to just leave, she smiled, curtsied, and hurried out. Mikey and I grabbed the two platters and carried them over to the coffee table. The chef had also prepared a pitcher of what looked like water flavoured with fresh fruit. I could definitely get used to this, I thought to myself.

As we removed the lids from the platters, I instantly started to salivate. The burgers looked amazing, huge juicy patties, topped with cheese, bacon, and some salad, all contained within a pretzel bun. And a small mountain of seasoned skin-on fries. I was in food heaven.

Thoroughly sated, we were happily relaxing on the sofas when there was another knock at the door.

"Come in," I said.

Looking over, I saw it was Felix, who glanced at the completely empty plates. "I take it everything was to your satisfaction, Master Josh?"

I found myself involuntarily thinking back to the sublime sensations of the food, which even though it was only burger and chips, was probably the best food I'd ever had. "Honestly, I have never eaten something so tasty in my life."

"I concur." Mikey rubbed his belly contentedly.

"Welcome to the world of spiritual food," said Felix.

"Spiritual food?" I asked.

This led to a conversation about different types of food, apparently spiritual food was made from magical beasts and Aether rich ingredients, usually from different realms. It could nourish more than just the body and sometimes even caused specific effects. I found myself picturing Felix online, ordering magical shopping from a cross-realm grocery delivery company and had to suppress the urge to laugh.

"Anyway, if you would like I can check you over now Michael? See what exactly the consequences are for giving you that pill," Felix asked.

I was curious myself; I still had no idea how I differed from a regular human, and it seemed like a great opportunity to find out some more about the world we were entering.

Mikey nodded nervously. "What do I need to do?"

"Nothing really, you will just have to lie down for a few minutes," Felix replied, "if you'd both please follow me, we will have it finished in no time."

We trailed Felix through the house, which proved handy as it allowed me to familiarise myself with more of the place as we went. It was like a maze, a veritable warren of hallways and doors and I knew it would be hopeless trying to find anywhere specific, at least until I memorised the layout. For now, I'd probably need a map! Finally, after several minutes or so of wandering, Felix pushed open the doors to a large martial arts dojo.

Several steps led to a mat covering one end of the room, the other side contained training aids, such as punch bags, wooden dummies and various rope wrapped posts. Numerous banners and pictures were hung on the walls and from the ceiling, depicting phoenixes, oriental dragons, and other mythological creatures. The largest, in pride of place at the centre of the room, was of a ferocious looking white tiger, and I knew at a glance that it depicted my ancestor, Baihu. The whole thing still felt unbelievable and, looking at the picture, I wondered how on earth he had sired human offspring. I hoped he had somehow taken human form, as the idea that one of my maternal ancestors mated with a tiger, was simply gross. I shook off the unpleasant image.

"What do I need to do?" Mikey asked.

Felix sat down cross legged in the centre of the mat and tapped the floor in front of him. "Just lie down here."

Mikey and I started to walk towards the mat but were interrupted by Felix coughing. He pointed at our shoes and at a series of cubby holes along the wall.

"Sorry!" we replied in unison.

I should have known better as shoes are always removed before entering a dojo. We took our shoes and socks off and once again proceeded to the centre of the mat, Mikey lay down, and Felix gestured for me to back off. I moved to the edge of the mat and sat waiting with bated breath for what was about to happen.

Before he started, Felix first gave us some information about humans with special abilities, so we had a frame of reference, patiently answering any questions we asked.

Essentially some, rare humans, are born with specific innate abilities, often due to some distant magical heritage, like me. But these things can also manifest in a previously mundane human who awakens later, either through training or, like Mikey, through a little helping hand. Also, when a person awakens there is sometimes a strong natural proclivity towards a certain element, which is usually a result of the nature of their heritage, but sometimes just happens completely randomly. Felix was basically going to check Mikey to see if his awakening had resulted in anything specific.

Felix knelt next to Mikey, and holding his hands above Mikey's supine form, his lips began to move in some sort of soundless chant. After a minute or so of chanting, a warm glow started to emanate from Felix's hands, which gradually suffused around Mikey's head, before slowly proceeding down his body until it reached his feet, at which point it dissipated, the whole thing reminding me of some sort of supernatural CAT scan. The whole process only lasted a couple of minutes and Felix motioned that Mikey could get up.

Mikey sat up and looked at him nervously, which was understandable as whatever Felix said could possibly affect his entire future.

"Well, Michael, at least for now; I am unable to detect any strange changes to your physiology, nor have any elemental preferences arisen from your awakening, so how you develop will be determined entirely by your own choices," Felix said.

Mikey looked pensive and maybe a little disappointed.

"Not the result you were hoping for?" Felix asked.

Mikey shrugged. "I'm not really sure what I wanted."

Felix smiled at Mikey's admission. "Who does at sixteen? You should look at this positively, you have complete freedom of choice with nothing steering you down a specific path. How you develop now is entirely up to you."

"I didn't think of it like that! You're right, I can be whatever I want to be!" Mikey said, suddenly looking like the cat who got the cream.

"Well, Master Josh, we are all done here for now, do you need help finding your way back?" Felix asked.

I thought about it for a second. "I think we may explore a little, is there anywhere we aren't allowed to go?"

"It's your house, Master Josh, so there isn't anywhere you're not allowed to go. I would, however, suggest avoiding the east wing second floor as it contains the staff's personal rooms."

"Oh, is that where your room is located?" I asked.

"Yes, I have the large suite on the end. One of the perks of being major-domo. If there is nothing else, I shall excuse myself."

As soon as Felix was gone, Mikey and I smiled at each other and looked around the dojo. I could tell that, even without discussing it, we agreed on our next plan of action, and the next half an hour or so was spent with us flailing at the various training items in the room. The decision to stop only coming after I had broken my third wooden post. I was sure that Felix wasn't going to be impressed when I explained what had happened. Proceeding out into the hallway, we wandered the house with no specific goal in mind, sticking our heads into countless rooms and growing increasingly bewildered over the unnecessary scale of the place. Half of the rooms, we couldn't even tell what their function was, no doubt they had some peculiar aristocratic use, and we just weren't cultured enough to understand, as they couldn't all just be living rooms!

Finally, after arriving back in my suite, we got a coke each from the minibar, and settled back on my bed to watch some TV whilst chatting about the day. After some initial hesitation, I eventually admitted to him what had happened in the park. I expected him to be horrified, as what I did to the dog was pretty fucked up, even if said dog was mauling a child. However, Mikey was pretty chilled about the whole thing and assured me that it was just lucky I was there to save the girl. At some point during the evening Mikey finally decided that he wanted to be a mage like Felix. I think telling him how Felix had manipulated the fire captured his imagination. However, with no real idea about how he would go about becoming one, we thought it best to shelve the discussion until we could ask Felix.

Chapter 8

I woke up bleary eyed to the sounds of Mikey snoring next me, if you can imagine a cross between a foghorn and a hedge strimmer, you will be close to the sound of a sleeping Mikey. Looking at my watch, I saw it was just after nine, which was honestly quite early for me on a Saturday morning. Staggering to the bathroom, I had a nice long shower and when I finally returned, Mikey was up and flipping through the TV channels.

"Sorry, shower wake you?" I asked.

"Yeah, but it's fine, lots to do today!" Mikey answered excitedly.

When both of us were dressed and showered, we took off through the house to track down Felix, eventually locating him in a dining room downstairs. He was talking to a few members of the household staff, who left soon after we arrived, presumedly to carry out whatever tasks Felix had issued. The three of us sat down at the table and waited for breakfast. The food was just as amazing as the previous night's meal, and it seemed that my appetite had increased considerably, possibly as a side effect of my newly awakened bloodline? Whilst we ate Mikey admitted that he would like to become a mage, which seemed to please Felix, who promptly offered to take Mikey on as an apprentice of sorts. All Mikey had to promise was that he would make time for a few hours of tuition each day and not use magic in front of regular humans unless his life was in danger. Honestly, I think Mikey would have agreed to far worse conditions for a chance to learn magic, but I wasn't about to mention that to Felix.

My situation was unfortunately more complicated, as I could have also elected to train as a mage, but I felt a strong preference for more physical skills and abilities, which, especially when combined with my bloodline abilities, meant I was better suited to be what Felix termed a Cultivator. A choice that was apparently the most common amongst the White family. This meant I had to therefore begin 'cultivating', whatever that was, and until a master was sourced, would have to try to muddle through by myself. Luckily, my father had apparently left a few items for me when he left, just in case he failed to return, which I hoped contained something to steer me in the right direction.

I knew Mikey was keen to start his magical tuition, but unfortunately for him, we needed to visit the Taylors first today to make them aware of the situation. Before we left, I agreed that Mikey could pick his own room for when he was over. Initially, he joked that a mage should get the tower suite, but after I counter-offered a garden shed, he quickly picked the suite next to mine. We left him in his new room, happily reading a primer on magic kindly gifted to him by Felix.

The whole drive to the Taylors, I tried to plan out what I would say, but by the time we arrived, I had completely given up and decided to just see how it went. It was strange, but as I knocked on the front door, I felt that as much as I loved the Taylors, I no longer considered this my home. Which might seem crazy, as I had only left yesterday morning. However, in the last twenty-four hours I had shifted into a separate world from the one my foster parents inhabited. A world of magic and wonder, but also one of potential dangers they would be unable to handle.

The door opened, mum Taylor saw it was me and smiled. "Josh! You don't need to knock," she said, before noticing Felix, "and this is?"

"Felix Aldridge ma'am." He bowed. "A pleasure to meet you."

"Such nice manners," mum Taylor said.

I had to stifle a chuckle as she flushed a little, clearly taken-aback by Felix's performance.

Coming to her senses, she quickly seemed to realise we were waiting for an invitation. "Sorry, do come in." She gestured into the house.

Mr Taylor was sat on the sofa watching the horse racing, which was one of his favourite pass-times. He was a kind and relatively simple man, his small flutters on the horses just about his only real indulgence and he won more often than not.

He looked over as we entered the room and immediately noticed Felix accompanying me. "Is everything ok, Josh?" he asked, the concern evident in his voice.

"Yeah, don't worry. Everything is fine, I just have some news to share. This is Felix Aldridge," I said in introduction.

As Felix offered his hand for a shake, I could see the tension start to ease from my foster-father.

I looked at my foster-parents and it took me a few moments to find the right words. "Some things have happened in the last twenty-four hours, and I need to tell you both, as it will affect all of us."

I lost count of the number of cups of tea we went through over the following few hours. The Taylors handled the whole thing with more aplomb than I would have credited them, initial disbelief turning to amazement and then concern. Even after my true identity and newfound wealth was revealed, they had been reluctant to cede guardianship of me to Felix, which truly warmed my heart. However, after a brief demonstration of Felix's abilities, it became clear to them that they were woefully ill-equipped to deal with the situation. I left to hugs and tears, with promises made that I would visit regularly, and content in the knowledge that I would always have a home there to which I could return.

The journey back to the estate was rather sombre, I knew I had done the right thing, but I was sad to leave behind the people that had helped me find myself again, and I vowed to make the Taylors proud, no matter what.

Chapter 9

Felix had left to begin lessons with Mikey, so I decided it was a good opportunity to check the items left by my father. Sat on a sofa within my rooms I stared at the velvet bag and innocuous leather book, which was outwardly rather plain and ordinary looking. Felix explained that only I could open them, something of which my father had made sure of, and they would require a drop of my blood to get past the enchantments. I attempted to nick my finger with my pocketknife, a gift from Dad Taylor, but no matter how much I pressed, the knife refused to pierce my skin, and eventually I was forced to stop as the knife felt like it would break under the pressure. Newly awakened bloodline again! After thinking about it I decided to try one of my canines, which had become slightly more pronounced. My tooth pierced the skin easily and I allowed the ruby droplet to fall onto the cover, there was a brief shimmer and then…nothing.

Assuming that it worked, I attempted to open the journal, and was surprised to find a brief letter to me, fall out from within. What it contained left me a little stumped.

Joshua,

If you are reading this before meeting me, then I am sorry to say that you are possibly the last surviving member of the White family. No doubt Felix has made you aware of your actual identity, however, the story Felix and indeed anyone else knows is somewhat different from the truth. I know that what I am about to tell you will only add to your confusion and for this I am truly sorry, but please know this was only to ensure your safety. You are in fact not my son, rather you are my nephew, the child of my younger sister Mara. This is a secret that must never be told to anyone, ever! I cannot emphasise this more, tell no-one! To do so will surely bring calamity to you.

All I can offer to help you on your journey, are the not-inconsiderable assets of the White family, plus this journal and bag, which should hopefully allow you to at least develop the ability to protect yourself. The journal and bag were provided by your actual father, whose mysterious identity I am sad to say even I am unaware. I only know that he was powerful on a level beyond any of us Whites and that he loved your mother dearly.

I am sorry we cannot be present to help to guide and support you, but know that as the last scion of our house, our hopes and love are with you always.

Your Loving Uncle

Stirling

Shortly after reading the letter, the contents lifted from the page and dispersed into the air. My uncle must have been serious about the secret, he didn't even feel safe leaving it written down. I honestly didn't know how to feel about the content. It was sad to know that I was probably alone and would never meet my mother, but nothing had really changed from my current situation, at least I knew her name now, Mara! I vowed that I would honour Uncle Stirling's wishes though; no-one would ever know, at least until I was strong enough to protect myself.

The identity of my actual Father was back to being an enigma, I didn't even know whether he was still alive. The letter seemed to create even more questions; if my father was so powerful, why would he allow everyone to die? Why did they die? Are they actually dead? With no clues, I knew I would just go around in circles. So, I decided to see what the rest of the journal contained.

My birth father was obviously not as sentimental as my uncle, as there was no letter from him, instead, what followed was more like a small compendium for Cultivators. Apparently, he was familiar with the White family systems and admitted that they were of a decent level, but my father recommended that I use the journal instead as it was far better, his words, not mine. Obviously, modesty was not one of his strong points. At least I knew something about him!

The initial chapter was a description of my Father's cultivation system, named The Primordial Yin Yang System, which sounded suitably pretentious! My Father lauded it as the number one cultivation method under heaven, but with zero frame of reference I had no idea if he was just blowing his own trumpet. It was largely a type of guided meditation, for how to draw in aether from the air through controlled beathing and circulate it through specific pathways, called meridians, within the body. During the process it would be converted to a personalised form of aether – Qi, and stored for use in my Dantian – a metaphysical space just below my navel. The bag, it explained, contained the herbs I would need to temper my body and other things to help me eventually unlock my father's bloodline, which if it was anything like my mother's, I wasn't sure I wanted to do!

Honestly, if I had read the journal a few days earlier, I would have just assumed it was some sort of pseudoscience quackery. However, now I found myself taking it deadly seriously, what a strange world!

It briefly described the first stages of cultivation, namely: Apprentice, Warrior, Spirit Warrior. Apparently, there were also further stages, but nothing would be revealed of those until necessary, fuck knows how the journal would know when it was necessary. Each stage had specific goals to achieve before being able to progress to the next. Apprentice, where I would start, was apparently about building the level of Qi my Dantian could contain by filling it, allowing it to expand, then rinse and repeat.

Deciding that I wouldn't lose anything from just trying it, I sat cross legged on the floor and attempted to follow the instructions and as my mind slowly opened, I was amazed that I could sense the aether flowing all around me. It was a strange sensation, as it was both invisible and non-tangible, but I could somehow feel it around me and moving through my body. Unfortunately, my initial surprise at being able to follow the method, soon gave way to frustration. As in the following hours I quickly realised that my Dantian, which, although shockingly, did seem to exist, was also fucking insatiable, determined to just keep on taking no matter how much Qi entered it. And with no description on the how big a Dantian was supposed to be, nor how long it would take to fill, I was essentially just going in blind and hoping for the best. So, I persevered, and finally after a few more hours it seemed I was getting somewhere, as a barely discernible mist seemed to permeate my entire Dantian.

At which point I was interrupted by a loud knock at the door. Feeling slightly out of sorts from sitting still for so long, I slowly made my way over and opened it to a thoroughly too excited Mikey.

"Bruv, look what I can do!" he said, whilst holding out his hand.

He started to concentrate so hard that it looked like he was constipated, and I had to stop myself from laughing. Suddenly a small ball of light flickered briefly in and out of existence above his palm.

"I am become Death, destroyer of worlds," he said with a beaming smile.

I started laughing at how excited he was. "That's epic, bruv."

And it was, because even if all he had managed was to imitate a dying torch, it was still magic and that was amazing.

I then relayed my own experiences to Mikey, and he was suitably unimpressed.

"Oh my god, that sounds so boring, are you really gonna spend so much time just sat meditating?" he asked. "Felix gave me an exercise I need to practise to progress, but it's more like a series of puzzles, so least it's fun."

"Yeah, it's not ideal." I found myself agreeing with him. I didn't want to waste my time just sat doing nothing, so in the future I would spend a couple of hours cultivating each night before bed and the odd extra bit when I had some free time. Hopefully, it would be enough.

"And you have to overfill this Dantainer thingy, again and again, but you spent all afternoon and didn't even manage to fill it once?" he asked.

"Dantian, and yep." I nodded. "But I don't think it is meant to be a fast process, so I'll just take my time"

"Well, rather you than me, whilst you earn a PhD in sitting on your arse, I'll be lobbing fireballs like Mario," Mikey said, whilst laughing and jumping around like the eponymous plumber.

It started laughing along with him, as I knew that cultivating would allow me to use abilities too, so I wasn't too bothered. Plus being a Cultivator had its advantages too, as despite a mage's ability to perform great feats of magic, I would be much more physically capable than they could ever hope to be.

"So, what do you have to do now?" Mikey asked.

"What do you mean?"

"Like, as the head of the White family, is there specific shit you should be doing?"

I suddenly realised I hadn't really thought about it. Surely, I would have some responsibilities? "I don't know bruv. But now you've got me wondering. Let's go and find out."

Chapter 10

After a good half-an-hour of searching, we finally tracked Felix down to the library, where he was sat reading. I realised I needed to get over my aversion to ringing the bell for assistance, otherwise I'd spend half my life looking for people in the house.

"Master Josh, how may I be of assistance?" Felix asked as we entered.

"Well, I'm not sure what I'm meant to do?"

"In what way?"

"With my life. Am I to just carry on as before but just live in a different house? Or is there something specific I should be doing as a White?"

"Those are valid questions, but truthfully, I planned to let you settle into your new life here for a while before worrying over specifics. You have been through a lot in the last few days, and I assumed you would need a period of adjustment before discussing things with you."

"I appreciate that, Felix, I really do, but I think that I need to know these things in order to adjust."

"A very prudent point, Master Josh. It seems I overlooked that fact. Perhaps we can discuss it over dinner?"

I hadn't eaten in hours so that sounded like a great idea to me. "Sounds like a plan."

Felix first arranged a lift home for Mikey as it was Sunday and therefore a school night! And shortly after that, dinner was served, and we talked as we ate more of the chef's delicious cooking.

64

We first covered the boring bits and luckily, there was no need to concern myself with the managing of the White's assets or finances, as we had professionals responsible for that, with Felix's oversight of course. With regards to what my family does, as Felix had previously mentioned, the Whites are one of the groups protecting humanity from hidden supernatural threats! Felix soon put a stopper on my bubbling excitement, however, when he informed me, in no uncertain terms, that I was not ready to be involved in that side of the business. Despite my arguments to the contrary, he was adamant that until I was sufficiently trained, I would not be included. Damn! And it got even worse, because Felix wanted me to continue the last few months at school and finish my GCSEs. Which honestly, I didn't even see the point of anymore, but it wasn't for long, so I reluctantly agreed, and in return Felix promised he would find me a trainer. Now we were talking!

He also made a point of mentioning that the level of aether energy is only far higher on the estate, due to enchantments around the grounds, that gathered and held aether from the surrounding area. I didn't see this as an issue, as I would only be cultivating at home, but what he said next shocked me.

Apparently, the Earth was once a veritable spiritual paradise, overflowing with aether, however around three thousand years ago, and no-one is sure why, the amount on the planet began to sharply decline, eventually dropping to its present-day levels. He explained that many of the ancient myths and legends were all based around fact, but that the dropping aether levels had forced most of these powerful creatures and characters to either leave Earth or enter deep hibernation.

It was funny, as like most people, I had always accepted that the age of intellectual enlightenment and science had just meant we had progressed past those myths, which were nothing more than remnants of a less developed time. It seems we were wrong. I was wrong.

"So, what would we have to deal with nowadays?" I asked.

"Lower-level threats. Creatures in fewer numbers and of far less capability. A supernatural world that can be kept hidden from the masses."

"Will it change back to how it was before?"

Felix drummed his fingers on the dining table. "Now that is the worrying part. Around eighty years ago, during the second world war in fact, the levels of aether suddenly began to increase again. Extremely slowly mind you, but enough to be noticeable. If it was to have continued at the same rate, we estimated it would have probably taken only a thousand years to return to a level above that of the estate. However, the rate has not remained constant and seems to be continually increasing."

"Shit! Surely that would lead to bigger threats?"

"Quite! However, it is not a simple issue. If the aether level reaches a certain critical point, the entire world be affected on a fundamental level. Not only will long dormant beasts arise, but some of the indigenous wildlife could awaken to aether use, including humanity. It would lead to a complete change to the nature of life on this planet."

"That's madness! How long do we have?"

"No-one can say, Master Josh, it could be a hundred years, it could be five hundred. Worst case, it could be as soon as the next few decades. It's rather hard to quantify with the ever-changing rate of the planets recovery, luckily, even after it happens, exposure to the richer aether environment will cause gradual change, it won't all happen overnight."

More at ease following the initial bombshell, I bid Felix goodnight and returned to my room. Sticking to my earlier plan I cultivated before bed, but a couple of hours of it led to no real change in my Dantian, I was forced to admit that I was in it for the long haul. I attempted to assure myself with the old adage – slow and steady wins the race! But it wasn't particularly comforting.

Before getting my head down, I had a brief skim through the rest of the journal, it was full of martial arts techniques suitable for different levels of cultivation. At the apprentice level there was an unarmed style named Emperor's Fist, a movement technique called Wind Step and techniques for various weapons, but with no experience using weapons, I would probably need to try some out before I knew which would suit me.

I did find it strange that many of the weapons seemed to be of a Chinese type, which led to many questions; are more cultural links to the mythical past retained in Asia? Also, Baihu, my supposed Divine Beast ancestor is part of East Asian mythology. So, why am I white northern European? Also, I know there are Mages and Cultivators, but what other ways are there of using aether? What about Norse, Greek or Ancient Egyptian myths? Were all ancient gods just powerful awakened?

With my head spinning from far too many questions, I slowly drifted into a deep sleep.

Chapter 11

The next couple of weeks passed by in a blur. School was the same as ever and I just did my best to focus throughout the day, although, History and Religious Studies suddenly became far more interesting. As I found myself eager to know more of the world's myths and fables, wondering which were based on truth and which were complete nonsense. The first time Damon had seen Mikey back at school he had looked stunned, fuelling my suspicions that he had something to do with the hit and run, but strangely, after a few days, he was back to being absent from school and I had no chance to confront him about it.

I spent a lot of time with Eleanor, our relationship developing nicely and most evenings Mikey came over for training with Felix or just to hang out and make hilarious plans for the future. Life was good!

It was also exciting because it would soon be the Easter holidays, and Felix was true to his word and had arranged an instructor to train me. They were due to arrive at the start of the holiday! I had even made sure to visit the Taylors every few days so they wouldn't worry. Everything was going smoothly until the final week of the school term; I should have known it wouldn't last.

*****

It was a Thursday afternoon and as I approached the Taylors house, I instantly noticed a strange car parked on the drive. Letting myself in, I called out to announce my presence, "Mum, Dad, it's me."

"We're in the living room," came the reply from Mum Taylor.

She didn't sound particularly stressed, so I calmly made my way in to join them. Two unfamiliar and suited men were sat on the sofa with cups of tea.

One smiled at me as I walked in. "Hi Joshua, my name is DI Dobson, and this is DS Hazelmoore." He gestured at the man next to him, who bobbed his head in greeting. "I was just telling your foster parents that I have a few questions for you, if that's ok?"

I nodded, unsure what it could be about. "Yeah, sure, sir, go ahead."

"I don't suppose you've seen Damon recently?" he asked.

"No, he hasn't been in school for several weeks, why? Is he missing?"

"No, not Damon, but his father is, as well as some of the family…business associates. When was the last time you saw him?"

"Damon?" I asked, thoroughly confused.

"No, his father." DI Dobson narrowed his eyes at me.

I shook my head, a little confused why he would ask. "I don't think I've ever seen his father. I've seen him dropped off in a black SUV before, but I haven't a clue who else was in it."

"You're sure?"

"I don't think I'd forget meeting someone, no matter how briefly. I don't understand, what has this got to do with me?" I asked. "Is this because of the scrap we had? Because I never hurt Damon, there're multiple versions of the footage online if you want to check."

"I believe you; we've already reviewed the footage. But it's odd, because Damon insists that you and Michael Westfield have something to do with it. He swears that

Michael was hospitalised in a hit and run and that you both blame his father for it."

"Hospitalised? Mikey's just fine, sounds to me like Damon has lost the plot," I said, trying to maintain my best poker face.

"Hmm, yeah, he is. According to Michael's parents, it was a case of mistaken identity at the hospital, but when we spoke to the hospital, they said that someone matching your description came to visit the 'not Michael'," he said making quotation marks with his fingers, "twice, in fact, and that shortly after the second visit, the seriously injured young man mysteriously disappeared from the hospital, and rather conveniently any CCTV footage of the time has been erased. It's all very—"

"Strange?" I said, interrupting him.

"Exactly, son, and if I'm honest with you. I'm not a big fan of strange."

"I don't know what to say, I thought it was Mikey when I visited, the school told me as much. The second time I visited because I felt bad for the lad. I'd been so glad it wasn't Mikey that I began to feel guilty, so I went back to check up on him again."

"And where did he go?" he asked, watching me closely for any signs of deception.

It was clear they didn't have any evidence; the detective was just fishing for information. Not that healing Mikey was illegal anyway. "Well, when I arrived, he had casts on his legs and was in no condition to go anywhere, so he definitely didn't just walk out," I said.

The DI tapped on his paper repeatedly with his pen. "Look, son, this is strange as all hell, and somehow you seem to be caught up in the middle of it. So, if there's anything you can tell me, to help me out, it will look better for you."

"Officer," I said, "can I be straight with you?"

"Of course."

"I don't particularly like Damon, but neither do most people, it's one of the pitfalls of being a jerk to everyone around you. But I haven't a clue what's happened to his dad, and in all honesty, the fact you are even questioning me about it seems absurd. Besides, everyone at school seems to think they are some sort of criminals, so surely there are far more likely avenues of inquiry than a sixteen-year-old high school student?"

It must have been clear to them that they weren't going to get any useful information out of me, as DI Dobson stood up to leave, followed closely by his partner. "Fair enough, son, thank you for your time. If we have any more questions, we'll be in touch," DI Dobson said, "oh, and thank you for the tea."

As we saw them out of the front door DI Dobson turned back to me. "If by some miracle, you are involved in what happened to the Stanley crew, I will find out."

I had nothing to do with it, so I just shook my head and shut the door behind them.

As soon as we were back in the living room, the Taylors didn't waste a moment before starting with the questions. I happily admitted that Felix had fixed up Michael and we snuck him out of the hospital, which drew a chuckle from them both.

"What about Damon's dad?" mum Taylor asked.

"Really, mum?"

"Well, I had to ask, you never know, it could have just been self-defence, they sound like horrible pieces of work."

"Yeah, they must be, especially if they're responsible for how Damon turned out. But it wasn't me. It's the first I've heard of it."

"Well, that's good enough for us." Dad smiled.

*****

After that one brief hiccup, things settled back into the routine, and by the time the final day of term I found myself hesitating over telling her the full truth about me. In the end though, I decided against it, it was still too soon into our

71

relationship to go shattering world views. Plus, Ellie was my first real girlfriend; I would tell her in time, there was no rush to complicate things.

After walking her home after school, we kissed, and I promised I would call her to meet up during the Easter holidays. Now how to explain the estate? Or would I not take her home? Nah, that would eventually seem weird, I'd already put it off long enough.

Before bed that night I finally had the long awaited first breakthrough to the second stage of Qi gathering, and felt I was fully ready to meet my new trainer in the morning. How wrong I was…

Chapter 12

When I awoke, the sun had only just reared its glorious head. Pulling back the curtains, I opened the window and breathed in the estate's aether rich air, marvelling at the beautiful dawn tapestry of blues and yellows. Following my breakthrough last night, I was eager to start training to test my new limits.

After a quick shower, I dressed in the outfit Felix had prepared for me, a set of Daoist robes, complete with plain black slippers. I wasn't sure how I felt about them, but at least they were light and comfortable.

Venturing downstairs to the dining room, Felix was already sat eating breakfast with a man I assumed was my new trainer. A combination of Hollywood movies and reading had obviously miscoloured my imagination, as I had envisioned a small, old, and hunched-over martial arts master. Some reclusive Daoist immortal venturing down from his mountain cave. The reality was somewhat different. At around six-foot-eight, he was over twenty stone of solid muscle and hair, so much hair! Standing up, he introduced himself in a strong Scandinavian accent as Master Ingmar Bronstad and like a human bear towering over me, he enveloped my hand in a strong handshake. Increasing his grip, but not to the point of crushing my hand, he grunted.

"Good, very good, you are strong," he said, "but you will also need to be here." He tapped my head. "Then, I can make you even stronger." He laughed.

73

I suddenly had an ominous feeling that Master Bronstad's training was going to be anything but pleasant.

Master Bronstad ate enough at breakfast for three adults, I had never seen someone who could pack so much food in. He must have eaten a dozen poached eggs, half an entire salmon, two grapefruits and a whole loaf of dark rye bread.

"If you want to be strong like a bear, you must eat like a bear," he said, whilst waving a huge lump of salmon.

I just nodded in agreement, whilst eating my, though still large, far more reasonable portions.

After breakfast we made our way to the dojo, Master Bronstad looked around, shaking his head at the facilities. "We will not be in here much, let's go to the outdoor training area."

I looked at Felix. "We have an outdoor training area?"

"Of course, allow me to lead the way."

As we made our way outdoors, I realised I had been far too lax in exploring the estate, who knew how many secrets this place had? The training area was a good ten-minute stroll away, in the middle of the woodlands surrounding the house. It looked, simply put, rather Neolithic. A circle of bare earth liberally coated in sand, surrounded by various log training contraptions, rock weights and random stone monoliths. Which seemed to have no purpose other than aesthetic. Caveman chic? I wasn't too impressed.

Master Bronstad, on the other hand, looked like a kid in a candy store. "Good, very good, here we will make you strong." he said with a giant smile.

Felix bade us farewell, and Master Bronstad turned to me. "Take off your shirt, you will not need it. First, we will warm-up and then I will test your capabilities, then we will break you."

I thought that maybe his wording was off, as English was not his first language. "You mean break through my limits?"

"No, your body will break." Master Bronstad grinned savagely. "But it will rebuild itself. Stronger!" he said, pretty much yelling by the end.

Brilliant, my new instructor was a lunatic!

Stripped down to just my trousers and slippers, the warm-up started off easy. Master ran through the woods, and I just had to follow him. For a huge man he was remarkably nimble. Every few minutes he increased his pace, which was fine, until about thirty minutes in. At which point he suddenly sped up so much, that I was essentially sprinting to keep up.

We must have been travelling at nearly forty miles per hour, which in thick woodlands meant that avoiding trees and roots required my full concentration. Five minutes later, my lungs were burning, and I was struggling. A momentary lapse in concentration, was quickly followed by my left shoulder clipping a tree and I was tumbling at high speed with no control over my direction. I lost count of how many trees I hit before finally coming to a bone-jarring halt. Lying on the damp forest floor and trying to breathe, every part of me hurt. Hearing footsteps approaching, I turned my head and saw Master Bronstad.

"You should have avoided the trees," he said whilst laughing his arse off.

I was hurt, pissed off and a little embarrassed, so I just scowled at him in response. From the change in the look, he gave me, I knew I had fucked up.

"You are angry at me for your own mistake?" he asked, "the warm-up is over, run back to the training area."

Realising that I couldn't let him down on my first day, I dragged myself to my feet and set off. When I finally arrived, Master Bronstad was already stood waiting for me, next to logs of various sizes.

"Pick a log, carry it for a full lap around the estate. Then you will repeat with the next log. When all the logs are gone, we move on," he said.

I was getting a little frustrated, for weeks I had been waiting to learn how to fight and utilise my Qi but Master Bronstad just wanted me to do caveman cross-fit.

"Are you going to teach me how to fight?" I asked.

"Yes, when you are strong enough."

"I'm strong enough now."

Master Bronstad scowled at me. "You whine like a child."

In all fairness, I was probably whinging, but I still felt the need to defend myself. "I'm only sixteen!"

"Yes, sixteen, so you are no longer a child," he said, before contemplating for a second and beginning to nod. "Okay then, we shall fight, show me how strong you are."

Eager to showcase my abilities, I grinned and held up my fists.

"Yes, let's have a good fight." He roared and launched himself at me.

Calling it a fight, would truthfully be misleading, as he pretty much just battered the shit out of me. He shrugged off my strongest blows like I was tickling him, whereas each time he hit me, well, I imagine being hit by a car would have hurt less. I'm also pretty sure he was pulling his punches. Finally, with my head spinning, I collapsed back on to my arse once again.

Cringing internally at the expected ridicule, I looked up to see Master Bronstad laughing. "Good fight!" He grinned, whilst wiping the blood from a split lip.

It was just two words, but they instantly wiped away any sense of embarrassment over my defeat and I found myself chuckling with him.

Instead of helping me up, he plonked himself down in front of me and looked at me seriously. "Joshua, do you know why Felix chose me to be your instructor?"

"Because you are strong?"

"That is true, but it's not the main reason. A life around regular humans, where you were always stronger, always faster, has given you a false sense of your abilities. I was chosen because you need to learn that…"

"I'm not as strong as I think I am?" I asked.

"No, you are very strong, more that there is always someone stronger." He smiled warmly at me.

I hung my head, a little dejected over the fact I had overestimated myself.

"You are sad?" he asked.

I found myself questioning how I actually felt. "No, not sad, more embarrassed, I guess."

"But you still wish to be stronger?"

"Of course, I want to be able to protect the people I care about." I nodded.

Then why are we sat around doing nothing about it?" he asked whilst getting to his feet.

Smiling back at him, I got up and looked at the logs. Let's do this, I thought. Deciding to start with the heaviest log, as I knew fatigue would make the exercise progressively harder. I squatted down and attempted to heave it up, but it was far heavier than I anticipated. Struggling with all my strength, I barely managed to get it off the ground, before having to let it drop.

"It's too heavy, what on Earth is it made from?" I asked.

"Nothing on Earth," Master Bronstad replied cryptically, "it is Iron spirit wood and weighs about two-hundred and fifty kilograms per cubic foot."

The log I had attempted to lift was about ten cubic feet, so must have weighed about two and a half tonnes, no wonder I struggled to even lift it! I made my way to the smallest log, which was closer to a round fence post, but still must have been around three-quarters of a tonne. Barely managing to get it up onto my shoulders to set off around the estate, it became immediately clear that running was not an option. Even walking it was nearly an hour before I had completed a full lap and by the time I got back, I was in agony, my back screaming for me to stop. Looking at the remaining logs, I had no idea how I could complete the task. Contrary to my expectations, it seemed Master Bronstad didn't actually expect for me to get the next log, instead leading me through an assortment of hellish exercises. When we finally stopped for lunch, several hours had passed and I was wavering on my feet.

Over the hour allowed for lunch, I thoroughly stuffed my face with copious amounts of meat, rice and fruit. Fully satiated, I could literally feel the strength returning to my body from the food and realised how spot on Master had been at breakfast. Noticing the food's effect, I decided to circulate my Qi according to my cultivation method too. Within a few minutes, most of the pain in my body was gone and I was ready for round two.

Opening my eyes, I saw Master Bronstad looking at me with a warm smile. "So, you figured it out?" he asked.

Internally I was cursing at his lack of guidance over the matter, but I decided to be diplomatic. "Why didn't you mention it?"

"I would have, eventually. But a lesson realised by oneself is often far more instructive."

"Fair enough, Master," I said, finding it hard to argue with his logic.

"Also, I wanted you to hold off from using Qi, as the longer you hold out, the greater the gains for your physical body. Qi's regenerative effects have a limit too, so although it's great for enhancing your body and speeding up the recovery of tired muscles, it will eventually fail to help, and you'll need actual rest. And any serious injuries will also take time to heal, even if they will do so far quicker than on a mundane, so making your physical body more robust will always remain a priority, even as your cultivation grows."

"I understand, Master." I nodded, vowing to myself I would only cycle Qi when I could no longer physically continue. At least I hadn't been suffering for nought.

After lunch, the relentless physical training continued for another few hours, until again I had got to the point where I was spent. Allowed to restore my condition through cycling my Qi, we then finally moved on to something exciting, unarmed combat techniques. Master Bronstad didn't have a specific martial arts style and after I quizzed him about it, was quick to tell me that he happily used anything that worked and discarded any useless fluff.

"You think you can learn to fight by performing forms or katas?" he asked.

"I thought that's a big part of how martial arts are learned."

Master grinned at me. "Okay, watch this."

Flowing immediately into a flawless wushu kata, Master moved with a grace that belied his stature. It was beautiful to watch, like a well-choreographed dance and I found myself wishing that I was able to emulate him.

Finally coming to a stop, he turned to look at me. "How was that?"

"Amazing!"

"And how many movements in that entire performance could be used as intended? In actual combat?"

It didn't take a genius to see what he was implying. "Very few?" I replied.

"Good, exactly." He smiled. "These things are good for teaching flexibility and flow. If you are particularly astute, they can even be used to explore the limits of your bodily control. All of which would make you a better fighter. But you will not learn how to fight from them."

Clearly my earlier assumption had come from a place of ignorance. English may not have been his first language, but he was perfectly fluent and eloquent. At least when he wanted to be!

The training after lunch was brutal and bloody. I learned different ways to strike, and how to utilise the mechanics of my body to maximise my speed, efficiency, and power. At least the use of the stone monoliths became apparent, who needed a punch bag when you could hit a rock! Even with my freakishly strong body, my hands were bleeding, my bones ached, and I was sure that they were riddled with stress fractures. Finally, around five pm, Master Bronstad said we were done with training for the day. He gave me a packet of herbs and instructed me to take a hot bath with them whilst cycling my Qi before dinner. Before leaving, I briefly questioned him about learning Qi techniques.

"If you give a powerful rifle to a veteran sniper or a new recruit, who will use it more effectively?" he asked in response.

"I understand." I nodded disappointedly, guessing that until I had the basics down, flashy Qi techniques would have to wait. After thanking him for his instruction, I made my way inside for some blissful rest.

Chapter 13

The next few days passed in a sweat-filled blur. I was getting stronger at an astonishing rate and by the third day I had managed to lug the one tonne log around the estate. Master Bronstad seemed pleased with my progress; he still easily kicked my arse when we sparred, but at least I tried to apply what I had learnt.

I was allowed a break every fifth day and arranged to spend my first day off with Eleanor. Felix offered to give me a lift into town and as we pulled out of the estate, we both noticed the problem at the same time; the aether level was nearly half of what it was in the estate.

"I thought it would take decades to get to this level?" I asked.

"That's what the evidence seemed to suggest, Master Josh," he replied, concern evident in his voice.

"What are we going to do?"

Felix scrunched his brows. "If this is happening on the scale of the planet, I am afraid there is very little we can do."

Knowing it could take years to affect any change, and that there was nothing I could do to stop it anyway, I put it to the back of my head so I could enjoy my day with Eleanor.

We met up at a local coffee shop, then spent the morning window shopping around town. Eleanor taking great joy in dragging me from store to store whilst trying on numerous outfits. It was a little boring, but I did enjoy seeing her twirling around in all the different clothes. It was also a nice change in pace from the previous few days and after a little persuasion from her, I even treated myself to a few items too.

Everything was going great until Eleanor led me to a small boutique store, located down a side road off the high street.

"Come on," she said, dragging me by the hand. "I love this place. Every item is unique!"

I could tell something was different as soon as we entered. It was only a small shop, full of what looked like high quality and expensive, hand-made clothing. It was a cool store and the middle-aged Asian lady behind the counter smiled when she saw Eleanor.

"Ellie, sweetie, great to see you," she said with a smile, however, when she noticed me her gaze quickly changed to one of abject terror.

I'm not sure how, but I could immediately tell that she wasn't human. "Are you okay?" I asked.

The lady quite literally flew around the counter and threw herself down into a kowtow. "Please spare me, milord, if I knew we would receive a visit, we would have prepared."

I was stumped, unsure of how to reply to that. Eleanor was staring at me in confusion.

"Please, madam, get up, there is nothing to apologise for," I said.

"Thank you, my Lord, thank you," she said whilst rising to her feet.

After she stood up, we all just stood there in an awkward silence, the shop owner still refusing to raise her head.

"Can, someone please tell me what the hell is going on?" Eleanor suddenly asked.

There were probably a hundred correct things I could have said, but instead, I just blurted out the first bone-headed excuse that came to me. "Maybe it's a cultural thing?"

Eleanor looked at me as if I was an idiot. "I'll ignore the lack of sensitivity in your comment, but I'm not stupid. Why would she call you milord?"

Our pleasant morning was quickly devolving into a nightmare scenario, and I had no idea if I should save it by being honest.

Eleanor huffed. "Fine, keep your secrets," she said, walking for the exit. "And don't bother calling, I had enough secrets from Damon."

Ouch! It was crunch time and so deciding the world would be changing eventually anyway, I decided to risk it. "Wait!"

Eleanor stopped walking and looked back at me, she looked genuinely sad.

"Please. Come back, I'll tell you," I said.

Sauntering back over, she looked at me expectantly. "Well?"

Taking a deep breath, I realised that there was little chance she would believe me, the truth was too far-fetched. So, I just came out with it, she would either believe me or not. "Well, honestly, the shop keeper isn't fully human."

"Are you kidding me, Josh? Being a bigot is your idea of telling the truth?" she asked.

I was shocked and a little offended that she would even suggest that. "No, not like that, she is something else, different."

She snorted. "Okay, I'll humour you. So, she's not human. And why did she call you milord?"

"Well, the thing is, technically, I'm not fully human either." I rubbed my head. "But, as to why she would refer to me like that, I'm sorry Eleanor, I haven't a clue either." I looked at the shopkeeper. "Can you help me out please, madam?"

The shopkeeper looked confused. "Milord, you honestly don't know?"

Clearly, moments like these were going to be a regular occurrence, as really, I was only slightly more informed than Eleanor. "I'm afraid that I only recently became aware of my own heritage, it's a long story."

The shopkeeper suddenly seemed far more at ease. "Well, you see, a few of us are extremely sensitive to powerful bloodlines."

"Okay, but why call me milord? And why prostrate yourself?" I questioned.

"Because, I have been around nobles before, but what I felt from your bloodline dwarfed theirs. So, I knew you were of an exceedingly noble background. And..." she hesitated.

From the look on her face, I could tell she was still scared. "Please, go on," I said.

"Well, you see, nobility tend to respond...violently to any perceived disrespect." She visibly quivered.

"That's awful, I'm truly sorry if I scared you," I said, mortified that I would be instantly perceived as a threat by other non-humans.

I guess deep down I liked to think of myself as a nice guy, so it bothered me that my mere presence had upset an old lady.

The shopkeeper smiled tentatively at me. "Such is the world we live in, milord."

Eleanor had remained silent throughout my conversation with the shopkeeper and was now looking at us like we were both insane. "I get it, this a set-up, isn't it?" she asked, "Mikey, you can come out now!"

"It's not a joke Ellie," I said, "there's a whole supernatural world, hidden within the one you know."

The look on Eleanor's face suggested she was wrestling with the idea.

"Does Mikey know?" she asked.

"Yes, and..." I hesitated.

"Spit it out then," she said, her growing frustration clear in her tone.

"Mikey isn't a regular human either, he...he's a mage. Well, an apprentice one."

On that bombshell, Eleanor had clearly reached her limit for crazy. "Look, this is all too much, I need some time, okay? I will call you," she said and started to walk off.

"I can prove it," I called out as she was leaving the shop.

Turning back towards me, she gave me a strained smile and walked out. It was understandable, I had just rocked her entire worldview. Wanting to be honest with people I cared about was admirable, but maybe I was being naïve and some things should just stay hidden. It was hard, as my entire life I had been surrounded by secrets, hell, I was still in the dark about certain things and I wouldn't wish that on anyone else.

The shopkeeper was sympathetic, she could probably tell I was upset and probably felt a little guilty for causing it, but it wasn't her fault. We chatted for a short while over a cup of tea, and I said my goodbyes. As kind as she was, it was probably a relief for her to have me out of the store.

Walking out into the fresh air, I wasn't sure if it was my imagination, but the amount of aether seemed to have increased a tiny amount again in just several hours. When Felix arrived to pick me up, I immediately asked if he noticed the same.

"You know, I think you may be right, Master Josh. Surely it doesn't bode well."

After my morning with Eleanor, I threw myself even harder into training, if it was noticed by Master Bronstad, he never questioned why. The rest of Easter break consisted of long days of training, followed by longer nights waiting to see if she would call. At least Mikey was always around, after learning from Felix he often stayed over, and we usually spent the evenings eating amazing food and unwinding by playing video games.

Towards the end of Easter break Master Bronstad said that my strength was increasing nicely and so it was time to add in some advanced training too, I begun to get excited, until he explained the 'advanced training'.

Master had sunk wooden poles into the ground with their ends sat at different heights and various distances apart. Running and jumping between them could have been fun and improved both my balance and co-ordination. Not fun, however, was completing the same activity in a two-hundred-kilogram training vest, whilst simultaneously dodging the random attacks of a crazy bear man and his metal staff. I never once doubted the effectiveness of his methods, but it hurt like a bitch and I found myself craving the nightly medicinal baths, where I could ease my bruised and battered body. I also suspected from the crazed smile on his face, that Master Bronstad took a sadistic pleasure in hitting me.

Eventually, the holidays came to an end and Eleanor had never called. Although, I found I was equally disappointed over the fact I would have less time for training. As torturous as it seemed at times, I was making great progress. Maybe I'm just a glutton for punishment? Whereas school, on the other hand, now seemed pointlessly trivial compared to the other amazing things I could learn.

"I'm going to be a mage, Josh, a fucking mage! I can literally make fire with my mind," he said whilst making a small flame appear and disappear above his open palm. "So I fail to see what benefit GCSEs are going to bring me in the future."

It was impressive how much progress Mikey was making, several weeks ago he could barely do anything, now he was a regular human zippo. He was right though, our life was destined to be unconventional, so why should we follow the normal paths?

"At least it's only a few more months. I mean, A-levels and Uni. are optional, so once we've finished our exams, we can do whatever we want," I said, trying to convince myself as much as Mikey.

"You say that, but some sort of education is mandatory until we are eighteen, plus my parents expect me to go to Uni. If I tell them I'm done with school, they'll go mental."

"So, tell them you have landed an amazing apprenticeship, where you will get qualifications whilst being paid," I said, "that's what I will be officially recorded as. An apprentice at one of my own companies."

He looked excited. "That could work! Dad is always going on about experience being better than qualifications, I could argue that this way I get both."

It was understandable, as Mikey's dad owned a successful chain of used luxury car salesrooms and garages. They were fairly wealthy now, but his dad had never forgot his working-class roots. His great-grandfather had emigrated to the UK from Trinidad with not much more than the shirt on his back, and all his money and success was hard earned, at least that was what he was always quick to tell Mikey and me.

"There you go, problem sorted." I smiled.

"Apprentices get paid, they will get suspicious if I have no money." He looked at me with mock puppy-dog eyes.

I started laughing. "You cheeky bastard, not only are you being taught by my family butler and provided a private suite in my manor. Now you want me to pay you too? Besides, minimum wage for apprentices is fuck-all."

He looked devastated. "Yeah, I guess I could get a part-time job in Maccies or something."

"Jeez, I was only joking, Mikey, of course I'll sort it."

Grinning at me, I could see the gears turning in his head. "And err, what would be the starting salary for this most excellent of apprentices?" he asked, gleefully rubbing his hands together.

Smiling back, it was too hard not to mess with him. "Well," I said, tapping on my chin. "You would only have GCSEs so you wouldn't be worth too much, but then again you are also my best mate and that is priceless. You will also be staying here whenever possible too, so I'd have to take rent off..." Mikey was staring at me, the eagerness evident on his greedy little face. So, I decided to put him out of his misery. "…shall we say, I don't know, two grand a week, Is that enough?"

Mikey's jaw dropped; I think it was safe to say he was happy, as he was still smiling when he got in his cab home. Heading back inside, I found myself thinking about Eleanor, and how awkward school would probably be in the morning.

Chapter 14

Even during term-time, I still had to train, so by the time I left for school with Felix, I'd already completed a punishing two-hour session, and even though my newest bruises were fading by the time I'd gotten out of the shower, I still felt tender.

In the car, I once again raised my point about the necessity of attending school, but Felix was apparently having none of it. It could have been worse, he could have demanded I did sixth-form or college too, so I wasn't going to push it. Besides, Felix was probably struggling enough having to fulfil two contradictory roles: servant and guardian. Maybe having me at school just gave him a break from the juggling act, but it also seemed that he was keen for me to retain some sense of normality, even though I wasn't bothered, as to me, that ship had long sailed.

Getting out of the car, I saw Eleanor across the car park, she looked over, but I just smiled sadly at her, nodded, and made my way into school. At first, I had waited for her to call, and when I realised she wasn't going to, I had been upset. But I had so many other things to deal with, that complicated romance was not top of the list and so I just threw myself into my training. It was her loss, I tried to assure myself, as I looked around desperately for Mikey. Okay, maybe I was still a little bothered.

The first day back at school proved to be rather dull and I found myself resenting the lost time that could have been better spent with Master, when I had become such a glutton for punishment?

I perked up after lunch, when I realised in the middle of a particularly boring Geography lesson, that I could cultivate whilst sat in class. It wasn't as effective as at home due to the lower ambient aether levels, but at least I no longer felt I was just wasting time. It did however lead to one awkward moment, as I tended to zone-out whilst cultivating and by the time I realised the teacher was asking me a question, it was clear by his demeanour that he had tried to get my attention several times. Oh well!

Finding a new use for my school time, life went on as normal and as the weeks passed by, apart from lunches spent with Mikey, my mind was rarely present. At first, my teachers were alarmed by my newly formed 'apathy', and I was called in for several talks about the importance of my upcoming exams, staying focused, blah, blah, blah. But, after we completed our final mock exams, they soon realised that I had been digesting what I needed to. After that, they just left me alone. I wasn't being disruptive, so they probably just chalked it up to puberty.

By the time that our exams rolled around, I was fairly content. Training was progressing nicely, and the increased amount of cultivation had allowed me to be sat firmly in the fourth level of qi gathering! Things were obviously going too smoothly for me, because as we were about to enter the hall for our first exam, Eleanor decided it was finally a good time to stop avoiding me.

"Can we talk after the exam?" she asked.

Shocked by the unexpected request, it took me a few seconds to fully process what she had said. "Okay." I nodded.

As we filtered out from the hall after the exam, I saw her sat waiting for me in the cafeteria. Sitting down opposite her, a flood of repressed feelings started to come out. I had no idea what to say, so I just waited for her to start.

"How have you been?" she asked tentatively.

Clearly the conversation was going to be a bit awkward. "Good, I guess, you?" I replied.

I could see she was wrestling with what to say and I didn't have the heart to watch her struggle. "Don't worry about it, Ellie, it's fine. We tried to see if we could be something more and it didn't work out. Even if you don't want to be with me, I'll always be your friend." I attempted to reassure her.

She took a deep breath and looked me in the eyes. "No. It's not fine! I liked you, like you, a lot! Then you came out with some crazy stuff, and that lady acted like it was perfectly normal, and suddenly I felt like the crazy one. Then you didn't talk to me again," she said, barely stopping to breathe, "so no, no its not fine."

Momentarily stunned, it took me a moment to find my voice. "You said you'd call, I waited, but you never did!"

Eleanor looked at me with an incredulous look on her face. "And you didn't think to call me?"

"I…I thought that you didn't want to speak to me. That you thought I was a nutter."

We sat in silence for a few moments, each waiting for the other to speak, finally Eleanor huffed. "Boys are so stupid," she said, her eyes misting up.

What do you say to that? In all fairness, in a way, she was right, I had no idea how to act in a relationship and didn't even think to call her, it was all too confusing. I knew I didn't want to see her cry though, so reaching over I took her hand in mine. "I'm sorry Ellie, but having a girlfriend was new to me. When you didn't call, I just figured you didn't want me around anymore."

Gently squeezing my hand, she half-smiled at me. "I'm sorry too. I didn't know what to think, so in typically useful Ellie fashion, I just did nothing."

"It was a lot to accept, either I'm crazy or—"

"Or, I had no idea about the world I've been living in," she finished for me.

Nodding gently back at her, I waited for her to continue, as something must have made her want to talk to me.

"At first, I still thought it was all some sort of set-up, or maybe you were just playing along with the delusions of the shopkeeper, it was easy at first. But the longer it went on, the more I realised that didn't make sense and I started to wonder if I was the one deluding myself."

"So, what changed?" I asked.

"I…I cracked, I needed to know, for sure, and I missed you so much." She squeezed my hands. "I went back to the store and spoke to the old lady; she was really sweet and she…" Ellie paused and took a steadying breath. "…she showed me! Her hand, it changed, right in front of me. It wasn't human, she had claws too Josh, claws! It took everything I had not to just run out of the store."

Part of me panicked. "Ellie, you should have come to me, what if it was dangerous?"

"I'd been to that store loads of times, Josh. It's been there for years, and I had to know," she said and looked down at my hands. "Can you do that? Grow claws?"

It was a good question. "I don't know." I shrugged. "Maybe, but I don't think the cafeteria is a good place to try," I said and started to chuckle.

Eleanor smiled and started to giggle along with me.

After we finally stopped laughing, I knew I had to ask the big question. "It doesn't change how you feel about me?"

Eleanor shook her head, pulled me towards her over the table and kissed me. It only then hitting me how much I had missed her.

"Do you want to come back to mine?" I asked.

"Whoa cowboy! We've only just got back together."

Panicking, I blurted out, "I didn't mean it like that!" Only then noticing from her smile that she was clearly messing with me. I could feel my face warming up, fuck, was I actually blushing? So uncool!

"So, you don't want me like that?" she asked.

92

"No, I mean yes, but that wasn't…" I noticed she was still smiling. "Damn it, you are cruel, Ellie."

Ellie started laughing. "I'm sorry Josh, it was just too easy. I have missed you."

"I missed you too," I admitted, "So would you like to come to mine?"

Smiling, she nodded in reply, and we left to wait to wait outside for Felix.

Ellie was a little shocked when I explained that we were waiting for my butler. And I found myself wondering how she would react when she saw my house?

Chapter 15

The car rolled between the opening gates and Ellie looked at me with a questioning gaze. Smiling at her I refrained from saying anything, and as the manor finally came into view, her jaw dropped, just like Mikey's. That was never going to get old!

"Who the hell are you, Josh?" she asked.

"I will explain when we get inside." I smiled, trying to act mysterious.

Her scrunched brow suggested I had probably failed in that regard, but at least she seemed willing to humour me.

When we were finally settled in my suite, we spent several hours chatting. I was an open book, freely going over everything about myself and all I knew about the hidden world. Finally, once Ellie was satisfied that there were some things, I knew no more about than she did, she grabbed me by the hand and demanded I give her a full tour of the house.

When she found out that Mikey had his own suite, she subtly implied that as my girlfriend maybe she should have her own one too. We had only just got back together, but I was happy and wasn't willing to argue the point. She did hit me though, when I suggested she could just stay in my rooms with me, you can't blame a lad for trying!

"Where are the secret passages?" Ellie asked.

"What secret passages?"

Again, with that look, like I couldn't possibly be so stupid! "Josh, this house is literally hundreds of years of years old, you're telling me that it doesn't have any secret passages or rooms?"

It was a great point, especially with the nature of our family, but truthfully, I had no idea. "I honestly haven't a clue, we would have to ask Felix."

"How have you lived here for several months, and not explored every inch of this place? Where is your sense of adventure?"

"I have been spending pretty much all of my free time training or recovering."

"You couldn't possibly have been training all the time? What are you, a machine?" she asked, looking at me incredulously.

"I did spend some free time chilling with Mikey, but apart from that, yeah, I was training non-stop." Looking into her pretty hazel eyes, it finally dawned on me why I had been so overzealous in my training, and I got a little embarrassed.

Ellie looked at me with concern. "That's a little hardcore, you need to take time to relax Josh, it's not healthy to never have a break."

"I know, it just…" I steeled myself, refusing to be ashamed of the truth. "…it helped me to not think about you."

The awkward silence that followed was quickly broken by Ellie. "I'm a fine one to talk, I got the same advice from my parents. For me it was revision, non-stop revision, I could probably recall the textbooks verbatim at this point." She threw herself into my arms.

As I held her, she asked, "Maybe show me where you train?"

"That I can do." I smiled enjoying the smell of her hair.

When we arrived, Master Bronstad was sat meditating in the arena and opened his eyes as we approached.

"Sorry to disturb you, Master, this is my girlfriend Eleanor, I was showing her around."

"Is this a new flame? Or are you the one young Josh was pining over, causing him to train so desperately?"

Damn! If she was a new girlfriend, that would have been just about the most awkward thing he could have asked, tact was obviously not Master's strong point! Although it did make me realise my personal feelings had been more obvious to those around me than to myself, bless them for not mentioning it. Before now at least!

Ellie, however, just took it with aplomb. "There's only one woman in Josh's life, at least as far as I'm aware?" She looked at me questioningly, her smile hinting she was joking. "Although, if that's the case, you should probably be thanking me then. For increasing his dedication."

Master Bronstad looked at her, then at me, and grinned. "Ooh boy, I like her, Josh, she's definitely a keeper, don't mess things up." He wagged his finger at me. "Well, it was a pleasure to meet you, miss Eleanor, I'll leave you two young lovebirds in peace," he said and was gone in a flash.

Shrugging off her obvious shock at his sudden disappearance, Ellie turned to look at me. "He seemed nice, if a little odd."

I found myself nodding along with her whilst thinking about what Felix had told me about Master Bronstad. "Yeah, and he's a great instructor. It's also amazing how well he has adapted over time, as social conventions were a little different for Viking berserkers fifteen-hundred years ago."

Ellie stared at me. "He's over fifteen-hundred years old?"

I nodded. "Yep, he was battling monsters around the world before some western civilisations even knew those parts of the world existed."

"I probably need to just stop being surprised about anything around you, don't I?" Ellie asked, clearly only half-joking.

We made our way around the training area, and I explained the use of the various items. Ellie had been doing gymnastics since she was a child, which is probably why she seemed more enthusiastic about the whole thing than most teenage girls would have been. When we got to the log weights, Eleanor attempted to move the smallest one and it would hardly budge.

"Damn, Josh, how much does this thing weigh?" she asked.

"That one is seven-hundred and fifty kilos."

"And you are expected to lift that?"

"Yep, and carry it for a lap of the estate?"

"Just how strong are you, Josh?"

I made my way towards the middle log, which was my current limit, excited that I had a chance to show off. After all, who doesn't want to impress their girlfriend?

"This is my current limit; it weighs one and a half tonnes." I heaved the log up onto my shoulders, my feet sinking slightly into the ground.

"I knew you were strong from the way you man-handled Damon, but I had no idea it was to this extent. Jesus, you could probably tear a man apart with your bare hands."

Mentioning tearing people apart, hit spookily close to home and I was suddenly bombarded with flashes of memories of the incident with the dog. Dropping the log down, I found myself breathing heavily.

Ellie ran over and put her hand on my arm. "Are you okay, Josh?"

Looking at Ellie, I knew I had to tell her. It was strange, as I hadn't even really thought much about the event since. Maybe I am wired differently? I thought to myself.

"Ellie, there's one more thing I need to tell you," I said.

Sat on the ground of the training area, I slowly narrated the events of that day. I did gloss over the grizzlier details, but I told her everything, including what we had done for Mikey.

After I finished, we just sat there in silence as she mulled over what I had told her.

"I like to think that I'm a good person and you know I hate unnecessary violence. But I'm not unrealistic, Josh, that dog would have killed that little girl. So, yes, the whole thing upsets me, but the thought of you not fighting back upsets me more. I know who you are in here." Ellie placed her hand on my chest. "You plan to risk your life to keep others safe, and I will be by your side whilst you do."

I just hoped that when it became people instead of animals that I was forced to fight and kill, that she would still feel the same.

Chapter 16

Our exams were soon over, and the end of school was fast approaching. Mikey eventually had his 'apprenticeship' agreed to by his parents and was looking forward to his new-found freedom.

I had offered the same thing to Eleanor, which she was enthusiastic about it, however her parents had been adamant that she complete A-levels before starting an apprenticeship, even if she no longer had any intention of going to university.

The evening before our last day of school, we were all sat having dinner and excitedly discussing the future, when Felix decided to drop a bombshell.

"Master Josh, Ingmar tells me that your training has reached a critical juncture, and if you're agreeable, he would like to take you on an outside training expedition?" he asked, whilst looking at Master Bronstad to continue.

Master looked at me. "It's true, Josh, an expedition would serve multiple purposes. You need to choose and learn a weapon, as well as begin to implement Qi techniques, and some exposure to the outside world will greatly solidify what you've learnt."

I was well up for a little adventure and a change of scenery for a few weeks sounded great. "Okay, so where are we going and for how long?" I asked excitedly.

Master Bronstad had clearly planned the whole thing out, as he didn't even hesitate to answer, "We'd travel to the Jade Wilderness realm and return in a year."

"A year!" I said, "and what is the Jade Wilderness realm?"

Master looked at me strangely. "Josh, a year is not long at all, barring an accident you will live for centuries, so you need to stop thinking of time in terms of mundanes. As for the Jade Wilderness realm, well, it's another world. Larger than earth, but still considered small within the larger cosmos."

I looked at Eleanor next to me and she reached out to take my hand. "You should go Josh, of course we'll miss you, but we'll be here when you return."

"I'm not against going, but I don't understand why I can't learn those things here?" I asked.

"You could, but a flower raised in a greenhouse will often die when exposed to the outdoors, do you understand?"

"I do." I nodded reluctantly.

"Good, only stress and danger will fully draw out your greatest potential," Master said, "plus, it will be fun." He gave me his trademark grin.

I grimaced at its unspoken promises of pain.

"Felix, is there any way that we could awaken Ellie before we leave?" I asked. "I would feel happier knowing that she is developing too whilst I am gone. If it's what Ellie wants, of course." I gazed at her questioningly.

Her excited nods made her opinion clear, and I turned to look at what Felix's response would be.

"I would be happy to try, Master Josh, however you have to bear in mind, not all humans are able to be awakened, most are destined for the life of a mundane."

Ellie's eyes dimmed a little at that. It was worrying to me too, as I couldn't imagine not sharing that aspect of my life with her. Plus, were she destined for the life of a mundane, the immense differences in lifespan would be almost impossible to overcome, potentially dooming our relationship before it had even really begun.

Felix arranged for everything in the dojo after dinner, unlike with Mikey, who awakened via the healing pill, we would attempt to awaken Ellie with a direct infusion of aether. Felix would carry out the procedure as he had extremely fine control and it would reduce the risk of any harm to Ellie. As Ellie lay, waiting for Felix to begin, I think everyone was nervous over what the outcome would be.

"Will it hurt?" Ellie asked as Felix was about to begin.

Felix held his hands out over her supine form. "No, not at all, most people describe it as a warm sensation, or they feel nothing at all."

As he began, I could feel the aether increase around his hands and slowly begin to trickle into Ellie. At first, nothing seemed to happen, and Ellie was expressionless. My heart started to beat faster, but just before I started to panic that nothing would happen, Ellie's eyes seemed to light up.

"I can feel it, it's cool, and pleasant." She laughed.

Felix continued for a few more seconds, and slowly withdrew his hands.

"Congratulations, Eleanor, it was a resounding success," he said.

We all cheered and I reached down to hug Ellie tightly, allowing the tension I had been feeling to leave my body.

Felix coughed, causing us to separate. "Now, Eleanor, I can do the same thing I did for Michael and test if you have a natural proclivity for the use of aether. Or you can simply wait and see how things develop?"

"I…I don't know, what would be best?" she asked looking around at all of us.

"Only you can make this decision, there is no right or wrong answer," Felix told her.

"I would like to find out, please. So that Josh will know what I'm studying whilst he is away." She smiled at me.

Her answer touched me, it was sweet of her to think of me, and she was right, I would have wondered about it the whole time I was away.

Felix carried out the same procedure he had with Mikey; however, the result was vastly different. Instead of aether dissipating as he moved his hands over her body, it pooled and rippled above her skin and an ever so slight coolness could be felt in the air, it was refreshing.

"Interesting, you are naturally attuned to an element. Which I'm sure everyone felt," Felix said.

"Ice?" I asked, based on the slight chill I felt.

"I understand your reasoning, but if her affinity was Ice, the chill would have been far more pronounced. It was Water, in all its forms. And from the way aether easily pooled around you, you will make a fine elementalist," Felix said.

Ellie looked thoughtful. "So, a mage like you and Mikey, but with just water?"

"Oh, no dear, not at all." Felix smiled. "Like anyone else, you may choose the path you take, whether that's to become a cultivator like Josh is doing, or a mage like Michael, or even another more exotic path. Being an elementalist just means that you have a deep affinity with an element, in your case water. And that any techniques or spells based around that element will be countless times easier."

"So, it won't limit me?" Eleanor asked.

"Well, it depends, if you trained to become a mage it wouldn't affect your ability to learn most spells, but some elementalists struggle with their opposing element, so in your case that would be fire," Felix answered.

Eleanor smiled at me. "I want to be a mage."

"That's awesome." I smiled back. "Would you be able to arrange someone to train Ellie?" I asked Felix.

Felix bowed his head. "I would be happy to, Master Josh."

I knew I could rely on Felix, so despite being sad at the thought of being away from her for so long, it was also exciting to think of how much she could progress in the year I would be away.

*****

The final day of school was a bittersweet affair, we were excited to be leaving school, but I would be leaving tomorrow for a whole year. Even though Eleanor would be returning in September to attend sixth form for her A-levels, we both made sure to say our goodbyes and thank our teachers.

After school, I stopped by the Taylors to let them know I would be travelling and wouldn't be contactable via phone; a fact they weren't too happy about. But I assured them that if there was an emergency, they could always call Felix. It was sad and we all got tearful as I hugged and kissed them goodbye. Felix had planned a farewell dinner for that evening, and I felt bad for not inviting them, but I didn't want them to know the finer details of the trip, as I knew they would only worry and try to stop me from going.

The dinner party was amazing, spent eating, chatting, and laughing with most of those I cared about. Ellie also got to try spirit food for the first time, which she loved. But as much fun as we were all having, I knew Mikey was staying over, so to have a little time alone before I left, Eleanor and I eventually excused ourselves from the table to go back to my suite.

After chatting for a while, we eventually started making out.

As things started to heat up, Ellie suddenly broke away from our kiss. "I'm sorry, Josh, I don't think I'm ready to have sex." Ellie nibbled her lip.

"It's okay." I caressed her face. "We don't have to do anything you aren't comfortable with just because I'm leaving."

"There's other stuff we could try?" She smiled nervously.

I didn't need to be asked twice.

Afterwards, we lay entwined on my bed sharing our thoughts and I felt completely at peace for the first time in a long while. It wasn't to last though, as around ten o'clock

Felix knocked to say he was ready to give Ellie a lift home. It felt too soon, as there was still so much that I wanted to say to her.

We gathered ourselves together, got dressed and made our way downstairs. Leaving the house, we slowly approached the awaiting car, and I pulled Ellie into my arms.

"I love you, Josh," she whispered to me.

"I love you too, Ellie. Wait for me." I kissed her before reluctantly letting her go.

Finally releasing my hand as she climbed into the car, Ellie turned with tears running down her face and smiled. "Always."

As the car drove off down the driveway, I quickly reached up, wiped my own tears away and steeled my face before turning to Mikey and Master Bronstad.

Master put a comforting hand upon my shoulder. "Feelings are not a weakness, Joshua, but being ashamed of them is."

Clearing my throat, I nodded at him. "Thank you, Master."

The rest of the night I spent with Mikey, he didn't pester me for any details about Ellie, for which I was glad, but he could clearly tell by the smile on my face that something had happened. His magic was progressing well and apparently Felix was pleased. I was happy for him and imagined that by the time I returned, he would be capable of some impressive feats. No. Both Mikey and Ellie!

By the time Mikey left for his own rooms it was well past midnight and I knew I didn't have time to cultivate, so I went to bed, drifting off to thoughts of adventure and the girl who would be waiting for my return.

Chapter 17

The next morning, after breakfast, Master Bronstad launched straight into a lecture on what to expect when we arrive. "The gravity is higher, about twice what you are used to on Earth, so it will take you time to acclimatise, as not only will your frame have to bear more weight, but your organs will also have to work harder too, especially your heart."

Growing increasingly excited, I couldn't help but ask, "Do I get to choose a weapon now?"

Master Bronstad rubbed his face with his palm. "Heavens save me from overenthusiastic youths. Yes, after this, you can choose a weapon."

My inner voice was screaming at me to fist pump, but I managed to control myself and nodded instead. "Thank you, Master."

We went over a few more details, but a lot of it was common sense that would apply anywhere, such as be mindful of your surroundings and be careful who you antagonise. I was especially looking forward to seeing the trees, which apparently grew to truly monstrous sizes. They sounded epic!

After what seemed like an eternity of lectures, the time I had been waiting for finally arrived. Felix came to lead us to the family armoury, but as we approached a bare wall in one of the downstairs rooms, I grew confused, until Felix began to tap the wall in a seemingly specific manner. The wall briefly shimmered, and a previously non-existent doorway was revealed. Upon its appearance, I found myself immediately recalling what Ellie had said.

"Ha, Ellie said there would probably be secret passages, but I never got around to asking," I said.

Pushing open the door, Felix chuckled. "Yes, Eleanor is a rather bright young thing, there are various concealed paths within the residence, some of which are the only ways to reach the vaults."

"Vaults, as in plural?" I asked, as we entered a dimly lit stairway.

"Yes, Master Josh. One of your ancestors was either extravagantly keen on organisation, or simply refused to keep all of his treasure in one place." Felix nodded; the exasperation clear in his voice.

"Before you ask. No, Josh, we are not going to take the time to explore the various vaults, we are on a schedule," Master Bronstad said, ending my quickly forming plans.

"I understand, Master," I replied, making no attempt to conceal the disappointment in my voice.

It wasn't worth arguing over, especially as the likely result would be some new hellish training method and its corresponding set of bruises.

The stairs went down quite a way, and I estimate we must have been at least thirty metres below the surface before we eventually stopped at the start of a single long tunnel. It was clearly man-made, but the walls were some sort of smooth dark stone with no distinguishable seams. Interspersed regularly were glowing blue orbs, from which I could sense the distinct feel of aether. Disconcertingly, the orbs only seemed to illuminate their immediate area and only lit when someone came relatively close to them. Which meant that the tunnel ahead seemed to be a dark abyss. As we grew further from the staircase, I looked back and noticed the orbs behind had also blinked out, giving the strange impression that we were in a small room with two end walls made of nothing but shadow. The endless repetition in the design of the tunnel made it feel like we were walking without getting anywhere, and I started to grow increasingly uncomfortable.

"Is that you growling, Master Josh?" Felix asked.

His question knocked me out of the strange funk I had fallen into, and I realised I had actually been growling. "Ermm, yeah, sorry, I didn't realise I do that."

Master Bronstad started laughing his arse off. "Have to get better control of those bestial instincts, son. I'm not sure how Ellie would feel if you started growling at her when you're horny."

I couldn't help but start laughing along with him, but then I suddenly worried, shit, was I doing it last night?!

"The tunnel is designed to make people uncomfortable, but if you weren't meant to be here, there would be far nastier surprises," Felix said as we resumed our walk. Honestly, if he was trying to reassure me, he was doing a bang-up job!

Eventually, the claustrophobic monotony of the tunnel was broken by an elaborate set of doors appearing on one side, and Felix came to a stop. They were made of some sort of white metal and covered with an elaborate relief; of human warriors battling an assortment of creatures.

"The White family armoury." Felix gestured to the doors.

"Aren't you going to open it?" I asked.

Felix shook his head. "Only you can open it, Master Josh."

Investigating the doors, I noticed that situated in the middle was a small blank plate with a tiny hole. I turned back to Felix. "Do you have the key then?"

"There is no key required, simply press on the plate."

I assumed that the door was most likely magic and so probably needed aether to open, but as I pressed my hand onto the plate, the sharp sting in my palm quickly disproved that idea.

"Fuck! You could have warned me!" I said.

"Sorry, Master Josh, I didn't think."

I could tell from the way he was clearly stifling a laugh, that he was lying his arse off. Smirking at Felix's painful attempt at a joke, I was briefly caught off-guard when the door suddenly illuminated, and with a whirring and clunking sound like a giant clock, the doors began to open, allowing me my first glimpse into the armoury.

It was roughly square and only about ten metres to a side, so not a huge room. And rather than the plethora of weapons I expected, there were instead various individual weapons on separate stands and plinths, with rarely a single type of weapon represented more than once. The entire back wall was also taken up by a display of six mannequins wearing sets of armour.

"There aren't as many weapons as I expected," I said.

Felix smiled at me. "Only the finest equipment is kept in here, Master Josh."

Master Bronstad snorted. "Son, there isn't a school or sect that wouldn't be willing to kill for the contents of this room. Hell, even many small kingdoms would wage war over these," he said, whilst lovingly, albeit disturbingly, caressing the handle of a particularly large axe.

Although the number of weapons wasn't huge, the variety was. "How do I pick the right weapon?" I asked.

"We could spend days debating the strengths and weaknesses of each weapon, and believe me, they all have them. But that's not why we're here. Try them, pick them up, swing them around and you'll know what weapon is best for you," Master Bronstad said, his advice both simple and unhelpful.

I was a little sceptical. "What if I like a weapon that doesn't suit me?"

"Bollocks! Know yourself and that is enough. Trust me."

Having faith in his words, I made my way through the room.

"Why did you avoid the meteor hammers?" Master Bronstad asked with a smile.

Knowing the reason, I was a little embarrassed. "Well, honestly, I think they are bit uncool." I waited for him to chastise my childish motive.

Master Bronstad laughed. "Good! That is exactly what I meant, trust your instincts. You don't like it? Then it's not for you, know yourself Joshua."

Filled with confidence from his support, I ignored most of the weapons and made my way to the ones that caught my eye. The first I approached was a Chinese Jian, the blade was about eighty centimetres long and three centimetres wide, with the last ten centimetres slowly tapering to a relatively fine point. I gave it a few test swings and it felt good. However, whilst swinging it, my eyes were drawn to another sword tucked away to one side, which looked to me, and my general lack of knowledge, like a mediaeval longsword. I felt a strange attraction drawing me towards it, so quickly returning the one in my hand, I walked over to check it out.

The sword was of a more western design than the previous one and its midnight-blue scabbard almost shone underneath the magic lighting. Its hilt had a simple gently curved cross-guard and a grip wrapped in what looked like black leather, abutted by an extended teardrop pommel. All the metal parts seemed to be made from the same dark grey metal, which in stark contrast to the scabbard, reflected very little light. It was perfectly understated, and the design resonated with me. Carefully picking it up, I was immediately startled by its weight, as it easily weighed twenty kilograms. Which, though nothing to me, would render it completely useless to a mundane human. Removing it from its scabbard, revealed a blade of around a meter long with a single fuller along most of its length. Despite the weight, the sword felt balanced and lively as I swung it, and I knew I had found my weapon!

"What type of sword is this?" I quizzed Master Bronstad.

"A bastard sword, is it the one?" he asked.

Looking at the sword in my hand, I nodded at him. "Yeah, this is the one, but why bastard sword?"

Master gestured at the parts of the sword as he explained. "A grip just long enough to be wielded two-handed, with a blade longer than an arming sword but shorter than your average longsword. It's neither a one-handed nor two-handed sword, but rather a bastard child of both."

The name made a lot of sense, and I liked the fact I would be able to use it both one and two-handed, something about that just felt right. Master Bronstad walked off to look around and I took the opportunity to finally speak to Felix about something I had neglected for far too long. "Have you uncovered anything about the death of my parents?"

"I have never stopped looking, Master Josh. The symbolism eventually led me to a cult of human supremacists named The Pure. They espouse the sanctity of remaining pure-blooded humans and the union of one woman with one man."

I shook my head. "How progressive! So, a bunch of murderous bigots then?"

"Quite, and what concerns me, Master Josh. Is the fact they knew the house held someone with a non-human bloodline. Which suggests that at least their information network is quite effective."

"We need to stop them," I said.

"Believe me, Master Josh, we shall completely uproot them."

"It's weird though, why murder my family but never come for me? Surely, I should be their target?"

"Yes, that is strange, I will see what I can find out whilst you are gone."

As Master Bronstad approached, I could feel my excitement growing. "Are we off now?" I asked.

Master Bronstad raised his eyebrow questioningly. "Do you not think you need to change? Your Earth clothes may look a little out of place, and maybe we should get a few provisions too?"

I instantly felt stupid, of course we would need supplies! Eventually, I elected for some brown brigandine with as little ostentation as I could find. Combined with my woollen trousers, cuffed boots and travelling cloak, I looked like I was on my way to a live-action roleplay convention, and I found myself wondering, not for the first time, how had I ended up in this bizarre situation. Looking over at Master Bronstad in his chainmail and leather, at least I knew I wouldn't be alone. With his massive height and great axe, he looked like a quintessential Viking berserker, and I pitied anyone who pissed him off.

No more than an hour later, we found ourselves back in the depths of the manor, fully provisioned and stood in front of a plain stone archway. The archway was set directly into the wall and looked like a simple architectural flourish, especially with the lack of any noticeable difference between the section of wall it contained and that surrounding it.

Felix raised his hands as he approached the arch and muttered something unintelligible, causing a plethora of strange runes to appear around it. Continuing with his mumbling and gestures, the runes illuminated one by one until, as the final rune began to glow, there was a flash of light and a swirling riot of colours filled the archway. It was obviously some sort of portal to the Jade Wilderness Realm, but just looking at it made me feel dizzy and I had zero interest in going anywhere near the thing.

"What are you waiting for?" Master Bronstad asked.

Then, without even waiting for my response, simply shoved me in. The last thing I heard before my world became a frenetic kaleidoscope was Master Bronstad say to Felix, "See you in five years old friend!"

Chapter 18

Five years! Five years! What the actual fuck, I thought to myself as I flew through the ever-changing vortex. He had told me we would be gone for a year! I spent the following minute or so furiously stewing over the ramifications and cursing my master, until I was suddenly, and rather unceremoniously, hurled out onto my stomach. Getting back to my feet, I dusted myself off and instinctively moved back from the portal, expecting Master Bronstad to exit in a similarly ungraceful fashion. Instead, I was mildly disappointed as he stepped out in a completely controlled manner.

I scowled at him. "Five years, Five fucking years! I told Ellie and Mikey I would be a year!"

"Keep your voice down!" he said, lowering his voice.

I instantly realised I'd been an idiot, as I had loudly announced our presence to anyone or anything within earshot and I hoped that there was nothing dangerous about to hear.

"I'm sorry, Master," I said, "but seriously, what the fuck?"

The portal suddenly crackled a few times before vanishing and we were instantly plunged into twilight. A tense few minutes passed as we quietly listened before Master was finally happy there was no immediate danger.

"Stop your whining boy, it will be five years for us, but only one for them, the movement of time is often different between realms," he said.

Honestly, I didn't find it that comforting. After all, we still had five years in this place! What about Mikey and Ellie?

"When I get back, I'll be twenty-one, but my girlfriend will only be seventeen!" I moaned.

Master Bronstad quietly chuckled. "None of you are mundanes, the changes you'll undergo in five short years will be negligible, I imagine by the time we leave you'll probably look exactly the same age as you do now."

"Huh," I huffed. "Still a bit weird!"

"Best get used to it son. When I first started cultivating, I became trapped inside a pocket world. It only took me a year to escape, but when I did, I found that a hundred years had passed outside and everyone I loved had been dead and gone for decades. That's why we tend to mainly associate amongst ourselves, time affects us differently and mundanes are too short-lived. I learnt that the hard way."

Even after so much time had passed, his old pain was still clearly evident.

"I'm sorry for your loss," I said sombrely.

Master Bronstad waved it off. "It's fine, ancient history now."

"So, what's the plan?" I asked, attempting to change the topic.

Master grinned at me and I instantly regretted asking.

"We train, we hunt, then train some more, but first we find somewhere suitable to stay for a while. How are you finding the higher gravity?" he asked.

I had noticed the difference, but with my strength it didn't really feel like too much of an issue. "It's not really affecting me too much."

Master Bronstad's only acknowledgement was a brief grunt and nod.

Knowing we would be setting off, I found myself looking forward to meeting people from another plane, what would they look like? And what language would they even speak? That could cause some problems.

"So, what direction should we head to find a settlement?" I asked.

Master Bronstad had a confused look on his face. "Settlement? We are staying in the wilderness, at least until you attain a certain level of skill with that." He pointed at my sword.

I really should have asked more questions prior to leaving, if I had known I'd be spending so long living like a forest hobo I may have changed my mind about coming. I could envision dreams about mattresses dominating my life for a while!

Choosing a direction at random, we set off into the forest to find somewhere suitable for a basecamp, whilst I tried to reconcile the twilight against the fact we had entered the portal mid-morning.

It was a beautiful place, and the trees were truly gargantuan, their boughs towering hundreds of meters above our heads. The sheer scale of the individual canopies meant that there was actually a fair distance between the trunks, which gave quite an open and airy feeling to what was actually a rather dense forest. Looking up at them as we walked, the leaves and colouration were hugely varied, some had traditional green leaves or needles, others more exotic tones of purples and blues. Every now and then, I caught sight of the moons between the leaves. There was at least two that I had spotted, one a bright grey like Earth's, the other was smaller with a warm orange hue. I was definitely not in Kansas anymore! The forest floor was soft underfoot and dotted with the occasional swathe of unidentifiable flowers and fungi, walking in a daze, I felt like I had entered a fairy wonderland.

"Beautiful, isn't it?" Master Bronstad asked, snapping me out of it.

"Yes." I nodded mindlessly.

"But it's also potentially deadly, so stop walking around like a moonstruck pup and pay attention to your surroundings."

Suitably chastised, I started to be more vigilant in my appraisals, noticing sounds I had neglected before. Most of them came from creatures out of sight, avoiding the two intruders to their homes. But as I started to pay more attention, I caught occasional glimpses of small animals, some furry critters similar to squirrels but with streaks of vibrant colours and six legs darted into cover as we passed, and the occasional bird eyed us warily from their perches high out of reach, ruffling their feathers threateningly as we passed.

As we walked, I noticed the sounds were suddenly becoming more muted, before eventually fading away entirely. The complete silence caused the hairs on my neck to rise, and I subconsciously reached for the handle of the sword at my waist. Master Bronstad turned to look at me and pulled the giant axe from across his back.

"Good instincts! Draw the sword and slowly back up towards me, we'll face them back-to-back," he said calmly.

Taking deep measured breaths to calm myself, I nodded as I drew my sword. "You do remember I don't really know how to use this thing?"

"Point goes in 'em, sharp edge cuts 'em. Don't worry about it, they're wild beasts not warriors."

"How reassuring," I muttered under my breath as we waited for the threat to appear.

We didn't have to wait long. Eight beasts slinked out of the shadows and they had us surrounded. They looked like Tigers, but with the sloped back of a hyena, and a wider flattened face. The fur on their flanks streaked with lines of scales, which looked alien on their otherwise mammalian body. They were clearly pack hunters, operating in a similar fashion to wolves. And slightly further back, a larger version stood, clearly the Alpha, maybe waiting to see what threat we posed before personally taking action? If it was, it suggested a scary level of awareness.

Master snorted. "Crastites, horrible little buggers, just avoid letting them get behind you. A ripped-up hamstring is not a pleasant experience."

No sooner than he finished talking, they came in fast with no warning, and as the first reached me, a second lunged in to try to catch me flat-footed dealing with the first. It was a good plan, but they had severely underestimated their prey. As I sliced clean through the head of the first, I kicked out at the second, whose body ruptured as it folded around my leg. At the sight, the Alpha screeched, and the remainder fled off into the forest.

Panting only a little from the increased gravity, I was quite underwhelmed from my first taste of combat on the planet.

"What was that about?" I asked Master Bronstad.

When he saw the amount of blood I was covered in, he started to laugh. "Just some low-level spirit beasts, little more threat than mundane animals."

"You knew, didn't you?" I asked, as I attempted to wipe myself down. "If you had told me, I would have held back a little."

"I didn't want you to hold back, I needed to see how you dealt with danger, with fear. You didn't freeze, nor lose control. I'm impressed, I think we'll make a fine warrior out of you."

Placated somewhat by his compliment, I could understand his reasoning. It was weird though; it was a tense situation and I had remained strangely composed.

"Yep, you did good son, but you need to clean yourself up, stay like that for long and not only will the smell become horrendous, but you'll also draw every predator around for miles." He smiled.

After cleaning myself as well as I could, it took us another half a day of travelling before we found somewhere suitable to stay. A river both provided a decent break in the ever-present canopy and would also provide an ample supply of fresh water for drinking and bathing. After so long walking, the water looked far too inviting and so removing our boots, we sat on the bank and allowed the water to soothe our travel worn feet. I knew there may be dangerous

116

beasts in the river, but the water was crystal clear, so we'd see anything approach, plus it felt so good that I was willing to take a risk.

"So, are we putting up our tents here?" I asked.

Master Bronstad looked at me quizzically. "We might be here a while, you want to live in a tent?"

"Well…" I stuttered.

"We'll build a treehouse," he answered, sparing me from my inability to form a coherent response.

Looking up at the trees, the first usable branches were around fifty metres off the ground. "Up there?" I pointed incredulously.

Master Bronstad had that look again, like I was being an idiot. "You'd rather build a cabin on the forest floor?"

"Well, it would be a lot easier." I nodded earnestly.

"Ha." He snorted. "And last all of thirty seconds, when a rampaging spirit beast comes past whilst you are dreaming about Ellie."

Visions assailed me, of being violently awoken as a cabin exploded all around me, which quickly convinced me that a treehouse was a much better idea. "A treehouse sounds nice." I smiled, my no doubt paling face causing Master Bronstad to burst into laughter.

After a rather sleepless night, caused by thoughts of being attacked whilst asleep, we started work on the treehouse the very next day. We had rope and basic tools and were surrounded by all the wood we would ever need. Strangely, Master Bronstad even produced an abundance of nails and hinges and I learnt to never underestimate his ability to plan ahead! Although, with the limited capacity of our packs, where he had gotten some of it from was a complete mystery, and one he was in no hurry to explain.

In the end, it took only two weeks to complete, but to say it was a hellish task would be a gross understatement, as all the timber parts were prepared on the forest floor, then hauled up the tree and assembled. When we started, I had no real idea what I was doing, but with continual guidance from

117

Master Bronstad, by the time we were finished, I was…well I was still no bloody carpenter, but at least I wasn't nearly as incompetent as when we started. Master had astounded me with how adept he was, but I guessed it made sense, as fifteen-hundred years of life would allow you to pick up quite a few skills. Sitting in the fruit of our labour when we were finally finished, I couldn't help but think that all the hard work had been worth it.

It was a simple single room cabin, but large enough for two beds and a small area to relax and cook. It was the sort of place any young boy would love to own. Even though it was fairly primitive, we planned to add things we needed over time and at least we had somewhere relatively safe to sleep!

Chapter 19

No sooner than the treehouse was finished, we moved straight on to my training. It would have been nice to relax for a week or so and enjoy our surroundings, but when I suggested it to Master, he just laughed in my face and pointed out that we weren't on a holiday. So, I found myself with sword in hand, being led through the basics of how to use one.

Within that little slice of arboreal heaven, weapon drills, footwork, and sparring became the entirety of our days. The regular excursions to hunt and forage my only breaks from Master's punishing regime. In the evenings, I would reflect on what I had learnt that day, further my cultivation, then sleep. Wake-up, rinse and repeat.

It was often painful and mind-numbingly repetitive, but it was working, and I was reminded daily why Master Bronstad deserved the honorific, as his fluidity in combat was astounding. His skill, coupled with the patience and dedication to correct all my mistakes, no matter how minor, led me to grow in leaps and bounds. Time passed, season after season, until, in the blink of an eye three whole years had passed in our forest haven.

*****

I subtly shifted my weight as he lunged, a lightning-fast parry carrying his sword past my left cheek as I stepped in and threw my right elbow towards his face. Master stepped back to avoid the blow, but I extended the arm into a horizontal slash with my sword, which he barely managed to block. Stepping back from each other, we circled, both looking for the slightest opening. But I knew there wouldn't be one, the title of master was earnt for a reason, so I decided to seize the initiative to try and create one. It was risky and could leave me exposed to a counter, so I knew I had to be careful. Thrusting my sword towards his chest, I could tell from his smirk that he knew it was likely a feint, but if he didn't want to be stabbed, he had to answer. His response came fast, a step back and to the side along with an overhead strike onto my blade, no doubt to drive mine into the floor and capitalise on how off-balance it would leave me. But I wouldn't allow that to happen! Immediately as his sword started its descent, I moved. In one fluid movement, I lifted my sword, and stepped across his strike. Catching his blade on mine, I used his own momentum and constant pressure on his sword to force his tip into the ground beside me. Suddenly within his guard, the split-second it took him to recover was enough and my sword was up and drawn across his neck before he even had time to react.

Master Bronstad wiped the line of ink from his neck whilst chuckling to himself. We had taken to using ink on the blunt blades as a training tool, as it helped to keep accurate tabs on where we were struck. The line on his neck was clearly a fatal blow.

"Son, there's no more I can teach you about how to use a sword," he said with a smile, whilst patting me affectionately on the shoulder.

I knew he was right, I had finally surpassed him in skill with a sword, although in all fairness, the sword wasn't even his preferred weapon and in a fight with nothing held back, I wasn't close to his match, even with my freaky physique. During our time together, I had learnt that Master was at completion of the Spirit Knight stage and was working on establishing his golden core to become a Sage. There may be some Sages left on Earth, no one really knows, but we do know there are very few at the Spirit Knight realm, which made him one of the most powerful men on our planet and I was exceedingly privileged to receive his tuition. So, I knew that if he had used Qi in our duel, I would likely be dead before I even managed to draw my sword, such were the benefits his cultivation level would provide.

Although, I was slowly catching up. The last three years had seen a massive jump in my own cultivation as the aether levels in the Jade Wilderness realm were far higher than on Earth, and I had finally finished the tenth level of Qi gathering. Each level had taken progressively longer, until it got to the point that I worried I might never reach completion. But now my Dantian contained a veritable ocean of mist, and any attempt to add to it was met with agonising pain, so I knew I had reached my limit.

"Master, I completed the apprentice stage last night," I said, eager to share my good news.

"You have completed all nine levels?"

"Nine? No, Master, I completed ten."

"No need for sarcasm boy," he said, rather sternly.

I looked at him confusedly. "I wasn't taking the piss, Master."

The shock on his face was apparent. "You sure boy? Ten times?" he questioned.

"Yes, Master, I'm sure I can count to ten." I laughed.

Master hissed through his teeth and looked at me with a mixture of concern and bewilderment. "Tell no-one of this, son, do you understand?"

"I do, but why?" I asked, confused that he would have such a strong reaction.

"Because it is a well understood metaphysical law, that all humans." He held up a hand to stop me from what I was about to say. "Including those with strange bloodlines, can expand their Dantian a maximum of nine times. So, the fact it's different for you. Well, I honestly don't know what it means, but I do know that it could bring trouble, understand?"

"Yes, Master." I nodded, and I meant it, as I had no desire to advertise something else was different about me.

Following the test of my sword skills, he next tested me on my use of Qi techniques. I had become quite proficient in my use of Emperor's Fist, which was a simple technique for using Qi to increase the speed and power of my blows. But I was even better with Wind Steps, which at my current level allowed me to lighten my body and reduce my own wind-resistance, enabling me to move several steps in almost an instant. After ten minutes of sparring, I started to struggle to maintain the techniques, burning through my Qi reserves far quicker than I could possibly replenish them. Eventually, Master noticed my fatigue and called for a stop.

"Good, you have a passable understanding of them both. Now, you must work on using them in quick bursts as required, rather than continuously. This will make far more efficient use of your Qi reserves."

"Thank you, Master." I bowed in respect. It was great advice but rapidly stopping and starting the skills would require far greater finesse and a lot of practice.

Master waved away my sign of respect as unnecessary. "Think nothing of it, son, having a competent student is a joy all its own."

The final technique I wanted to demonstrate was a weapon skill. It was called Focused Strike and involved projecting Qi into a weapon, which would enhance its ability to overcome an opponent's energy or physical defence. Which is important as cutting into a lesser material with a sword is relatively easy, but try cutting into something equal to, or even stronger than the blades material and you would simply ruin your sword; there is a reason that maces and hammers were the historical weapons of choice for mundanes against plate-mail! Now, I had faith that my sword was far from ordinary, but add aether into the equation, bringing energy shields, arcane abilities, tempered bodies, or even random esoteric materials, and suddenly any enhancement to a swords ability to cut made a lot of sense.

Making my way to a large fallen branch, I began to move my Qi through the required channels, allowing it to flow out of my hands and into my sword. The only outwardly visible sign of the technique was that the swords edge began to glow, but this was so slight that it just looked like the blade catching the light. I lifted the blade and with a single strike split the branch cleanly into two parts.

Master was clapping. "Great, we'll make a fine arborist of you yet." He laughed. "And with how long it took to prepare the strike, you better hope that any enemy is as still as that stick."

I instantly deflated and could feel my cheeks start to colour. "That's true, Master, but I swear, I can utilise it far quicker if necessary, and every time I use it, I get a better feel for the sword, and it becomes that much more fluid."

Master raised his eyebrow. "Well, you're a gifted swordsman, of that there's no doubt. Maybe one day you could even reach one-with-the-sword, the legendary first step in becoming a true swordsman, so keep at it."

Happy that I had made sufficient progress in my skills, the discussion then turned to the next steps in my cultivation, and I knew from the journal left by my father that the warrior stage would involve tempering the body to better withstand the increasing Qi density of the following stages.

"This is where you're a bit weird," Master said, "Your physical body has already passed the level of others who have completed this stage, so I'm not sure what affect the usual medicinal baths and herbs would have."

"It's fine, Master, I've already checked. The journal explains what I need to do, and I already have the herbs. Apparently, they'll both temper my body and start to unlock my bloodline."

Master looked at me in confusion. "I don't know what you mean. Your bloodline has already awoken, your body and hair are evidence of that."

I shrugged and wondered if the journal was perhaps referring to my father's bloodline, could you have more than one? I didn't know, but I doubted my father would try to hurt me.

"Just be careful, ok, and if anything goes wrong, call for me?" Master instructed.

Standing above the bath of scalding hot water, I took out the small bag left by my father. The journal explained which items to use in the bath and how to use them, and looking at the list, it was clear they weren't ordinary items, they weren't even all plants! There was an item for each of the five elements and they all had rather ridiculous sounding names. Reaching into the bag, I retrieved the items according to their descriptions within the journal: Golden Sun Flower for Fire; Moon Lily for Water; Divine Jade for Earth; Sky Mithril for Metal; and Purple Lightning Bamboo for Wood. Each of the items were contained within what resembled a soap bubble, but one that was remarkably strong and pliant.

The small bag itself was a wonder, and clearly some sort of magic was at play as it was far larger inside than out. However, the items I removed quickly overshadowed any awe I felt towards the bag. The Golden Sun Flower was beautiful and seemed to be composed of actual dancing flames, and I was sure that without the globe it would have burnt me. The Moon Lily was completely translucent and black, and just looking at it made me shiver from the cold. The Sky Mithril was potentially a sliver of white metal, but it was hard to tell because it was rotating at such a high speed that it looked like a small tornado. The Purple Lightning Bamboo, true to its name, was purple and mauve, and surrounded by coruscating blue arcs of electricity. The Divine Jade was perhaps the least visually impressive as it simply resembled a large opaque emerald, but when I gazed upon it, I was somehow filled with whispers of solidity and stability over great epochs of time. It was humbling.

The power within the five items was obvious and exposing my body to them was honestly starting to feel like a really fucking bad idea. I knew that the more I hesitated, the harder it would become, so I stilled my thoughts and decided to have a little faith. Copying the symbols onto the tub, I had no idea what they meant, but I knew they were probably important, and so I made damn sure they exactly matched the examples given in the journal. After giving my work a final careful check, I was satisfied the symbols matched and climbed into the bath, placing the five items onto the surface of the water in the proscribed pattern.

The journal detailed what would happen, so I thought I had prepared myself, but fuck me was I wrong, I was definitely not prepared! As the items touched the surface of the water, the spheres surrounding them dissipated and they spontaneously connected to each other in blazing lines of energy, forming a ring and a pentagram. The journal had explained the two symbols represented the cycle of creation and destruction between the elements, but I had just thought it weird that the pentagram recurs as a mystical symbol in so many different cultures.

The items began to dissipate, and the water began to boil as first their energies transferred into the bath, and then into me. The pain was so intense, that I thought for sure I was dying. Rivers of primordial energy flowed through me, reducing my body to the smallest of particles as it passed. As I felt my body fully disassembled, I briefly wondered how I was even present to witness the process without a body, but the thought was short lived, before I was lost again in the white-hot pain of being rebuilt. First my nervous system and skeleton were assembled and the pain from the exposure of my new nerve endings was almost too much to bear. As my spirit cried out at the overwhelming agony, something began to pulse in answer from within my slowly reconstituting blood. The pulse grew stronger and stronger, and I felt my consciousness begin to expand, there was a brief sensation of disconnectedness and relief, and I left my body behind.

Rising into space, stars flashed past my vision and as I accelerated onwards through nebulae and galaxies, time lost all meaning as I revelled in the stark beauty of it all. Gazing around, I became aware of other beings sharing the void with me. Some were relatively benign, the way they gently swam through space reminding me of planet sized whales. Others furiously clashed, the blows from the astronomically proportioned creatures de-stabilising space itself and the resulting shockwaves tossing me around like a leaf in a storm.

As I drifted on, I became acutely aware of a giant tentacled creature, my attention drawn to the trail of devastation it left in its wake. I looked on in shock as everywhere it passed stars were extinguished and planets were reduced to husks of filth and corruption, that caused my spirit to recoil in disgust. But as I noticed it, so too did the eldritch creature become aware of me, and I could feel its malevolence and hunger, its sheer desire to consume me, as it reached across space in search of its tiny new prey.

Its multitude of eyes pinned me with their gaze and horrific limbs stretched to envelope me, but as I made peace with my inevitable end, I was spared by the sudden appearance of a white light before me, that shielded me from its grasp. A flash emanated from the light and the creature recoiled from it, but it was no use; the eldritch creature simply ceased to be. It was all so quick that I couldn't understand what had happened. I tried to sense the remnant echoes of the phenomena, but it was too far beyond me, the mysteries it contained making little sense. The bright light turned its attention to me.

As the light faded, the vague shape of a man was revealed within and even though I could not make out any details, I felt completely exposed before the figure, like there was nothing I could possibly hide from his gaze. Yet I wasn't afraid and was instead filled with an overwhelming sense of familiarity.

"You're not ready to be here!" his voice reverberated inside my mind. There was no malice in his words, just cold certainty.

I had so many questions that I wanted to ask him, but before I even had a chance, he waved a hand, and I was travelling back, even faster than I had left. Completely disoriented, I slammed back into my own body and the tub exploded, leaving me naked and gasping on the forest floor.

As I opened my eyes, I could vaguely discern clouds gathering above the canopy, with a rainbow of colours arcing through them and I was filled with an ominous premonition, surely, I had been through enough? No sooner than I had managed that first coherent thought, a lightning bolt arced down from the sky into my prone body, but contrary to my expectations, the first strike didn't hurt at all, and instead I was filled with warmth and the sensation of my new muscles easing.

Because of that first strike, I had thought that maybe it wouldn't be so bad, but by the sixth, my muscles had contracted enough to almost pull me apart and I had thoroughly changed my mind. I wasn't sure how much more I could endure, and by the ninth and thankfully final strike, I was left charred and screaming. The last thing I recalled before fading into oblivion was Master's worried face as he gazed down upon me.

Chapter 20

I opened my eyes to sunshine flickering through the canopy above me and the gentle sounds of nature around me. Everything was just more…vibrant. I turned my head towards Master, who I could hear whistling from the side of a crackling campfire.

"Finally returned to the land of the living have you, son?" he joked, but I could see he was weary, as if he hadn't slept much. Which was odd, as it would take a lot to wear out a Spirit Knight.

Pushing myself up into a sitting position, I felt myself for any discomfort. There wasn't any, which was strange as I remember the state I was in when I passed out and I'm pretty sure I was physically smoking. In fact, I felt positively amazing, almost like a new person, which in all fairness, my body quite literally was.

"What happened?" I asked.

"You mean, other than illuminating the forest for miles, before exploding the medicinal bath and being struck repeatedly by lightning?"

"Ermm…yes?" I ventured hesitantly.

"Well, after the little show you put on, I had to gather up our stuff and carry your foolish arse as far and quickly as I could. After about three hundred miles or so, I figured we'd gone far enough and so I set up camp here and tried to fix the damage you had done to yourself, that was over a week ago. So, boy, what did you do?" he questioned me.

I shrugged helplessly. "I have no idea, I just followed the instructions in my father's journal, it didn't say the effects would be so...exaggerated, thank you for looking after me, Master."

Master huffed and waved off my thanks. "Well, whatever you did, it certainly pissed off the heavens." Seeing the obvious confusion on my face, Master shook his head with a hopeless look upon his face. "If I had to guess, I'd say that was tribulation lightning. Now, that's just a guess, as we only have written records, but it fit the descriptions. Although it's not meant to happen until someone attempts to pass the Saint stage."

"Sorry, Master, I had no idea that would happen. But why did we flee?"

He looked at me like I was an idiot. "Those tribulation clouds were miles wide, to the point I worried even I'd get caught up in the thing. On top of that, all the aether for who knows how far was first sucked up by that bloody medicinal bath, and then by those clouds. I thought it looked like a natural treasure being born, and you can damn well bet that if I thought that, then someone else would have and there'd be people crawling all over to find it. So, still think we should have waited around?"

"Aww, you think I'm a treasure," I joked, attempting to dodge the question and lighten the mood.

At first, he scowled, then he smiled, which eventually turned into a full-on belly laugh.

"I needed that," he said, rubbing his face. "I am glad you're ok, son."

"If I'm honest, I feel better than ok, I feel amazing," I said.

"Well, after that bloody spectacle, I hope it was worth it. So, what was tempered?"

I looked at him, confused by what he meant.

"You don't know?" he asked exasperatedly. "Well, I hope it was at least a few things, because if you have to do that five times, then we are in trouble."

"Whoa…, Master." I held up my hand to slow him down. "Why the fuck would I have to do it five times?"

Master held up a fist. "Blood, Bones, Muscles and tendons, Organs, and finally the Twelve meridians," he listed off, raising a finger for each item. "A body tempered five times a Warrior makes," he said sagely.

"Well, I'm pretty sure I won't need to do it five times," I replied. "I felt it, my body was completely broken down and rebuilt including all *twenty-two* meridians. It was bad, really bad, I think my bloodline is the only reason I survived the process."

"That's something at least," he said with relief. "Wait, did you say twenty-two meridians?"

"Yeah, I take it twelve is the norm?"

Master took a moment to compose himself. "Boy, it's not just 'the norm'. Every human has twelve, so, I'm pretty sure, it's safe to say you aren't human." He rubbed his face with his hands.

"Yeah, no need to remind me, we already know that. Neither were any of the Whites," I said defensively, gesturing at my ridiculous hair colouring.

"No, son, they may have had traces of a divine beast's bloodline, but they were still human, and every one of them had twelve meridians, just like the rest of us."

"Well…I…I don't fucking know." I shrugged, truly getting a little fed up with all the unknowns.

Master placed a reassuring hand on my shoulder. "It's fine, son, it doesn't change who you are, we'll figure it all out eventually."

"Thank you, Master."

He nodded. "Stirling wasn't your father though, was he?" he suddenly asked out of nowhere.

That was meant to be my biggest secret, but if I lied to him, I knew it would erode the trust between us and if I couldn't trust him, then who could I? "No, he was my uncle," I admitted.

"Ha, you're Mara's boy! I knew it, you had her eyes." He smiled. "You know, she was like a little sister to me."

It was amazing to know that he had been close to my mother, but my attention was stuck on just one part of what he'd said. "What do you mean had?" I asked.

Master threw me a mirror. It looked like my face gazing back at me, just an idealised version. My jawline was slightly more angular, my cheekbones a tiny bit more pronounced. It was subtle but my looks had definitely improved. The other changes though, were unfortunately less subtle. My pupils were no longer just blue, the edge was ringed in a metallic silver. And my previously white hair now had a subtly pearlescent luster, the blue stripes slightly metallic looking just like my eyes. Great, I looked like the unholy love child of a Nordic god and a fucking anime character! Knowing my eyes used to be like my mother's, I felt a hollow pit in my stomach from losing something I never even realised I had. Shaking off the bitter thought, I wanted to see if my blood was any different, now I had started to unlock my father's bloodline. Biting the side of my finger, I had to squeeze it quite firmly to get a single drop of blood out. It was still red, but more viscous and it sparkled slightly, like glittery nail polish. Fuck my life! Master Bronstad came over to observe it and looking at me, he started smiling.

"Don't even start!" I warned him.

"Maybe…" he started, whilst choking back his laughter. "Maybe…you are part pretty unicorn!" he sputtered out whilst absolutely pissing himself at me.

His laughter was contagious, and I soon found myself laughing along with him.

Master suddenly started to look at me strangely. "We should see how strong you are now."

I was game, I could feel my body was basically brimming with power. Before we left, I had basically plateaued at lifting the one-and-a-half tonne log without using Qi and I could already lift the two tonne one when I augmented my body with it, but I assume with my rise in cultivation that would have increased over the last three years. Most human cultivators could apparently lift between two and three tonnes after fully completing the Warrior stage and I was keen to see how I compared.

We didn't have any definitive weights with us, so we just chose progressively larger rocks. Master Bronstad was stronger than a typical spirit knight and said that he could lift around three tonnes without Qi and about ten with! So, we took turns, to see how long I could keep up. The results were surprising, Master eventually started to use his Qi, but at that point I still didn't need to. When we found a rock that he was barely able to lift, I attempted it and was also barely able to lift it, I kept trying for larger rocks until I maxed out with Qi at what we estimated to be about twelve tonnes, the first ten or so lifted with just my body alone! Even though my low cultivation only allowed my Qi to augment me a little, once my cultivation grew...damn!

"You are a monster!" Master beamed at me. I guess, after fifteen-hundred years, he was still a Viking at heart. "I would guess that you are now far physically stronger than a sage. Once they augment with Qi, I am not sure, but yes, you are definitely a monster!"

"I guess I'm not as defenceless anymore, monsters here I come!" I laughed whilst shadow boxing around.

Master's face suddenly became deadly serious. "Don't get too cocky, son, strength isn't everything, you are far behind in your Qi cultivation and techniques. Against even a weaker, yet dangerous opponent you could still easily die!"

I couldn't refute his claim, I wasn't invincible and so, suitably chastised, I sat down and had a look at Master's map. I could see he had annotated the portal and our treehouse, so luckily, I had a frame of reference to work from. We were situated within a continent named Antaris, which, even though it was slightly larger than the contiguous USA, was only the north-western part of the Antanel Empire. Only the major cities were annotated, and after Master had already carried me around three-hundred miles, the nearest -

Stormhaven, was easily another thousand miles away. It was all guesswork, but it was the best I could manage with the limited information available. Where is GPS when you need it?!

I hoped we would encounter smaller towns and villages on our journey and get more specific directions, plus after three years of only wildlife and Master Bronstad for company, as much as I loved him, I was in desperate need of some interaction with other people. When we first arrived, I had assumed there would be an occasional encounter with others, whether parties out adventuring or hunting, or even gathering plants and herbs. Yet, three years later, not a single soul had ever passed our way. A fact that had previously annoyed me, that had actually turned into a great stroke of luck, as there was no one who could identify us as the people who lived in the little treehouse.

As we were gathering our things together to set off towards civilisation, I became aware of voices approaching in the distance, there were three or four of them, but I couldn't understand the language they were speaking. Before they got to us, Master threw me a tiny jade tablet.

"What do I do with this fucking thing?" I asked.

"Place it onto your forehead and send some Qi into it, and don't be rude."

Doing as he said, and feeling like a complete fool, I placed the tablet against my forehead and sent a small sliver of Qi into it. My mind was immediately filled with a rush of concepts, pictures and unfamiliar words. As I came out of my brief daze, I was amazed to realise I could understand the language spoken by the approaching group.

"What was that?" I gasped.

"A memory jade, filled with the common languages of the Jade Wilderness realm, far quicker than trying to learn a language the normal way."

I had to agree, it was a slightly surreal experience but also pretty epic, I had gone from understanding one language fluently to fourteen, imagine if I could find some of those for skills and techniques!

We sat back down by the fire to have a tea whilst we waited for them to arrive and as they finally came within eyeshot, I saw that there was five of them, clearly a party of adventurers on their travels. They looked like a group on their way to a LARP convention, with a traditional setup you would expect to find in an RPG: There was a large middle-aged male warrior in full plate armour with a shield and flanged mace; what looked like a younger female warrior in chain mail with a large sword; a beautiful woman in red robes, perhaps a mage, who had pointy ears like an elf! A young man in white robes, a cleric or some sort of healer maybe? And the last dude, of a similar age to the cleric, was not chatting with the others, just skulking behind them with a bandolier full of throwing knives and two nasty looking daggers on his hips. Clearly that was why I thought there were four, Mr Emo Rogue obviously wasn't very talkative.

As we saw them, they also saw us, and I could see they instantly became guarded, but we didn't get up from where we were sitting, they had nothing to fear from us. Not that we were afraid of them either.

"Hoy, the adventurers." I waved cheerfully.

The man in white robes immediately waved back with a smile. As they approached, the rogue remained further back and I could tell, they were still wary.

"Join us for tea?" I offered.

The party hesitated for what to do, but the man in white robes immediately joined the circle around the fire. "Thank you for the hospitality, please allow me to introduce us. We're the Intrepid Ramblers, an adventuring party based out of Stormhaven, and I am Oziah, priest and bringer of Kandora's light."

He then proceeded to introduce us to the rest of his party, they had a Paladin of Zanos called Marcen; Hernda was apparently a free warrior, whatever that meant; Shay-Ara was an Elven sorceress; and the roguish character was called

Nayvar, whom he described as an Explorer, although from Nayvar's dress and general demeanour, I imagined that was just a polite way to avoid saying thief or assassin.

After several minutes sat around the fire, it became clear to both sides that neither of us planned to launch an attack, at least not immediately. So, we all started to relax and chat a little, well, apart from Nayvar.

"So, are you heading to look for the treasure too?" Marcen asked.

It wasn't clear whether he was fishing for information, or simply forthright, although with the role of paladin I would have assumed the latter. Either way, we had no interest in looking for the 'treasure' and so I had no reason to lie.

I shook my head. "No, we were out here training, and discussing whether to head to Stormhaven, when you arrived."

The rogue gave a snarky little laugh, as if he didn't believe a word I'd said. But before I even had a chance to say anything, the paladin beat me to it. "He speaks the truth Nayvar."

I looked at him in confusion. "You can tell if someone is lying?" I asked, thoroughly impressed.

"Discerning truth is one of my gifts from Zanos. Part of my duties are those of a Justiciar, the ability helps to separate the guilty from the innocent."

Looking at the man, I wondered whether he was also responsible for the punishment too, but it didn't seem appropriate to ask. I found myself wondering how divine gifts would work. Were Gods real? I thought they were just powerful cultivators, but maybe that isn't always the case. They seemed like a decent bunch, and I felt a little guilty for not telling them they were on a wild goose chase, but there was no way I was going to create a risk to Master and me.

"And you have no interest in joining us in our hunt for the treasure?" Shay'Ara asked, her voice was light and pleasant with an almost musical quality, it was enchanting.

135

"I'm afraid not, I crave a taste of civilisation and where I go, my student goes," Master quickly interjected; probably afraid I would wish to follow the beautiful elven maiden.

Which quite funny, as from the redness of his face, he was far more enamoured than I. Not something I would have expected from someone of his age, well, if the body's still willing, or so they say! Plus, in all fairness he didn't look a day over 40.

"We respect your choice of course, but before we leave. In your time out here, did you perhaps notice anything that may be of use to us in our search?" she asked.

Fuck! This could be tricky, especially with a human lie detector.

"Hmm," Master grumbled whilst nodding, which I took as a sign for me to zip it. "A week or so ago, there was a huge disturbance in the area and all of the aether around was drawn towards that direction." He gestured in the direction from which we'd come.

Smooth, Master, nothing but the truth! But if they found our treehouse and the remains of the bath, I did worry if they would have any way of associating it with us.

"Thank you, it's a specific direction in which to look, a shame you will not join us, but it matters not. Shall we?" she posited to the rest of her group.

A few grumbled replies were given, and they all got to their feet. Rising to see them off, I cupped my fist in farewell. "Safe hunting," I said.

They all nodded in reply and set off into the trees, towards our old camp! Knowing that staying around could potentially create more problems, we looked at each and smiled, I could tell Master was probably thinking along similar lines; if a paladin could sense the truth, who knew what kind of hiding ability a rogue could have, maybe he was still around. So, with no visible sense of urgency, we slowly gathered our camp and set out towards Stormhaven.

We had the map, but Earth compasses did not function with any degree of reliability, so we were largely

136

using the movement of the sun to navigate, which worked to a point, but, with the constant tree cover, was only enough to ensure we remained travelling more or less South-East. Our hope was that we would eventually come to signs of civilisation, whether roads or towns and from there the way would reveal itself, at least that was the plan. Now, a thousand miles is not a huge distance and on Earth many people are used to travelling that far via modern transportation. However, I assure you, were you on foot, a thousand miles would seem a lot further. A fit mundane human could possibly sustain about thirty miles of walking per day, and it would still take them thirty-odd days to cover the distance, if they could even maintain such a punishing pace for so long. Luckily, we are not mundanes and we were also not planning on walking.

We had travelled for just under four hours when we saw our first sign of civilisation and at a pace of easily thirty miles per hour, we had probably covered nearly one-hundred-and-twenty miles to reach it. I felt we could have gone even quicker, but we were in no rush. Regardless, I was smiling from the thrill for most of the journey, these abilities were never going to get old!

Chapter 21

The town was around two-square miles and completely enclosed by a forty-foot palisade made from the giant indigenous trees, with a mile or so of grassland surrounding that. It had probably been cleared to give the wall guards a clear view of threats approaching from the forest, but it also provided usable space. Some of which was being used as pasturage for a local type of cattle, and some as arable land, with numerous fields of flourishing crops. Overall, from a distance, it gave a pleasant impression, and it wasn't until you looked closer that you noticed details suggesting things may not be as idyllic as they first appeared.

Uniformed spearmen guarded the perimeters of the pastures and fields as the farmhands worked, and the palisade was surmounted at regular intervals with large, manned ballistae. As we walked along the hard packed dirt road towards the gate, the guards eyed us warily, but after deciding we weren't a threat, immediately turned their attention back towards the treeline. Their level of attentiveness suggested a threat from the woods was ever-present. Having dealt with numerous beasts during our time in the woods, I understood some of what was out there and knew they were right to be vigilant. The local predatory flora and fauna would happily tear through mundane people as well as low-level awakened, which between them, even in this realm, made up the largest proportion of the population.

At the gate, two guards were stood, one at either side, and as we tried to enter, the right-hand one stepped out to bar our way. Although he kept his spear at rest at his side, his nervousness was evident, not that I could blame him, as with a huge axe strapped to his back, coupled with his large stature, Master is quite imposing.

"What brings you to Traveller's Rest?"

So, the town was called Traveller's Rest, at least that was one question answered. Master stepped forward and removing a coin from a small bag, passed it to the guard. "We are travelling to Stormhaven and wish to purchase supplies, an inn would be nice too, as it has been far too long since I slept on a decent bed."

Quickly pocketing the coin, the guard's anxiousness disappeared with it. "Ol' Bren's shop will give you a fair price, you can't miss it, it's the first shop down the eastern street off the town square. As far as Inns, we have a few, but if you've the coin for it, the Jaded Mystic is the best in town."

"And where would one find this Jaded Mystic?" Master asked.

The guard chuckled as he answered. "Forgive my laughter, I meant no offence, you'll understand when you see the inn, it's in the Northern part of town and stands out somewhat."

The guard stepped to one side and thanking him for his help, we stepped into the town.

It was how I imagine a medieval town would have looked, except clean and without the foul smells. The buildings were relatively uniform constructions of wood and stone, none more than three stories, the streets well cobbled and even. The overall pleasantness meant it had the feel of a theme park or movie mock-up, and served to make the experience slightly surreal. As we made our way towards the centre of town, the place was bustling, whether folk going about their daily business, hawkers selling their wares, or small children playing in the streets. After three years in the forest, it was both overwhelming and heart-warming to see day-to-day life again, but the casual use of magic within a few shops as we passed reinforced that I was actually far from home.

The closer we got to the town centre, the larger the buildings became, with smaller shops and houses giving way to large stores, taverns and inns. The merry making of their patrons was audible as we passed, evidence that drinking was not just an evening activity.

The town square itself was surrounded on three sides by posh-looking shops, and restaurants with al fresco dining, and numerous people could be seen quietly enjoying their food and drinks. At the North end, a building with a large clocktower dominated, most likely the seat of the town government, which overlooked a large stone stage that sat upon that end of the plaza.

As we stood enjoying the sights, we must have caught someone's attention, as a group sat outside one of the restaurants stood and approached us. They were being led by a young man who looked to be around eighteen or nineteen, so of a similar age to me. Dressed in fancy black robes, he carried himself towards us with a confident gait. His followers were similarly clad in black, but wore mismatched armour and carried weapons that looked poorly maintained.

"I want your sword," he said, as they arrived in front of us. "How much for it?"

What an obnoxious prick! "It's not for sale," I replied.

One of the larger of his followers stepped forward and snarled at me. "If you know what's good for you, you'll offer it as a gift to our young lord. He has been accepted as an outer disciple of the Black Gate sect and is not someone you can afford to offend."

The pride in his voice was as evident as the foulness of his breath, and the little lordling was positively preening under the praise. The whole situation disgusted me. All around us, people were stopping their conversations and turning their attention to the unfolding drama.

"It's not for sale," I repeated, forcing down my growing anger.

His followers drew their weapons, but the young man raised an arm to halt their advance. He gestured towards the stone stage with his chin.

"Perhaps, we can solve this in a more civilised manner, it wouldn't do to upset the town guard after all. The winner gets the sword?"

Looking at him, I raised an eyebrow, my curiosity perked.

"The sword is already mine, so what would I gain from winning?"

Placing his hand within his robes, the young man pulled out a small coin purse. "One hundred gold coins."

There were a few gasps from the spectators, and I turned to look at Master, who simply smiled and shrugged at me. It looked like I had his blessing, and we were about to be a little bit richer.

"How do we do this?" I asked.

The young man licked his lips and shouted, "A duel is declared! I call upon the Imperial magistrate."

A few seconds passed before the doors of the clocktower building swung open, allowing a woman to exit. She was dressed in regal looking plate-mail decorated with golden filigree. Walking to the stone stage, she hopped onto it without pause.

"Who has summoned the Imperial Magistrate?" Her bellow filled the entire square.

Fuck me, that was probably loud enough to be heard outside the town gates and I could tell that she was not someone to be underestimated. The young man began to walk towards her and I took this as my cue as well. Joining the Imperial magistrate on the stage, she took her time to look us both over before speaking.

"What are the terms of the duel?"

"Winner takes the stakes, to the death," the young man said before I had a chance to say anything and sneered at me like he had caught me out.

141

The Imperial magistrate looked pointedly at me. "And both parties agree to these terms?"

I turned to look at the guy. "Are you sure about this?" I asked. He was a bit of a prick, but a fight to the death seemed a little extreme and I'd never killed anyone before.

The prick laughed at my question. "Is the filthy peasant a coward? That's ok too, I'm sure we could find less pleasant ways to deal with the issue."

Well, I gave him a chance. Turning back to the magistrate, I answered, "I do." Whilst wondering how I had so quickly gotten in to such a situation? This realm was even crazier than I realised, it was like the wild west!

"And what are the stakes?" the magistrate asked.

"One hundred gold coins from me against his sword," he said, the greed in his eyes obvious as he gazed at it.

I nodded my acquiescence to the terms and the Imperial magistrate withdrew a scroll from somewhere, upon which she proceeded to record the terms of the duel.

"Names?"

"Treliom Montaine," the lordling answered.

"Joshua White."

"Affiliations?"

"Black Gate sect."

"None," I replied, it didn't seem prudent to announce I was a member of the Baihu clan, who knew if it would even be recognised or if it would cause some sort of drama.

Holding the scroll to Treliom, he took out a dagger and pricked his finger with it and used the blood to mark next to his name on the scroll. Imitating him, I used my canine to do the same, hoping the magistrate wouldn't notice my blood was any different. Luckily, she merely rolled up the scroll and placed it away without even glancing at it.

"When I say begin, the duel will start, and neither shall leave the stage until I declare a victor, is this understood?"

We both nodded and the Imperial magistrate jumped from the stage. I looked around, we had gathered quite a crowd, news must have spread whilst we were talking to the magistrate.

Switching to focus solely on Treliom, everything else faded into the background. He was muttering something under his breath, an incantation of some kind most likely, and as the Imperial magistrate gestured for us to begin, he raised his hand, which glowed with a sickly green light.

"Tear him to pieces," he screamed.

On his command, three green portals opened on the floor in front of him from each of which a beast came snarling out. They were some sort of undead hounds, with putrescent flesh hanging off them, their tongues lolling from frothing mouths of vicious looking teeth. As one, they launched themselves at me, their milky eyes proving no impediment to locating me. The crowd roared in approval of the grisly sight, and as they arrived within striking distance my hand closed upon the hilt of my blade. As terrifying as they looked, they were ultimately just simple animals, three steps and three strikes and I only had to deal with him, the beasts bisected corpses left on the floor behind me. The crowd was silent as I advanced towards Treliom, whose face was full of undisguised rage.

Howling, he ran at me, and made a wild swing with his newly drawn sword. If he wasn't such a detestable human being, I may have spared him. But from our brief interaction, it was clear that he was as much a plague to society as the abominations he summoned. A single wind step and strike as I passed him and it was over, his body and head separating as they dropped.

The crowd erupted with cheers, which instantly annoyed me. Treliom may have deserved it, but a young man had just lost his life and the crowd just treated it like sport. Ignoring them, I made my way to the magistrate to collect my winnings. She threw the bag of coins to me, which I caught and hung on my waist.

"It seems I worried unnecessarily." The Imperial magistrate smiled.

143

Clasping my fist, I bowed to her. "I thank you for your concern anyway, magistrate."

"Be careful of the Black Gate sect Joshua White. The sect won't care about the death of a single outer sect disciple, but his fellow disciples may. The Montaines could pose a problem too."

"Thank you for the advice."

The magistrate leapt from the stage but turned back to me upon landing. "It's Hannah, by the way, Hannah Olisias. My name that is."

It may have been my imagination, but I swear her cheeks flushed a little pink before she quickly resumed her walk. Master approached me through the dispersing crowd, and we made our way towards the Northern part of town in companionable silence, I had just killed my first actual person and was unsure how to feel about it, supplies could wait.

Chapter 22

The Northern part of town was clearly more affluent, the houses larger with their own grounds. As we passed, I caught occasional glimpses through gaps in the walls and spiked metal fences. Their well-manicured lawns, fantastical topiaries and water features providing further evidence of the wealth of the inhabitants. Each of the estates had their own household guards too, who watched us warily until we moved out of sight.

When we eventually found our way to the Jaded Mystic, we smiled at each other, understanding why the gate guard had laughed. There wasn't a single ounce of moderation to the odd building, its ground floor split organically into three towers that occasionally intertwined before shooting off at strange angles. However, it was the fascia of the building, rather than the unusual architecture that truly bewildered me, it was completely covered in intricate carvings depicting the same sorcerer in various exploits: battling armies or marvellous creatures; casting spells of magnificent proportions; or indulged in orgies! Even everyday activities were present: the sorcerer sat reading a book; or taking a bath. It was apparent that whoever the sorcerer was, he didn't suffer from a lack of ego.

Entering the inn, we were immediately greeted by the Maître d', who was dressed in an elaborate aqua brocade tunic, with his hair and moustache fastidiously groomed. With our stained and worn armour, and general level of dishevelment, I was acutely aware of how out of place we must have seemed in such an establishment. The maître d' on the other hand, took it all in his stride, and I guessed they must be used to travellers sometimes arriving in such a state.

"Gentleman, how may I help you?"

"We were informed that this is the finest establishment in Traveller's Rest, so we would like two suites," Master replied.

"Of course, I assure you, sirs, there is not a finer establishment for hundreds of miles. We offer luxurious rooms, fine dining, drinks from around the empire, as well as a range of complementary services for our guests."

After three years in a pretty basic treehouse, the promise of some well-deserved luxury sounded like heaven.

"You would have had me with just hot baths and a laundry service." I laughed, whilst tugging on my ripe clothing. The Maître d', rather diplomatically elected not to comment, though I could swear I saw a hint of tension in his polite smile.

The gate-guard had been right, this was only a place to stay if you had the coin, as two nights for two suites came to four gold coins. Which did include food and services, but any exotic drinks would be extra. To put this in perspective, Master had explained that an ordinary inn would cost around a few silvers per night, at which a meal would vary from only five to thirty coppers. So, four gold coins could have afforded us months at a cheaper inn, but as we made our way up the grand staircase to our suites, I decided I didn't care, we deserved it after so long in the wilderness.

The suite was amazing, if a little ostentatious for my tastes. Reminiscent of pictures I had seen of the interior of Buckingham Palace, it was all gilt work and antique looking furniture, and every detail of the décor positively screamed wealth. The opulent bed beckoned to me, but I had lots to do before I could succumb to its call, not least of all a bath with actual soap.

Luxuriating in the ginormous roll-top bath, I gazed up at the ceiling fresco, in which the same sorcerer frolicked with mermaids and sea creatures. I found myself wondering who the sorcerer was and if he was even still alive? Maybe he was off on yet another adventure? Despite his egotism, I hoped he was, if even half of the exploits were real, the world would be lessened by the loss of such a colourful individual.

After far too long in the bath, a brief struggle ensued as I attempted to shave. Apparently, tempering my body had also left me with hair that now resisted cutting. Eventually, after blunting three of the complementary razors, I finally resorted to using my sword, which as well as being completely unwieldy, felt rather sacrilegious. So, if I was to remain clean-shaven, it looked like I would need to procure an enchanted razor or dagger of some sort.

I then took full advantage of the laundry service, which was extremely fast and efficient, my items returned in under an hour. Sorting through the now clean clothes and armour, I cringed, as three years of training and battle with forest beasts had left them barely wearable. They were honestly little better than rags and I felt the dire need for replacements. Not that I had an issue resembling a wandering vagrant when necessary, albeit a particularly clean one, but our future interactions with the natives would be influenced by how we looked. Even that twat Treliom may have thought twice before acting if we looked like more than just peasants, as upsetting someone with a potentially powerful backer could quickly prove fatal.

Electing to wear my least awful outfit, I reluctantly left the luxury of my suite and made my way back downstairs. Master was sat at the bar enjoying a frothing tankard of some sort of ale, his armour looking only mildly better than my own.

"Master, we need to purchase better clothes and armour," I said, gesturing to my clothes.

Master looked me up and down. "You may son, but there's still plenty of life in my armour," he argued, patting his breastplate before taking a massive quaff of his ale.

"Master, you look like a murder hobo."

Arguably, my timing could have been better, as being made to laugh whilst drinking had all the effect you would expect, ale was promptly ejected from both his mouth and nose as he sputtered whilst trying not to choke. Finally managing to cough up what he had involuntarily inhaled, he glared my way, only to find me doubled over pissing myself, which then quickly caused him to start laughing again. A lack of sense of humour was luckily not one of Master's flaws.

The bartender simply watched it all with a wry smile, but, as we finally managed to regain some semblance of self-control, asked, "Can I get you a fresh ale, sir?"

Which of course just set us back to laughing.

Eventually we composed ourselves, and the bartender helpfully provided directions to a store that catered to higher end clientele.

It was only a short walk to Enbrose's Pavilion, and as we entered the store, we were immediately accosted by a short rotund man dressed in intricate gold robes.

"Welcome to Enbrose's pavilion, purveyor of only the finest adventurer's attire and accoutrements. I am Enbrose, how may I be of service today?"

Alliteration aside, the delivery was obviously well-rehearsed, and Enbrose himself managed to seem approachable rather than obsequious.

"We need your finest armour and clothes, but fit for travel and combat, not just prestige," Master replied, clearly more accustomed to these situations than me.

Enbrose orbited us, nodding and muttering to himself as he did.

Finally coming to a stop in front of Master, Enbrose smiled at us. "Budget?"

Master pulled out a small coin purse and shook a dozen or so tiny rocks into his palm, they had a slight glow and with the way Enbrose's eyes lit up, they were clearly valuable.

"I have just the things," Enbrose said, rubbing his hands together in gleeful anticipation.

Wasting no time, he scurried off to gather up items and I took the chance to enquire about the rocks.

"What are they, Master?"

"Spirit stones, they can sometimes be mined from areas of high aether density, usually around the convergence of leylines or the like."

"I take it they're valuable?"

"These are only Minor spirit stones, least of their kind, but they're still worth around a thousand gold each."

"Holy shit!" I exclaimed. "Why?"

"Because they are extremely rare and contain a lot of pure aether, son."

My mind boggled at the information, why the fuck did I waste so much time absorbing aether from the air when I could have used the stones? Surely Master could use them too?

"Wouldn't we be better off keeping them? Using them?" I asked.

"If they were all we had, then yes," Master whispered, winking at me.

"Would have been nice whilst I spent all those nights slowly cultivating." I grumbled.

Master laughed at my annoyance.

"Son, if you tried to use these during the aether gathering stage, you would have made a nice mess of your meridians if you didn't just outright cripple yourself," he said, leaving me thoroughly placated and a little embarrassed.

Around ten minutes later Enbrose reappeared, waddling over whilst struggling to carry a literal mound of stuff. Placing the heap down, he then proceeded to sort and lay out specific items in front of each of us.

"For the young lord, this Elven armour seemed appropriate. For you, star-steel plate and chainmail made by the barbarian forge-masters of the Untal steppe. With matching tabards of Antarian spider silk."

Looking at the ornate half-plate armour, it was clearly the work of a master, a combination of a bright silver metal and dark blue reptile skin, hopefully it was as functional as it was beautiful. I picked up the chestplate to inspect it more closely, shocked by how light it was.

"The steel is enchanted to be light but strong, and the leather is from an ice drake. Armour fit for an Elven prince," Enbrose said enthusiastically.

"Where did you get such fine armour," I asked suspiciously.

"Around forty years ago, through a greatly fortuitous trade, or so I thought at the time. Apparently, a band of adventurers had found it in some ancient Elven ruins deep in the woods. They sold it to another merchant, and I purchased it from him, damn near ruined me too."

"Not as fortuitous as you thought?" I asked, my curiosity perked.

"No! Because, for forty years, no-one has been able to afford the blooming thing! Until today!" He rubbed his hands together, positively beaming from ear to ear.

The bastard, he had me by the short and curlies, I wanted the armour, and he knew it!

Master was also inspecting the armour in front of him, it was also a set of half-plate, of dark grey metal and though it had less embellishment than mine, still looked masterfully crafted, it also had fewer gaps in the protective metal plates due to the addition of heavy looking chainmail. Nodding as he thoroughly checked each piece, when he was finally done, he looked up at Enbrose, who was licking his lips in nervous anticipation.

Then the haggling began, and I stepped back, thoroughly out of my comfort zone with such an affair.

"How much?" Master asked.

Enbrose immediately launched into another tirade about the providence, before he was promptly cut off by Master.

"How much?"

The frustration over not being allowed to finish his sales pitch was evident on his face, however this didn't stop a gleeful smile from appearing as he named his price.

"Hmm...let's see...five stones for the elven armour, two for the Ultan, fifty gold a piece for the tabards. Seven and one hundred all in."

"Five stones," Master offered.

Enbrose immediately started blustering. "Five stones, five stones! Are you trying to rob me? Seven stones dead," he countered.

This went on for another good few minutes, the language becoming more colourful with each new round, before they eventually settled on a price of six stones. Both seemed happy with the price, although from the grin that split Enbrose's face, I felt like he definitely came out on top. Which was more or less confirmed after we informed him that we were also in need of some fine boots, robes and cloaks, and Enbrose happily outfitted us with the rest completely on the house. He didn't seem like the charitable type, so clearly, he'd finally made a tidy profit on his old investment.

Dressed in our new robes, we left with our armours wrapped up in the new cloaks. A smiling Enbrose gaily waved us off, probably waiting for us to leave so that he could dance for joy around his shop over his new-found fortune. If he wasn't simply going to pack up shop to live a life of luxury on his six thousand gold coins!

Our next stop was to find a smith, as Master explained to me as we walked, top end armour was usually enchanted to automatically adjust its fit when supplied with aether. Within reason anyway, child sized armour would obviously never fit a giant. However, the straps were another story and would need to be adjusted for fit by a trained armourer, and hopefully we could find one who knew what they were doing.

Enbrose had assured us of the ability of a certain dwarven smith, and following his directions, it wasn't long before a skyward trail of smoke was visible, accompanied by the tell-tale cacophony of metal striking metal. By the time we arrived outside the smithy, the din was almost unbearable, and I hoped for their sake that no-one lived in any of the nearby buildings.

Entering, as if the intense heat wasn't enough, we were abruptly presented with the muscular bare back of a red-headed dwarf swinging a huge hammer. Standing all of four feet and change, they were almost as broad as they were tall, and whilst walking around them to gain their attention, mine was suddenly, and shockingly, drawn to the huge and pendulous breasts swinging in time with the strike of the hammer! Finally noticing us, the smith turned to look at us, whilst I attempted to look everywhere else other than her now fully exposed chest.

"What'sa matter boy, never seen a pair of tits before?" she asked with a big smile on her face, as she wiped the sweat from her brow.

Covered in soot from the forge, she was pretty despite her build, with rosy cheeks and a mischievous glint in her eyes. I had no idea whether casual nudity was a cultural norm for dwarves and so with no desire to embarrass myself, turned to look at her whilst attempting to pretend the situation didn't bother me at all. Noticing the sweat running down her chest, only to drip off her nipples, I felt my face grow warm and knew I'd failed miserably. Fuck my life!

"Shouldn't you have an apron on to protect you from sparks?" I asked, immediately realising that was probably a thought that should have stayed in my head.

"Nah, it chafes me teats." She chuckled, flicking her nipples as she did.

Now, I'm not a fucking prude by any stretch of the imagination, but at this point, the combination of the dwarf's blatant exhibitionism, and how thoroughly impractical and absurd topless smithing was, had left me thoroughly tongue-tied. So, I looked to Master for some all too necessary support. What I received instead, was the sight of a fifteen-hundred-year-old Viking with the beaming face and twinkling eyes of a lovestruck teenager, brilliant!

"Like what ya see?" the smith asked him, making no effort to hide the amorous intentions in her eyes.

Having had enough of the developing situation, I finally managed to find my voice before I became an unwilling spectator to some carnal gymnastics.

"We need the straps adjusting on our new armour."

Snapped from making goo-goo eyes at Master, she bent down to pick up a loose linen top from a table, which she thankfully pulled on, before addressing me again.

"Let's get ya sorted then, so then the big un can sort me." She winked.

Electing to ignore the comment, I untied the bundle and presented the armour. The change in her demeanour was instant.

"Where'd ya get that boy?" she asked, her tone almost frantic.

Holding out her arms reverentially, I handed her the armour. The smith closed her eyes and slowly ran her hands over the armour, occasionally pausing with her head cocked as if listening to something only she could hear. Eventually opening her eyes, she looked at me expectantly.

"From Enbrose, and at nearly five thousand gold coins, it was daylight robbery."

She simply smiled at my answer. "This ain't no armour you'd be 'aving for any amount o' coin."

"Even from the elves?" I asked.

Laughing, she passed the armour back to me. "No elf made that, that was old when this world was still new."

"Who made it then?" I asked.

The dwarven smith shrugged. "Who knows." And held out a hand for me to shake. "Clara," she said.

Taking the proffered hand, I shook it, her hand was callused, her grip like iron. "Josh," I replied.

Putting the armour on for Clara to adjust, I allowed some Qi to flow into it. The armour responded instantly, writhing around on me like it was alive, it was not a pleasant experience and I had to fight back the urge to pull it off. The metal flexed and flowed, the scaled leathers contorting, before finally stopping as abruptly as it had started. The armour now fit like it was made for me, and holding up my arm, I inspected the vambrace as I clenched and unclenched my fist.

"Fuck me, even the Ice-Drake skin adjusted," I exclaimed in shock.

"Pfft, if that's Ice-Drake skin, then I'm a fooking gnome." Clara chuckled.

Looking at her expectantly, I waited for further explanation.

"Where's ya imagination boy, that be Dragon skin!"

"Dragon skin!" I almost shouted.

Clara's eyes widened in alarm. "Keep it down boy, wars have been started over less than that there armour."

"And yet you don't want it?" I asked, feeling a little suspicious.

"Things like that 'av a way of endin' up exactly where they wanna, nae dwarf is foolish enough to get in their way."

"You act like it has a mind of its own," I said jokingly.

Clara's expression was deadly serious. "And who's to say it ain't?"

Sliding my tabard over the top, I donned my sword and cloak and turned to check myself in a nearby mirror.

Master was looking me up and down, and after adjusting my cloak slightly, patted me on the shoulder. "You cut a fine figure, son, your mother would be proud."

Simultaneously both happy and sad at his comment, I just nodded, unsure of how to reply. The gentle smile on Master's face evidence enough that he understood. Looking at my reflection, I was pleased, I don't want to blow my own trumpet, but I looked good, like a high-born warrior from a fantasy RPG.

Happy that I no longer required Clara's services, I thanked the smith for her help and agreeing to meet Master later, left the two of them alone to better 'acquaint' themselves.

Chapter 23

With no real destination in mind, I decided to wander the town and see where my feet took me. The difference made by my outfit was immediately evident, the curious gazes no longer lingering as they had before. But, as pleasant as the town was, after an hour or so of walking aimlessly, I eventually grew bored and hungry, and decided to stop at a tavern for some food and drink.

Happily eating my mystery meat stew, my relaxing afternoon was rudely interrupted by the appearance of five dodgy-looking bastards, who I immediately recognised as Treliom's followers, and they didn't look like they'd come for a nice chat.

"You shouldn't have messed with the Montaine family, boy." The lead thug snarled at me as they approached.

I looked over to the passing guards for assistance, but pointedly avoiding my stare, they sped off as if they suddenly had somewhere far more important to be. The useless fuckers! Oh well, it looked like I was on my own.

"The guards won't help a jumped up little pissant like you, look at ya, wasting the young lord's coin to make ya'self look all important, now, be a good boy and hold out ya neck for Crandor."

Drawing my sword, I stood up, thoroughly pissed-off that I hadn't even got to finish my meal. I was still willing to see if I could avoid bloodshed, although I didn't hold out much hope, as anyone who refers to themselves in the third person is probably a little touched in the head.

"You don't have to do this Crandor, walk away and no one needs to get hurt."

The thugs laughed, baying wildly as they surrounded me.

"Such a naïve young fool." Crandor practically hissed. "Lord Montaine's son died on my watch, the only chance to keep our heads, is to bring him yours."

If Treliom was a son of an important family, then there was no chance they'd be spared for such a colossal fuck-up, whether they took revenge or not. They probably knew it too, but they were desperate, and killing me was the only hope they could cling to. They came in fast, giving me no further chance to reason with them.

I launched my table at the two on the left and circled around to the right, knowing that if I was surrounded my chance would drop precipitously, so my best bet was to try and ensure they were in each other's way. Parrying the first thugs slash, my follow-up took his arms off at the elbow and I immediately sped past to the one behind him. A quick thrust to his throat caught him before he could even react and he dropped, using his hands in a futile attempt to stem the blood now gushing from his throat. Disengaging, Crandor was suddenly upon me, his blade growing ever faster in tandem with the madness growing on his face. He wasn't a bad swordsman, and what he lacked in skill; he was more than making up for with pure ferocity. Whilst dealing with the deluge of Qi enforced strikes from Crandor, I noticed the last two thugs had recovered from the table and were moving to flank me. My momentary lapse in concentration allowing Crandor to land a solid kick to my midsection, which launched me through a bunch of tables and chairs to a bone-jarring stop against the tavern wall. Luckily, the kick had an unintended positive side-effect. I had flown at least twenty feet, and quickly rising, now had some space from my assailants. Crandor had clearly put some force into that blow, as I was left slightly winded even with my new armour, and I realised that even if my newfound strength had made me more robust, it had done little to increase my weight. Crandor was the clearly the most dangerous opponent, so I knew I needed to end the other two first so I could concentrate on him without any distractions. Quickly strategising how to achieve this, I realised I hadn't even been using any Qi techniques, the first two thugs hadn't required any and then I was pressured so heavily by Crandor that I hadn't thought to. It was evident that for all my time fighting beasts and sparring with Master, I still had very little experience fighting other warriors.

Using wind-steps, I was upon the two thugs in a flash, my sudden increase in speed left them flustered and I cut them both down before either had a chance to react. Then it was just Crandor and me remaining. Without hesitation I moved to strike him down as I had his companions, however Crandor was on a completely different level to them and moved just as quickly as me. After several brief exchanges we separated, and it was clear he had now gained some control over his earlier rage.

"Surprised, boy? You're not the only one with a movement technique."

Honestly, I was a little shocked, he was far more capable than Treliom had been, and unlike the other trash, if I failed to take him seriously, he was truly capable of ending my life. It was an unpleasant feeling, but also exciting, as fighting foes like this was the only way I would improve. So, pushing down my growing anxiety, I started to analyse what I knew. He had me beat a little in cultivation level, the density of the Qi I could feel empowering his strikes attested to that, but I was far physically stronger and the more gifted swordsman. Eventually his aether reserves would run dry and then I would have him, I could try to simply physically overpower him, but he was a slippery fighter, so there was no need to take the risk when attrition would work.

"You've no chance, brat, I was killing peo…"

Leaping at him, I gave him no chance to finish his spiel, we weren't in a movie. The annoyance on his face was plain, as was his rising anger. Which was exactly what I wanted, the more unhinged he became, the quicker he would burn out. It worked, and after twenty or so furious strikes, I could feel him slowing, his blows weakening. He had caught me several times in the duel, but they were only glancing blows to my arms, which my armour easily stopped. Each of my parries started to carry him further out of line and finally, I could feel he had reached his limits. Sensing he was about to disengage to catch his breath, I finally allowed my own Qi to burst from my core, the sudden change in rhythm allowing my riposte to catch him, my blade half buried in his chest.

All was suddenly still, until the momentary silence was ended by Crandor's sword clanging to the ground, as frothy blood sputtered from his mouth. There was a brief instant of shock and terror in his eyes, then he gave a faint smile, and he was gone. Eyes now vacant, his body dropped, and my sword slid free. Wiping the blood from my blade, I gazed down at Crandor's corpse. He was a worthy opponent, and the body on the floor could just as easily have been mine, so I gave him a swordsman's salute. A simple sign of respect and one his ability if not his character deserved.

Sheathing my sword, I looked around me at the surrounding carnage. Oh, shit! We had totalled the seating area, and I'd left a Josh shaped dent in the tavern wall. I knew there was no way I was going to get out of paying some sort of reparations for the mess. Crashing adrenaline levels and the sudden change in pace left me feeling slightly worn out and I rubbed my head in annoyance at being left to deal with the aftermath. Well, it may be a pain, but it was better than being dead, I thought whilst looking down at Crandor's body.

The gathered crowd eyed me warily, as if I was a wild animal that may decide to bite one of them. Although, based on the five bodies littering the ground, maybe they were right to, but fuck it, it was them or me.

Noticing Master amongst the spectators, I made my way over to him.

"You've made a right royal mess here, son."

His statement was accompanied by the sound of numerous approaching feet, and turning to look for the source, I noticed a platoon of Guardsman headed our way. Of course, now they wanted to get involved! They were being led by Hannah, the Imperial Magistrate from my earlier duel, and as they grew near, a sweaty, flustered looking man made his way quickly towards them out of the crowd. The reason immediately became clear as he began to rant to Hannah about the state of his once beautiful tavern. Emboldened by the presence of the guards and magistrate, his attention quickly turned to me.

"Thrice-damned ruffian, look at the mess you have made of my establishment!"

Any desire to apologise and pay for the damages faded fast as my anger grew and looking at the reddened face of the buffoon in front of me, I failed to suppress the growl that rumbled from my throat.

"You would expect a man to simply offer up his head?"

My growling clearly did me no favours, as the Guards' hands tightened on the hafts and hilts of weapons. Aware of the threat they posed, my actions echoed theirs, but the quickly escalating situation was diffused as Hannah raised a hand.

"Stand down," she commanded.

Seeing a lack of reaction from the guardsman, the look on her face immediately turned to annoyance. "I SAID, STAND DOWN!" she bellowed.

That seemed to do the trick, and as the guardsman relaxed, I found myself releasing a breath I hadn't even realised I was holding. Then she turned towards the proprietor, who seemed to shrink under her stare.

"Well? Answer the question."

Clearly, the man had not expected to be the sudden object of her attention, and it took him several seconds to compose himself.

"No, Lords no," he said, visibly wilting at the admission.

Nodding in satisfaction, Hannah's gaze then turned to me.

"And you, Joshua White, do you believe that any reimbursement is due to this man."

Looking at the downcast eyes of the proprietor, I glanced around at the scene, wondering if I could have handled things differently. The man had been angry because his livelihood had been affected, and even though I had not instigated the fight, I should have probably just apologised for my part, instead of acting like an indignant child. It was probably leftover adrenaline affecting me. With everybody still waiting for my response, I walked from corpse to corpse and gathered their coin purses. The kills were mine and so were the spoils, such was the way. With all five collected, I made my way towards the proprietor and handed the coin purses to him.

"This should cover their part," I said, and removing a single gold coin from my own purse, handed it to the man. "This should cover my own."

The man alternated his shocked gaze, between me and the contents of his hands. Looking inside the coin purses, a moment passed as he seemed to sort through his thoughts, before, sighing, he shook his head.

"Thank you, young man, but this is far too generous," he admitted, attempting to pass the gold coin and several of the purses back to me.

The man went up in my estimation by several notches, he could easily have just taken the money and ran. Instead, he was honest, which spoke volumes about his character. Reaching out, I closed his hand around them and smiled at the man.

"Take the rest as my apology for being an ass."

Looking at my face, probably for any sign of deception. He nodded and smiled, which I assumed meant he didn't find any.

161

"Looks like my little tavern will be getting a bit of an upgrade, thank you, young man."

"Right, everyone can disperse, there's no more to see here!" Hannah loudly announced.

Crisis averted, the crowd dispersed, and I was left standing with just Master and Hannah, who looked at me with a wry smile.

"Only one day in town and I've already been called out do deal with you twice, anyone might think that you're a trouble-maker."

It was clear from her tone that she was joking, but a little reassurance never hurt.

"Definitely not, ma'am, I've just been a little…unfortunate."

"Ma'am? Damn it, I'm not that much older than you!"

My attempt at being polite failed miserably and I wasn't entirely sure why.

"Sorry, you're the first imperial magistrate I've met."

I could see the gears turning in her head as she decided what to make of me.

"You're not from the Empire, are you?" she asked.

Looking for Master's approval before responding, he gave me a barely perceptible nod.

"No, we're not from this realm."

I guess, she'd probably expected us to be from another country, as her jaw literally dropped.

"Wha…how…is this a joke?" she stammered out.

Based on her reaction, cross-realm travellers were uncommon, and I wondered why Master had never mentioned it?

"I will come and find you tomorrow," she said before suddenly rushing off.

I turned to Master. "Do you think she'll be a problem?"

Master gazed in the direction she had left. "No, I don't think she wishes us any harm."

After the day's excitement, the evening was thankfully more sedate, with just a lovely meal and quiet conversation at the Jaded Mystic before retiring early to bed.

Chapter 24

After breakfast, Master and I left the Inn to find a merchant caravan station. At a jog, we could have probably run to Stormhaven in well under a week, but Master said that travelling with a merchant caravan was something that every adventurer should experience at least once. Honestly, I wasn't convinced.

The caravan station was bustling, with numerous porters moving goods from a large warehouse onto wooden wagons twice the size of any ever used on Earth. I wondered what kind of animal would be used to pull such monstrous contraptions. Three richly dressed merchants stood at the sides, passing instructions to foreman, who then barked orders at the porters, along with colourful insults, generally about how slow and useless they were. It was organised chaos at its finest, and the fact the merchants were stood doing largely fuck all, was no surprise whatsoever. Just like back home, it seemed the wealthier you were, the less actual work you did.

Approaching the merchants was a little odd, as other than their clothes and age there was little to distinguish between them, they could easily have been clones at slightly different stages of life. Uniformly overweight with short thinning hair, their beady eyes tracked us as we walked over, probably calculating from our attire whether there was any money to be made. The eldest looking one stepped forward and smiled.

"Good day, fine sirs, welcome to Mandelhill brothers trading, how can I help you?"

"We require passage to Stormhaven," Master answered.

"Very well, working or leisure?"

We'd discussed this on the way over and, luckily, Master agreed with me. Being ready to fight if necessary was fine, but I had absolutely no desire to spend the entire trip taking orders from a merchant or guard commander.

"Leisure," Master answered.

Smiling at our request, the merchant hollered, "Tribbs!"

Now we were simply potential passengers, the interest with which the Mandelhills looked at us vanished, and the other two quickly resumed their instructions to the foreman.

Soon after, a tall narrow-faced man, who I assumed to be Tribbs, strutted towards us out of the warehouse. He was dressed simply in a green woollen tunic and brown breeches, but the clothes were clean and his boots well-polished. I took it as a good sign, as if he was as fastidious with the caravans as his own dress, we would likely be in good hands.

"These gentlemen require transport to Stormhaven," said Mandelhill senior.

Bowing wordlessly to the merchant, Tribbs turned to us and beckoned. "Please follow me, sirs."

Happy to be leaving the merchants and their loading yard, we were led to the other side of the warehouse, where five caravans were lined up. Just as oversized as the wagons, their detailed woodwork made them resemble Romani Vardos on steroids, only painted with more muted earthen tones. They were awesome!

"Which one will we be travelling in?" I asked excitedly.

Tribbs grinned at me. Rubbing his hands together, he looked like a medieval Mr Burns, and I was wholly disappointed when his next words weren't 'Excellent!'

"Well sir, that depends on how much you are willing to pay."

"What's the difference between them?"

He gave me a knowing smile. "It would be far easier for you to just take a look, sir."

We made our way through the various caravans, there were three varieties, the first one contained eight bunk beds allowing for a total of sixteen passengers. Each bed had its own windowed nook and a trunk for storage. A single bathroom with a toilet and shower was shared between all the passengers, but the fact a wooden caravan had a working bathroom at all was amazing. The joys of magic! The second, had only four beds, with the extra room allowing for a small sitting area and stove, it was also a little better appointed, with furnishings of a higher quality. Unlike the first, the bathroom was also fitted with a bathtub. The final caravan was ridiculous, largely dominated by a single oversized bed, its every filigreed detail overly ostentatious. It was a travelling suite fit for a prince or princess and not suitable for us at all.

"How much?" I asked, pointing at the second caravan we had checked.

"A gold per person, or five gold for sole use, a wagoner and food is included in the price."

No wonder people tended to work as guards on caravan runs, only the wealthiest people would be able to afford to throw that much gold around! I bet even a berth on the economy wagon would be too expensive for most. Luckily for us, money wasn't an issue. Sharing a wagon with strangers was also something to consider, as sharing a wagon with two strangers could potentially be fun but was just as likely to be a complete nightmare.

Clearly Master wasn't willing to take the chance over three gold coins. "We'll pay the five," he said, handing over the coins. "When do we leave?"

"Sunrise on the morrow, journey to Stormhaven is around thirty days."

Leaving the place, I couldn't help but wince at the thirty days travel time. With how quickly we could have covered the distance on foot, it seemed like a huge waste of time.

As we passed through the gates, I was surprised to see Hannah stood there waiting for us.

"I'm coming with you," she said.

"Why?" Master asked, beating me to it.

"I want you to take me with you when you leave this world."

Left a little shocked at her answer, she continued before we even had a chance to reply. "I can bring you under the Olisiases banner whilst you are here and being part of my official retinue could open more opportunities for you. Please, I will definitely make it worth your while," she said, a little desperation creeping into her voice towards the end.

Master shook his head. "That doesn't answer why you want to leave this realm with us."

"Freedom," Hannah replied, without missing a beat.

"You'd be just another girl in our world, with no clan to rely on," Master said.

Hannah got a faraway look on her face. "Sounds amazing."

"Freedom's as good a reason as any." I smiled. "But not a soul can know, as I doubt your family would let you go without a fight."

Hannah nodded her assent. "Thank you, you won't regret this."

We agreed to meet at the caravan in the morning and left to gather up supplies. Although Tribbs had mentioned food would be included, it was always best to be prepared. The rest of the day was uneventful and despite the luxury of the Jaded Mystic, I was growing bored in the town and was itching to leave.

The next morning, we were up well before sunrise in order to arrive at the caravan on time. We made sure to thank the Maître d' before leaving and I took the opportunity to ask about the sorcerer in the carvings whilst I still could.

"Who is the sorcerer?" I gestured at one of the reliefs.

"I wondered whether you would ask, sir. Most do. He was my grandfather Tan'taranel, one of the greatest sorcerers the Empire had ever seen. For centuries he adventured, protecting us all and asking nothing in return." He looked around to see if anyone else was present, before leaning in and continuing in a quieter voice, "The imperials began to fear his power and he was betrayed. My whole life, Grandfather had been such a carefree and happy man, but the last time I saw him…his lust for life was gone, hence the name of the Inn."

Telling the tale of Tan'taranel clearly upset him, and I felt bad for bringing up something so obviously painful.

"I'm sorry, it sounds like he was an amazing man."

With a bittersweet smile, the maître d', held out his hand for me to shake. "You seem like a good man, Joshua White, be careful when you get to Stormhaven, the empire is a pit of vipers, and not a place for good men."

As we walked out of the inn, his final remark had tempered my excitement over Stormhaven, and reminded me to be more careful. As my dad had liked to say, *the nail that sticks out gets hammered.* Thinking about him helped my mood and I found myself smiling. What I'd found out about my birth hadn't changed anything, they would always be Mum and Dad to me. I would get stronger, find out who was responsible for their deaths, and they'd pay. And I'd find my sister too, I knew she was still out there somewhere, I could feel it. With a renewed sense of purpose, Master and I made our way to the awaiting caravan.

Chapter 25

The first two weeks of the journey were a monotonous blur, the view from the caravan windows just endless repetitive forest, and so I'd spent the majority of my time quietly cultivating. My current goal, at the Spirit warrior stage, was to absorb more aether and condense my Qi into a liquid form, which my newly tempered body and meridians were now able to contain. It had quickly become apparent just how much aether this would take, and so Master had finally allowed me to make use of the spirit stones. When I wasn't cultivating, I'd spent a lot of time making small talk with Hannah as it turned out she is only a year older than me.

"I swear it doesn't feel like only fifteen days, I'm starting to go stir crazy in this caravan," I said.

"Ha, this is nothing, you should try spending most of sixteen years stuck in a clan compound, only allowed out for official events or the occasional supervised trip," Hannah replied.

She made it sound awful, but I'm sure it couldn't have been that bad. "Really? I bet that 'compound' was a lot bigger than this though?" I teased.

Hannah gave a wry smile. "Yeah, my family's one of the seven major noble clans, so it's actually a similar size to Traveller's rest, but…"

"What the actual fuck?" I couldn't help but interrupt her. "Your family compound is the size of a town? And you were comparing it to this little fucking wagon?" I asked incredulously.

"Yes, a bit larger actually, and I was about to explain before you, rather rudely, interrupted me."

She was right, I had been rude. "I'm sorry, I guess being in this box is getting to me."

"Apology accepted, and as I was saying, it was the same because I felt trapped, it may have been huge, but it was still a cage."

Imagining being stuck in a single small town with no freedom to leave, I realised how awful it could have been. "So, what changed?" I asked sympathetically.

From the way she looked at her hands before speaking, I assumed she wasn't used to opening up. "I never really had friends as a child, only siblings and cousins to play with, and as we got older even those relationships soured into constant competition for status and resources. It quickly became clear that I was the most gifted youth in the main branch, but I had no interest in the social side of noble life, as all the preening and fake compliments sickened me."

"I don't blame you, I would have hated all that nonsense too, and for what it's worth, you have a friend now," I said, attempting to reassure her.

"Thanks." She smiled. "Besides, it all worked out in the end. You see, my cousin Aveena had always been a social butterfly and was far more popular than me, so when I came of age, her mother, my Aunt Vorexia, took the opportunity to ensure she remained in the clan spotlight. At my first clan meeting as an adult, she suggested that some time spent as an Imperial Magistrate would aid my development and be good for the clan." Hannah started to laugh. "She probably thought I'd rail against the idea, but instead I saw a way out. So, when the patriarch asked for my opinion, I offered some nonsense about how it would definitely benefit the clan and me. They all agreed, and I was out of there the following day. I've never looked back," she said, positively beaming by the end.

"I'm glad it worked out for you, I imagine most people think it's all great as noble, but it clearly has its..."

I was interrupted as the caravan came to an abrupt halt. Which was strange, as the stops were all pre-planned, and I knew we hadn't been travelling long enough to have reached the next. So, deciding to investigate, we headed outside. Ahead of the lead wagon, there were a group of unsavoury looking men and women, who in true Robin hood fashion, had used a tree trunk across the road to bar our way forward. The caravan guards were clearly professionals though, as they were already stood with their weapons drawn, ready to engage as necessary.

As we passed the stationary caravans, I thought it would be strange if they'd all arranged themselves out in the open, so I looked for any signs that we were surrounded. It quickly became clear that there were also numerous bandits around us, attempting to use trees and bushes to hide and failing spectacularly, so possibly on purpose.

As we arrived at the front of the lead wagon, Hannah, wasting no time at all, immediately started to shout, "Honestly, what is wrong with you all? To rob a merchant caravan on an imperial highway, especially one flying the flag of an imperial magistrate, were you all dropped on your heads as babes?"

I wasn't sure whether she was brave or stupid, but either way, it was funny as shit, as Hannah was completely fearless. The bandits as expected, didn't seem to find it as funny, nor did they seem to care one iota about her status.

"Listen 'ere ya lil' bitch, we don't givva fuck oo ya are, ya pay the toll, or ya die," said a scrawny bandit at the front.

The merchant on the other hand proved far more diplomatic, making it abundantly clear this was a regular situation, and that he even recognised the bandit leader.

"Now, now, Strenger, you know the Mandelhills always pay the toll," he said, throwing a purse towards the bandit.

Strenger juggled the purse in his hand. "Price 'as gone up."

The previously calm merchant finally started to lose his cool. "The price was agreed by your boss, it's not for you to decide."

Licking his lips, Strenger smiled. "I's afraid da boss 'ad a lil' acsee-dent in 'is sleep. I's da boss now, an' da price 'as gone up." Looking at Hannah, he leered. "An' I'll be 'aving dat lil' thing as ma new toy."

Now, I was all for paying a few coins to avoid a little bloodshed. But when Strenger announced his plans for Hannah, my temper flared, and I decided the piece of shit was going to die.

"Here's how it's going to go!" I bellowed. "Strenger is an idiot, and he's going to get you all killed, probably sooner rather than later. So, today I'll do you all a favour, we'll pay you all the agreed price, but he's going to die. It's up to you whether you want to join him."

Strenger started to laugh, I didn't. I did, however, notice the bandits start to slowly back away from him, which did make me smile, it looked like they didn't much like him either.

"Well, looks like they're smarter than you." I chuckled, gesturing at his companions with my head.

Finally, Strenger stopped laughing, and looking over his shoulder noticed the bandits had distanced themselves from him. Turning back to me he snarled.

"Ya piece of shit, I'll fucking kill ya."

Drawing two daggers from his side, he launched himself at me like a whirlwind. The man was all speed but no skill, a quick application of wind steps and I was past him. He walked another couple of steps before his body even realised it was dead, then he dropped in two separate pieces, his head rolling to a stop underneath Hannah's foot. I waited to see how the bandits would react, whilst wiping his filthy blood from my sword. Finally, one of the female bandits gathered the courage to slowly approach, and everyone waited with bated breath to see what she'd do. Passing me, she approached Strenger's body and bent down to take the coin purse from his corpse. As she stood up, she spat on his body, the anger on her face evident.

The bandits burst into cheers, and I was left a little dumbstruck at their unexpected reaction. Gazing over at Hannah, she looked just as confused as I felt.

The female bandit approached me with bloodshot eyes. "Thank you," she choked out as she passed me the coin purse.

In an orderly fashion the bandits then proceeded to move the tree off the road and retreat en-masse back into the forest. After watching them leave, I approached the merchant to return his purse, expecting to see relief on his face. Instead, it was sadness I saw, adding to my growing sense of confusion over the whole situation.

"What exactly is going on here?" I asked, deciding not to beat around the bush.

"The…" The merchant was clearly about to say one thing, but then noticed Hannah's presence. "Nothing, I'm just not keen on violence, thank you for your assistance." He attempted a smile and then trundled back to his seat on the wagon.

By the time the convoy set off again, Hannah and I were back inside, mulling over the oddity of the bandits. "It makes no sense, the merchant should have been happy to receive his money back," I said, "plus, she thanked me."

"Yeah, and as capable as you are, I don't think they left because you scared them off. It was more like they never planned for violence anyway," Hannah reasoned.

I got up from my seat. "Fuck it, I'm going to speak to Mandelhill."

Hannah started to rise too. "I'll come with you."

"No, you stay here, he didn't hold his tongue until he saw you," I said.

"But he knows we are travelling together."

"True, but I still think it's better I go on my own."

The merchant was sat looking pensive when I arrived at his wagon. Jumping up, I took a seat alongside him. "I never got your name?" I asked.

The suddenness of both my appearance and question seemed to catch him off-guard.

"Oh…well…Lorton," he stammered out, offering me a hand to shake.

Taking his hand in a firm grip, I attempted to smile reassuringly. "Josh, Joshua White."

I assumed it must have been something important bothering him, as although he was the youngest of the three brothers, he still looked to be about thirty, and with years of experience as a travelling merchant, he shouldn't rattle easily.

"So, Lorton, are you going to tell me what the fuck that was really about?"

After a deep sigh, he steeled himself and stared at me. "I don't know what you're talking about?"

I couldn't blame him for lying, after all I was just a paying passenger, but there was no way I was willing to be brushed off so easily. "Look, Lorton, I just had to kill a man, and even though he was clearly a piece of shit, something was off about the whole thing."

"Is this where you threaten me?" he asked.

The fear on his face was obvious, but so was his resolve, and I respected that. Although if I'm honest, I was a little offended by his assumption. "No, of course not, I'm not going to hurt you just to satisfy my curiosity!"

"Then why would I say anything?"

"Because it will save me wasting my time to run after the bandits and find out. I imagine if I run, I could probably reach them and be back in under an hour."

At first Lorton looked amazed, like I'd said something he hadn't even considered, then he chuckled mirthlessly. "You would too, wouldn't you?" he said, hanging his head dejectedly. "I knew the Imperial Magistrate would be trouble, but we couldn't just refuse her transport. Years of trading, over in an instant."

Now I knew it was something serious. "Well, in all honesty, that depends on what was really happening, plus Hannah isn't a bad person."

Lorton looked at me incredulously, like he was trying to decide whether I was naïve or an idiot. "She is an *Imperial* Magistrate, and those people were outcasts. Donating money to them is a capital offense."

I think he misread the smile on my face, as he immediately took offence. "You find this funny? Are you so heartless?"

"Fuck, no!" I said, "It's just, Hannah won't give a shit, she doesn't even really want to be a magistrate. Why would helping outcasts be a crime anyway?"

"Because they were declared outcasts by the empire. Most fled unpayable taxes, others simply had something a noble took a fancy to and had jumped up charges levied against them. Whatever the reason, they ran to survive, and were declared outcasts for it, no Imperial town or city will harbour them now."

I knew Imperial rule would have some flaws, but people being persecuted for no reason whatsoever was unacceptable. I needed to find out if this was systemic, or just the work of a few rotten individuals. Hopefully it was the latter, and a little noble 'pruning' would alleviate the situation!

"Surely, not all of them are innocent though? Strenger definitely wasn't."

"You'll always get a few bad apples in any large group, and he was one of the worst, but most are just regular folk trying to survive, many with children to feed and protect," he said defensively.

It was clearly a complex situation, but if he was right, the Mandelhills were taking a big risk to do the right thing and that made them pretty cool in my book. I guess I'd judged them unfairly when I assumed they were just money grabbing merchants and I realised I needed to be less judgmental based on first impressions. "Well, if that's the case, I think what you are doing is commendable, and I'm sure Hannah would feel the same. Plus, Hannah's an Olisias and the major clans are often at odds with the Imperials."

"You know her well, this Olisias?" he said with distaste. "As the noble clans are responsible for as many outcasts as the Royals."

Truthfully, I hadn't known her long at all, and the Mandelhills situation made me worry I wasn't as good a judge of character as I'd always believed. "Well enough." I lied.

"For their sake and mine, I hope you do."

So do I, I thought to myself as I left him to his worries.

Upon my return to our caravan, Hannah looked at me expectantly, obviously eager to be clued in. Deciding to just put her out of her misery, I quickly admitted the truth. "They weren't bandits, they're imperial outcasts."

Hannah instantly flared. "Why would they help outcasts? I may not have really wanted to be a magistrate, but I will do my duty to protect our people, this shall not stand."

Her righteous fervour shocked me, but it also helped to reassure me that I hadn't been wrong about her character. She actually cared about the people.

"It's not like that, Hannah, these people aren't criminals, they're mostly victims of Noble corruption," I said.

Hannah took a moment to contemplate what I'd said. "And you believe that?"

"I do." I nodded.

Hannah pursed her lips, and I could tell she was thinking of how to help. "I could petition the royal family to investigate the claims."

"You honestly think they'd sort it?" I asked.

"I…I don't know."

"What would your family do?"

Hannah sat in silence for a while mulling over the question. "Our patriarch is a decent man, and I'd like to think that he would be fair…" She hesitated.

"But?" I prompted her to continue.

"We would close ranks, family comes first," she admitted, visibly deflating.

"Yeah, I thought as much."

"Ok, so what's the plan?" she asked.

Thinking about it, I realised 'kill those responsible', wasn't much of a plan. I then started to worry about how comfortable I'd become with killing people. Looking at it objectively though, I was now part of a world with a different moral code, so the fact I wasn't crippled with guilt was a good thing. Plus, the nightmares plaguing me for years were no longer as frequent, which I'd definitely call a win! So, did I adjust to this new life a little too easily? Undoubtedly, but fuck it, I still felt like myself, and I wasn't acting like a homicidal maniac, so I reckoned I was fine. Although, I had been quicker to lose my temper, so that was something to keep an eye on…

"Josh, the plan?" said Hannah, interrupting my self-reflection.

"I…I don't really know," I admitted.

Master stood up and approached the two of us. "This isn't a holiday-camp Josh, you will continue the training I have planned," he said pointedly.

I was sure he hadn't mentioned a definitive plan before, in fact, he'd been pretty chilled in letting me decide on some things, but ultimately, I was the student, and he called the shots. "Understood, Master."

"Good. You shall continue to Stormhaven and join the Adventurers' Guild. There you'll carry out any quests that appeal to you, which will allow you to further hone your skills. I originally had successful completion of an A-rank quest as the criteria for us to leave, but with your recent growth, I've changed my mind and want you to complete an S-rank one."

"An S-rank quest? Isn't that a bit much?" I argued, having no idea how difficult it would actually be, but almost certain that it would be no picnic.

Master waved off my concern. "I'm confident you'll manage, and the quicker you do, the faster you get to go home." He grinned. "I'll investigate the situation with the outcasts and when I'm done, I'll come find you."

If I'm honest, I was torn, as much as I was enjoying our trip and wanted to help the outcasts, I was also keen to return home as quick as possible. I missed my friends massively, and more importantly, I needed to take revenge for my parents, adoptive or not. I felt I had already gotten strong enough to protect myself from any threats back on Earth, and the need for revenge was always there inside, quietly burning in the background. For three more years now, it had sat there festering, and I was sure my frustration over it was at least partially responsible for causing my quick temper. So yeah, I felt torn in several directions, plus, if I said I had no anxiety about being left alone on a foreign world I'd be lying.

I knew I had to say something, if I didn't, eventually I'd snap. "Master, I love and respect you like family, but I need to go home. The thought of my parents being unavenged, it's…it's eating me up." I was fighting back tears by the end of my admission.

Master walked up and put a steadying hand on my shoulder. "I won't tell you not to take revenge on those monsters, it's your right to do so. But always remember son, as important as it is, it's just one task of many. Don't let that one thing define who you are, otherwise, you let them take more than just your parents."

Sometimes I forget how old Master is, then he helps to put things into perspective so easily, and I can see the wisdom fifteen-hundred years of life, love and loss can bring to a person. He was right, I'm more than a sad backstory, I want revenge, yes, but I want to get stronger for me, to push myself as far as I can go, to be the sword that protects and defends those I care about and those unable to defend themselves. That is what I want to define me. As I reached the peak of my self-realisation, something seemed to snap in my perception of the world and everything became clearer, became more. Things that been stumping me in my swordplay and Qi techniques, suddenly began to make more sense and I quickly sat to meditate on them before the sensation faded.

Opening my eyes, I saw that it was now night-time, and Master was smiling at me. "If it wasn't for the fact that you're my student, I would be getting more and more envious of you," he ribbed good-naturedly.

"It was amazing, I understand…more," I said.

Master nodded. "A moment of instant enlightenment, treasure it as they are extremely rare. You will come to learn that martial comprehension is just as important as cultivation, and you will reach bottlenecks in it just as you would in your cultivation."

"Mmm," I grunted in agreement.

"So, don't leave us hanging boy, what did you achieve?"

Standing up, I reached towards the hilt of my sword, and focusing on my understanding of what the sword meant to me, began to draw it. It's hard to describe the sensation, but as the sword left the scabbard, an aura of sharpness arose with me at the centre and cuts began to appear on surfaces all around me.

"Shit, boy, put the sword away, quick!" Master yelled at me.

Jamming the sword back in its scabbard, the aura disappeared as quickly as it came. Looking at Master, I saw he had a look of great shock and was slightly pale.

"What, Master? Are you ok?" I asked.

It took Master several moments to compose himself before he was finally able to speak. "You have reached one-with-the-sword," he said, his tone ominous.

I couldn't understand what the problem was, it seemed worthy of celebration to me. "I think so, during my brief enlightenment many things became clearer."

"What you have done should be impossible, son."

"Surely others gifted with the sword could?"

Master shook his head at me. "It's not simply a matter of talent with the sword. Understanding of higher order powers, such as Rules and Laws, requires a level of comprehension that's thought to be only available to those whose soul has been strengthened by the transition to Saint."

Master looked at Hannah, who was stood there with her jaw literally hanging open, grabbed my shoulder and dragged me off into the woods. Clearly, he didn't want anyone else present for the conversation.

Only when we had travelled about a mile into the woods, did Master finally allows us to stop.

"Different numbers of Qi condensation, twenty-two meridians, metallic blood, a soul stronger than it has any right to be at your age. You, Josh, are both a wonderful enigma and an absolute nightmare. If someone nefarious was to know all of that and get their hands on you, well, I don't even want to imagine."

The idea of being dissected and used in such a way was pretty terrifying, but I was no pushover. "At least I am able to defend myself, Master."

"Yes, I reckon no one at the same level could pose a threat to you, hell, with your natural strength and sword intent you would even be able to fight Spirit Knights and maybe some Sages, but what about particularly strong Sages? What about Saints? Or, gods forbid, those above Saints?"

"Are there people at that level in this realm?" I asked, shocked, especially considering the strongest known experts on Earth were particularly powerful Spirit Knights like Master.

"Who knows what hidden experts are within any realm? It's common knowledge that each of the great clans has several elders at the level of Sages and at least a half-Saint level guiding them. The Royal family itself is definitely headed by a Saint cultivator. But who knows what characters lay hidden in the dark? And this is only one small empire at the far west of just one planet."

I chuckled self-deprecatingly. "There's always a sky beyond the sky."

"Yes, son. Really, we come from a barren wasteland as far as aether is concerned, but don't be disheartened, you are terrifyingly strong for your age and who knows, maybe your upper limit will be to soar under any sky. But you must be careful, as the martial world is full of crouching tigers and hidden dragons, and the strongest fist makes the rules."

I nodded my acknowledgment. "So, what is sword intent anyway?"

Master's mouth scrunched up as he thought about how to answer. "Now, I only know the theory, but like I mentioned, there are apparently higher order powers known as Rules and Laws, and these are the fundamental basis to how all of existence operates, a part of the Great Dao. I believe that aura you released was Sword Intent, where you are essentially using your will to manifest a tiny part of the Rules or Laws that govern what a sword is and what it does."

"So, my sword intent almost functions like a sword?" I asked, completely gobsmacked.

"More or less, that's my limited understanding of it anyway," Master replied.

I couldn't help but look at a nearby tree trunk and concentrate on trying to cut the tree.

"What are you doing son? You look like you're straining to have a shit?" Master chuckled.

"I'm trying to cut the tree with my Sword Intent."

"I'm no expert, but I think you would probably need a far greater understanding of the Sword Laws to achieve something like that. You are probably tapping into a very limited aspect of it, using your sword as a medium and enhancing its ability to cut. At least for now."

"Yeah, you're probably right," I admitted, thinking that made sense. But I couldn't help but wonder how deep my understanding of the Sword Laws could be pushed? Maybe one day a wave of my hand could cut like a sword. I thought

181

back to the creatures I'd seen battling in the void, I was now certain they must have been utilising Laws in their attacks.

After returning to the caravan, I immediately noticed that Hannah was looking at me like a mystery that she had to solve. I didn't think there was any maliciousness in her gaze though, just pure curiosity. Master soon left to investigate the outcasts, leaving me with a huge amount of wealth in a small storage pouch, something I'd only learned existed when Master finally admitted where he had been carrying all the supplies that we had used to construct the treehouse. Gods knows why I had originally been stuck with an oversized backpack, probably because it amused him!

For the remainder of the journey, I immersed myself wholeheartedly in cultivation, single minded in my endeavour to increase my strength as quickly as possible and my efforts weren't in vain, as by the time we neared Stormhaven I had finally managed to condense my first Qi Lake and pushed it through its expansion, which meant I was officially a level two Spirit warrior! It had been expensive though, as I had burnt through one hundred of the minor spirit stones. Which as the equivalent of one-hundred-thousand gold coins almost made me weep! I was a little worried too, if it was going to take more and more spirit stones to break through, did I have enough? And if I didn't, where the fuck would I get the aether?

Chapter 26

The city of Stormhaven perched on a vast promontory, that stuck out into the sea separating Antaris from mainland Antanel. Even from a distance I could see the waves crashing around the headlands base, which gave testament to their sheer size and ferocity. Considering the weather was actually quite pleasant, I dreaded what they would be like during a storm and the name of the city suddenly started to make a whole lot more sense. Stormhaven itself was even more impressive than I'd imagined, but the actual height of its towering granite walls only became apparent as we got closer, and they dwarfed the oversized caravan as we proceeded through the gate, leaving me to feel like Jack entering the giants castle for the first time. Everything, from the gate to the portcullis, ominously hovering around a hundred metres above my head, were exactly as you'd expect from a medieval castle, just at an inhuman scale. I thought I'd seen some scary beasts in the wilderness, but the thought of what could need such a scale of construction made me shudder.

As we finally passed through the gatehouse, it became clear that the only things at such a scale were the walls and the towering keep in the distance, the rest of the buildings were of a normal size, like people had just found a castle made by giants and decided to build a city within its courtyard. If that was the case, I hoped the original builders had no plan to return, as they'd probably see creatures of our comparatively Lilliputian size as no more than a vermin infestation. I quickly shook off the disconcerting thought, as

183

by the looks of the city it had existed for a long time and there'd be fuck all I could do to stop them anyway.

The caravan wound through the city before finally stopping in the grounds of a small estate in what I assumed was the merchant district, and we were quickly overrun by porters, working efficiently to divest the wagons of their cargo. I didn't bother watching where it was all to be taken, I had finally arrived and was eager to explore the city. So, after thanking Lorton for transporting us, I started to make my way back into the city, well, I tried to at least, but I didn't manage more than a few steps before I was stopped by Hannah.

"Where are we going?" she asked.

"We?"

She looked a little upset by the comment. "Yes! *We,* don't forget you promised to take me with you when you left," she said, "Plus, I have many connections in Stormhaven. Which will make your life a lot easier."

"Hannah, I have no intention of breaking my promise, and when I leave, you will definitely be coming with me. But I'm not travelling around the city with an Imperial magistrate. Your position may open plenty of doors, but we both know it will probably shut even more."

She looked like she was stewing over a difficult decision. "Just give me a few hours? Then we can go wherever you want."

I looked at her seriously. "Are you sure? I don't want to waste time fucking around."

"I'm sure," she nodded

"Fine," I agreed, instantly hoping I wouldn't come to regret the decision.

Walking through such a vast city on foot would have taken days, so when Hannah stopped us to hail a carriage I had no issue with it, although I did find it funny that we were basically taking a horse-drawn taxi, even if they weren't regular horses. By carriage it still took an hour to reach our destination, which was a splendid looking building displaying, what I had learnt to be, the Imperial crest. It was far grander than any of the surrounding buildings, in a completely unapologetic demonstration of its importance.

Whilst Hannah was allowed further into the building, I was stopped by the guards in the atrium, and as I watched Hannah disappear off into the depths of a hallway, one of the guards approached and beckoned me to follow him. He led me into a basically furnished side room, holding several men and women sat around quietly chatting. Whatever they had been talking about, all the chatter stopped immediately as we entered and they switched to eyeing us nervously, tough crowd!

Looking at the guardsman, I raised my eyebrow quizzically. "Waiting room? It's a bit…sparsely furnished." I joked.

I thought I was being funny, my comment completely harmless, but the guardsman didn't seem to appreciate my levity. "It's by the grace of the Imperial family that servants are even provided with a room, usually your kind would be forced to wait outside for their betters." His words oozing disdain.

"I assume there has been some misunderstanding, I'm nobody's servant. Do I look like a servant?" I growled, his attitude annoying me.

The guard looked me over and I allowed my travelling cloak to part and reveal more of my armour underneath, he looked at my armour, then up at my face.

"A well-dressed servant, perhaps Magistrate Olisias' favourite boy-toy," he answered.

Then it clicked, the bell-end was jealous, he probably pined over Hannah every time he saw her and then she waltzed in with me. Oh well, fuck him, his insecurities were not my problem.

Chuckling to myself I just took a seat, he wasn't worth causing trouble for Hannah. The guard sniffed imperiously and left to go back to his duties, and I only had to wait for

185

about ten minutes before Hannah finally made an appearance.

"I take it you had no issues?" She chuckled.

I noticed that she was no longer dressed as an Imperial magistrate, though she was still geared for combat, with an ornate brigandine cuirass with metal pauldrons and metal greaves over her boots. It was functional but the small details ensured it remained quite feminine and I was sure the get-up cost a pretty penny.

"The guard was a prick," I said, "I think he has a thing for you, so I just ignored him."

"Davros is a minor noble with ideas above his station, still, the Arch-magistrate asked me to thank you for your self-control."

"No problem," I said, although I did find it strange that the Arch-magistrate was aware of my presence. "Wait, did you say his name was Davros?" I laughed.

"Yes, I don't understand why that is funny, Davros is a strong name and is fairly popular."

With zero frame of reference, my first thought of screaming 'exterminate' in a mock mechanical voice would have only added to her confusion and so I had to quickly reel in that desire. "Just knew another dickhead with that name on my world, small universe." Nailed it!

She looked a little unconvinced, so I quickly moved on, as distraction is always a good option. "So, what's with the new gear?"

"I took an extended leave of absence, a sabbatical if you will. Told them I want to do a spot of adventuring."

"And they were okay with that?"

"Why not, we aren't prisoners and are allowed leaves of absence, especially those of us who are nobles and often have other duties too."

I guessed it functioned somewhat like the Armed Forces back home. "Fair enough, ready for an adventure?" I asked.

Her smile suggested it was a great idea.

The Adventurers' Guild was only a short carriage ride from the magistrates building, as the guilds and seats of bureaucracy were in the same region of the city. On the way we passed Guilds for every role and trade you could think of, even Beggars had a guildhall! Which seemed ridiculous, as Gods knows how long they had to beg to pay for that! The Adventurers' Guild was apparently somewhat special though, as it was the only Guild you could join as an existing member of any other, and had only a single purpose, the issuing of quests.

"Who issues the quests?" I asked.

"Anyone, from individuals all the way up to Empires or even coalitions of Empires," Hannah replied.

"That's insane, surely there must be an astronomical number of quests then?"

"Yep, everything from simple ones to recover a lost item, all the way up to defending borders and fighting off threats to countless lives."

"And anyone can join and take a quest?"

"Yes, but your adventurer rank dictates what sort of quests you can take. You'll understand more when we arrive."

It was obvious that Hannah was getting annoyed by my constant barrage of questions, plus the carriage driver was giving me the occasional funny glance, probably because most children would know the things I was asking. So, I was forced to rein in my curiosity.

The grounds of the Adventurers' Guild were immense, more like a country estate, with numerous small encampments in the grounds, all flying flags to denote the identity of their Adventuring party. It felt like a music festival, just one where everyone is armed and possibly capable of magic. So maybe more like a grand LARP festival, are they a thing? I feel like they should be. Either way, I was getting distinct Glastonbury vibes and I liked it, there was even music drifting in the air, from random people playing instruments and having impromptu singalongs. The flags were great too, there were ones displaying the obvious:

mythical beasts or weapons and the like. But I preferred the weird ones, my personal favourites from the ones I could make out were one with a bespectacled snail smoking a pipe, and one with what looked like two well-dressed housecats engaged in a dance, a foxtrot maybe? Fuck knows, but it definitely made me smile.

Hannah caught me smiling. "I wouldn't let them catch you smiling at their flag like that."

Interrupted from my reverie, I glanced over at her questioningly.

"That's the Dancing Cats Band, a coterie of bards and one of the most ruthless, bloodthirsty groups around."

"But their flag is so nice!" I protested, only half joking.

The Guildhall itself, looked like a gothic cathedral, complete with flying buttresses and spires, it even had a huge stained-glass window illuminating the grand hall, except instead of biblical scenes or Christian saints, it depicted pure carnage. Warriors and mages were engaged in battle with a huge monster, all eyes, teeth, and tentacles, with the wounded and dead strewn all over the battlefield.

"Fuck me, they don't hold back with the details!" I found myself exclaiming.

"It's the battle with the Antanel Gorgoth. Whilst an expedition was exploring a coastal ruin, they chanced upon it sleeping deep below the earth. After they accidentally woke it from its slumber, it went on a rampage."

"Not a morning person then," I joked, trying to lighten the mood.

"Twenty villages and seven towns destroyed, leaving millions dead and even more with their lives in ruin. It took an army of thousands of adventurers to finally bring it low, very few of which survived, so not very funny really."

I must have seemed like such an arsehole. "Sorry, I didn't know," I said ashamedly.

Hannah sighed. "No, you didn't, but when things are depicted with reverence like this, it's because they are important. A remembrance."

188

"I will be more mindful, I honestly thought it was apocryphal. Like displays of parables we have in similar buildings back home."

Hannah just smiled and nodded understandingly, and I made a mental note to be more culturally aware, incidents like that could easily have been avoided if I wasn't so ignorant. Every day's a school day!

Registration was relatively straightforward, there were a whole bunch of manned desks, set up like tellers in a bank back home, so I joined a queue and waited for my turn.

"Purpose for your visit?" a gaunt older elf asked as I approached his desk.

"I wish to register as an adventurer please."

"Polite too," he said, surprise evident on his face.

"And most people aren't?" I asked, genuinely curious.

"Unfortunately, impoliteness often tends to go hand in hand with position or strength."

"Good manners cost nothing, at least that's what I was taught."

The elf gave me a kind smile. "Let's get you sorted, fill out this form. Then we will test you and issue you your badge."

I quickly filled out the form, it was relatively basic, and didn't ask for anything particularly troublesome, apart from the place of origin, but I didn't need to lie, so I jotted down Surrey, England, Earth. Which drew a brief puzzled look from the elf, but he processed it all the same, and then I just had to sit and wait around for my turn at the test. About an hour later the same Elf came and beckoned me to follow, leading me to a large set of doors.

"The test is in stages, and you just need to fight until you can no longer continue. If at any time you shout stop, the test will immediately end, and your score will be the last completed level. Remember, your life will actually be at risk, so you would be wise to know when to stop," he explained.

"Don't worry sir, I know my limits and value my life."

189

The old elf squinted at me, probably trying to ascertain if I had actually taken his words seriously or was just paying him lip service. Seemingly satisfied it was the prior, he smiled. "Less of the sir, you can call me old Dez or uncle Dez."

"Ok, I'm ready, Uncle Dez."

The doors opened and I entered a large square room about fifty metres a side. I could seven warriors were stood against the wall on the opposite side, their armours marked in rune formations, which seemed to grow ever more complex from the first to the last. I thought it was fairly safe to assume that the warriors likely corresponded to the various levels I could pass.

A voice sounded out from all around me, "Are you ready?"

Drawing my sword from its scabbard, I announced to the air, "Ready." Even if talking to no-one in particular left me feeling like a bit of a melon.

The first warrior leapt from the wall and made his way towards me, as it got closer it became clear that the armoured warrior was in fact some sort of automaton, and the face within the helmet was entirely featureless other than two glowing red jewels in place of eyes. Approaching the doll, I noticed that although the thing was not particularly fluid in its movement, it was capable of sudden bursts of speed. Which I learnt as it attempted to strike me with its sword. Deftly moving out of the way, I followed up with a straight kick to the chest of the doll which launched it clean across the room. The lights in its eyes dimmed and I noticed that its chest was caved in from the kick. Perhaps I should have held back a bit, whoops!

The following four dolls were equally unable to pose a threat and were finished in short order, but doll number six provided a sharp uptick in the challenge, as it was far more fluid in its movements and its speed and weapon skill were easily capable of catching me off guard. It was also better able to emulate the use of aether techniques than the previous dolls which caught me by surprise, and the bout quickly devolved into a blur of flashing steel, until I finally managed to force the doll off balance and behead it with the aid of a timely application of wind steps. It was the first time I had to use my own techniques in the fights, and I realised that the final doll was no doubt going to be even more capable. My heart was racing with excitement over the impending challenge, and I had to take several deep breaths to centre myself and calm down.

"A-rank achieved. Do you wish to continue?"

Uncle Dez hadn't bothered to make an announcement after the previous levels, lending weight to my assumption about the difficulty of the next opponent.

"Yes," I said, not taking my eye from my next opponent for a second.

It was lucky I was so vigilant, as the next doll went from being stood against the rear wall to swinging its oversize axe at me in an instant, covering the forty metres or so between us as quick as I moved using wind-steps. I managed to parry the axe to the side, but the strength of the new doll allowed it to recover in an instant and it was back on me. We flashed around the room, a cacophony of clanging steel, my greater skill with the sword allowing me zero advantage over the sheer ferocity of the axe-wielding doll. Rune-empowered strike with the axe met every attempt I made to injure it with my own qi powered focused strikes. As the fight wore on, it became apparent that not only did the doll match me in physical strength, but I could feel my own reserves of Qi beginning to deplete, and I got no such sense from the doll, who seemed to draw its power from the very room within which we duelled. If things continued, I had no doubt that I would run out of energy long before the doll, and then I would be left pitting only my physical strength against the doll, which, considering it matched me in that regard, would not end well for me. Especially, as I was only keeping up with its speed by constant use of wind-steps.

There was only one way that I could win the fight, and if I wanted to complete an S-rank quest like Master instructed, I couldn't hold back. Slipping easily into the state of one-with-the-sword, the summoned Sword Intent caused my edge to sharpen, my strikes to cut deeper. Scores began to appear on the armour of the doll just from being near me due to my unpolished control, but it was working, as great chips began to appear on the axe of the doll, and I began to drive it back through my sheer will to cut down my foe. With a monumental final effort, my sword edge became incandescent, cutting clean through both axe head and doll alike. Only when my opponent tumbled lifeless to the floor, did I finally allow my guard to drop and was left sweating and gasping for breath.

Completely spent, I took a knee to recover, and my arms barely had enough strength to re-sheath my sword. Even though it was just an automaton, the doll was the most challenging fight I'd ever had, and I'd emerged victorious. Despite my fatigue I roared in celebration, the urge both primitive and instinctual. Damn feral bloodline! At least there was only Uncle Dez around to hear it, although I was honestly too tired to care even if there was anyone else.

A few moments later, the doors opened, and Uncle Dez walked in, looked at the puppet on the floor and then at me.

"Don't see that every day." He chuckled.

"It's not going to be a problem, is it?" I asked worriedly.

"Nope." He waved off my concern. "A display like that in the Imperial palace would be a problem, they don't like any potential threats to their rule. But the Adventurers' Guild stands apart, we protect *all* the people of the realm, so the stronger our members are, the better. Now, let's get your ID badge."

Uncle Dez seemed excited, so I just followed along, eager to get it done, so I could get a room somewhere, eat until I was full and then pass out, preferably in that order. Hannah came over as soon as she saw us, and we moved into a room where the other examinees were also waiting to receive their IDs. Seeing we were happily settled, Uncle Dez quickly scampered off into one of the adjacent rooms.

"How did it go?" she whispered.

"Good, I passed, but it was exhausting."

She looked at me confusedly. "No, I mean, obviously you passed, but what level?"

Before I had a chance to reply, a young man in finery ambled over, obviously a noble of some sort. I swear it seemed like they were plaguing me everywhere I went, and I was far too tired to deal with any bullshit.

"Hannah, long time no see, what brings you here?" he drawled.

"Oh, hello Yancy." Hannah frowned. "I'm accompanying my friend Joshua to be registered."

"Joshua? I don't recognise the name, to which house do you belong?"

"I don't, just someone Hannah met on her travels."

"Accompanying a commoner, how quaint, well, I just received my upgrade to B grade adventurer, youngest of my clan to do so," he said with a smug smile, and gestured to a small silver badge on his lapel which bore the Adventurers guild crest; a crossed sword and staff surmounted by a shield. The shield itself was embossed with a single rune equivalent to a B in the realm's common script. The look of pride on his face was only matched by the level of condescension with which he looked at me, and I instantly wanted to punch him in his smug face.

"Congratulations Yancy," Hannah offered politely.

"Why thank you, I should probably let you know that Father intends to visit soon, to arrange a marriage between us. The glorious linking of our two great clans." He smirked. "Some things will always be out of reach of the common man. Like Hannah, and this." He slowly tapped on his adventurer's badge.

Hannah had gone pale, obviously the news of a possible arranged marriage had come as a great shock. Before I could say anything though, Uncle Dez reappeared.

"Be seeing you Hannah." Yancy laughed and trotted back to his friends, probably to continue boasting of his achievement.

"Follow me," said Uncle Dez, "I'm afraid Miss Olisias will have to wait in here for you, I'm sorry."

I placed a hand on Hannah's shoulder. "Don't worry, after we leave, there'll be no one around for him to marry," I whispered.

Hannah instantly perked up a little. "Good point, thanks Josh."

Nodding back at her, I followed Uncle Dez into a small side room. It was a wood trimmed office with a lady sat behind a particularly weighty looking desk. She stood as we entered the room and, rather oddly, looked like a stereotypical schoolteacher, complete with wire rimmed glasses, ruffled blouse and plaid skirt. I *would* have said she looked to be around fifty, but in a world with aether, that meant she was probably anywhere from fifty to fuck-knows. I also noticed she wore a similar badge to Yancy, only hers was gold and bore an A upon it, so not just an administrator, but an adventurer too.

"Please, take a seat." She gestured to the empty seat across from her.

Taking the proffered seat, I adjusted myself to get comfortable and waited for her to continue.

"It's truly a pleasure to meet you Joshua, I am Arch-Mage Valerie Legorrin, and I serve as the head of the Adventurers' Guild's Stormhaven branch. Dezarel has made me aware of what transpired during your test, and I must say that I am suitably impressed. Which is not something that happens too often."

"Thank you, ma'am, it's a pleasure to meet you too."

"Before we hand over your ID, we are awaiting the ratification of your test results by the central branch, which shan't take long. In the meantime, I thought it would be prudent to both assure you that your abilities will be treated with the utmost confidentiality and inform you of the gravitas

194

of what you have achieved. Do you know what it means to be an S-rank adventurer?"

Brilliant, it looked like they were going to find out just how ignorant I am. "All I know is that it will allow me to take S-rank quests."

"Yes, that's true, however S-rank has a few extra…quirks, shall we say. Within all the realms that the Adventurers' Guild operates, members of A-rank and above are accorded the same rights and privileges as nobles, and as an S-rank, you would be treated as a Duke. But as a representative of the Guild, you must in turn also hold yourself to a certain standard of behaviour. Do you understand?"

"I do ma'am, I always act according to my conscience and would not wish to bring the guild into disrepute."

"Splendid, I think we will get along just fine Joshua."

"You mentioned other realms?" I asked.

Valerie smiled mysteriously. "Yes, we noted that you listed an unfamiliar location as your place of origin. I take it Earth is another realm?"

I nodded my affirmation.

"How exciting! You will have to tell me about it some time. But I digress, yes, you will find a branch of the Adventurers' Guild on most lower realms and even many of the higher ones."

The information was a little shocking, it seemed the Adventurers guild was a far larger entity than I had given credit to and I found myself wondering how someone of my level of strength could receive an S-rank if the guild existed in higher realms too.

"Of course, the ranks we confer only apply to the lower realms, you would need to be re-evaluated if you ever managed to ascend to a higher plane."

Well, I guess that answered that for me, still, membership would provide some decent perks and who knows if I would ever ascend to a higher realm?

At that moment, a golden globe on Valerie's desk illuminated and a voice emanated from it.

"Conference of S-rank to adventurer Joshua White is approved by the Adventurers' Guild, all branches will be duly notified."

Following the announcement, the top of the globe opened, and a small badge rose from it, which Valerie took into her hand. The globe then returned to its previous state and Dez and Valerie smiled at each other before she handed it to me.

"Before you take it, know that should the realm be in danger, you will be expected to help protect it, the same as any other adventurer."

"I understand." I nodded. "I wouldn't let innocent people die if it was within my ability to stop, even before I joined the guild."

"An admirable attitude, now allow some of your energy to enter the badge and it will bind to you."

I sent a sliver of Qi into the badge and felt a vague connection to it, it was the same as the other badges I had seen, but made of some bright white metal, it also did not have the S I was expecting, showing only the Adventurers Guild crest.

"Expecting an S?" Uncle Dez asked.

I chuckled. "I was actually."

The next few minutes were spent letting me know some more of the perks my new rank granted, before I finally left to catch up with Hannah. They had tried to be as concise as possible as I think they could tell I was anxious to get back to my friend. Before leaving the room, I adjusted the badge to a ring, which was apparently one of the features of all guild badges and placed it upon my left pinkie. Luckily it had no trouble adjusting itself over the dragon skin gauntlet. I was also impressed that A-rank and above badges also served as dimensional storage devices. They only had a few cubic metres of space, but it was still awesome, and far larger than the money pouch Master had given me, no more having to lug a pack around!

After thanking Valerie, Uncle Dez accompanied me back out to where Hannah was sat waiting. "Did you want to take the test too?" I asked, realising I should have thought to check earlier.

"No, I'm not quite ready to pass for B rank, so there's no point. How did it go?"

We were rudely interrupted, when, probably after noticing I was once again with Hannah, Yancy decided to swan back over. I wasn't sure what he was even still doing here, probably still show-boating to his adoring groupies.

"So, you're a member of the Adventurers' Guild now? Well, remember to pay your respects to your seniors," he said, gesturing at his badge. The man was clearly a buffoon.

Not even dignifying him with a response I just raised my guild ring to him.

"Not even graded! What are you going to be? A bag carrier? Surely even trash can reach F-rank?"

I was too stunned to even reply, clearly the dude was more stupid than I had assumed, luckily Uncle Dez didn't miss a beat.

"Yancy Trevion, as a B-rank adventurer, I refuse to believe you would be so ignorant of our insignias, and if you are, I suggest you educate yourself. Now, are you going to apologise? Or should I escalate the situation?"

Yancy looked like a fish, his mouth repeatedly opened and closed but no words came out. Finally managing to compose himself, he bowed to Uncle Dez. "I apologise, Master Dez, I did not mean to cause offense."

Uncle Dez looked at him as if he was a fool. "Not to me, boy! To Master Joshua."

The look of confusion on his face was clear and although the guy was a buffoon, I honestly started to feel sorry for him and decided to spare him any further embarrassment in front of his friends. Plus, making a potential enemy out of one of the major clans, especially over something so trivial, seemed ill advised.

"It's fine, Uncle Dez, we are leaving anyway." I waved it off.

"As you wish, Master Joshua."

Leaving the stumped Yancy behind us, Uncle Dez escorted us to the exit. When we were finally alone, Hannah grabbed my hand and stared at the ring. "Is it true?" she asked frantically.

"That I'm an S-rank adventurer? Yeah, I guess so."

Hannah started to laugh. "That's brilliant, I had no idea you were that strong, and although it's not fool-proof, it will definitely make the major clans weigh up the cost before taking you out."

"What the fuck, Hannah! Why would they want to kill me?"

"Use your brain Josh, a powerful warrior with no allegiances could be a threat to them."

"And even though I have no malicious intent towards them, they'd remove me just in case I someday did?" Once again, I was astounded at how cut-throat the vast cosmos was, I needed to stop being so naïve and remember that everyone was a potential threat.

"Exactly, either roping them in or eliminating potential threats whilst they are still weak is standard practice for the clans." Hannah advised.

As much as it pained me to admit, the action made a perverse kind of sense.

"You wouldn't believe how many geniuses are killed in the cradle Josh, it's sad, but talent counts for nought in front of overwhelming power."

Chapter 27

The Adventurers' Guild definitely looked after their S-ranks, I'd receive a monthly stipend and luxurious housing was provided in all major cities. In the case of Stormhaven, this was an estate for use by any itinerant S-rankers who happened to be in the city. I stayed away from the place like the plague, as if word was passed around that it was occupied, I could only imagine how many people would show up at the door to hobnob, and I had no interest in getting dragged into Imperial politics. It was bad enough that Yancy may have learnt about my identity, but at least the Trevions didn't rule here. Stormhaven, as the capital of the Bendorff duchy fell under their purview, and I doubted that Yancy would pass on my information to them, as with their competitive nature, clans would probably keep such stuff close to their chest. At least that's what I hoped, either way I wouldn't be openly announcing my identity, and instead booked a room in a pleasant hotel in the merchant's district.

Far away from the social hangouts of the upper class but still offering a certain level of quality. I could have probably gone even further and got a room somewhere in the poorer areas, but I would soon be heading out on a mission to Gods knows where, so I elected to treat myself whenever I could. Yeah, it may seem stupid, but spend any length of time sleeping on the floor or a piece of shit bed and I assure you that you'll appreciate a good one like I do!

At least showers were never a problem, because as medieval as things looked on the surface, magic was so ubiquitous that even the poorest of commoners had access to clean water and indoor plumbing. I'm not a germophobe, but I swear, if it was actually like the middle-ages, with everyone stinking, filthy and full of lice, with people literally throwing their shit out into the streets, it would get old real fast, and I would not be a happy fucking bunny.

After several days chilling and exploring the city with Hannah, which in my defence was amazing. I realised I had been procrastinating and went to pick a quest. The Mission Hall in the Adventurers' Guild was busy, with hundreds of people both accepting quests or handing them in. Luckily, it was split by rank and the section for A and B rank quests had far fewer people. The quests were listed on devices that functioned pretty much exactly like a modern tablet and the fact someone had produced something so analogous to electronics using magic astounded me. Clearly, they were the work of master artificers and probably not mass producible or I would have seen them before, but I did find myself wondering why there were no electronics in this realm? Complex mechanical engineering seemed conspicuously absent too, outside of a few large scale clocktowers. Did the availability of aether retard other forms of development? I made a mental note to ask Master when I next saw him.

There were at least fifty A-rank and around two-hundred B-rank quests available, and ones that had already been selected were annotated as such. Although, multiple teams could select the same one and whoever brought back the specified proof of completion would receive the credit, which I had no doubt sometimes led to conflicts between them. I decided it would be prudent to attempt a few A-rank quests before looking at the S-rank ones, as I had no idea how difficult they would prove, plus I would be completing it on my own, whereas others would complete them as part of a party. The initial plan was for Hannah to accompany me, but after finding out she was still only C-rank I was forced to shit-can that idea, as with her level of strength it could quickly prove fatal. Hannah was not happy about that decision, but I think it was less because she genuinely wanted to come and more that she was still afraid I would ditch her, and she'd lose her ticket off-realm.

Eventually, I settled on a quest to investigate the disappearance of people from within a small city to the north named Berevar. It was located on the shores of Lake Antaru, which, at around three-hundred-and-fifty miles across, was of a similar size to the North American Great Lakes. Berevar was a slightly shorter distance from Stormhaven than Traveller's Rest, but not fancying just running everywhere, I needed to arrange transport. Preferably not in a caravan this time, as they were far too slow! According to the notes it was initially issued as a C-rank quest, but as more and more experienced adventurers disappeared too, it had eventually worked its way up to A-rank. So potentially, something very dangerous was happening in Berevar. Perhaps foolishly, I found myself getting excited at the thought and wanted to get straight on it. Accepting the quest, my name was added to the list, and I noticed that an A-rank party had also accepted it a week earlier, I just hoped they wouldn't have finished it before I arrived. After travelling all that way, that would be just my luck.

After a brief investigation, I learned that several methods of air travel were available to Berevar and I could even rent a flying beast to ride, like a fucked-up version of a hire-car back home. That was apparently the quickest option, but having never even ridden a horse, starting with a giant flying animal seemed like a recipe for disaster, not to mention I had no faith whatsoever in being able to successfully navigate my way, and if my bearings were even slightly off, I would just fly right past it and then it would take fuck knows how long to actually get there.

And so, I found myself at the Western curtain wall marvelling at the city's airship port, whose huge cantilever construction overhung the more unfortunate buildings close to the wall, relegating them to perpetual shade for much of the afternoon. I briefly found myself wondering if there was an inn there, as it was conveniently close to the port and would no doubt be quite cheap because of the lack of sunlight. I made a mental note to check upon my return. The winding metal staircase up to the port provided a fantastic view over the city, although luckily, I had no issue with heights as with only the most basic of handrails, I imagined being so exposed at over a hundred metres up would have been terrifying for many.

The port itself was just a huge slab of stone, which, with how it just jutted clean out of the wall with no extra structural support, seemed to defy what I knew about physics, and I suspected more magical chicanery was at play. There were numerous berths along its edges for airships to moor, but only six of various sizes were presently docked. I had honestly expected them to resemble the airships back home, zeppelins with a big, elongated balloon and pod underneath. However, these were just like huge wooden sailing ships, complete with furled sails. The largest was bigger than any ship-of-the-line ever was and the smallest not much bigger than a schooner, but they could be easily differentiated from their sea-based counterparts by the masts, which were shorter and seemed to have only a single long spar towards the bottom, and numerous small stubby wings that protruded out along their main decks. They also had larger windows, probably to allow a better view for the passengers. The 'wings' looked like they would be completely ineffectual for providing any actual lift regardless of speed, so perhaps they were just to stabilise the things in the air? Fuck knows, but they must fly somehow, as whilst docked they sat suspended in the air for no apparent reason whatsoever. Just another example of knowledge from back home being relatively useless.

I approached a large booth in the middle of the platform, which I assumed was the ticket office, but with how accurate my assumptions were recently proving, it was just as likely to be a fucking tombola stand, because why not?

The booth had several manned positions and after a short queue, I approached a window with a friendly smile only to receive a sullen glare for my efforts.

"Ya gonna waste both our time jus' smiling at me like a simpleton?" he grumbled.

Obviously, the man was being a bit of a bell-end, but maybe he was having a bad day, so I decided to give him the benefit of the doubt.

"I need to get to Berevar, I wondered if I could get a ticket, please?"

"Are ya taking the piss lad?"

"No, sir. I've never taken an Airship before."

The man looked at me for several moments, probably deciding if I was joking, before rubbing his face and sighing.

"Berth four for Berevar. Passage is arranged directly with the ships."

Taking out a gold coin, I placed it on the counter. "Thank you for your help." I smiled and walked off.

I made it several steps before I heard, "Wait, lad!" Turning around, the man was beckoning me back over.

He leant forward in a conspiratorial manner. "Don't be so quick t' flaunt ya wealth in front of Airship crews, son. Some're honest as they come, others are pirates in all but name and ya never know which ya gonna get. It's an awful long way down over some shiny baubles," he whispered.

I guess he wasn't such a bad sort after all, just a grumpy and likely underpaid city worker. "Thanks for the advice, sir, I'll bear it in mind."

The airship waiting in berth four, the 'Canny Hawk' according to its nameplate, was in the middle of the pack for size amongst the airships present. Akin to a frigate of old, its robustness was reassuring compared to the tinier vessels, especially considering the very real threat from aerial predators. Its larger deck also allowed for a number of ballistae to line each side, each of which looked like they could do some serious damage to any beast foolish enough to try its luck.

Disappointingly, the man stood at the foot of its gangplank was dressed more like a cuirassier from Cromwell's New Model Army, complete with metal pot helmet, rather than in the piratical fashion I was hoping for. Seeing me approach, he instantly gave me his best 'salesman's' smile.

"Looking for passage, fine sir?"

"To Berevar, Guild business," I replied, flashing my ring. He had a brief look of confusion, probably over the lack of rank on the ring, but quickly shrugged it off. From both Yancy's actions and now this guy, it seemed that an S-rank was not particularly well recognised, perhaps because there are so few of us? Or maybe he just thought I was a weirdo who liked flashing my jewellery at people!

"Twenty silver for a seat in the passenger cabin, a gold gets you a small private cabin."

"How long is the flight?"

"Depends on wind and whether we have any issues on the way, but no quicker than twenty hours."

I briefly thought about it and decided on a private room, it would be nice to sleep without worrying about a slit throat, maybe I was being a little paranoid, but better paranoid than dead. I'd found less sleep was becoming necessary as my cultivation increased and maybe I'd eventually not need to sleep at all. For now though, it was probably best to stay as fresh as possible for the quest, as with so many people missing, fuck knows what I'd encounter in Berevar.

"A private cabin please," I said, handing over the coin.

"Right you are, sir." He placed my payment in a large pouch hung from his waist and passed me a small wooden tag. "Ship leaves in an hour, just find any free cabin inside the forecastle, they're all the same."

Nodding my thanks, I made my way up the small swaying gangplank, once again thankful about my ease at height. Several crewmembers could be seen on the maindeck, coiling ropes, and doing other odd jobs, but there were nowhere near the numbers I'd imagined were needed to crew such a large vessel. I guessed that with an hour still to go, they were still relaxing in their own berths.

The forecastle had only a single wooden door in its centre leading to a hallway with five further open doors on each side. I made my way to the furthest door on the left, hoping that its forward position meant it would have one of the best views ahead, and I was not disappointed, the angle of the window allowing a great forward view out over the city. Locking the door to the room, I took a seat on the bed and began to quietly cultivate whilst I waited.

I was interrupted from my meditation by shouts from outside, and realised the ship was readying to take off. Not wanting to miss it, I made my way outside and up the stairs that led to the top of the forecastle, taking a spot against the railings where I hopefully wouldn't get in the way.

The sails began to glow and unfurl up into the air. Illuminated patterns were revealed upon the sails as they rose, which, from their visible glow, I assumed to be some sort of magical formations. Fully open, the sails were gargantuan, easily twice the height of their respective masts and almost diaphanous, like halves of hot air balloons made from dragonfly wings.

With a brief pulse from the formations on the sails, the airship began to steadily rise further into the air.

"First time on an airship?" Came a rough voice from the steps.

Looking over I saw a large man walking towards me, he was also dressed like a cuirassier, similar to the gangplank attendant, only with a black over cloak and plumed tricorn hat, its shockingly iridescent feathers from some exotic and unidentifiable bird.

"Yeah, she's beautiful." I offered my hand for the man to shake. "Joshua White, adventurer."

"Well met, Joshua White." The man smiled and gave my hand a brief but firm shake. "And yes, that she is! Lazalio Heb, captain of the Canny Hawk. I like to make the rounds to introduce myself to all the passengers, and after I spotted

you making mooneyes at my ship, I thought I'd see you first."
He chuckled.

I laughed along with his good-natured ribbing, the banter refreshing and reminding me of home. A little polite small talk followed before Lazalio excused himself to go and greet the other passengers, leaving me to look out over the railings as the ship rose further and further into the air.

We quickly rose well above the heights of the giant trees before finally levelling off. I have no idea how high we were, but I knew the trees were hundreds of metres tall and looked tiny down below. I briefly wondered whether I would survive such a fall, as with the raised gravity here, I'd probably have a terminal velocity far higher than on Earth, likely over two or three hundred miles-per-hour. Crazily, I decided that with my newly tempered body, especially if I reinforced myself with Qi, I would possibly be okay, but it wasn't something I was in a hurry to test!

The vista was incredible with the variously coloured trees covering as far as the eye could see like a multicoloured carpet and being able to see so far gave me a tangible sense of just how vast the Northern Wilderness truly was.

The ship itself remained fairly stable in the air, with only a subtle sense of the buffering by the wind. Something of which I found myself glad, as twenty hours on a constantly swaying ship would be awful. When the ship finally began to move forward, I noticed it wasn't particularly fast, which explained why it would take so long to cover the five-hundred miles or so to Berevar. Happy that I had seen enough, I made my way back to my cabin to wait out the journey.

Things were quiet until about twelve hours into the flight, when the sounds of alarmed voices disturbed me from my cultivation, looking out my window I could see several winged creatures heading towards the ship. As they drew closer, I managed to get a better view and could see they were limbless winged serpents of some sort, their bodies long and sinuous like a snake. I couldn't imagine them being good news for the ship though, as the smallest was around thirty feet from nose to tail, the largest closer to fifty, each with far more girth than any Earth snake I'd ever seen. Their large wings seemed to be modified forelimbs like a Bat and were connected via the wing membrane down half of the creatures' sides. Their wingspan easily matched their length and vicious looking talons extended from their tips. As terrifying as they looked, I recalled the number of large ballistae on board, and was hopeful that the crew could deal with the nasty things.

The first volley of bolts tore through the sky, their tips glowing like red embers suggesting they were far from ordinary. Unfortunately, the creatures were extremely agile for their size, weaving between the bolts with graceful finesse and of the entire volley only a single bolt struck true, penetrating deep into the midsection of one of the two smaller creatures. A great plume of viscera blew out from the back of it, testament to the effectiveness of whatever enchantment the bolts held, and the beast fell from the sky, shrieking as it went. It seemed it had suddenly become a race between how quickly the remaining two creatures could get to the ship and how fast the crew could reload. With zero desire to be stuck in a cabin if the airship went down, I strapped on my sword and made my way out on to the deck to see if I could help.

Other passengers must have had the same idea, as when I arrived outside various mages were already stood launching blasts of eldritch and elemental energies at the creatures. Many of them hit, but it seemed that the scales of the creatures were resistant to magical attacks, with most leaving scorch marks and little else. The greatest damage came from attacks that hit the membranous wings, which were far more fragile and left with large smoking rents wherever the spells had struck. The crew finally managed to reload and launch a second volley which took out the second smaller creature, but after the largest managed to avoid the bolts yet again, it was clear the crew wouldn't have time to reload before it would reach us.

Retracting its wings against its body, the creature dove at the deck like a giant serpentine javelin, and as it crashed into the deck, the railing and several of the ballistae exploded into a hail of metal and wood chips. Any of the crew or passengers unfortunate enough to be in its way were instantly reduced to a messy pulp or launched, screaming, out into the open air. The battle devolved into pure chaos as the people drew their weapons and attempted to slash and bash at the beast, however the scales proved no less resistant to physical damage than they were to magic. It was instantly clear that this beast was of a level far above that of the crew or any of the other passengers. Each swipe of the beast's tail flung more people about, the unlucky ones finding themselves in freefall, and even those that landed upon the ship in no condition to continue the fight. Drawing my sword, I launched myself at the beast, managing to make a large gash along its side. The pain from the blow enraged the beast and it ignored everyone else to whip at me with its tail, I attempted to dodge the thing, but it was simply too long, and I realised too late that I should have jumped! The thing hit like a truck and launched me like a fucking cannonball into one of the masts, which gave an almighty cracking sound from the impact. Climbing dazedly back to my feet, I briefly wondered if the ship would stay in the air without a mast, but the creature didn't give me any further time to worry about that, as it gave up on trying to bash me around in favour of swallowing me whole. I managed to sidestep out of its path using wind-steps, which caused it to strike the mast instead, but, added to my earlier impact, the extra damage pushed the mast past its limit and with awful snapping sounds it began to topple over. I had to jinx it didn't I? Luckily, the collision seemed to stun the creature too and whilst it shook its head, I scrambled to pick up my fallen sword, and sliced into its neck with an almighty two-handed swing. Unfortunately, my commitment to the attack meant I had not been paying attention to its tail, which clipped the back of my head, sending me pretty much face first into the deck. My head was swimming from so many blows in such a short space of time and I knew that I was probably nursing a major concussion. Luckily for all of us, I could see from my prone position that I had managed to cut through most of the beast's neck before it nailed me, and so it lay thrashing and twitching in its death throes.

Happy that the creature was no longer a threat, I tiredly rolled on to my back, only then noticing a plump middle-aged woman in a white robe running towards me. I didn't feel any malicious intent from the woman, so as she began to mouth an incantation, I watched in idle curiosity as a pleasant feeling white glow begun to suffuse the both of us. Within moments, my soreness began to disappear, throbbing head included, and I was left in awe of the woman's amazing ability.

Finally getting my bearings, I noticed mages wrestling with the mast, some had summoned great vines, to wrap around it and arrest its fall, whilst others were controlling powerful wind spells, which buffeted around it, in an attempt to lift it back into place. I gazed up into the eyes of the healer and received a gentle smile in return.

"Thank you, ma'am, it means a lot," I said.

"Think nothing of it, it should be me thanking you."

Pushing myself up into a sitting position, I waved off her reply. "I'm sure the crew would have dealt with it."

"No, young man, they wouldn't have, that was a level four Amphithere. Once it avoided the ballista bolts, there wasn't another on board that could deal with it."

I was a little shocked as a level four beast was equivalent to a Spirit Knight, but beasts generally far outpower humans of the same level, so it would easily take a party of A-rank adventurers to take down a level four! "Amphithere, huh, so that's what the things are called? Well…I just did what I had to."

"And I for one am glad that you did. For someone so young to have such power, forgive me if its rude to ask, but just what class are you?" she asked, curiosity gleaming in her eyes.

Master had explained that classes were used throughout many realms, as they were an easy way to categorise skillsets, and allowed people to slip straight into party roles, just like in an RPG. The awakened could simply self-identify as a Class based on their abilities, or take the name from class stones, which impart a relevant cultivation method or the mage equivalent, as well as some accompanying skills, in a similar way to the memory jade I used to lean the local languages; like a starter-set for the awakened. Basic class stones are readily available in most Adventurer shops, with more prestigious or specific ones given out as part of apprenticeships, providing the newly awakened easy routes to start their growth.

The class stones did have a problem though; the methods provided would only allow for growth to a pre-determined level. Once they hit that cap, if someone wants to improve further, they need to find either a higher-level class stone that's compatible with the previous stone's system or use a separate cultivation method like the one provided to me by my father. And that's the real kicker, as the best skills, class stones and systems are already in the hands of large organisations, be they sects, clans, or families, and they apparently guard them like a dragon would its hoard. Especially, if they own a high tier cultivation method or mage system, which would never be shared with outsiders and is often as much a part of an organisation's identity as the signature skills they practice.

The pessimist in me couldn't help but wonder whether class stones were just a handy tool for limiting the growth of the masses? Not that everyone could reach the pinnacle anyway, as talent would weigh in as much as resources. Whatever the answer, I realised how lucky I had been to receive such a great cultivation method from my father. Regardless of their limitations, I thought I should probably see about acquiring some class stones to take home, as if aether levels did rise to a high enough level on Earth, it may be handy to be able to easily empower some others to help deal with any issues that crop up.

"I'm sorry, I know I probably shouldn't pry, forget it," the woman apologised, mistaking my silent musings for having taken offence.

"No, it's fine, I don't mind. I'm a Warrior class, Arcane Swordsman," I said, as I decided on a name for a class that best suited my skillset.

"Winnifred, but my friends all call me Winny. I always wanted to help people, so when I was lucky enough to awaken, I jumped on the chance to become a Cleric and now I heal as many as I can, well, can't stop, lots of people to heal, so little ability to do it."

"Amen to that, sister." I smiled.

Taking my time to get myself back together, I thoroughly cleaned the blood from my sword, whilst watching the people bustle around me. The crew were consummate professionals, with triage of the injured and dead occurring alongside swift repairs to the Airship. I was impressed, they knew their stuff. I could also see that I'd been correct about losing a mast, as we were losing a significant amount of altitude, but the process was relatively slow, and when we eventually halted, we were still several thousand feet above the tops of the trees.

As the mast was finally hauled back into position, green runic characters glowed upon it and the two parts of the mast fused back together as if nothing had ever happened, which I thought was rather nifty. As soon as they were free from their burden, the mages responsible for saving it, all dropped panting to their knees, the degree of effort they had expended clear in their exhausted expressions.

Realising I had been sitting and watching like a lazy bastard, I got up and looked for the captain to see if I could help. Lazalio Heb, was stood on the poop deck surveying the damage to the ship whilst quietly passing orders to his officers.

"Captain, I wonder if there is anything I can do to help?"

Interrupted from organising repairs, Lazalio had a look of annoyance on his face, which quickly turned to a melancholy smile as he noticed it was me. "Joshua White, thank you, lad. Thank you. If you hadn't acted...I dread to think what state we'd be in, likely as not just a pile of debris."

The earnestness of his thanks was humbling and honestly made me a little uncomfortable, as many had lost their lives in the fight and the mages had worked themselves to complete exhaustion to save the mast, whereas I just swung my sword a few times. It didn't seem fair. "I fear you give me too much credit captain, it was an expensive victory paid for with the blood of many brave souls."

Lazalio smiled sadly. "Aye, that it was, and they too will be remembered, with compensation paid to their families. But don't sell yourself short lad, as likely none on this vessel would be here now without you and its only right and proper that we give our thanks."

I could feel my face reddening a little with embarrassment, but I knew excessive humility would probably just come across as false. "In that case, you are welcome captain. Is there anything else I can do?"

"We have everything in hand, perhaps see if you could provide any assistance to the wounded."

Nodding, I left them to their work and made my way over to help with the wounded, acutely aware of my lack of experience in these types of situations. I could have helped the injured off my own initiative as I had several batches of healing potions that I purchased for my quest, instead I just sat watching and then looked for guidance on what to do. Suddenly Master's intentions for me became all too clear, I was a complete greenhorn and it had most likely already cost people their lives.

There seemed to be only the one cleric on board, whether there were more prior to the attack I didn't know, but Winny already looked tired and probably wouldn't be able to heal too many more people before she simply passed out. The number of healing potions onboard were limited too, due to how expensive they were, which explained why many were left with only basic ministrations such as bandages and tourniquets, in the hope to just keep them alive until their awakened bodies could start to heal them.

Wasting no time, I began to help the most seriously injured drink healing potions from my own supply. The effects were immediately evident, bringing people back from what was in many cases literally Death's door. Knowing they could save my life I'd spared no expense when choosing the level of potions and looking at their effects they were well worth it. It was just a shame that at a gold coin each, potions of such a level were only really an option for the excessively wealthy, different world but same rich poor divide!

Well, I was rich and if I could save a life for a single gold coin then that was money well spent in my eyes, so half an hour and fourteen potions later and I had saved all that I could, with anyone remaining nursing injuries too minor to necessitate a potion, or already dead before I had a chance to get to them.

I'd never fought with a group before, but it was tragically clear to me that even seconds counted in these situations. Maybe I could partially blame my earlier inaction on shock and concussion, but ultimately it was mostly due to my lack of battlefield experience, and I swore I'd pull my head out of my arse in the future. I'd do better, be better, I owed the dead at least that much.

"You did a good thing, Josh," Winny said, patting me on the back.

"Yes, *we* did, but next time I'll do even better," I replied.

It turned out that Winny was the ship's Cleric, and after handing over my remaining thirty-six potions, which left her a little dumfounded, I returned to my room to meditate. Ultimately, combat on such a scale had proved to be pure fucking chaos, nothing like the solo combat I was more used to, and I needed to still my mind to process what I could learn.

The ship must have been back up to speed almost immediately, as the following morning, after a sorely needed sleep, Berevar had become visible from my window nestled as it was against the shimmering waters of Lake Antaru.

Chapter 28

As the airship dropped towards the city, we were afforded a fantastic view. As just a regular regional city, Berevar was far smaller than Stormhaven but in no way any less impressive. It was composed almost entirely of gleaming white rock and the architecture was beautiful, with sinuous spires and arches. Barely a single straight line was visible which gave the city an almost organic feel, like the bleached remains of a giant coral reef.

"No-one else builds quite like the Elves," Winny said at my side.

I thought about the stereotypes for fictional Elves on earth and their supposed affinity with the natural world. It seemed the stories held a kernel of truth, at least if their sense of aesthetics was anything to go by. I wondered if Carl Jung was correct and there was some sort of vague collective unconscious, its presence colouring our fiction with hints of the ancestral knowledge it held, or perhaps it was less esoteric, just cultural tales passed down through the ages, diluting and changing in their journey through time but never completely forgotten. Were there Elves on Earth at some point? If there was, where are they now?

The airship alighted alongside the dock, which was a graceful lattice framework with individual staircases for each berth. Thanking the crew for the passage, I left the Canny Hawk behind and made my way out into the city. My first bit of business was to find an alchemist or apothecary, as I had donated all of my potions to the airship and, after seeing how

215

effective they had been, thought it would be foolish to carry on without any.

Confusingly, even though the city was built by Elves the largest population still seemed to be humans, with a few Dwarves here and there, interspersed occasionally with members of races that I couldn't even identify. Some were still vaguely human in form, just with beast-like qualities such as furry ears or excessively large teeth, but others were completely alien. When I passed by what looked like some sort of slimy slug-woman, slithering along with four tentacles instead of arms, it took all of my self-control to not just stand and stare. No one else had even batted an eyelid and I didn't want to be that guy!

In all fairness, there *were* far more Elves walking the streets than in Stormhaven and the city on the whole was more diverse, I just found the number of humans surprising. I guessed that maybe humans just have a higher birth-rate, as there was over eight billion of us back on Earth. I say us, even though it was looking increasingly likely that I wasn't actually human either. Well, I look human, mostly!

After wandering ineffectively for some time, I finally gave in and asked for directions from a rather polite city guard, and soon found myself outside a large store, rather boastfully, named Berevar Heavenly Medicines. Luckily, healing potions and spells worked on most species, regardless of their physiology, as they largely worked by infusing a large dose of life-attributed aether into the body. So, even though I might struggle to find an alchemist able to make pills for my progression, healing potions or ones that generally dealt with aiding the body would rarely be a problem.

Walking through the door caused a bell to ring, reminding me of small stores back home and the familiarity was strangely comforting. The grinning face that popped up from behind the counter however, quickly destroyed the illusion. It was green and wrinkly, with far too many pointy teeth in its overly wide mouth, its huge droopy ears reaching all the way to its shoulders. And its eyes, fuck me, its eyes!

They were huge, yellow and reptilian, complete with nictating membranes, which disconcertingly weren't even synchronised, as they slowly and creepily slid back and forth across the giant yellow orbs. Now, I refuse to judge someone by how they look, but I will happily admit that it took all of my self-control not to flinch at the sudden and unexpected sight.

"Are you just going to stay in the doorway, sir?" The creature asked, his genteel manner and pleasant warbling voice completely at odds with his scary appearance.

"Ermm, no, of course not, sorry," I apologised, walking towards the counter.

"First time seeing a Goblanvolk?" he asked gently.

"That obvious," I said ashamedly, "I'm sorry."

The wide grin never left his face. "Don't be, exposure to new races can often be shocking, the key is not letting your initial reaction determine how you act thereafter," he advised like a kindly old teacher.

"Very true." I nodded. "That sounds like something my Master would say."

"Sounds like a wise man."

"Yes, he is." I smiled.

"Well, how can I help you…?"

"Josh."

"Trantolius," he introduced himself with a small bow of his head.

A few minutes later and I was all stocked up, unfortunately Trantolius had nothing that could aid my cultivation, not that I really needed it, but he really knew his healing potions.

"Trantolius, I'm here in the city to investigate people going missing, I don't suppose you've heard about it?"

"Forgive me, Josh, but you seem a little young to be investigating such a case, especially considering the fact that the people who went missing were all children and adolescents."

217

It seemed the case was quite well known locally, although I did find it odd that no mention of the victims ages was made on the quest information in Stormhaven.

"I'll be careful," I assured him.

"Well, just make sure you are, I don't know what is going on, but it reeks of foulness, something awful has happened to those kids, I'd stake my reputation on it," he said ominously, "If I was you, I'd start with the parents, maybe they'd know more."

Thanking him for the potions, I got directions to the local Adventurers' Guild, thinking they may be able to help.

The Berevar branch was far smaller than that in Stormhaven, but still sizeable enough to accommodate the large volume of foot traffic in and out of the building. Approaching one of the duty clerks, I showed my ring and was granted immediate access to all of the information held by the local branch.

There were originally thirty-two people reported missing, all aged between seven and nineteen, and since then a further ten adventurers had also disappeared whilst investigating the case. I immediately disregarded the missing adventurers, as it was likely they were only victims due to the investigations they were carrying out.

There was no obvious commonality between the original victims other than the age range, some were too old for it to be a paedophile, but that didn't necessarily rule out some sort of sexual predator. However, the lack of a specific gender or type seemed to suggest that was less likely, as from what I knew, those sorts of predators tend to have quite specific preferences. The victims also had various socio-economic backgrounds, and if they just needed youngsters, it would have been far more sensible to prey only on the poorest areas, as they have the least guard presence. Hell, they could have even just snatched up some homeless kids as there's always plenty in large cities, which suggested that there was definitely something specific about why those children were chosen in particular.

Trantolius was right, I needed to speak to the parents. I was starting to feel like a private investigator, and it was clear that being an adventurer could involve far more than just swinging a sword, I guess in a world with guards instead of cops, adventurers were often the detectives, and I can't say I didn't like it!

Luckily the victim's details were all on file, so it wouldn't be too hard to find them. One of them, a fifteen-year-old girl named Jiana Caffley was from a successful merchant family, and as one of the wealthiest families in the city, the Caffleys' compound was easily located, the huge iron-fenced estate guarded by their own private retainers. Finding it may have been easy but gaining access had proven slightly more problematic, as the gatehouse guard was reluctant to let me in without an appointment. Which was understandable, as I could have just been any random nutter. Luckily, once my identity as an S-rank adventurer was confirmed, I was quickly escorted to an anteroom within the property and allowed to wait for Mr Caffley to become available.

I wasn't kept waiting for long before Mr Caffley bowled into the room. His well-coiffed brown hair was greying at the temples, evidence he was pushing well into middle age, but he still cut a powerful figure, as much a warrior as merchant, if I had to guess. Being the head of a large enterprise, his facial features were well schooled against any excessive display of emotion, but I nevertheless got the impression of tiredness from the man.

"And to what do I owe the honour, Master Adventurer?"

"I'd like to ask you a few questions about Jiana."

"I thought as much, but forgive my rudeness, what could you possibly ask that I haven't already answered to numerous other adventurers?"

He stared at me, waiting for my answer and I didn't begrudge his attitude. I'd be fucked off too if I'd lost my daughter and all I had received was questions and no answers.

It was weariness that coloured his words. He was a man with vast responsibilities, torn between duty, grief, and hope.

"I am sorry Mr Caffley, I can't say I understand what you're going through, but I'm sure it's awful. Hell, I can't even promise that I'll find Jiana," I said, gambling that such a powerful man would appreciate the no-nonsense approach. "But I can promise I won't give up, and as an S-rank, I have far more hope of surviving for long enough to find out what the fuck is happening in this city."

Mr Caffley stared at me as if he was taking my measure, and I guess he was content with what he saw. "I appreciate your candour, ask away."

Now, I had been thinking more on my way over, about less mundane reasons that children may be kidnapped. I remembered Master saying that I would be treated as a treasure trove of cultivation resources, so maybe that's what these missing teens were?

"Did Jiana have a unique physique or constitution that you know of?"

"No, not as far as I'm aware."

Damn, well that was maybe one idea ruled out. The only other possible commonality I had been able to think of between so many different types of children was their health, and perhaps they all suffered from the same sort of magical affliction?

"Was Jiana ever treated for an unusual illness or condition?"

The surprised look on his face suggested that she had.

"Ermm, yes. As a small child, she once became deathly cold, and we couldn't warm her no matter what we tried."

"And how was she treated?"

"Our regular family apothecary managed to identify the cause. Jiana had somehow been exposed to a plant with an extremely Yin nature. It took a series of treatments, but it was eventually resolved."

"Ever find the plant responsible?"

"Ermm, no, we didn't. We were just happy she was healthy again."

"And no one else suffered from such a malady in your household?"

"No, just Jiana."

That was strange, as such a plant would cause issues for everyone exposed to it and surely there was no way a small child would have been left unsupervised near anything potentially dangerous, which suggested the exposure was possibly intentional and targeted.

"Any chance I could have the name of the apothecary?" It may just be nothing, but at least I had a potential avenue to investigate.

On my way out, Mr Caffley had been rather keen to remind me that the apothecary, Madam Wang, had been serving the city for decades and had a stellar reputation. But that was the benefit of being a stranger, local reputation didn't count for fuck all to me, I'd just go where the clues led. I honestly felt like Poirot, and I was loving it!

Over the following two days I eventually managed to track down twelve of the parents, one flat-out refused to speak to me, but after questioning the rest, I found that all of their children had been treated by Madam Wang at some point! Twice may have been coincidence, but that many was definitely a pattern. The other point that suggested foul play was that Madam Wang's costs were normally quite high, yet she had offered pro-bono treatment to each of the poorer families. Now, maybe she is just a lovely lady who likes to aid the needy, but after experiencing how dark this world could be, I was naturally sceptical of any altruism. Maybe I was too jaded for someone of my age, but fuck it, preparing for the worse may just save my life. Either way, it was time to visit Madam Wang.

Chapter 29

Madam Wang's establishment was a large oriental pagoda in warm reds and golds, its smell of medicinal herbs and incense, that permeated into the surrounding streets, pleasantly removed from the usual disinfectant and bleach common to modern hospitals.

The foyer was staffed by a white-robed young man, who quickly approached as I entered.

"How may Madam Wang be of service to you?" he asked, his tone almost reverent when he mentioned his employer.

"I have a few questions for Madam Wang about the missing kids," I said, deciding to be upfront about my purpose as I wasn't accusing anyone of anything, not yet at least.

The young man however seemed rather quick to jump to conclusions, his face scrunched up in a rictus of displeasure. "You dare to cast aspersions towards the great Madam Wang?" he screeched, his spittle spraying at me.

Now, I wasn't sure if he was over-reacting due to a guilty conscience or simply due to his, clearly unhealthy, level of admiration towards Madam Wang. Either way, I had been polite and wouldn't tolerate such an attitude.

"You forget yourself!" I bellowed, "I have made no accusations and merely wish to ask a few questions," I continued in a slightly more reasonable tone.

"Send him through Herman," echoed out from deeper within the pavilion in the raspy voice of an elderly woman.

Albeit reluctantly, the visibly shaken Herman opened a door and beckoned me to enter, he didn't seem inclined to lead the way. Oh well, he wouldn't be in that state if he hadn't been such a prick. The short corridor led to a set of double doors, that were already stood open for me and, rather alarmingly, bore carved scenes of graphic torture and violence. Completely discordant with a house of healing.

"The suffering of the unworthy," the same raspy voice announced from the room beyond.

Entering, I was greeted by the sight of a small, hunched figure busily sorting through a messy table covered in various plants and fungi. Seemingly content to ignore my presence, the figure just carried on at her task, occasionally grunting over items of apparent interest and placing them into a separate pile. Madam Wang was not what I'd expected, it felt like I'd stumbled across one of the Shakespeare's weird sisters preparing to brew a fresh cauldron.

"Scenes of suffering don't seem very appropriate for an apothecary," I said, attempting to draw her attention.

"And you'd know about suffering would you, boy?" She cackled like an archetypal witch.

Images of my murdered family flashed before my eyes, and I found myself clenching my fists involuntarily. Straightening up, Madam Wang finally stopped what she was doing and looked around at me. She only looked to be in her sixties, so nowhere near as old as I'd first imagined, and with how attractive she remained; I could easily imagine how pretty she would have been in her younger years.

"It seems like you are quite familiar with pain. I'm sorry." The empathy on her face seemed genuine, although a minute previously I had believed her to be an old krone, so clearly, she knew how to act a part.

"It's fine, shit happens," I replied, unwilling to share my inner demons with my main suspect. "Why were you pretending to be an old hag?" I quickly changed the subject.

"Just a bit of harmless fun," she retorted, although I swear, I saw a brief flicker of annoyance pass over her face.

I wasn't sure if she was a master manipulator, weaving some ploy I was unable to understand, or if I was just massively overthinking the whole situation. "Do you know why I'm here?" I asked.

"Why yes, it's about my treatment of the missing children. At least that is what I was led to believe."

So, someone had already tipped her off. I would have liked to have known whom though, as it could only have been one of the parents.

"Exactly, during my investigations I found out that all of the missing children were treated by you at some point, which if I'm honest, seems a little too coincidental."

"Well, of course it does deary. We only wanted children who'd received my necessary ministrations. Only the sweetest fruit for my Lord"

She cackled wildly, hunching over as her face began to distort into that of a wicked old krone, I guess that explained her earlier annoyance at my comment, the prettier face was the actual disguise.

"Sweet, sweet Child, tell Aunty Wang about your suffering," she rasped, and I could feel a palpable impulse to lay bare the darkest secrets about myself, like invisible worms in my head silently assuring me that everything would be better if I just surrendered all my pains to her. Clutching my head, I focused on pushing the feeling out.

Continuously cackling, Madam Wang stretched out her wrinkly hand, which began to glow with a sickly green light, and I had a feeling that whatever she was doing, it was nothing good.

"Give in child, free yourself from pain," she said, the pressure in my head increasing massively.

The pain became so intense that I dropped to my knees, and Madam Wang began to slowly hobble towards me, drawing a nasty looking kris from beneath her cloak that I did not want anywhere near me. Summoning all my willpower to push her tendrils out of my mind, something stirred within the depths of my subconscious and with a surge of pure psychic power, her presence was blasted from my mind. The relief was instantaneous, and although I felt a little lightheaded, at least my mind was my own again.

"What have you done?" Madam Wang shrieked at me, blood running from her facial orifices as she clawed wildly at her head. "What have you done?" she repeated desperately, removing clumps of skin and hair as she continued to claw away at herself.

Her visage became ever more gruesome, until finally, after gouging out her own eyes with her fingernails, she simply curled up on the floor, quietly whimpering the same question over and over.

Now, admittedly I had seen some messed-up things in my past, but even I was shocked by the brutal nature of Madam Wang's breakdown, plus, looking at the state of her, I couldn't help but wonder about the power that had caused such a backlash of her own ability. Whatever it had been, it had no doubt saved my life, and if that was what she had planned for me, it was hard to have too much pity for her.

My respite wasn't to last though, as Herman barrelled into the room, any fear he may have felt towards me quickly forgotten upon seeing the state of Madam Wang.

"I will help you, Madam, please be okay, let me get some medicine," he jabbered frantically.

"Yeah, that's not going to happen, that fucking monster got exactly what she deserved!" I yelled, as there was no way in hell, I was letting her recover.

"Monster!" he shrieked, "MONSTER! You're the monster! A petty little thug like you could never hope to understand the glory of our Lord's work. Madam Wang is a blessing to this world, delivering the worthy to their places in His great work! You will pay, you will pay!" he ranted, literally spitting as he did.

Reaching into his robes he pulled out a small red jar, which as he popped the lid off, released a noxious smell that drifted over to me. It smelt like sulphur, blood and death, and I knew it was bad news. But before I had a chance to react, he emptied the entire contents into his mouth, crunching away on whatever it had contained.

The grimace on his face suggested that it tasted as bad as it smelt and not wanting to give him time for whatever he was aiming to achieve, I made my way over to him sword in hand. Herman hunched over screaming as his flesh began to wiggle and distort in a horrifying fashion and I sped up in an attempt to reach him quicker. It wasn't to be though, as before I could get close enough to strike, a wave of red energy emanated from him, lifting me from my feet and propelling me across the room, straight through a wall and into an adjacent one. Luckily, the walls were quite thin, but the furniture that I had smashed through had been far less forgiving and there wasn't a part of me that didn't ache. It was the second time in just a few days that I had been launched in such a manner and as I forced myself to my feet, to say I was thoroughly pissed-off off would be an understatement!

The view that met me through the hole in the wall however, quickly doused any anger I was feeling. Herman was gone and in his place was what I could only describe as a Demon, complete with dark red skin and curving ram-like horns. At easily eight feet of bulging muscles, I found myself gulping involuntarily and trying to decide whether to fight it or run. No. Running wasn't an option, if that thing got out into the city, it would be a calamity with countless lives lost. I was responsible for the creature appearing and I so I had to put it down. My sword hummed in my hand as if it agreed with me, which was new. It also began to glow of its own accord, seemingly eager to combat whatever foul abomination Herman had become. Stepping back through the hole I'd made in the wall, I was immediately struck by a feeling of wrongness that surrounded the creature, like it wasn't meant to be here, and the very World rejected it. I was happy to oblige its wish.

Holding nothing back, I launched myself at the Demon, which roared in response and raised its claws to meet me. The shockwave from the impact caused an explosion of air which tore through the surrounding structure and even with my inhuman strength, I struggled to hold on to my sword. The creature's claws sparked as my sword ran along them and as it began to push me back, it quickly became apparent that it actually had me outmatched in physical strength, which was a first for me. From the sounds of snapping and creaking from all around me, I knew that the building was doomed and did not want to be around when it collapsed. I disengaged from the creature, using its own force to aid my wind-steps in fleeing the building, slashing at every support I passed. The Demon was not very quick-witted and just stood there as I fled, and I hoped that even if the collapsing building couldn't finish it off, which seemed doubtful, it would at least injure it.

Barely making it out onto the street in time, the building collapsed behind me, producing a sweeping cloud of dust as it did. For a moment there was silence, and I urged all those gathered in the streets to flee.

"Get away!" I shouted, "There's a Demon inside!"

The people looked at me as if I was mad until I flashed my guild insignia. "I am S-rank adventurer Joshua White, if you wish to live, FLEE!" I bellowed the last.

My desperate yell finally seemed to get through to them and most began to hurry out of the area, however it wasn't until a deafening roar came from deep within the rubble, that even the most curious began to run. It was too late for some, the Demon launched itself up from the rubble and the explosion of debris struck many of them in the back, and they dropped bleeding to the floor, their conditions unknown. The commotion had also finally drawn the town guards over, which clearly took longer than it should have, but I couldn't help but wish it had taken them even longer. At their level of strength, they would be little more than fodder for the beast.

The guards stood transfixed at the sight of the demon, but to their credit, they quickly snapped out of it, forming up with spears and shields to the front, whilst several dragged any injured townsfolk behind them.

"What manner of creature is that thing?" asked the captain of the guard.

"Fuck knows," I replied, "It used to be Madam Wang's assistant, Herman."

The Demon was scratched to shit from the collapsed building, but the wounds were superficial, and it gazed at the assembled forces with complete indifference. I had expected it to immediately start on a rampage and wasn't sure if the fact it hadn't was a good thing or not.

"Madam Wang and Herman were responsible for the missing kids," I continued.

The guard looked shocked. "And you are?" he asked.

"Joshua White, S-rank adventurer, I was investigating the case."

"Right, well, my lord, how should we go about this?" the guard asked.

"I need you to stay back and help with the injured whilst I confront the beast. It's really fucking strong, probably level five, so I'm not sure you'll be able to help me fight it."

The guard visibly paled. "Gods above help us." Gathering himself together, he yelled, "Everybody back, clear the area, carry the wounded if you have to, Gravius, report this to the city lord immediately."

I interposed myself between the Demon and the guards as they aided the evacuation.

The Demon smirked at me, so human-like it was disquieting on such a terrifying face. "Your efforts amuse me. I am in no rush little man, after I feast upon your flesh, I shall enslave this city in the name of my Lord. Millions of helpless souls just waiting to be devoured." He gestured around with arms wide open.

Fuck, I guess Herman hadn't become a mindless Beast, which would have been far easier to deal with.

I tried to think of a witty comeback, but I had nothing, plus fuck it, words were cheap, steel would speak louder. So, once again, I launched myself at the Demon, but this time purposely avoiding a direct clash of strength.

I feinted a slash and as the Demon swung wildly in response, it quickly became clear that for all its strength, it still only had Herman's skill and apparently, he was an awful warrior. Every strike I landed, carrying Sword Intent and empowered with my own Qi, left large gaping wounds in its flesh and it roared its displeasure at the pain. Yet, as I weaved away from its own lumbering swings, it was disheartening to watch the wounds knit closed, even if the process was being inhibited somewhat by the lingering Sword Intent. Especially as I knew that any hit it landed on me, would fail to heal near as quickly. I was dancing on the edge of a knife, and I couldn't keep it up forever, as my own energy stores were also continually decreasing.

Eventually, it happened, a single slip-up, a dodge away a hairsbreadth too short, and the Demons claws carved furrows across my chest and left arm, it wasn't good. So much for my magic fucking armour! The cuts to my arm were deep enough to almost completely sever my bicep and the arm hung useless at my side. I jumped backwards to create some distance and quickly tearing a piece of cloth from my cloak to tie around the wound, was forced to use my right hand and teeth to get it cinched tight. Demon Herman slowly stalked towards me, smiling as it panted to get its breath back, as if it knew it had me.

"I will enjoy watching you suffer for what you did to Madam Wang, let's see how you squeal as your lifeblood slowly leaves you."

I admit it wasn't looking good, but encouragingly, I noticed the wounds on the Demon were no longer closing nearly as fast as they had, so even it had limits. Steeling myself against the pain of my wounds, it was time to see who would hit theirs first.

As we came together again, I was forced to use my sword one handed, but every blow contained all the force I could manage, no longer sparing any concern for how quickly I would burn through my energy reserves. The wounds I left became deeper and bled more freely, and it may have been my imagination, but I swear the fucker seemed to be getting visibly smaller. Realising his predicament, Herman threw himself at me in an attempt to catch me in a bear hug. His sudden rush caught me off guard, and slowed down by my own blood loss, I couldn't manage to avoid it. All I could do was hold my sword steady in front of me, impaling him up through his belly as he grabbed me.

The demon's arms wrapped fully around me and as his huge talons pierced into the flesh of my back, I could feel the breath being slowly forced out of me from the crushing embrace. I tried to force my sword up into his chest, but felt his claws push deeper into my back in response. The pain was almost overwhelming and when I choked up a mouthful of frothy blood it became clear he had managed to puncture my lungs. I was starting to drown in my own blood and as my strength started to fail me, my hand dropped involuntarily from the hilt of my sword. Tilting my head back, I looked up to see him tilting his own, clearly about to make an almighty bite into my head. I couldn't let it happen; it would be the end of me. In that split second, his actions had left his own throat exposed and so, not wasting my only chance I pushed back against the claws in my back and forced my own mouth forward biting into his neck. Thank God for overdeveloped canines! With an almighty wrip, I tore a huge chunk of his neck and throat out, gagging on the foul taste as I tried to spit the filth from my mouth.

Herman immediately dropped me to the floor, all thought of me quickly forgotten as he clutched at his neck in a desperate attempt to stem the loss of blood. He had no chance. From the look of how his eyes were practically popping out, breathing had also become a bitch. Ha, served him right, let's see how he fucking liked it! The hilt of my sword was still sticking out from his abdomen, but with the dwindling amount of oxygen in my blood, I didn't have the strength to take it. It seemed it would be a race between whether bleeding out or asphyxiation would get me first, but even barely clinging to consciousness, I was determined to at least watch that monster die first.

Suddenly, my curiosity was perked by numerous green and white orbs flying towards me. I didn't have the energy to panic, and I was completely impotent to get out of their way anyway. Luckily, they weren't malicious, and my curiosity quickly turned to bliss as the healing effects of the spells washed over me. Some were purifying, forcing the demon's foul corruption from my wounds, others repairing and knitting damaged flesh back together, which itched like hell. That first breath I took as my lungs began to function properly again was the sweetest I'd ever had, only slightly ruined by the following seconds spent hacking up leftover blood from my lungs.

Dragging my dishevelled arse up to Herman, who was amazingly still clutching his neck, I started to worry whether the fucker might actually survive if left long enough. I wasn't about to give him that chance. Moving as quick as I could, which wasn't particularly fast at all, I pulled my sword from him and swung as hard as I could at his neck. In my weakened state and with his hands wrapped around it, it was like chopping down a fucking tree, so it took a fair few hacks before finally his head and a large part of both hands fell free to the floor. If that didn't kill him, then fuck knows.

Totally exhausted, I briefly raised my sword into the air in triumph and fell backwards onto my arse.

Chapter 30

The following few minutes were chaotic. The captain of the guard had returned and was busy leading the search for further survivors, a problem compounded by the semi-collapsed state of the surrounding buildings. As much as I had tried to contain the fight to the rubble of Madam Wangs pavilion, combat is messy, especially with a creature like that and so inevitably some stray energies had flown into the surrounding environment. I felt rather guilty about it, as at the time it hadn't even entered my thoughts, but in all fairness, Demon Herman was basically a force of nature and if I'd let him be, it would have been far worse, his self-admitted plans for the city had made that crystal clear.

All around me healers rushed around, returning many survivors from the brink of death. Tabards identified some as part of the town guard, but most were just random adventurers and civilians, coming together in a shared desire to minimise the loss of life. Learning from my previous error, I hadn't rested either and was back on my feet as soon as I was able to, helping to shift larger pieces of rubble and swiftly administering healing potions to those that required them. I was so fatigued that the only thing that kept me going was sheer willpower, fuelled by the pit in my stomach, that grew every time we were too late, and another body was placed off to the side.

When a lifeless child pulled from a building, I couldn't help but imagine them in their last moments, terrified and alone as the world collapsed around them, they could have been no more than eight-years-old. A victim of the fight, of my carelessness. Silent tears began to run from me after that, dripping from my nose and chin as I continued to dig, desperately hoping to find some redemption in locating any others still alive.

I was eventually pulled from my digging by a gentle hand upon my shoulder. "Everyone is accounted for, my lord, it's okay, you've done enough."

Blinking the dust from tear-stained eyes, I looked around to find the captain of the guard, his eyes full of sympathy. I looked over to the row of bodies, who someone had respectfully covered in sheets, there were six people who hadn't made it, but my gaze lingered on the one with the tiny form.

"No." I shook my head. "I haven't." I gestured around wearily.

"Permission to be frank, sir?" the captain asked.

"Captain, I'm just an adventurer that happens to be a little better at kicking arse. I wouldn't want it any other way," I said tiredly.

The captain smiled at that. "Today has been a tragedy, there's no doubt about it, but if it wasn't for you, it could have been far worse and if my eyes don't deceive me, you aren't much older than that child we will soon be burying. So don't beat yourself up young man, it's a cruel world and you did the best you can, no one can ask for more than that."

"I…I…Thank you," I whispered, his reassuring words helping more than I could articulate.

"No problem, now go get yourself cleaned up and we can talk about what to do next."

I brushed myself off as best I could and made my way over to a nearby water bowser, the cold water felt great as I cleared the dust and grime from my face. The captain was right, wallowing in self-recrimination and guilt wouldn't help anyone, I had done my best and had barely survived myself. I would better honour the dead by finding the scum who orchestrated the whole thing, this Lord they mentioned. But it was worrying, as whatever had caused Herman's transformation, it was definitely not ordinary, and a person cable of producing it would likely be extremely dangerous. I just hoped that whatever it was, there was only a limited supply, as fighting a group of them, or even one more skilled, had a good chance of ending badly, for both me and the Empire's citizens. Oh well, one step at a time.

Making my way back over to the captain, I saw he was caught up in a discussion with several other important looking guards and a bunch of adventurers.

"Find anything useful?" I asked as I approached.

"And you are the one responsible for this mess, I assume? Do you have any idea how much money this will cost the city to repair?" shouted one of the guards in more elaborate armour.

I turned to the captain and completely ignored the fool. "Anything?"

"Yes, we found Madam Wang's corpse under the rubble, on her body she carried the insignia…"

"Don't ignore me, boy, I am the city guard commander. Gerbol of the Melikants!" he yelled, "and you will treat me with the appropriate respect. Now, how do you propose to compensate me for all the property damage your scuffle has caused."

"Property damage? Six people lost their lives due to that creature, one of which was a small child," I said, unable to stop the growl that followed my words.

"Yes, six dead commoners and a child as likely as not to become a streetwalker or thief, how tragic." He sneered. "Now, HOW WILL YOU SETT…"

I didn't give him a chance to finish his sentence, the rat faced bastard flailing and choking as I held him in the air by his throat.

"What happened here was a tragedy, lives were lost because some evil fuckers decided they could get away with doing whatever they wanted. And when scumbags like you completely disregard the lives they take, you enable their actions and it disgusts me, you disgust me. Now, I am going to put you down and you will fuck off out of my sight before I tear the limbs from your body and have what's left of you delivered back to your clan. Do you understand?" I roared, barely containing the rage inside me.

He nodded profusely. "Good," I said, throwing the wretch to the ground.

No one made a move to help him, even his own subordinates, whose glares, I am happy to say, were filled with the same disgust I had for the man.

Gerbol spluttered and hacked as he climbed to his feet. "You w…" he started to say, the words dying on his lips as he faced me.

It was lucky he stopped talking, I was a second away from making good on my threats, the consequences be damned. Red-faced and muttering, Gerbol turned around and left about as quickly as he could without running.

"Your actions will not have endeared you to his clan, the other human clans may also take offence, believing you to be challenging their authority," a graceful female elf interjected.

I looked over to her, my rage slowly dissipating. She was one of the adventurers I had seen working arduously at healing the injured. "What authority?" I winked, honestly way past caring about hurting some nobles' sense of self-importance.

"And may I ask why, when you were obviously carrying strong healing potions, did you not use one on yourself during the fight?" she asked.

"Ermm, yeah, I kind of forgot about them in the heat of battle." I scratched my head embarrassedly.

The look on her face was calculative. "You are new to this aren't you?"

"Yeah, this is my first quest," I admitted, "Is it that obvious?"

"Your combat abilities are outstanding, but such a mistake reveals you as a rookie," she said in honest appraisal.

235

I nodded in agreement, she was spot-on, so there was no point denying it.

The elf gestured to her two companions, and they walked off a short way and began to discuss something.

"Well, if it's any consolation, I think you did amazing, rookie or not," the captain said and held out his hand. "The name's Randall."

I clasped his wrist in a warrior's shake. "Josh," I re-introduced myself, grateful for the way he was clearly trying to lessen my embarrassment.

Apparently finished with their little conflab, the elf led her team back over.

"We would like to offer for you to join us on this quest. As you may have guessed, we're the Gilded Tarrions, the A-rank team that accepted this quest in Stormhaven," she said.

It wasn't a hard call, a team by my side would have made it a far easier fight, even just a healer to fix me up would have been a game changer. Not to mention the skillsets the other members may have, and with how bad things could possibly get, reinforcements could only be a good thing. Plus, I was sure I could learn a lot from an experienced team and lessen the damage from any mistakes I would make, so a win all around.

"Glad to be aboard." I grinned. "Is this everyone?"

"No," the elf said, "We also have Taria lurking around somewhere, I'm sure she will make an appearance at some point."

The next few minutes were spent on introductions to my new team. The elf was called Shay'Ilvia, a sorceress specialising in light and nature magic. The Dwarf named Dragmar wore a robust looking set of full-plate and was apparently a Fury Knight, whatever that was? I felt a little guilty, as in his armour the combination of his short stature and excessive girth reminded me of a metal teapot, but I wasn't foolish enough to mention that to him! The third, was a quiet human Archer named Landioss whose scale armour distinguished him from your typical Ranger type, so I assumed he was some sort of battlefield archer. When the last of them, Taria, finally made a brief appearance, she was revealed to be a dusky-skinned and dangerous looking human who appeared to be not much older than me. No doubt her Assassin class may have been disconcerting for some, but I actually found it somewhat comforting that there would be a badass killer watching our backs from the shadows.

"I met another elven sorceress a while back, her name was Shay'Ara, is Shay a family name?"

"In a way." Shay'Ilvia smiled at my comment. "All elves who wander outside use the prefix Shay in place of their family name, our true names returned to us only upon our return. One could argue that all wandering elves are a family of sorts."

Her response actually created more questions than it answered, after all Old Dez never gave Shay as part of his name, but I didn't want to keep pestering her about her culture, as despite her amiable nature, we'd only just met, and I didn't want to sour a budding friendship through some cultural faux pas.

"So, where to next?" I asked.

"I may be able to help with that," Randall interjected, "I was about to mention it, but Commander Gerbol interrupted me. We found insignias on the corpses of both Madam Wang and Herman." His tone becoming serious.

"Well, don't leave us hanging, man, what were they?" asked the previously taciturn Landioss.

"The Blood Whisperer Sect," Randall said, drawing shocked gasps from all but me.

I didn't have a clue who he was talking about, but even if the name wasn't enough of a giveaway, I could tell from everyone's reactions that the sect was bad news.

"So, what should we do about it?" I asked, keen to not draw attention to my lack of common knowledge.

"What can we do?" Dragmar asked in his gruff voice. "Take on an entire sect ourselves?" He laughed.

"We could approach the sect and see what they say?" I offered.

The others looked at me incredulously. "You want to march into a dark sect and question them?" Shay'Ilvia asked.

"I don't see why not, why are they still around if they're so bad?"

"The balls on this one! I love it!" Dragmar laughed, slapping his leg.

"All that is known of their activities is mere hearsay and rumour. Dark sects thrive in the shadows, otherwise a force would have been mobilised to deal with them before," Shay'Ilvia said.

"Well now we have proof," I stated.

Shay'Ilvia shook her head. "Proof that two members were involved, far from enough to declare war on the whole sect."

"Madam Wang had other employees in the city, we could round them up," Randall suggested.

I found myself nodding at Randall's idea. "We will need to be quick, if they were involved, it's likely they've already fled," I said.

The following hour was spent in a mad rush investigating the names of her other employees, luckily Madam Wang's was relatively well known amongst the local residents and after the chaos she and Herman had caused, everyone was quick to offer up whatever information they could. Successfully confirming the identities and descriptions of three additional employees, we quickly split up to track them down.

Miles Derevaglio was who I had been assigned to find, and it was well known that he hailed from Bunter's End, a small beast-kin ghetto at the edge of the slums. I didn't waste any time waiting for a carriage, instead taking off through the city streets using wind-steps, pushing my speed to its absolute limit.

Unfortunately, by the time I arrived, black smoke rising from the area suggested I was already too late. Tracing its origin to a specific building, I held my cloak to my face and forced my way inside.

Pushing into the living room, the heat was stifling, and I knew if I hadn't rebuilt my body there was no way I could have entered, as everything was ablaze, flames travelling up the walls and licking at the blackened ceiling. Visibility was minimal, but through the smoke and burning furniture I managed to make out a body on the floor. Crouching down to get a better look and avoid the worst of the rising smoke, I could see he had been dead for a while, likely from the nasty looking wound on his chest, the dark pool of blood it had created beneath him congealed and bubbling from the heat. Realising I would be getting no answers from a corpse, I quickly left, before the fire brought the building down on top of me.

Bursting out into the streets I took a deep cooling breath and swore that I would never run into a burning building again if I could help it, my skin left red and sore wherever it had been exposed to the heat.

Curiously, I noticed my dragon-skin armour remained cool to the touch, and I guessed that, even in death, it retained some of the dragon's rumoured imperviousness to fire. Gazing down at my chest and left arm, I could see that the damage caused to it by Herman had also finished knitting closed, the quality of the self-repair enchantment further reinforcing how much of a lucky find it had been. Yet, as I admired the way light played across the deep blue scales, I couldn't help but grimace over how much worse my wounds may have been without it, as the fact he had managed to slice into me despite such fantastic protection; was a testament to just how fucked-up his demonic claws had been.

The body inside had matched the description of Miles Derevaglio, a young man who fetched ingredients from suppliers around town for delivery to Madam Wang, and the fact he had been murdered suggested he may have known something and was silenced to keep him from sharing it. But who was the assailant? Our investigations hadn't taken long, plus I had raced here, and yet still they were ahead of me, so they must have wasted no time before beginning the clean-up. I hoped that one of the others had more luck than me.

Arriving back at the ruins of Madam Wangs, I awaited the rest of my new party. One after another they all filtered back with similar stories to my own, and I couldn't help but think that the city's water mages would be busy today with so many fires to put out. Other than the sect insignias, we had been left with nothing and I was unsure of how to proceed.

I was about to ask if anyone had any ideas when Taria sauntered out from a side alley, leading a bound and gagged figure.

"Found this cretin attemptin' ta leave the city at the Southern gate. I reckon e's worth a queshun or two," she said, kicking the man to the floor. "Saw smoke, figured I's late, ran to the gate, 'e came out stinkin' o' blood and smoke, so I nabbed 'im, put up a right fight, 'ad to get a lil rough."

That was a bit of an understatement; he looked like she'd pummelled the shit out of him.

"How'd you know he'd use the Southern Gate?" Randall asked curiously.

"Din't, others were too far, jus' a lil bitta luck." She shrugged.

Well, that was either the understatement of the year, or she had just beaten and tied-up an innocent man. I hoped it was the former, although I had a sneaky suspicion that Taria wouldn't lose any sleep either way.

Leaning over, I pulled the gag from the guy's mouth.

"You will all suffer, the Lord cleanses all through his divine ministrations," he shrieked

Great, another whack-job! Although at least it proved that Taria had nailed it.

"Who is this Lord?" I asked, by now genuinely curious.

"We do not speak his name," he said seriously, "but his great work is for all. Through our suffering we are purified, in our pain we are uplifted," he intoned with religious fervour.

240

"Is this Lord anything like the monstrosity Herman turned into?" I questioned.

"Monstrosity! You dare blaspheme against mankind's true face given form?" he ranted, "Our Lord has a special place for people like you." He tried to spit at me, and I was forced to quickly side-step to avoid it. What a fucking charmer!

Walking over to Shay'Ilvia, I leant down to whisper into her ear. "What is the name of the Blood Whisperer Sect leader?"

"Reynard, Reynard Olisias," she whispered back.

Fuck me, an Olisias! I tensed up, wondering what Hannah knew about all this? Oh well, there was nothing I could do to change it.

"Are you okay?" Shay'Ilvia asked quietly, noticing my reaction.

"Yeah, I'm fine, just I have a friend who's an Olisias," I replied, feeling no need to hide it.

I turned back to the glaring captive. "I will have to go and speak to Reynard directly then."

"Who?" he asked feigning confusion; he wasn't a very good actor.

"It's fine, I'm sure Hannah would introduce me."

"The prophet's sister?" he asked.

Clearly, he wasn't the sharpest tool in the shed, but even so, when I smiled at him, he was at least smart enough to realise he'd fucked up.

"The Prophet? Sounds important." I started to laugh, joined shortly after by everyone else.

The laughter infuriated the man, and he immediately began to rant again, it was all the same stuff as before and so I just ignored him.

"I can't believe that actually worked." I chuckled.

"Actually, it's probably not as unlikely as you would think, they seem like a cult of some kind and the intellectually challenged make easy targets for conversion," Shay'Ilvia said, sounding sad that the less fortunate would be preyed on in such a way.

She was right, but it would be foolish to hope that all of them would be so stupid. The desperate and disenfranchised are just as vulnerable to predation from groups like that, and unfortunately, a place like Antanel would leave people like that everywhere. Plus, with the sorts of beliefs these people seemed to hold and their reverence for the demonic, they would also have a seductive draw towards budding psychopaths or even just plain horrible cunts, who were keen to explore a more vicious and less-travelled route to power.

"I need to speak to Hannah, find out if she knows what her brother is doing," I said.

"And if she does?" Dragmar asked.

"I will do what I have to. It could be her brother is flying solo, or, worse-case scenario, her whole clan is involved. But until I speak to her, there's no point speculating."

"That ain't da worsed case scenario," Taria said. We all looked at her questioningly. "Well, maybe loadsa nobles are involved, or…the Imperial family." She grinned.

Her suggestion was sobering, and I only hoped she was well off-base, or the empire was well and truly fucked.

"We need to report the quest as completed to the Guild as well, we don't get paid otherwise." Dragmar said.

"But it's not complete," I argued.

"Yes, it is. Madam Wang was taking the kids, who is now dead. The conspiracy it has led us to is a whole new quest and needs to be discussed with the guild. They will re-evaluate the situation and may issue out a new one, or they may keep it off the books. We shall see upon our return," Shay'Ilvia advised.

It made a certain sense, if the parameters of a quest changed too much, its grade as well as reward would need to be changed.

242

"Okay, we'll need to take that back with us." I gestured to Herman's corpse, which had not been moved from where he fell. "Maybe someone at the guild will be able to help identify what exactly he became."

Chapter 31

Dez inspected Herman's corpse, his lips curled in distaste at the abomination. Valerie looked at him questioningly. "I'm right, aren't I?"

"Hmm, most likely," he said, and taking a pouch from his pocket, removed a small dried yellow flower which he proceeded to crumble onto Herman's arm. Wherever the flower dust fell, small sparks of black energy began to jump from the corpse and the arm began to revert to its original form.

"Yes, as I feared. You are right Val, it's demonic corruption. Someone has figured out a way to quickly turn people into pseudo-demons, though the transformation would not have been permanent. This man would have likely returned to normal within several days, and the reversal would have been fatal."

Thank fuck! With just a few days, a creature of that level would be able to cause untold destruction, but it was still better than having them around permanently. From the relieved look on Valerie's face, she was likely having similar thoughts.

"So that thing was actually a Demon?" I asked.

"It is, but only superficially, and it's worrying, as it suggests that true demons or demonic cultivators are behind this."

"What's the difference between a demonic and regular cultivator?" I asked, a little puzzled.

"A demonic cultivator uses Yin aspect aether to cultivate," Dez replied.

This confused me a little, as from what I understood of Yin Yang theory, many aspects would be classified as Yin; the Moon, darkness, and the cold to name but a few, but they were used quite freely. My own cultivation method even required a balance of both Yin and Yang.

"But so do many cultivators," I said curiously.

"Indeed, but what sets the demonic cultivator apart is their use of abhorrent methods to acquire aether. Rape, torture, basically any activities that when repeated over time create a Yin environment are used, with no compunction whatsoever. More to the point, they actually enjoy these practices, revel in them, rather than just use them out of necessity. Just like actual Demons."

"I get that some people are twisted, but there must be some benefit to it?"

"It is a fast route to power; unlimited, aspected aether is an alluring temptation."

He wasn't wrong, I was blasting through spirit stones to raise my cultivation, and even though I needed much more than the average cultivator, others wouldn't have my wealth, largely relying on pills, herbs, and the very environment for assistance. Enlightenment aside, which would only be required for the higher stages, progression would be a slow process without resources.

Master Bronstad was a prime example, he is not devoid of talent, but as he has explained to me, progress apparently became much harder the older you grow. Had he access to unlimited aether in his youth, it is likely he would have reached Spirit Knight whilst still young and continued to grow beyond. Instead, he is stuck struggling to form his Core due to his advanced age. So, an alternative source of aether would be attractive to many, regardless of any moral implications.

"Well, what are we going to do about it?" I asked, eager to put a stop to such abhorrent practices.

"I will be issuing a large-scale quest. To investigate the source of Demonic corruption into the Empire and purge it, as the Blood Whisperer Sect is too big for a single party to confront."

"Would the element of surprise not be better?" I asked.

Valerie shook her head with a serious expression. "Surprise will not suffice if the sect fully mobilises, we will also need numbers."

I nodded, seeing the logic of her decision. It looked like it was going to be a major operation. "Do you have any more of those flowers, Uncle Dez? They may come in handy."

"I do, but I am afraid they will be of no use against a living version."

"Oh well, guess we'll have to do it the hard way then." I chuckled mirthlessly.

*****

Tracking down Hannah didn't take too long; she was enjoying her leave whilst sat outside of her favourite café. Her face lit up as I approached, and I dreaded to see how that would change from my news. I took a seat opposite her, and she wasted no time in quizzing me about my adventures, her face running through the full gamut of emotions as I explained what had transpired in Berevar, finally stopping on shock when I revealed what we had discovered about her brother's sect.

"Talk to me Hannah," I gently prompted.

"What do you want me to say? That you're right, my clan is a bunch of monsters preying on the innocent?" she asked indignantly.

"I don't know, I just thought you might know more, especially about Reynard, he is your brother."

"Hmmph," she huffed and went quiet. I didn't want to upset her further, so I gave her time to process, taking the fact she hadn't simply stormed off as a good sign.

"I haven't spoken to him in nearly six years," she eventually said with a sigh.

I was familiar with family drama, but that seemed a little excessive. "Why not?" I asked.

"When I was little, I looked up to Reynard, he was much older and always kind to me. Often making time to play, offering words of encouragement, or sneaking me a sweet treat," she said, smiling at the obviously fond memories.

"He sounds like a good big brother," I offered quietly.

"He was."

"What happened?" I asked, my curiosity well and truly stoked.

Hannah held up her clan insignia for me to look at, it was a heraldic bird of prey of some sort gripping a spear in its talons. "Each clan has a class which has come to represent the very identity of the clan. For the Olisias it's the Winged Knight class, which has strict requirements on a person's physical aptitude."

"And you met the requirement?" I asked, guessing where this was headed.

Hannah sighed and nodded sadly. "First person since the current patriarch, everyone was so excited, but my brother, he got so angry. I thought he'd be happy for me, but instead when I told him, he became spiteful.

"He failed where you succeeded?" I hazarded a guess.

Hannah nodded. "I knew he hadn't met the requirements, but I didn't think he'd be envious, not towards me, I was his baby sister!"

"What class is your brother?"

"I don't know, after failing the requirement for Winged Knight, he forsook the other class stones offered by the clan, instead electing to search for a system on his own. But you already suspected that didn't you?"

"Yeah," I admitted, it was most likely he was practicing some foul method provided by his patron. "I know it's not easy to hear Hannah, but I reckon your brother wanted you to join him, that's probably at least part of why he was so pissed off when you took your class."

Hannah visibly paled at the thought, which seemed like a good sign. "I would never, it's…evil!"

I believed her, so it was probably lucky she became a Winged Knight, if he had confronted her with his plans, her refusal to go along with them probably wouldn't have ended well.

"I hate to ask this, as I know it puts you in a horrid position, but are there others in your clan to whom your brother is close?"

"My Gods!" she exclaimed, clearly realising something.

"What?"

"My uncle Trantell, the patriarch's youngest son. I always saw him with Reynard, and I never thought anything of it."

"So, he could be involved?" I asked.

"Yes, but more than that, he is Vorexia's husband, Aveena's father."

"So, maybe you were ushered away from the clan at your brother's request?"

"Hmm, I guess it's possible," she said, not looking particularly convinced. "I should return home and speak to the patriarch; he needs to be informed about Reynard."

We agreed to meet back at the Adventurers' Guild once my quest was complete, I had promised I wouldn't leave without her, and I intended to honour it. I just hoped that she wouldn't have any issues back at her clan, as who knew how many others were involved? As I watched her go, I prayed that not accompanying her was the correct decision, but I had a different task to complete. Besides, she was a strong warrior in her own right, and I had faith in her abilities.

Outside the adventurers' guild, the Gilded Tarrions were encamped within a large group, easily two-hundred adventurers strong, Dez and Valerie amongst them. The thought of marching to battle as part of such a large party was exciting, but I worried about how I would fit into the plan, as I had no idea about large group tactics. Hopefully they'd be happy for me to just get stuck in.

"Nice of you to finally make an appearance," Dragmar said, in a blatant attempt to defuse some of the nervous tension in the air.

"Ha." I chuckled. "And I wish I was bringing better news, but it's likely that more than just Reynard is involved from the Olisias clan."

"Well, we best make a move then, before they can mobilise extra support for the sect." Dez counselled.

"BREAK CAMP! WE LEAVE IN FIVE," Valerie bellowed.

"Jesus, Valerie! You scared the shit out of me!" I said, my heart pounding from her sudden shout.

The camp instantly became a hive of activity, with each party quickly disassembling their camps. It was impressive to watch, as there hadn't been a single grumble of discontentment, just a flurry of well-practiced actions. It was reassuring, these people knew their business.

"What is Jesus?" Dragmar suddenly asked whilst stowing away some kit, the others turned to look at me, equally curious about my answer.

I had to stop myself at laughing at his serious tone. "Err...The son of God, crucified so our sins would be forgiven, spread a message of love and forgiveness."

"Which God?" Landioss asked, fuck my life, this was harder than I thought it would be.

"The unseen creator, omnipresent, omniscient, omnipotent, some refer to him Jehovah, others as Yahweh, Adonai, Allah, Jah and many others, including just simply God," I said attempting to answer as best I could.

"Never heard of him," Dragmar said.

I chuckled at his deadpan response. "I think maybe Yahweh is as much a concept as an actual being," I offered, hoping to nip the conversation in the bud, as I was woefully ill-prepared to explain Earth's Abrahamic religions to people from a world where Gods make actual appearances. Luckily, they all seemed satisfied with my comment, as after a few considering nods they carried on with whatever they were doing previously, whilst I made a mental note to avoid the subject wherever possible in the future.

The camp was fully packed in well under the five minutes given by Valerie, with each party neatly assembled and awaiting further instructions.

"Now what?" I asked.

"Should be here any minute," Valerie replied, whilst gazing in the direction of the Guild building.

The sails appeared first, shimmering as it rose over the roof of the Guildhall. It was an almighty airship, one of the huge ship-of-the-line kind, its figurehead the adventurers' guild crest.

"So that's the guild ship then?" I asked, thoroughly impressed.

Valerie nodded. "The Intrepid, one of the finest ships in Antanel," she said, positively beaming.

"For some reason, I thought we'd take a regular ship across the sea," I said.

Everyone looked at me in confusion.

"And spend the whole time fighting off sea serpents?" Dez asked. "We'd be down at least half our party before we even arrived. Only the foolhardy or desperate would risk travelling out onto the deep water."

I had seen mention of serpents on my map, I just hadn't realised it was so bad. "So, no-one sails regular ships anymore?" I asked.

"No lad, of course they do, just not across the Antaris strait, the volcanic vents on the seafloor create ideal conditions for the serpents to breed," Dragmar said, "No other place in the world holds the foul wyrms in such numbers."

Just a few winged serpents had nearly ended my trip to Berevar in disaster, so if there were hordes of their aquatic brethren waiting for us in the water, travelling in the sky suddenly seemed like a splendid idea.

"Gone a little pale there, son," Dragmar commented, and I briefly explained my previous encounter.

"Ha, yep, that'll do it, voracious bastards the lot of 'em," Dragmar said, eliciting nods and chuckles from everyone.

Chapter 32

She may have been the size of a blue whale, but the Intrepid cut through the sky like an eagle. With only an hour or so until sunset the view from onboard was a riot of pinks and purples. The orange moon, which I had learnt was named Luvari, already hanging high in the sky awaiting the appearance of its larger sibling Luvaro, it was beautiful. According to Hannah, there is also a wandering third moon - Luvar, but it only makes an appearance once every few years, and its infrequent appearance is usually celebrated with a huge party. I couldn't understand how such a weird orbit was even possible, so I just chalked it up to more magical fuckery, either that or Hannah was pulling my leg!

The journey was blissfully uneventful, and I spent my time enjoying the view and quietly cultivating on the deck. Cultivating occupied much of my free time now and if it wasn't for how calming the process was, I don't think I would have been so disciplined, regardless of its benefits. I could feel the quantity of my Qi teetering on the threshold of another level, and so, quickly drawing as much as I could from a fresh spirit stone, I forced my way into the third level of Qi condensation, my meridians baptised once again in the flood of the greater quantity of liquid-like Qi; stretching and widening them. As the euphoria from the breakthrough passed and I allowed my Qi to settle back into my Dantian, I couldn't help but wince at the amount of empty space once again present due to its latest expansion. But I wasn't disheartened, as I knew I was making rapid progress, my cultivation completely at odds with Master's experiences and his description of hard-to-overcome bottlenecks. I had barely felt any resistance as I progressed, and I briefly wondered whether I would.

I also took time to reflect on what I'd come to realise in my time in Antaris; far more was at play when determining combat ability than a person's cultivation level or stage as a mage. I could fight above my level and so could Herman after he transformed, so it was fair to assume others could too. The Adventurers Guild assessment was a better indicator of ability but even then, it was only of limited use, as a fireball from a C-rank sorcerer may be less powerful than one from an A-rank, but it could still ruin my day. And in all honesty, if the Guild test dolls had been able to fling spells about, I may have not even achieved S-Rank, as being a melee, the test largely played to my strengths. It was a sobering thought. Plus, it wasn't like everyone was a member of the guild and wore a badge handily announcing their rank anyway.

When we arrived over the aptly named Isle of Ash, vast plumes of volcanic smoke could be seen in the distance being continually belched into the atmosphere by Ban'vel; the island's largest volcano. The Blood Whisperer Sect was apparently nestled within the basalt fields at its base, which seemed like a stupid place to put a sect to me, as the constant deluge of ash and rocks from the volcano probably made for a Hellish environment. I definitely wouldn't want to live there, but I guess it did seem fitting for a Demonic sect, although maybe I had that backwards, as surely a Yin environment should be cold? Fuck knows.

Wyrmvale, our destination, soon became visible, it was the largest settlement and only city on the island. Largely constructed from local stones of ominous dark greys and blacks, its jagged spires of volcanic glass stood out in stark contrast as they occasionally sparkled in the mid-day sun. I had no doubt that it was inhabited by normal everyday people, just trying to muddle on like every other city, but it definitely looked like it had been ripped from a gothic horror novel. As we descended to the airdock I wondered if Ban'vel would leave the city perpetually choked on layers of dust; I had no desire to be covered in the stuff. Not to mention that breathing that shit surely couldn't be good for the lungs, volcanic dust is nasty.

I needn't have worried, when we got to about a hundred metres above the city, we passed through some sort of magical field that surrounded it, which I guessed was to keep the ash away. My skin tingled as we passed through the barrier, it wasn't unpleasant, but was deathly cold and made my hairs stand on end. The barrier was amazing, and I wondered why it wasn't covered in ash, although rendering the city into complete darkness as the Ash accumulated wouldn't have been ideal.

"A marvel of magical engineering," Dez said.

"How is it not covered in Ash?" I asked, hoping to get an answer.

Dez pointed to the perimeter of the city, where piles of Ash were being loaded onto huge wagons and driven off into the distance. "The barrier is pyramidal and cools anything which it encounters. The quickly cooled ash slides down the frictionless barrier, where it is collected and carted away."

"Amazing!" I said, astounded at their ingenuity. "But it can't be a pleasant job, being responsible for gathering and transporting the Ash."

Dez's face darkened a little. "No, it's not. The majority of people tasked with it are criminals. There are few worse punishments in the whole of Antanel, than being sent to work the ash pits of Wyrmvale."

It was sad to see such a magical marvel tarnished in such a manner. "Surely there was a magical solution to the accumulated Ash too?" I questioned.

Dez nodded. "Of course, it is by design. Conveniently serving to provide employment for the lowest social strata of the city, whilst also giving a convenient place of exile for anyone the nobles want out of sight."

It made a perverted kind of sense, but also essentially turned the city into a penal colony of sorts. "Why build a city at all then? They may as well have put a prison here," I asked.

"Wealth." Dez smiled mirthlessly. "There are Beasts to fight here that you'll find nowhere else in the Empire. And it's also rich in fire aspected aether, which means it's quite popular amongst fire cultivators and mages. But they aren't the main reasons." he grinned at me knowingly.

"Don't leave me hanging," I said impatiently.

"Spirit...stone...mines!" he said, deliberately pausing after each word for emphasis. No doubt he had seen me burning through them in my cultivation and knew I'd be interested.

He was right, it was abundantly clear to me that I could never have too many. "Spirit stone mines, here?"

Dez nodded. "A major leyline runs through the island. So, the mines are hugely productive and one of the largest sources of Antanels wealth."

"How can I get some?" I asked eagerly.

"The same way one would procure any item of value, buy or trade for them."

He left out stealing them. Though whether that was purposeful or not, I had no idea, either way I was thoroughly unimpressed by the Antanel empire. It was rife with corruption and the rich-poor divide easily matched the worst of countries back home. So, I decided that after I completed this quest, I was going to liberate some spirit stones straight from the noble's pockets and fuck the lot of them! The thought of some greedy little noble panicking over his lost spirit stones made me smile.

"You're planning something stupid, aren't you?" Dez asked, my silent grin no doubt betraying my thoughts about the potential criminal endeavour.

"Ermm...of course not, I'm not that dense," I lied.

Dez looked at me skeptically. "The last person to steal some, they left screaming on a post at the city gate. After they tortured and flayed her," he said, the warning in his tone obvious.

The awakened can be capable of surviving injuries that would quickly kill a mundane and I shuddered at the thought of how long it may have taken her to die.

"Eleven days she screamed and whimpered at that gate," Dez continued, almost as if reading my mind. "They administered potions to keep her from dying, just the right amount to extend her suffering without fully healing her."

The medieval brutality was sobering, even for this fucked up world. "That's one hell of a deterrent," I admitted, it was and had even given me pause. For a second. I still reckoned it was worth the risk if I could get enough spirit stones, but I would have to guarantee a metric fuck-tonne to make it worthwhile.

I could tell Dez still wasn't convinced I wouldn't try something, but he just shook his head. "To be young and foolhardy, just don't drag us into anything."

"Don't worry, the mission comes first," I said.

"That's all I ask." He smiled.

As the Intrepid came to rest in its mooring, Valerie came walking over. "What are you two conspiring about?" She joked.

"Just how many spirit stones I can manage to rob from whatever nobles are in charge of the mines," I retorted cheekily.

She looked at me and then Dez, who simply shrugged resignedly in response. "I'll pretend I never asked," she said, "but remember it's a joint venture, and although every major clan has a finger in it, it's ultimately the Antanel's pie, and that's a lot of very powerful people to piss off," she warned.

I hadn't known either of them for long, so their concern for me was heart-warming, even if I was a little surprised about their lack of resistance to the idea of theft in general. But I guessed seasoned adventurers are used to operating in morally grey areas, plus they knew even better than me how cruel nobles could be, so it made sense they wouldn't shed a tear about them being robbed. I was sure that if I'd mentioned a plan to steal from the poor and needy, then it would have been a completely different conversation. Not that I ever would, I may be…morally flexible, but I'm not a complete arsehole.

Our whole group quickly assembled on the streets of Wyrmvale, receiving cautious stares from any of the locals who passed. Which was understandable, as although they were used to seeing parties of adventurers, they were likely never in such large numbers. The locals, Wyrmvalians? Were a hard, dour looking people with barely a smile in sight and even the few children that passed were subdued in their behaviour, no doubt a consequence of living and working in such a grim place. The sheer depression that could be seen everywhere was awful and before I realised what I was doing I found myself in front of one of the passing children, she must have only been around eight or nine and her hollow little eyes were completely devoid of joy. I removed a bag of candy from my guild ring and her eyes finally showed some emotion, her wonder plain at something appearing in my hand as if from thin air. I attempted to pass her the bag, but she instantly recoiled, making herself as small as possible.

"It's ok little one, it's just candy," I said and popped one into my mouth. "Take them." I offered the bag again.

The girl eyed me warily. "I ain't givin' it away for a bag o' sweets, Ma says me maidenhood is worth sum'ink."

What the fuck was wrong with this place? No small child should think like that, is that what these people were reduced to? It may be because I was an orphan, but I struggle when I see young kids suffering, it wasn't right, someone should be shielding them from the filth of the world. It was heart-breaking and made me so very fucking angry.

I struggled to not let any hint of the anger I was feeling show, as I didn't want to upset her, she wasn't the target of my anger. "It's ok, I don't want anything, we are leaving now, I just thought some candy might cheer you up, as you seemed a little sad."

She reached out and gingerly took the bag from me, clutching it protectively to her chest. "Ev'ryones always sad 'ere. Thankya mister." She smiled forlornly and scurried off down the street.

Taking my place back amongst the Gilded Tarrions, no one said a thing to me as we made our way out of the city, my actions having caused an awkward silence. It wasn't until the city was well behind us that Shay'Ilvia walked up beside me.

"That was a kind thing you did back there." She smiled.

I snorted. "Maybe, but it doesn't change anything, that place is awful."

"Don't underestimate the little things, today you reminded that girl that not everyone is a monster, and brightened her life, if only for a moment."

"I just wish I could do more, make things better for them."

"How old are you, Josh?" she asked

"Nineteen," I replied absent-mindedly.

She gasped and covered her mouth in shock. "You're still a babe!"

I chuckled at her words, but she placed a comforting hand upon my shoulder. "Oh child, this world is not perfect, but take it from me, Josh, there is far more good than you know. I have seen much of it in my centuries of wandering."

She was right, everywhere had shitty places and I couldn't let one bring me down. Do what I can, help whom I can, that's what I could do. "Thanks, Shay'Ilvia," I said, and I meant it.

Chapter 33

At the pace we travelled, the journey to the Blood Whisperer Sect had only taken a day, and most of the creatures had been smart enough to leave such a large party well alone. The main hindrance was the Ash constantly bearing down on us, as with a potential battle at the end of the journey, no one had wanted to spare the aether to shield us. So instead, we raised our hoods and tied scarves around our faces to minimise how much we breathed in. When I asked why we hadn't just taken the Intrepid directly to the sect, Dez happily informed me they didn't want it to get unnecessarily damaged. Personally, I would have taken a bit of damage to the airship over trudging through a giant smoking fucking ashtray, but then I didn't have to pay for its repairs.

Several miles from the Sect, the temperature began to steadily drop for no discernible reason. Being so close to active volcanoes, often with lava oozing down from their peaks, the chill felt alarmingly discordant. By the time we actually stood beneath the walls of the Sect, it was cold enough that condensation from our breath had begun to freeze upon our scarves and any exposed metal was left painfully cold to the touch.

The Sect itself was quite small, resembling a motte and bailey castle more than the walled town I was expecting, although admittedly my perspective may have been slightly skewed from staying at Stormhaven with its inhuman scale. It shared the same Gothic aesthetic as Wyrmvale, only far more sinister. Braziers of spectral green flames stood aside the gatehouse, the same bilious colour faintly illuminating the windows of the keep as it towered above the palisade walls. Great obsidian gargoyles perched atop the crenelations, gazing menacingly down upon anyone who approached, and with the lifelike savagery contained in their faces, I couldn't help but worry they would burst to life and sweep down upon us.

The keep itself would have been hauntingly beautiful, if not for the dozens of mutilated people, writhing in pain whilst impaled upon stone thorns along its sides.

"Fuck me! if that doesn't scream evil lair, then I'm a bloody giant," Dragmar said, his perfectly timed joke serving to alleviate some of the growing tension amongst the group.

Some, but not all, as along the assembled line, I could see hands hovering over hilts and helms being donned, whilst others instead clutched symbols of faith, offering quiet words of prayer to whatever gods they venerated.

"What now? Do we just knock?" I smiled wrily, gesturing at the gates.

As if in response to my question, booming sounds emanated from the gatehouse, and accompanied by the clanging of heavy chains, the great doors of the Sect slowly began to shudder open.

"In your parties, shield-warriors to the front," Valerie commanded.

The group instantly responded in a flurry of well-practised motions, heavily armoured members drew their weapons and moved to the front, archers, sorcerers, and healers quickly forming up behind them whilst readying spells and incantations. I guess that was one benefit of classes, everyone knew their roles. Definitely food for thought!

With a small shudder the gates finally opened, allowing a small party of twenty or so black-robed figures to exit. They were led by a regal looking man, who in his blood-red cape and ornate black armour resembled a romanticised medieval vampire, and as much as it pains me to admit, looked pretty fucking badass, especially with the scary looking polearm he was using like a walking staff. From the family resemblance, it was clear he was the sect-leader, Hannah's brother Reynard. A single wordless gesture from him and their small party came to a stop around twenty metres from us.

"To what do we owe the pleasure of a visit from the Adventurers' Guild?" he said, smiling charmingly. "And led by the Stormhaven branch leaders no less, you honour us." He bowed towards Valerie and Dez.

"There's no need to play coy, Reynard, the debacle in Berevar has led us to your door, as well you know it," Valerie retorted.

"Ah, but without manners, we are no better than beasts are we not," he said, whilst pointedly looking at me.

"Are Demons not beasts?" I chuckled.

A brief twitch of his eyelid was the only sign that my words bothered him, quickly gone with the return of the same easy smile.

"I would have thought a descendant of the great Baihu would have been more sympathetic towards a Demons more…feral urges, you are after all a fellow predator, are you not outworlder?"

I would have liked to say his words didn't bother me, but no one in this world should have known about my heritage, as I had never mentioned it to anyone, even Hannah. From the beaming smile he gave me, he had easily noticed my shock. Reynard was dangerous, exceedingly so.

"And how did you come by that information?" I asked.

"My Lord knows many things, though even he is curious about the other bloodline flowing through you. So, he offers you a single chance Joshua, walk away, return to your world and leave this one to him. You cannot hope to stand against his power."

It seemed a fair deal, but that's why I could tell there was more to it, so I decided to take a gamble "No, he's not curious, it makes him nervous." I guessed.

261

Reynard's face twisted with rage. "You dare to presume our Lord is scared of the likes of you?" he snarled, all traces of his earlier feigned pleasantness gone.

His anger was all the confirmation I needed. "No, not me." I smiled as I drew my sword. "But I'd wager that my dear old dad would make him piss his demonic pants. And besides, your Lord isn't here. I only have you to deal with."

"Hahahaha," he cackled wildly. "So be it, let us see the capability of one of their whelps."

The robed figures behind him instantly attempted to put something from their robes into their mouths, no doubt the same thing Herman had used. Luckily, our group had been fully briefed beforehand about the substance and two quickly fell to Taria and another assassin, who, appearing behind them, slit their throats before they ever had a chance to take the pills. Another seven fell to a mass of spells and arrows, which still left eleven, but it was a damn sight better than dealing with twenty of the abominations.

"I've got Reynard!" I announced and sped towards him utilising wind-steps.

He raised his glaive to meet my charge and I could instantly tell from his aura that he was above Master in his cultivation, so definitely a Sage. Luckily, his aura was slightly unstable, so it was likely he had only recently risen, which was probably why he hadn't used the transformation; he was strong enough to not need it, especially with its fatal side-effect.

His Qi techniques were savage in their ferocity, his glaive sending out crescents of ruby energy in a berserker rage that it took all of my strength to deflect. And he wasn't a mindless beast either, rather a highly skilled warrior efficiently channelling his rage to augment his own considerable skills. If it wasn't for my ability to use sword intent, the fight would have been over as quickly as it started, with me hopelessly cut down beneath his vastly more powerful Qi techniques. We danced around, a blur of energies and clashing steel, but it was always me on the back foot, barely managing to match his greater power through my finesse with a sword.

Luckily, I wasn't fighting alone, and waves of support spells impacted me, enhancing my speed and strength to ever higher levels. The buffs allowed me to finally match him in power, enabling me to use my greater weapon skills to leverage the advantage. Reynard roared his displeasure, which must have been a Qi technique of some kind, as although I steeled my aura in defence, it still launched me away from him.

Jumping to my feet, I could feel a small trickle of blood from my ears as Reynard casually strolled towards me, twirling his glaive.

"You are stronger than someone of your cultivation has any right to be boy," he said, "but it won't be enough."

One moment he was casually strolling towards me, the next I felt a sharp pressure and explosion of pain, as he was suddenly in front of me, the point of his glaive embedded in my abdomen. He snarled in frustration over his failing attempts to push the weapon deeper, but luckily my armour was showing its colours, resisting the penetration. Lifting my leg, I kicked off him, wrenching myself from his weapon as a timely healing spell washed over me and began to restore the damage he had done. Fuck yeah, having a healer around was awesome! He turned in the direction of the spell caster and I feared he was going to target them, but he didn't have a chance, as a bombardment of offensive spells landed on him in a coordinated attack. I looked over to see Valerie and Dez orchestrating a group of sorcerers in their concerted efforts, and as wave after wave of lightning and incandescent firebolts consumed Reynard's figure, I watched in grizzly fascination as the man fell, smoking, to his knees. For a single fleeting moment, I dared to think that we had won, until the brief illusion was shattered by a rough wheezing chuckle. Climbing back to his feet, Reynard was a mess of blistered and charred skin, but the fact he was still alive troubled me, what would it take to put the fucker down?

That worry quickly turned to dread as his body began to bubble and distend, slowly growing in size as his injured flesh sloughed away; to reveal pristine crimson skin beneath. Fuck my life! ram-like horns erupted from his temples, and I knew I couldn't give him a chance to complete his transformation. I flew at him as fast as I possibly could, attempting to strike him down whilst he was still recovering, but my efforts were in vain. A casual backhand hit me at such speed that I failed to defend myself, the sheer force of it leaving me sprawled out, dazed and barely conscious.

He would have likely finished the job too if he wasn't immediately distracted by another cascade of spells. It's amazing how useless a concussion can render you and I barely managed to fumble the stopper from a healing potion. As I poured its contents into my mouth, my head cleared almost instantly and as my jaw popped unpleasantly back into place, I briefly hoped that regrowing my teeth would be as easy as healing flesh.

I picked up my sword and as soon as there was a pause in the barrage of spells, I launched into a series of strikes at him, his injured state finally allowing me to land some serious hits. Enormous gashes bled freely, even as his previous injuries began to heal, but strikes that would have easily bisected a normal man left only rents in his toughened demonic flesh. Eventually, his monstrous recovery enabled him to start using his glaive again and we were once again locked into a dance of death, only his bleeding wounds slowing him enough for me to keep up. Wounds that I was now struggling to add to, which were also closing at a speed visible to the naked eye.

"Just keep him busy for thirty seconds Josh!" I heard Valerie shout.

Now thirty seconds might not seem a lot, but I can assure you, when you are locked in mortal combat against a stronger opponent, thirty seconds feels like a fucking lifetime!

As wound after wound slowly stopped leaking his precious lifeblood, Reynard was getting stronger and faster, catching me with cuts and glancing slices as quickly as our healers could close them. The constant cycle of wounds opening, and closing was leaving me ever more fatigued and almost inevitably, I began slowing as he sped up. When I finally heard Dez shout, "Now, Josh, get away!" I was hanging on through sheer willpower alone, with barely enough energy to fling myself away from him.

The only thing that saved me from being caught was the timely appearance of a runic circle beneath his feet, which instantly arrested his movement. I'd like to say that I retreated valorously from my enemy, but there was no sight of a warrior's bearing in my desperate scramble, on my back, like a wounded fucking crab! When I finally felt like I'd moved a safe distance, I collapsed, completely spent and thankful for the chill in the air that was cooling me as I lay heaving for breath. Slowly hauling myself back to my feet, I watched in rapt fascination as further circles and symbols appeared, entrapping Reynard from both above and below.

As Reynard raged impotently against the arcane forces holding him in place, the circles all began to slowly rotate in alternating directions, exerting ever-increasing restrictions on him. And eventually he was unable to move whatsoever.

"You will pay f—" he started to say, before even his ability to speak was robbed from him.

I found myself wondering what the goal of the spell was, until I noticed movement starting in the sky above. Great storm clouds formed, swirling along with the rotation of the largest runic circle. Tremendous clashes of thunder sounded, accompanied by great flashes of lightning in hues of blues, purples and white. The sheer power being harnessed was dreadful and filled me with awe.

As the storm grew in intensity, I finally took a moment to assess the rest of the battlefield and it was a scene of pure carnage. The Demons had all been brought down by the adventurers, but at far too steep a price. Numerous bodies of adventurers lay around the Demons' corpses, the disproportionate number of living sorcerers and healers a grim testament to the heroic sacrifices made by the many warriors, who acted as their shields. Sadly, I noticed the mutilated bodies of Dragmar and Taria amongst the dead, but whilst Reynard still breathed, there was no time to mourn.

The spell in the sky was building to a crescendo and as it accumulated its heavenly force, my hair began to rise in the swiftly ionising air. There was a brief moment of silence, and then a single lightning bolt descended so fast that, beyond the flash, the only evidence of it happening was the eardrum shaking thunder that trailed in its wake. I don't think I will ever forget the sheer power promised by that crackling roar, nor Reynard's screams as he became its target. The air felt like it was buzzing, and the bolts kept falling in a harsh staccato rhythm, leaving afterimages on my retina of arcs the width of buckets, and I was forced to avert my gaze in order to save my sight. My ears rang as Reynard's screams turned to whimpers, and his whimpers eventually to silence.

When the bolts finally stopped falling, the sudden calm was almost disorienting, but I didn't hesitate and launched myself at him, my sword flashing out at his unguarded neck. I needn't have bothered, the moment my sword made contact, his blackened corpse disintegrated into nothing more than motes of ash, carried away by the cold wind and its faint ozone scent. Clearly, he was already long dead, which was unsurprising after he'd been repeatedly used as a lightning rod, but I had been unwilling to take any chances, as us cultivators are a resilient bunch and those demonic bastards especially so.

The crunch of approaching footsteps made me turn around, Valerie and Dez looked rough, with remnant trails of dried blood from their noses, eyes, and ears.

"Are you okay?" I asked concernedly.

"We'll live." Dez replied wearily. "The strain of that spell was a lot to bear, even shared between us all. Most were not so lucky."

I looked over to the circle of mages who had produced the spell. Numerous healers worked frantically to save a few of them, but the majority remained untouched where they sat. Their eternal rest the sad result of working a grand invocation that was simply too much for them.

"They knew what would happen, yet they did it anyway with no hesitation. True adventurers!" Valerie quietly began to weep.

Tears fell freely from Dez's eyes too and he placed a comforting arm around her. I left them to their grief and made my way around the battlefield, providing aid wherever I could. Eventually, I ran out of potions and was relegated to providing basic first aid, oftentimes this was enough to keep people alive until healers could complete the job, sometimes sadly not. When we had finally finished with our ministrations, less than sixty of us remained of the over two-hundred adventurers who had set out, it was a pyrrhic victory at best.

I made time to give my condolences to Shay'Ilvia and Landios, but it felt like a hollow gesture to people in the depth of grief. They had been a party for many years, working their way up through the guild ranks together, whereas I was a relative stranger. I was unsure if the Gilded Tarrions would look for new members and continue, but I hoped they would at least find a modicum of peace in whatever they decided.

Gazing towards the open gates of The Blood Whisperer Sect, I drew my sword and made my way towards them. I wasn't going to ask anyone to come with me, they had already sacrificed enough. However, it turned out I didn't have to. The sound of feet jogging up behind me let me know that I wouldn't be going in alone. Turning around I saw Valerie and Dez, Shay'Ilvia and Landios, and behind them I saw even more rising to their feet and making their way over, until only the most injured remained behind with several guards and healers to keep them safe.

"Don't look so surprised, young Joshua, we're the adventurers' guild and we still have a job to do," Dez said.

Looking around at the gathered faces I could see grief and tiredness in equal measure, but tempered by a fierce resoluteness, to do what needed to be done, to see things through. This was the real adventurers' guild, and I was filled with an overwhelming sense of pride to belong to it. No words were needed, a single swordsman's salute and I turned and led our party into the waiting doors of the sect.

Chapter 34

None of us knew what awaited us inside the sect and so we approached in formations, fully ready should combat break out again. It was likely there were more disciples, as a sect would surely have more than the twenty Reynard had brought out to confront us. Most likely he only brought out the more powerful elders to drive us off, but not knowing what awaited us left a palpable tension in the group as we passed through the gates. Oh well, into the belly of the beast!

Compared to what we feared, what actually greeted us in the courtyard was rather anti-climactic. Around one-hundred disciples were on their knees in neat lines, I didn't sense any threat from them, but then again, I didn't from Herman until he transformed, so I didn't drop my guard for a second, fearing some kind of ruse. A pair of older men waited at the front of the disciples and slowly approached us as we entered, empty hands held out to their sides.

"I am the sole elder remaining in the sect, please don't hurt the disciples, we offer our unconditional surrender," said the elder of the two.

The other was acting aloof from the whole debacle, but a barely contained anger was clearly visible on his face. He was also not wearing sect robes either, instead attired like a noble.

"And you are?" I asked him.

"Trantell Olisias," he practically spat, "I was here to visit my nephew Reynard, the man who you murdered outside."

269

Well fuck, this was going to be awkward. Luckily, Valerie stepped forward, which was probably a good thing, as my tolerance for bullshit had hit a record low.

"Reynard Olisias was executed for his crimes against the peoples of this realm," she said, obviously not bothered about being diplomatic.

"My nephew was a baron, who only the imperial family had the right to judge. I will have your heads for this." He raged.

"I am Arch-Mage Valerie Legorrin, head of the Stormhaven branch of the adventurers' guild. With the full authority to dispatch any and all threats to the people of this realm," Valerie retorted, unwilling to budge an inch.

Trantell sneered at her. "A threat to the realm? I think not, you overstep your mandate!"

Valerie just shook her head. "Colluding with demonic higher powers, orchestrating the kidnapping of children, should I go on?"

"We shall see what the imperial family have to say about this?" he said and made to walk past us. I stepped into his path, blocking his way.

"You would bar my way, commoner? A noble simply visiting his family at a sect."

"Let him go," Valerie ordered.

"But he's clearly one of them," I argued.

"Maybe, but we have no proof, and we can't just punish an Earl for his…questionable associations."

My hand tightened around the hilt of my sword; the man was clearly involved with all the monstrosities committed and I itched to strike him down for it. But Valerie was right, I had no proof and killing him without it wouldn't be justice, it would be cold-blooded murder, and I wanted to be better than that. Reluctantly, I stepped aside and Trantell waltzed out scot-free with a cocky smile on his face, the bastard.

Most of our group stayed with Dez to deal with the surrendered disciples, a few joined Valerie and me to enter the keep to see what we would find.

It was not as I expected, well, I mean it was still eerie as fuck, illuminated as it was by the green flames within the sconces, but it was also neat, tidy, and richly appointed with luxurious tapestries and paintings. From the corpses that decorated the exterior, I had expected more of the same; open blood stains and visible carnage, whereas instead it was like a normal aristocrat's keep. Although he was an evil piece of shit, I guess Reynard still enjoyed his creature comforts.

The illusion of normality was only shattered in two rooms: The great hall, whose great chandeliers and throne were made entirely of bones, which was not clichéd at all! And what must have been the castle chapel, whose altar contained a great red statue of a nasty looking Demon, who I could only assume to be the Lord they all kept mentioning, and to say it was creepy, would be a gross understatement. The plinth below the statue was awash with flesh blood, atop numerous older, dried stains, evidence of gods knows how many people that were bled out at its feet.

As I entered the chapel, I swear it felt like the statue was looking at me, attempting to peer into my very being.

"Don't come in here," I warned, holding my hand up to waylay anyone else from entering.

"You dare to enter my domain after slaying my prophet?" a booming voice echoed around the chamber, "You're either very brave or very stupid. Either way, you won't be leaving."

A pressure built up inside me as it spoke, like the attack from Madam Wang only far more direct and powerful. I instantly face-planted and the pain from hitting the ground would have probably bothered me if it didn't feel like my consciousness itself was losing cohesion. It's hard to describe, but it felt like my very ability to be me, my very soul, was being pulled apart. As I began to slowly lose awareness, that same familiar power welled up inside me again from my subconscious and battered the intrusion away, allowing me to return to clarity. The Demon Lord's rage filled howls filled the chapel, as his statue began to crumble, and vast cracks appeared around the room. Clearly the whole place was going to collapse, and I scrambled to get out before it did.

"I will not be denied!" The Demon Lord cackled maniacally. "We will meet again, worm, and I will tear your entire realm apart." As his voice faded out, the entire chapel started to crumble.

I looked around me, the others were all collapsed outside the chapel, it seemed that being exposed, even indirectly, to the attack on me had knocked them out cold.

Valerie was the first to awaken, climbing groggily to her feet. "What the hell was that?" she asked, rubbing at her head.

"Bad news," I replied, thinking about the power contained in just that small projection into this realm. "Really fucking bad news."

Slowly, the rest climbed back to their feet, apart from the one who had been nearest to the door. Who seemed alive, but in some sort of coma, as despite numerous attempts to heal her, she wouldn't wake, and I hoped the damage wasn't permanent. Everyone was shaken from the experience and so only Valerie and I continued to explore, the others instructed to carry the injured woman outside to see if anyone else was able to help her.

After entering the dungeons, the first thing we came across was the torture chamber, which had no doubt been used as part of the sect's foul cultivation methods. There was no-one alive and what had been done to the poor little souls, whose infant corpses littered the room, was nothing less than nightmare fuel. But it was also in the dungeons that we finally found the only ray-of-light within the whole awful fucking expedition.

Inside large cells were scores of children that the sect had snatched from around the empire, including some of those missing from Berevar. Most had injuries and all were at various stages of starvation and dehydration, but they were alive. As we gently coaxed the cowering kids out, I couldn't hold back the tears of joy quietly running down my face, washing my soul clean of some of the filth I had been exposed to in the monstrous place.

Leaving the castle, I was surrounded by a tiny horde of children who refused to leave my side, many of which could have been no older than eight. I had a little girl on my shoulders, a toddler in my arms and numerous others clinging to my cloak, they were covered in their own waste and malnourished, but they were safe.

A large tent was erected to shelter the survivors and it was decided that a party of adventurers would accompany Dez to return and fetch the airship, but first I wanted to deal with those who surrendered, which caused some issues.

"We should execute them all," I argued and not for the first time.

"They are prisoners, we can't just execute them, it's inhumane," a female cleric named Dalia replied.

"Have you seen their cultivation chamber? What they've done?" I asked, trying my best to reel in my growing temper.

"Ermm...no," she replied hesitantly.

"Then I suggest you all go and have a good fucking look before we continue this discussion."

And that is what we did, every remaining member of the expedition filtered in to see the chamber in the dungeon, some came out with faces full of rage, others looked haunted, almost everyone wept.

"They were children, babies!" Dalia sobbed. "I didn't know."

After that, the prisoners were summarily executed and not a soul disagreed.

The journey back to Stormhaven was rather sedate, an entire airship full of people in quiet mourning and recovery. No one spoke of the horrors we had witnessed, nor questioned what we'd done as a result, it was just another uncomfortable necessity in an unforgiving and cruel world, nothing more.

However, the experience worried me, how would aether change the Earth? Would that be our future? When psychos and predators are afforded a route to tangible individual power, would they behave themselves? Bollocks would they! It was going to be pure fucking chaos. Far worse than even here, which had millennia for a stable aether-based society to emerge, and yet was still riddled with violence and oppression. I tried to put the troublesome thought to the back of my head.

Chapter 35

As the airship drifted down to the rear of the Stormhaven Adventurers' Guild, numerous guards could be seen in formation below. Many bearing Stormhaven livery, but others instead adorned with the Olisias crest. Trantell Olisias stood at the forefront accompanying a man I failed to recognise, and I knew that we were about to have trouble. The expression on Valerie's face was one of pure fury.

"How are we going to play this?" I asked her.

"The city lord is an old friend, he will allow me to speak my case, though he may not like what I have to say about guards being brought onto Guild grounds," she said, clearly making no attempt to hide her anger.

"Maybe try to not lose your temper Val?" Dez advised gently, and from the look she gave him, I was glad that he was the one to say it.

She huffed and scowled at Dez, but he merely smiled gently back at her, and her anger quickly dissipated. "You're right of course, my friend, as usual." She sighed, making me envious of her level of self-control.

As the airship came to rest on the ground, the gangplank was lowered over the side, and Dez, Valerie and I proceeded down to meet the waiting city lord.

"Val, this is a right hornet's nest you've stirred up, you'd no authority to execute a noble, and a baron no less," the city lord said, his frustration evident. "I have to take you all in for questioning. Please don't make this any harder than it already is."

"We executed a den of demon worshippers," Valerie attempted to reason with him.

"You had no right to pass judgment on your superior, my nephew was an imperial baron and where is the proof he was a demon worshipper?" Trantell asked.

"You're quite correct, Your Lordship," Valerie said, pointedly enunciating every syllable. "But as a branch head of the Adventurers' Guild it is within my remit to investigate any and all threats to this realm, and it was under his authority that Reynard was executed," she added, pointing directly at me.

Trantell looked down his nose at me. "And who gave him the authority?"

"Joshua White is an S-rank adventurer, fully ratified by the guild. As such he is afforded all the rights and privileges of a Duke within every nation of this entire realm," she said, practically shouting towards the end.

Trantell's face dropped as he realised things were not as simple as he'd believed. "He had a right to a trial by his peers," he argued.

"Quite," Valerie agreed, trying, and failing to keep the grin from her face. "Only, he rather tragically decided a fight to the death was a better option than arrest."

Realising he was going to get nowhere, Trantell glared at the city lord, who merely shrugged helplessly in response, and then stormed off without another word, followed closely by the Olisias guards.

"He won't just let this go you know, Val. That man is pure poison," the city lord said.

"Aren't all noble clans the same, Wally? Except for the Bendorffs, how you lot have managed to stay honest in such a nest of vipers is beyond me," Val replied.

"It's a simple difference in viewpoints, Bendorffs are taught that we are noble because we serve and protect the people, the other clans believe that because they are noble the people should serve them. An important distinction. But thank-you for the kind words, although I do seem to recall I have practically begged you to stop calling me Wally," he said with a smirk.

"Sorry." Val chuckled, obviously not sorry at all. "Allow me to introduce Marquess Waldrose Bendorff, city lord of Stormhaven and one of my oldest and dearest of friends. And *Wally*," she made a point of purposefully accentuating the name, "this is Joshua White, our newest S-rank adventurer."

"You're angry that I brought my guards aren't you," Waldrose asked.

Valerie gave a little huff.

"It's a pleasure to meet you Marquess Waldrose," I interjected, pointedly ignoring Val's desire to act like a petulant teenager, which although weird and a little out of character, was actually quite endearing, in-keeping as it was with the silliness often shown between long-time friends.

"Please, just Waldrose is fine," he said, holding out a hand to shake.

"My friends just call me Josh." I shook his hand.

"Apparently, some of my friends call me Wally, but please don't do that." He smiled, providing some much-needed levity after the drama Trantell had tried to cause.

Whilst the other adventurers disembarked, Val regaled me with stories from their days actively adventuring. Waldrose had been part of their party, The Wandering Fools, and they had only stopped after many decades when the other two members of the party went missing. They tried for years to track them down, but with zero success, eventually Dez and Val moved into administrative roles and Waldrose assumed the role of a city lord within his clans Duchy. Waldrose didn't mention it, but clearly, he had chosen Stormhaven to remain close to his best friends, which I thought was sweet.

"This isn't going to end well Val." Waldrose rubbed his head wearily. "Trantell is an arse, but he is a well-connected arse, by all accounts he is close friends with the second prince."

"Do you think the second prince is part of the same demon worshipping cult?" I asked.

"I hope that Trantell was only associated with them at all due to his relationship with Reynard. But the thought that more of the Olisiases may be under the sway of a Demon is worrying, and if members of the imperial family are too…"

"Then we are in serious trouble," Dez finished for him.

"What should we do?" I asked, feeling a bit in over my head.

"The only thing we can do," Val said, "Carry on as normal and know they'll be coming for us."

"Return with me to my mansion, it will be safer for you all," Waldrose asked.

The offer was kind, but I had no intention of bringing my troubles to someone else's door. "Thank you for the kind offer, Waldrose, but I have things I need to do."

Val looked worried. "You mean to leave Stormhaven?"

I nodded. "I need to check in with my Master."

"I understand, just be careful, as strong as you are, you're not indestructible," Valerie said.

I'd only known her a short while, yet her concern for me was obvious, it was touching.

"I will, Val, don't worry." I nodded.

Leaving the three of them to discuss their plans, I said my goodbyes and made my way back to my room at the inn. I needed to find Master, and I also had to speak with Hannah at some point, as we had just killed her brother. That conversation was not going to be awkward at all!

Fighting Reynard also made it clear that I still wasn't strong enough to deal with all the potential threats. So, I needed to get stronger! And the easiest way to do that would be a prolonged period of cultivation. As much as it would be boring and I wanted to get home, I couldn't rush dealing with these demonic cultivators. With the powers involved, if I rushed, I may never get home at all.

In the carriage ride back, I never noticed anyone following me, but my paranoia over the possibility made me travel to a different location, some distance away from my inn. After paying the carriage driver, I took off at my greatest speed using wind-steps, there were no doubt many in the empire who would be able to keep up with me, but there was no way that would include any random rogue put to the task of stealthily following me.

When I got back to the inn I paid in advance for three months, much to the shock of the innkeeper who happily took my coin. I could tell he was concerned that something weird was going on, but after briefly explaining that I would only be using the room to cultivate, he was rather happy, I guessed to an innkeeper a meditating guest was about as trouble-free as he could get.

Sitting cross legged on my bed, I had no idea how many spirit stones I would need, so I poured out most of those that Master had given to me onto the floor. There were thousands and the pile was easily as large as the bed I sat upon. If spirit stones were as heavy as regular pebbles of the same size, I'd have worried about the floor collapsing under the weight! Fuck knows what Master would say about me using them on such a large scale, but ultimately, they were my family's wealth and needs must and all that.

Clearing my mind of distractions, I reached out and began to extract aether from the stones stacked all around me. As the aether poured into me, I slowly slipped into a mindless state, aware only of the flow of aether into my body and its assimilation by my cultivation method. As time passed, my mind frequently alternated between analysing my techniques and how I had utilised them, and long periods of thoughtlessness. I was constantly aware of the growth of my Qi Lake as I converted and condensed more Qi, my Dantian expanding repeatedly. Once, twice, thrice, it was taking longer each time and eventually an uncontrolled thought crept back in; concern that I was rushing my growth, but a subtle feeling gently emanated from my subconscious that all was how it should be, quieting my thoughts once again. After the seventh expansion it was no longer suitable to call it a Qi Lake, it was huge, a vast ocean of Qi, but still I persevered.

Finally opening my eyes, I had reached the tenth level of Qi condensation in one fell swoop and knew my next step was foundation establishment, allowing me to officially step into the realm of Spirit Knight! The problem was that I had no idea how to do it and was forced to consult the journal.

Once again, the book somehow sensed my growing cultivation, allowing me to view the section for Spirit Knight, but unfortunately, where the guide had been extremely explicit in describing the procedures for the earlier realms, for foundation establishment the explanation offered a combination of description and vague advice.

My Son, you are now well on your way to becoming a true cultivator. Foundation establishment is merely the path from liquid Qi to forming your solid Core. Where previously you have gathered, then condensed and expanded, now you must compress to increase the viscosity of your Qi and pass it through your meridians to strengthen them. The denser you can make your Qi, the greater your Core will be. I will not tell you the mechanics of how this should be achieved, as how you do it should be entirely personal. But I can say that you will merely need to visualise it and enact it through your will. Remember, you are the master of your own inner world, use instinct and whatever method feels right to you. Just as the tallest of buildings must have the greatest foundation, so must you, for the rest of your cultivation shall be built upon it.

That didn't really help too much, but at least knowing that it paved the way for Core formation gave me guidance I didn't have before. When I had spoken to Master about these things, I got the impression of specific pre-determined steps leading to the systematic construction of a Core, I wondered if I should pass on my father's wisdom in using a more instinctual method?

Closing my eyes, I allowed my consciousness to drift into my Dantian, the ocean was calm, and I knew that it wouldn't compress on its own, but what method should I use, could I make a whirlpool? Contracting my Dantian as I did? Maybe. Could I attempt to freeze it? Perhaps, but ice is solid yet less dense, so that wouldn't work, plus that would be all Yin with no balance. I wasn't getting anywhere, and I knew that it couldn't be a completely rational process, I mean it could, but then I'd be disregarding my father's advice about instinct. So, stilling my thoughts, I immersed myself in the ocean itself.

I realised I had been looking at things too literally, it wasn't actually a liquid at all, that was just a metaphysical representation formed by my perception of the density of the energy. It did remind me of a primordial sea, but instead of life, it was an origin for the Core that was yet to be, yes, that felt correct! It was an origin, the idea, the concept, was a seed that began resonating with something else within me. My blood! The Qi began roiling in great waves. What was the Origin of things to me? Despite being exposed to the supernatural and spiritual world, I still thought in terms of scientific theory, as it was hard to disregard a lifetime of learning, no matter how short that time was. I just needed to reconcile the two.

To me, the Big Bang was the origin of all things and I felt that resonated with the Daoist idea in the Dao De Jing: Dao begetting one, one begetting two - the Yin-Yang, two begets three, three begets the myriad things. Maybe what science was attempting to understand as the source of the big bang was just the Dao, but they could never understand due to an incomplete understanding of reality? As scientists on Earth would not know to include aether and the role it plays in the universe, nor the Dao due to its pseudo-religious connotations. The physical and the spiritual, one could not exist without the other, the physical providing substance, the spiritual the meaning. I drifted with my thoughts, my ideas and beliefs colouring my journey, sometimes I was aware of the process, consciously guiding it, but I didn't understand the actual science of the Big Bang, no-one on Earth did, so I surrendered myself to the process and allowed my instincts and the singing of my blood to lead me.

When, the process finally came to an end I saw a spiralling whirlpool in my Dantian, well what do you know, there was a whirlpool in the end! But what was driving the whirlpool made me stop in my tracks, there was something at the core of my Dantian, or maybe it was correct to say a lack of something. It was a fucking Black Hole! The void-like home of a singularity was living inside me. It was working, the Qi was increasing in density as it was pulled into the black holes orbit, but some of the Qi was also disappearing as it passed the event horizon. Fuck, fuck, fuck, what was the end game here? Would I be left with no Qi and a Black Hole? Plus, don't they explode at the end of their lives? What would happen if the Black Hole exploded in my Dantian? I felt a pulse of reassurance from my subconscious, which stopped my growing panic, but also freaked me out a little as it had recently been acting like it had thoughts of its own. Then I realised, my father was right, I could still use the Qi orbiting the black hole, and instinctively knew that if I wanted, I could snuff out the black hole in a heartbeat with just a thought. It wasn't an actual black hole, just an idea, a visual representation of my limited understanding of something of infinite density, the singularity. I was an idiot. So, now calm, I began to rotate the Qi through my meridians and back to my core, the increased viscosity made it harder, and I could feel my meridians trembling with the strain, but with each pass they adapted further, the process working them like exercise would for my muscles.

I opened my eyes with a smile, I was officially a Spirit Knight, Master was going to flip out at the speed of my progress. Then I noticed that there were only a few hundred spirit stones left on the floor, yep, Master was definitely going to flip out!

Chapter 36

After a quick shower I went back downstairs to speak to the innkeeper, time had lost all meaning whilst I had been cultivating and I needed to know how long I had been up in the room. The innkeeper saw me approach and his mouth literally hung open in shock.

"Hi, you look a little surprised to see me?" I asked.

"No...well, yes, it's just been a long while is all," he stammered out.

I had a horrible feeling I wasn't going to like where this was going. "How long was I up there?"

The innkeeper looked a little panicked. "Well...you see I didn't want to disturb you as it seemed important when you arrived, and no offence intended, but you looked like you would be good for the money, so I just left you to it." He didn't even pause to take a breath during the whole speech.

"How long?" I repeated, trying really hard to not let my growing panic turn to anger, especially towards a man who it seemed had likely done me a massive favour, when he could have just as easily banged on the door and kicked me out when my payment had run out.

"Ermm, I think that as of last week, you have been in that room for eight..."

"Eight months!" I blurted out.

The man shook his head vigorously. "No, sir, eighteen months."

Oh my god! Eighteen months, eighteen fucking months, I felt like screaming, God knows what my friends thought. They probably thought I was dead, fuck, fuck, fuck!

"I'm truly sorry, sir, I didn't want to disturb you as everyone knows that interrupting someone whilst they are cultivating can have huge side-effects, if I had known I would have made an effort to wake you."

I took a deep calming breath. "No, thank you, sir innkeeper, you have extended me a great kindness, I just got a little flustered about my friends is all. How much do I owe you?"

"Well…you didn't take any meals, so how you're still alive is beyond me," he said, the last bit mumbled at barely a whisper I just managed to pick up.

I smiled at him. "Yeah, me too if I'm honest, although I am really hungry."

Looking a bit embarrassed that I'd heard him, he cleared his throat and carried on. "That leaves fifteen months and a week at long term rates of two silver per night, we'll just call it one-thousand silver. Or ten gold of course." He looked at me and swallowed nervously.

I wasn't going to short-change the man and sorted fifteen gold coins into a small pouch and handed it over. "There's fifteen gold coins in there, as a normal guest would have to pay for food, which you lost out on, plus extra just for being kind enough to not disturb me."

The innkeeper took the pouch with unsteady hands and looked inside, happy with what he saw, he quickly secreted the pouch away inside his tunic. "Thank you, sir, thank-you."

I nodded and turned to walk away but was stopped in my tracks by the innkeeper.

"Sir, sir," he whispered, "I almost forgot, two men came looking for you, the first was a shifty looking fellow, came not long after you checked in, I guessed he was up to no-good, so I told him you'd stayed here for a while but suddenly left in a hurry. It's always best to tell half-truths to their type, spot a lie a mile away they can. The other was a giant bear of a man, with an axe, came about four months ago he did, said he knew you were here and asked me to tell you he would be at…the flame's…The Flame's promise, yes that was it!" he said, "The Flame's Promise in Tang'reyat, with Hannah, don't know if that means anything to you."

The innkeeper didn't know how much that meant to me, he'd protected me as a complete stranger and then told me about my Master and friend.

I held out my hand for him to shake, palming a spirit stone to him as I did. "Joshua White is my name, if you ever have any trouble whatsoever, go to Valerie Legorrin at the Adventurers' Guild and tell her you're a friend of mine, she'll be able to help."

"Francis Bagwell." He shook my hand with a smile. Then he briefly glanced surreptitiously at what I passed him and looked like he may pass out, before quickly clenching his hand shut so no-one could notice. "Is that?" he whispered hesitantly.

I just nodded and smiled, as I left, I could hear Francis behind me quickly walking out the back, no doubt to squirrel away his newfound wealth.

Tang'reyat, why would Master go there? And take Hannah with him? Fuck knows, there was no point wondering, I'd find out when I got there. The carriage to the airship port didn't take long and I was in luck, Tang'reyat was a regular destination so it was only a couple of hours until the next Airship would depart.

Whilst waiting I realised that I needed to satisfy my rumbling stomach, sooner rather than later, as it had started to feel uncomfortably like it was digesting itself. Which was understandable I reasoned, considering I had subsisted solely on spirit stones for well over a year, something I hadn't even realised was possible. A short walk from the port were a variety of restaurants, no doubt capitalising on traffic to and from the port and so I just chose one at random. By the time I had eaten my fill I had consumed at least one of every dish on their menu, and the restaurant staff were no longer looking at me like the god-sent patron they had an hour earlier. Instead, they shuffled around nervously like they were in the presence of some ravenous beast in human skin, who may decide they were the next course. Deciding I had thoroughly overstayed my welcome, I settled my bill and made my way back to the port. The restaurant had quickly locked up behind me, probably because I'd eaten my way through most of their supplies.

The airship to Tang-reyat was a medium schooner sized vessel and rather than taking a room, I opted for a seat in the passenger compartment. Although I hadn't been fully aware of how much time I had passed in isolation at the inn, I felt that a little company for the journey would probably do me good. The passengers were an eclectic mix of many species, some of which I couldn't identify, and other than the few that kept to themselves, most were happy for a chat over a cup of tea.

The journey would have been completely pleasant until, whilst stepping out for some fresh air on the deck, I noticed someone that I recognised. Yancy Trevion, major noble and major bell-end was hanging around with a couple of friends. Over eighteen months ago his family were pushing for a marriage to Hannah, so it was possible he was her fiancé now. It may have been pure coincidence, but the fact he was also headed to where she was located suggested he hadn't given up on the arrangement, even if she wanted none of it.

Personally, I couldn't be arsed to deal with the prick, unfortunately Yancy quickly noticed me, and his face lit up like all his Christmases had come at once, idiot! He swaggered over to me with his two friends in tow.

"So, we meet again, Joshua the adventuring commoner," he said whilst sneering at me. Honestly, who would actually say that? He sounded like an aristocratic villain from a Victorian novel.

"I refuse to believe that you aren't aware that I am now to be treated as a Duke in this realm, Yancy, especially after last time," I replied.

"Quite, but once a commoner, always a commoner, nobility is in the blood you see."

"Surely you're not that ignorant Yancy, you're only a noble because one of your ancestors claimed that status at the point of a sword."

"Maybe, maybe, but after countless generations the nobility still stands, and we ensure the blood runs true," he said with a smarmy smile.

I was a little gobsmacked, did he just defend inbreeding? "What do you want Yancy?" I asked, not bothered enough to try and explain the basics of genetics to a fool.

"Ah, I have been remiss in my duties. You are unaware of my joyous news, I have recently been admitted to the Black Gate sect and these are two of my fellow inner disciples, Lyren Babcock." He gestured to the lad on his right, before pausing dramatically and smiling ear-to-ear whilst introducing the one on the left. "And Niels Montaine."

I had thought he looked a little familiar. "Black Gate Sect, Montaine family, huh, small world," I said, cursing my luck, as I was kind of hoping I'd dodged that bullet!

Niels just quietly stared at me, and I wondered if he was going to make a move. "You killed my little brother," he said, and I wasn't sure if it was a question or a statement.

"Was your brother Treliom Montaine?" I asked, even though I was already sure of the answer.

"Yes."

"Then yes, I killed him in an official duel in Traveller's Rest."

"Why?" he asked, and I could tell he was genuinely curious.

I held up my sword by its scabbard. "I had something he wanted and so he wished to kill me to get it, he failed, not a pleasant man was your little brother."

"No, he was a human-shaped beast, a truly terrible person. And Crandor?"

"Crandor was a decent fighter, a worthy opponent, he tried to kill me out of desperation. Looking back, I think that maybe he knew he wouldn't have been spared by your family and was simply looking for a warrior's death."

"You killed a member of the Black Gate sect Joshua White and now you've come out of hiding, we will have you answer for that." Yancy smiled sardonically.

"This is how you all feel?" I asked, looking at Niels, who wasn't at all like his brother.

Niels sighed wearily. "I have no doubt that my brother was in the wrong, countless people still suffer nightmares over the things he did, but he was my brother and honour dictates I attempt to avenge him."

We walked into the middle of the deck, where there was more space, and the three of them spread out before me. Yancy was an arse, but his shitty personality wasn't enough to warrant his death, Lyren had been quiet, but his eyes betrayed a resoluteness that I could respect, and Niels was the only one who truly had cause for true enmity with me, but he seemed like a decent guy, and I didn't want his death on my conscience.

"Do you know what this is?" I held up my Guild signet ring. "Surely, you now know what it signifies, Yancy?" I asked, trying to stop any needless bloodshed.

Yancy laughed. "Even an S-rank adventurer will struggle against two As and a B at the same time.

Lyren's face suddenly had a look of concern for the first time.

"He never told you, did he?" I asked.

Lyren shook his head and stared daggers at Yancy. "You never said he was S-rank!"

"Before we do this, I have a request," I said.

Lyren and Niels looked at each other. "Go ahead," Niels replied.

"I wish to know, what kind of sect is the Black Gate?" I asked.

Niels took a moment to think about it. "It is a wondrous place, nestled on the slopes of The Horn, its furthest reaches sit amongst the clouds, looking out over the great wilds below. Countless people live there, so of course some have dark souls, just like my brother, but most try to live good lives, at least as good as they can on this path of death that we all tread. A place of hopes and dreams and failures, of people chasing strength to protect what they love. The Black Gate sounds ominous, but only to those who don't understand its meaning. Led by our sect master, the great hero, Narrel Beastbane, we stand between the gates of death and the people of Antaris. And, more than that, it is…home."

Niels and Lyren looked at each other and smiling sadly, drew their weapons. They couldn't beat me and apart from Yancy, the other two knew it. Neither wanted to, but they would fight me anyway, Niels because I had slain his brother and Lyren because he would fight alongside his friend. I felt a stab of pain in my chest, in another life these two could have been my friends.

I raised my hands and fell into the first position of Emperor's Fist, I was out of practice with it, but I had no other unarmed techniques and was sure that if I held back, I could simply incapacitate them.

"You would show us such dishonour! Draw your weapon," Yancy screamed.

I shook my head sadly. "You know nothing of honour."

And I was amongst them, my now thicker Qi pulsed through my body, and using wind-steps felt as if I rode the very air. To my perception it looked like they were moving through molasses, a few precise strikes and they were all unable to continue fighting. But they were alive, their broken bones would soon heal, and I was richer for sparing them.

Yancy was howling and rolling around whilst holding his broken leg, Lyren was out cold, and I slowly made my way to Niels who was taking deep steadying breaths whilst cradling his broken arm. As I stood in front of him, I bowed as low as I could. "I slew an evil man, but he was your brother and so I ask for your forgiveness."

"Look at you, begging like a lowly dog, I knew you had no honour," Yancy howled.

"Shut your mouth Yancy, you disgrace us with your words!" Lyren said, having woken up, although the outburst was a little surprising from the previously taciturn man.

Niels shuffled over in front of me. "Master once told me that if honour does not originate from the heart, then it is merely dogma. At the time I thought I truly understood, but now I realise I merely confused romanticising for understanding. There is nothing to forgive Joshua White, thank you for sparing us and guiding me to the truth." With a pained grunt from the effort, he likewise bowed in reflection of me.

"Look at you both, acting like filthy peasants." Yancy laughed maniacally.

Rising, I offered my arm to Niels and helped him up then slowly made my way to Yancy.

Yancy spat at my feet whilst holding his leg. "You have shamed yourself for all the world to see. And what has it gained you? I will still be marrying Hannah, mark my words, commoner."

I chuckled mirthlessly; I couldn't help it. I had no contempt for Yancy, I just pitied him. "Yancy, what is the value of the life of a good man?" I gently asked him. He just sneered in response. Nodding to Niels and Lyren, I made my way back to the passenger cabin, noticing that a crowd of spectators had gathered at some point.

As I was about to enter the cabin an elf sat upon the quarter deck called out to me. "Young hero, what is the answer? What is the value of the life of a good man?"

I looked up at the elf, he was dressed in dark leathers and had a plethora of daggers strapped to his body. They weren't for show either, I could tell he was dangerous. As the crowd all looked to me for my answer, my eyes never left the elf.

I smiled at him. "Fuck knows, but I reckon it's a damn sight more than a humble apology."

The crowd all chuckled at my response, all except for the elf, who merely tilted his head in respectful acknowledgment.

Chapter 37

Tang'reyat was a beautiful city and its vast spires, covered with colourful onion and helmet domes, reminded me of Russian orthodox churches. Which, oddly enough, caused a twinge of homesickness, even though I'd never even been to Russia.

On the airship I'd read a city guide of Tang'reyat, which explained its unusual status and flamboyant architecture. The city is home to a diplomatic consulate of The Mage Republic, which was the larger nation to Antanel's East. The territory of the consulate encompassed the whole city as well as some of its surrounding lands and the region was entirely administered by them. So, even though the island remained part of the empire and Bendorff duchy, upon crossing into the city, I had officially entered foreign soil and was just glad there was no passport system, or I would have been well and truly fucked!

There was still a customs office at the port that needed to be passed through. Luckily, the customs officials just hammered out the typical questions: purpose of your visit? How long you planned to stay? Etc. So I just answered as best I could and was quickly ushered on, I got the impression that, within reason, they didn't actually care what was said as long as people didn't seem too nervous or sketchy.

The Mage Republic as the name suggests is run completely by mages, and is a hugely respected nation, with no aristocracy, supposedly little nepotism, and a magical meritocracy. The country also prides itself on providing magical tuition to anyone who is capable, even foreign citizens. Which resulted in Tang'reyat housing the most prestigious magical academies within Antanel, chief amongst these Scorfinn University and the far more long-winded and pompously named Azarem Academy of Spellcraft and the Deep Mysteries.

Many of the Empire's greatest mages and sorcerers received instruction within their illustrious halls and to bear one of their qualifications afforded great esteem to the recipient, much like Oxbridge degrees back home. Again, just like Oxford and Cambridge, the various students, and alumni of the two institutions were in constant, mostly friendly, rivalry. With the regular competitions between them a celebrated part of the annual social calendar. Although, from what I had read, these competitions were accompanied by excessive fanfare and festivity, resulting in events closer to Mardi Gras than The Boat Race!

Due to the presence of the academies and the availability of foreign goods, the city was a multi-cultural hive of activity. All the streets I first passed were one giant bazaar, a riot of colourful canvasses, noises and smells. Hawking merchants called out to those who passed, offering goods from across the realm or promises of hidden treasures to be found amongst their wares. Spicy and savoury scents from street food carts made my mouth water, and fine incenses and enchanting music drifted out from darkened dens, offering rest and solace to weary travellers. I felt like I was immersed in a story from one-thousand-and-one nights, it was amazing.

Yes, it was amazing, but I wasn't a fool. So, as I wandered around, allowing myself to enjoy the place, I also made sure to keep my guard up, my perception tested against the sensory overload and semi-daze that the bazaar was intended to cause. The bright and pleasant façade of the flower, alluring and overwhelming, causing you to miss that the nectar being offered was often from a carnivorous plant. Call me paranoid, but I had no doubt many naive travellers had been stripped of their purses, or worse, within the shadows of the vibrant predator that was the grand bazaar of Tang'reyat.

Despite enjoying my brief exploration, I knew that wandering around aimlessly and hoping to simply stumble upon The Flame's Promise would be a fool's errand, so I decided to look for a guide. I could have spoken to a guard, as I had seen them fairly regularly in their matching armour and unmistakeable ottoman-esque helms. But, just like Stormhaven and I had no doubt other cities of Antanel, there were a number of street urchins around, whether foundlings or simply from the poorest of homes, they could be seen begging or carrying out simple tasks for the barest handful of coins. The more daring ones darted swiftly between legs, attempting to lift an unsuspecting mark of their purse before disappearing into the throng of passersby.

I noticed one finish unloading an entire cart of produce onto a market stand, only to receive a single copper coin in return for their labour. When the young boy saw the solitary coin that had been placed on his palm, he wasn't even mad, just sadly despondent, no doubt used to his labour being so undervalued. The rotund merchant wasn't done though, as apparently it wasn't enough to just underpay the poor kid, he had to humiliate him too.

"Well, what do you have to say?" The greasy merchant chuckled.

The kid instantly started panicking and clutched his measly pay to his chest. "Thank-you, honourable merchant, may all your trades enrich your house," he said as respectfully as he could manage.

I had seen quite enough; I'd found my guide. Stalking over to the two, the merchant noticed me and thought I had come to speak to him. An understandable mistake, as in my richly appointed armour and travel-cloak, I looked every bit a noble, and what business could a noble have with a common street rat?

"How can Ibrazil help such a glorious young warrior as yourself?" The merchant's sour breath reeked, even over the copious amount of cologne he wore.

I had little respect for a man who would treat a child in such a manner, especially one who had chosen to work when it would be far easier to try and take what he needed, like so many others did in his situation. "I wish to speak to the boy," I replied.

If Ibrazil felt any displeasure over my choice, he masked it masterfully. "Of course, Master Warrior." He bowed. Ibrazil was one of those most dangerous of men, the kind who would smile and extol your virtues, whilst surreptitiously slipping poison into your drink.

I took a knee in front of the kid, he was filthy, his clothes little more than rags. "Young man, what's your name?"

The boy was trying his best not to shake but couldn't stop his voice from trembling. "St..Stelman, Stelman White."

I placed my hand gently upon his shoulder to try and calm him. "A strong name, I'm Joshua, Joshua White, so it looks like we share the same family name. Perhaps it's fate that has brought us together." I smiled. "Do you know these streets well, Stelman?"

"Like the lines of dirt on me palm, sir," he said, puffing up proudly.

"Well, I'm need of a guide, so would you be willing? I will pay of course, in fair coin."

The boy considered it briefly, he wasn't an idiot and was probably well aware of the potential danger an armed stranger could represent.

"No funny business?" he asked.

I shook my head. "On my honour."

Stelman stared at me, no doubt looking for any signs of deception, but whether he decided I looked honest, or his desperation simply won out over wariness, he held out his grubby hand. "Where do you need to go?"

"The Flame's Promise, you know of it?" I asked, shaking his hand.

He nodded and beckoned for me to follow.

As we were leaving Ibrazil finally decided to interfere. "If you take my labourer, who will we get to move our stuff?"

I honestly couldn't be bothered to deal with his bullshit and flicked him a silver coin. "That should cover it."

Ibrazil greedily rubbed the coin between his fingers. "That will cover the labour, but I am a busy man, what about the cost of my time spent finding a replacement?" He laughed mockingly.

"I suggest you choose your next words very fucking carefully, merchant," I said.

Ibrazil looked at me and I stared back as he weighed his options. "Forgive me, sir, I mistook the coin for copper, a silver is very generous," he mumbled.

"Smart choice." I smiled. "Come, Stelman, lead the way."

We walked off into the crowd, leaving Ibrazil muttering curses under his breath.

I had been following Stelman for several minutes or so before he finally found his voice. "Ib's a dangerous man, you shouldn't have angered him, he acts the part of a market trader but he's not."

I must admit I was a little curious. "What is he then?"

"Thief, loanshark, killer, loads of things. Half the stuff he sells is what he's taken from those who couldn't pay."

"Thank you for the warning, but I don't think we'll have to worry about Ib, he's smart enough to know when someone is more trouble than it's worth," I said.

"If you say so, mister," Stelman replied, but I could tell he was unconvinced.

The Flames' Promise was an attractive four storey building, with an outdoor beer-garden, and as I watched the scantily clad staff lead some of the patrons inside, it became immediately evident that the place was no inn. No doubt Master would love it, but I wasn't so sure about Hannah.

I passed two silver coins to Stelman. "I don't think this is a place for a child, Stelman, make yourself scarce and meet me back here tomorrow."

"I ain't afraid of seeing a little pussy," he argued defensively.

Honestly, his outburst shocked me, but it probably shouldn't have as I didn't even want to imagine what sort of things he'd been exposed to on the streets.

"How old are you Stelman?" I asked.

"Eleven."

"Well, I think you're a bit too young for a place like this."

"Not too young to be offered a silver coin for a blowie."

"What?" I snarled.

"I didn't do it!" he quickly said, probably mistaking my anger and disgust to be directed at him.

I forced myself to calm down. "It's ok, Stelman. I'm not mad at you, I'm angry at the people that prey on vulnerable children," I said gently.

Stelman shuffled on the place looking down at his feet. "Everyone knows who they are, but no one cares as long as they stick to us street rats. One of 'em even took my sister, never seen her since," he said with a sniffle.

I rubbed my face with my hand, this was going to complicate things, I knew it, but I couldn't do nothing. "Who took her?" I asked, dreading the answer.

"The Melikant's crew."

So, someone from a major noble clan, fuck it, that wasn't so bad. I was worried it was the ambassadorial staff, now that would have been a proper headache.

"I'm not making any promises, Stelman, but I will try and get your sister back, okay?"

"If you get my sister back, I will be your man forever," he said, "On my honour," he added, repeating my earlier phrase back to me.

It didn't take much effort to arrange a private room for Stelman, they were even happy to organise a bath to be drawn and fresh clothes for him, it's amazing what a little coin can do. They were initially suspicious of my motives, but after I mentioned I would like to avoid exposing him to the more risqué side of their business, they eased up. No doubt used to far stranger things than someone taking pity on a poor street rat.

Once Stelman was happily sequestered away and I didn't have to worry about him, I enquired about Master and Hannah, and was led to a suite on the third floor. Entering the room, I was confronted with the sight of Hannah relaxing in a large roll top bath. Copious amounts of bubbles stopped me from seeing more than I should, but I still averted my eyes.

"I'm sorry Hannah, I didn't know you were bathing. I'll wait outside," I said to the wall, pointedly not looking at her.

"You disappear for over a year and then casually stroll in whilst I'm taking a bath! Being a bit forward, aren't you?" she asked.

"Yeah, I'm sorry, I'll come back in a bit." I rubbed my head awkwardly.

Hannah started giggling. "It's fine, I wasn't being serious, you can't see anything anyway."

The sound of splashing water as Hannah stepped out from the bath sent my imagination immediately into overdrive and I couldn't help but envision what was below those bubbles! Now, I don't consider myself a creep, but as a hot-blooded lad, I will happily admit it took a real act of willpower to not take a sneaky peak.

"It's fine, you can turn around now," Hannah said.

Her hair was still damp, and she had merely pulled on a bathrobe. I suddenly felt like my blood was on fire.

"Are you just going to stand there and stare at me?" she asked coyly.

Slightly embarrassed, I coughed lightly. "Sorry, just a little surprised is all, how have you been?"

She looked troubled. "I've been better," she admitted.

"If it's anything I can help with, just say the word," I offered.

"Thanks, Josh. You know, if you enjoy what you see. It's yours if you're brave enough to take it!" she replied, abruptly changing the subject.

"I...I do like you Hannah, but I have someone waiting for me," I said, more flustered than I'd like to admit.

Hannah smiled at me. "You're cute when you get embarrassed. Don't worry, I was just messing with you," she said, and it may just be my ego speaking but I swear I saw a brief tinge of disappointment on her face.

Fuck, I mean, maybe I was just projecting my own disappointment, Hannah was a stunner and if I was single, I would have torn that robe off at her invitation and...stop, best to not go there.

"So, it's been a while, how did you end up here with Master Bronstad?" I asked, trying to steer my thoughts in a less sordid direction.

"It hasn't been great, just as Yancy said, the Trevions came to propose marriage and my clan agreed, when I got a message to return home to plan the ceremony, I went to look for you. Instead, I found Ingmar and we came here as other than leaving the country, it's as far from clan control as I could get."

Things were getting complicated, I just wanted to go home, but it looked like it wouldn't be so easy. I had to extricate a young girl from one of the Melikants, and the Olisiases were probably on the hunt for Hannah. Two major clans and two major pains in my arse.

I explained the situation with Stelman's sister and Hannah was visibly disgusted, immediately wanting to help.

Hannah suddenly had a serious look on her face. "They're not the biggest problem."

"No?" I asked, genuinely curious about what could possibly be more of a concern than avoiding two major clans.

"No." She shook her head. "Following the disturbance in the wilderness, the imperial family have been determined to get the natural treasure. The imperial guards have been investigating all of the teams that came back. One of the teams who were questioned said they met two strangers in the wilderness, their descriptions matched Ingmar and you."

Fuck, we were worried that this could happen, but it had been long enough now that I just assumed we were in the clear.

"So, they know who we are?" I asked.

"I'm not sure, but it won't be long now, as they've already tracked down that you were at Traveller's Rest, because I was there, and I've already been called in for questioning about it."

"Fuck, that's not good."

"I take it the treasure is actually with one of you then?" Hannah asked.

"There is no treasure!" I replied. "It was my breakthrough in body cultivation that caused the commotion!"

"Oh!" she exclaimed, and the look on her face would have been comical if we weren't in such serious trouble. "Well, can't we just explain that then?"

"To cultivators, my body is a treasure Hannah," I said.

"Well, it's not bad." She winked at me. "But referring to yourself as a treasure is a bit egotistical, no?" She laughed.

I looked at her as seriously as I could. "I'm not joking Hannah. Alchemists are always looking for rare reagents and stuff from spirit beasts, my blood and body can be used in the same fashion."

Hannah looked positively revolted. "That's disgusting, they'd consume you?"

"I'm not sure, but I don't think it would end well for me. Never underestimate the lengths to which people will go in search of power."

Hannah was biting her lip; I could tell there was something she wanted to say but was afraid to do it.

"What is it?" I asked

"It's nothing, don't worry, I should get ready," she said and smiled awkwardly before leaving for one of the adjacent rooms.

That was a bit weird, I thought, before my musing was interrupted by Master finally making an appearance. "Well, son, you seem to have gotten us into quite the predicament!" he said.

It was good to see him again, but he looked tired. "Yeah, Hannah filled me in. On the plus side I managed to complete an S-rank quest," I said, "So once all this business is done with, I suggest we get the fuck out of dodge!"

Master huffed. "Honestly, with the mess we're in now, we'd be leaving whether you'd managed to or not."

I couldn't help but feel guilty. "Sorry, Master, I've put us both in danger."

"Don't talk nonsense, son, danger's part of the life, that's why we came here," he said, "although, things have gone a little off-piste," he added with a grimace.

"Yeah, things have definitely gotten…complicated," I admitted.

Master grinned at me. "Oh well, it just adds training value, if we can get through this, I reckon you'll be prepared for anything Earth might throw at you."

I found myself agreeing with him. Plus, as dangerous as things were, it was also kind of exciting. Rescue an innocent, then avoid capture and escape back home, all with an attractive native warrior in tow!

I explained the situation with Stelman's sister and Master agreed that we should do what we could to help. We were in enough of a bind anyway, so doing the right thing would make little difference to us, but a world of difference to the young girl. I didn't think he'd object; Master was an ancient viking, but his long years of life had taken him to a place far from his original raping and pillaging lifestyle. I generally tried not to think about that, it may be repulsive to me, and probably even to him now, but I was not so sanctimonious to judge the people of the past by modern standards, that would be ludicrous, better to learn from it and not repeat it. From what I'd witnessed and our conversations, I'd learnt that Master's moral code was quite like my own now and so I knew that even if it was dangerous, he would never let a young girl suffer at the hands of a pervert.

"So, what's the plan, son?" Master asked.

I thought about how we could go about it, sneaking in and out would have probably been the best option but I had no training in infiltration and neither of us were particularly built for stealth. "I reckon we just walk in and take the girl, if anyone tries to stop us, we…"

Master raised an eyebrow. "We what?"

"We ask them to step aside, politely, of course." I smiled, whilst tapping the hilt of my sword.

Master guffawed. "Now that's the sort of plan I can get behind!"

Chapter 38

Now, I admit the plan may have been quite simple, but we weren't idiots, so we quickly hashed out some further details. Whilst Master and I rescued the girl, Hannah would secure an airship that we could take straight back to the portal location. With so many people after my blood, probably quite literally! We knew we wouldn't have time to find somewhere safe for Stelman and his sister, so we would be taking them with us too, hopefully they wouldn't object. As much as I would have liked to stay and experience more of Tang'Reyat, every hour we stayed was an extra hour that my enemies had to find us, so in the early hours we would all set out and blitz through the operation, hoping that speed and darkness would aid us in our endeavours.

The wait was full of nervous tension, Hannah assured me that the docks were always full of smugglers and other unsavoury characters, so tracking down a dodgy airship crew wouldn't be a problem, especially if the price was right. Besides, if it was, she said she would just commandeer one, what a legend!

Master looked around the bar and gazed out of the windows, the few patrons still partying looked worse for wear and other than a few shady characters hustling from shadow to shadow; the streets were largely empty. He turned to look at us and nodded. "It's time."

Wishing each other luck, we took off to our tasks. Not a word was spoken as we swiftly made our way through the streets, I could see how nervous Stelman was by the way he wrung his hands together or shuffled his feet whenever we stopped. I would have preferred for him to accompany Hannah, but we needed him with us to identify his sister, which was too important a task to be left to mere description. As cruel as it sounds, if we failed to locate the girl, there was no chance for a second attempt and so we were dragging him along with us.

"It'll be ok Stelman, just stay behind us in the background, we'll only call you out when its safe," I tried to assure him.

"I…I know, I can do this. For my sister," he replied.

I gave him a nod of appreciation, brave kid.

Due to Tang'Reyat being, for all practical purposes, a part of The Mage republic, the Melikant clan's estate in the city was more moderate than it otherwise would have been. It still had its own private grounds, but they were well under an acre, more in keeping with a large, detached house back home.

The two guards at the gate seemed to be paying very little attention to their surroundings and I could tell that neither of them was particularly powerful. Rather than attempt to negotiate entry, a quick use of wind-steps placed me between them, and before they even had a chance to react, I knocked them both out with swift blows to the head, carefully controlling my strength to not kill them.

"They'll have a nasty headache when they wake," Master commented as he approached.

"Yeah," I said, "but I didn't want them to alert the household and it's better than being dead."

Master nodded. "Good job."

It may have been only two words, but Master was a warrior with centuries of experience and so recognition from him always filled me with pride.

We stalked our way up to the main house, there were two more guards at the doorway and so I used the same tried and tested tactic, gently lowering their unconscious bodies to the ground. Sounds of partying came from inside, no doubt

Lord Melikant was entertaining. I hoped it was just a bunch of his noble friends and not people from the local diplomatic community, as that would complicate matters.

The door was unlocked and, after pushing it open, we entered a large unoccupied entry hall. When a side door opened, I was sure we had been discovered, but it was merely a servant carrying a tray of hord 'oeuvres, who quietly nodded to us in supplication, before proceeding on with her burden. I looked at Master for how to proceed and he simply shrugged as if to say he was happy to follow my lead.

I decided that we needed more information, and the best bet would be the servants, if the lord of the house was such a deviant, then most likely the servants would be well aware of the fact and probably suffering as a result of it. I headed through the door the servant had come from, which led into a busy corridor full of serving staff waiting with empty trays for more drinks and food from the kitchen.

"Stelman, come here." I beckoned him forward.

The servants all looked at us curiously, worry clear in their eyes.

"Please do not be alarmed," I said, attempting to reassure them. "We're not guests, but we have no intention of harming anyone, we simply wish to locate a young girl who was abducted by the lord of the house."

"Tell them about your sister," I asked Stelman.

He proceeded to describe his sister to them whilst they shuffled nervously on the spot. Finally, one of them, who looked to only be about seventeen herself, stepped forward hesitantly.

"Is…is her name Daalu?" she asked with a quivering voice.

"Yes, that's her! Have you seen her?" Stelman asked excitedly.

The young servants face dropped, tears falling quietly from her eyes.

"It's okay, what's your name?" I asked as gently as I could.

"Tilly," she said.

"Keep your mouth shut Till, you'll get us all in trouble," said an older male servant.

Master glared at him. "Open your mouth again and I will cut you down where you stand," he said, taking his axe from his back.

The man visibly paled and I looked back to Tilly. "It's okay Tilly, please tell us what you know, I won't let anyone hurt you," I said.

Tilly looked around at the others. "Will you please take us all with you?" she asked.

I looked at Master and once again he just shrugged. Fuck it, in for a penny, in for a pound. "Okay, but when we leave, we leave fast, no nonsense, and no stopping for your stuff, understand?"

They all looked at each other and nodded, I could see the excitement growing on their faces, clearly, they were little better than prisoners.

Tilly took a moment to steel herself. "He calls them his toys, young boys and girls that he takes and plays with until they get too old. Then he loses interest, and he makes us work here as servants and playthings for guests." She looked distraught and ashamed; they all did. She turned to Stelman. "I'm so sorry, sometimes Master gets too rough with his toys, they…they break. Daalu was such a sweet thing, but she didn't make it."

Stelman shook his head in denial. "No, no, she can't be, I came to rescue her…" he continued to rant to no one in particular, lost in his grief. Master wrapped the boy in a great bear-hug, and his crazed rants turned to simple sobs.

The scene was heart-breaking. I looked at Tilly, and saw she was crying, many of the servants were. "Are you sure?" I whispered.

She nodded to me. "I had to clean up afterwards," she said with a haunted look in her eyes. "We cremate them in a furnace, Lord Melikant doesn't want them buried on the grounds."

I wasn't going to push her for more information, to do so felt cruel. I was also struggling to keep a lid on my growing rage, there was no fucking way this was a secret, no, the fact that they were used by guests when they grew too old for the Melikant meant a bunch of people were culpable.

"What about tonight?" I asked, trying to keep the anger from my voice. "Are the guests expecting you all to serve them as usual?"

Tilly nodded, looking down at her feet. "Yes, it is a private party for Lord Melikant's friends, they're almost as bad as he is."

I turned to Master. "Get them all out, Master, don't look back, I will meet you at the airship."

He stared at me, and I could tell he knew what I was planning, but he simply placed a hand on my shoulder. "Do what needs to be done, son, I'll get them there."

I stood in the hall watching as the servants quietly filtered out of the house and I realised that even the oldest was younger than me. Finally, only Master was left, carrying a sleeping Stelman who had cried himself to sleep. No further words were needed between us, Master just nodded resolutely to me and left. I drew my sword and headed into the party.

What followed was a dark business, pure savagery that I will not describe, as I have no desire to glamourise my actions. It was merely a grim necessity. I will say that Lord Melikant himself did not die easy, he suffered, that I made sure of. You may think me a monster and maybe I am, but I will sleep easier knowing at least thirty monsters of a different kind would never see another sunrise, and the children of Tang'Reyat would be safer for it. And that's enough for me.

I caught up with Master at the port, it seemed that many of the servants had decided to keep following him once they were free of the house, and the small crowd looked conspicuous for the time of night; completely ruining our plan of a quiet and unnoticed exit from Tang'Reyat! I could see Hannah arguing with a sketchy looking guy and made my way over to see what the problem was.

"…that there would be five passengers, not fifteen, so it's going to cost you," the man said, clearly growing agitated.

"They are…unexpected, and I am happy to pay for them. I just think ten times the cost for three times the passengers is ridiculous," Hannah argued.

"The extra is for the attention you are bringing to us, now either pay or fuck off, up to you," he said, clearly having enough of the conversation.

I thought it was best to interject, as we needed to get gone. "Just pay the man Hannah, it's fine."

"But its extortionate!" she complained.

"Maybe, but we brought trouble to his door and that has a price. So, give the man the money and let's get the fuck out of here," I said, not willing to brook any discussion.

"Fine." Hannah huffed and handed over the coins.

Less than five minutes later we were all aboard and heading out of the city at full speed, our destination Bandevar, a small fishing town on the northern coast and the closest settlement to the Portal's location. We couldn't fly directly to the portal as the tree cover was just too dense and using ropes to lower passengers wasn't feasible due to the height of the great trees, the ship didn't have any ropes long enough. I could have probably jumped down, so could Master and possibly even Hannah, but Stelman and the servants, not so much. Most were mundanes and the rest had barely awakened, so their bodies wouldn't withstand being carried down as we jumped, we weren't in a superhero movie, the inertia and whiplash would plain fuck them up.

I found myself looking at the lads and lasses we had acquired from the Melikant estate, what would we do with them? Stelman would come with us, we'd agreed on that, but what did they want to do? I didn't want to unwittingly turn a rescue into a kidnapping!

I had an idea, but I only wanted volunteers, so I gathered them all up and spoke in hushed tones to not draw too much attention. "You're probably all wondering where we are going?"

There was a general nodding of heads, so at least I knew they were all listening. "Before I answer, I need you all to refrain from any outbursts over what I say, okay?" Once again, I was surrounded by nodding heads and I started to feel strangely like a teacher.

"We are returning to our own realm," I said, there were a few stifled gasps, but everyone did as I asked and kept quiet. "Any who wish to come are welcome, those who don't will be left in Bandevar, don't worry, we won't leave anyone destitute, any questions?"

There was a general air of excitement and Tilly stepped forward. "What would we do there? Be servants for your household?"

"Well," I said, rubbing my head. "I thought that for those willing, I could set you up with somewhere to live and a stipend, in return you could let me know if you notice anything strange going on in your area."

The idea of an informal spy network had just come to me, it would give them something productive to do whilst integrating into our world and help keep me informed about potential cases to work.

The lad who'd tried to stop Tilly speaking earlier stepped forward. "Will it be dangerous?" he asked, and they all looked at me expectantly for my answer.

"I hope not, I'm not asking you to run an investigation or do anything to put yourselves at risk, just let me know if anything seems weird."

Most of them quickly agreed, a few had family left and wished to stay behind for them, but Tilly had other ideas. "Can I stay on in your household as a servant?" she asked nervously.

I reckoned she just wanted to cling to the sense of security my rescuing her had brought, poor thing. I didn't think Felix would have an issue with an additional pair of hands and hopefully once her confidence was raised, she would make plans for herself. "I don't see that being an issue Tilly, but we don't keep servants like that, all members of our household staff are paid employees, free to leave whenever they choose." From her beaming smile, I don't think she even cared, she was just happy to be kept around. "Although, there is something I would like you to do for me, as a favour."

She looked at me nervously, a slight wariness in her gaze as she chewed her lip, but still she nodded.

"I would like you to look out for Stelman," I said, looking at the slumbering boy. "He has lost his big sister and will often be alone in the house, he will need someone to be there for him. Can you do that for me, be there for him, like a sister?"

Tilly nodded vigorously through misted up eyes. "Yes, milord, I can do that, I will be the best big sister ever."

"None of that milord business please, just Josh will be fine."

The next few hours were fun as I explained about Earth and its differences, most of which left them speechless, and I couldn't help but feel that this whole spy network thing could possibly work out rather well.

Chapter 39

Maybe it was too much to expect smooth sailing, but all my hopes for just that were dashed when, shortly after we turned to follow the Northern coastline of Antaris, two large airships appeared ahead of us. It was far too specific to be a coincidence, no one could have guessed so accurately where we would be heading, someone had betrayed us. I looked at the faces around me, Master I trusted with my life and Hannah was my friend. The group we'd just picked up had no idea where we were going until recently, so they couldn't have arranged for someone to head us off in time. That left the airship crew as the likeliest culprits, but the look of shock on the captain's face seemed genuine to me, so if it was one of his crew, I doubted he was in on it.

I looked at Master. "Who do you reckon?"

He also looked around and seemed equally stumped, eventually just shrugging. "Does it even matter at this point?"

I chuckled mirthlessly. "Nah, I guess not." I looked at the captain. "This isn't what you signed up for, what do you want to do?"

The captain grinned back at me. "If we handed over passengers at the first sign of trouble, we wouldn't be able to operate for long in this line of work," he said, before adding with a yell, "Would we boys?"

"No!" they all yelled back.

"Besides, no way those lumbering fuckers will catch us." He smiled.

The crew all pulled masks up around their faces and moved rapidly about their business; great black covers were hauled down and over the sides and the figurehead, obscuring any identifying markers; clearly this wasn't their first rodeo. Additional smaller masts and sails were added to the ends of the stubby wings, and I briefly wondered about the effectiveness of such small sails, but no sooner had they unfurled than our speed skyrocketed, and I had to stumble to maintain my footing.

"Let her fly lads, let her fly," the captain hollered.

We were between the waiting airships and beyond them before they even had a chance to turn, but not before I briefly caught the gaze of a man stood on the prow of the larger ship. It was only the barest of moments, but from the lack of concern and humour in his face, I knew we were fucked. It was the look an adult has when amused by the antics of children.

The airships were eventually left behind as little more than specks in the distance when our boost began to wane, and we returned to normal speeds. The man I'd seen hadn't even tried to stop us, like someone who knew he would have us anyway and didn't even need to make any additional effort to do so.

Master stood with his axe in his hands, our gazes met, and I knew he had seen the same thing.

"This isn't going to end well," he said gravely.

"If they know our destination, he can easily catch up to us, we need to put down as soon as they're out of sight and let the airship carry on to Bandevar without us," I said, "The wilderness is huge, as long as he follows the airship or if we get deep enough into the forest, we can lose him."

"It's nearly a thousand miles to the portal from here, we can cover that fast enough, but the others will be too slow, it would take us over a month at a pace they can maintain," Master argued.

Hannah looked worried. "We should just stick to the plan, it will be fine, we've left them way behind."

"No, you don't understand, Hannah. The man on that ship was beyond all of us," I argued. "So, we get closer and risk he is waiting for us below or do it now?"

Master looked at our companions "He could already be below us."

I thought about the blasé look on the man's face. "No, he wasn't in a rush, he could probably have boarded us as we passed if he was. I think this is just a game to him, he will wait to catch up until he has to, now is our best chance."

"So, we leave them behind?" Master asked wearily.

"We can't do that, it's not right," Hannah argued.

I looked around the ship, hoping to find an inspiration, anything to get us out of the situation, then it hit me, I was strong as fuck, I could carry easily bear the weight of everyone, I just needed a way to carry them, it was crazy, probably a bit stupid, but it might just work. "Captain!" I yelled.

"Yes lad?" he replied.

"I don't suppose there's a boat on this ship?" I grinned.

"Aye lad, we have a jolly boat, hasn't been used in years though, and it doesn't fly, bloody things probably not even watertight either."

"Doesn't matter, we need it, now. And don't worry, I'll pay for a replacement."

Ten minutes later, I found myself stood on a peninsular watching the airship quickly taking back off towards Bandevar, hoping that no one had noticed its brief descent. I looked over at the guys and girls hastily positioning themselves in the small tender and couldn't help but chuckle to myself despite the impending crisis. Master grabbed the prow of the boat behind himself, and I grabbed the stern.

Master looked over his shoulder at me. "You ready, son?" he asked.

I nodded in affirmation.

"You might all want to hunch down; it may get a bit windy." I warned them and we were off.

We accelerated slowly to not cause anyone to fly out of the boat, but within a few minutes we were travelling through the forest at the top speed we could maintain, which was easily over sixty miles-per-hour. We could have gone faster, but even with the huge gaps between the tree trunks, the forest would have been hard to navigate without injuring the passengers in the boat.

I'm not going to lie, I had the biggest smile on my face over the sheer absurdity of it all and the passengers also seemed to think it was hilarious, well, the ones who weren't growing green from motion sickness.

And so, for hours we zoomed through the great wilderness, two men carrying a wooden boat full of people at speeds a rally driver would have been proud of. Occasionally I risked a glance over at Hannah, who looked a little troubled, but I just put it down to the stress of our escape as when she noticed me looking, she merely smiled, shaking her head at how ridiculous we looked.

Eventually, we stopped a mile or so from the portals location and prepared to return home. Whilst Master and I used spirit stones to replenish our spent reserves as quickly as we could, Tilly and the others hurried around making sure everyone had something to eat or drink. Stelman had finally awoken during our run and after his initial shock, seemed to take a little joy from it, something he sorely needed after the news he'd been dealt. Watching him follow Tilly around like a puppy and assisting her, I realised that I'd definitely made the right call there, they would be good for each other.

We had travelled hundreds of miles into the wilderness, so no matter how strong that man was, there was no chance he could find us, as to cover such a vast area with spiritual sense would take a cultivation level far above saint and so I found myself relaxing a little.

Then I noticed Hannah again, she was looking at the group happily eating and chatting away, but she didn't look happy or relaxed, she looked sad...and guilty. I noticed she was fiddling with something in her hand, and looking closer, I saw it was her magistrate's badge. I hadn't seen her do that before and suddenly had a really bad feeling.

Hannah noticed me watching her and looked at me, tears welling up in her eyes. I got to my feet and slowly approached her. "Why, Hannah? I thought we were friends," I asked, attempting to keep my emotions from spilling out.

"That man is the Grand Inquisitor, the head of the Imperial inquisition. They...they took my mother, said they'd kill her if I didn't co-operate," she admitted, tears running freely down her face.

Well, fuck, any anger I felt over her betrayal instantly deflated, who wouldn't do awful things to save their own mother? "How long do we have?" I asked.

"I...I don't know," she said, her voice quivering.

"Not long enough," came a cold voice as the grand inquisitor stepped into view from behind one of the trees.

Around forty years old, his lank black hair and goatee were speckled with grey, the purple caftan he wore was trimmed with intricate golden filigree. Coupled with his alabaster skin and eyes so dark they were almost black, he cut an imposing figure.

"What do you want?" I asked.

"Maybe I wish to bring you to justice, young man, as quite a few nobles have died at your hands after all. Haven't they?" He looked at me questioningly. "I jest of course, his imperial majesty is rarely bothered when something happens to help keep the major clans in their place."

Hannah stepped forward hesitantly. "I did as you asked, Lord Inquisitor, what about my mother?"

The inquisitor looked at her with disdain. "Do I look like someone who would babysit a silly old wench? I gutted her like a sow for daring to birth a traitorous swine of a daughter."

Hannah fell to her knees dejectedly. "But...but I never betrayed the Empire."

"You are friends with the man who ruined my Lord's plans, and the empire only exists to serve Him. A clear

315

betrayal. Not to mention you then betrayed your so-called friends too, you are the very definition of a traitorous swine." The inquisitor laughed, visibly delighting in Hannah's suffering.

"So, you haven't just come for the treasure?" I asked.

"Oh no, his imperial majesty clearly desires the treasure, but that is beside the point. I have been solicited by our Lord," he said, the look of pride on his face disgustingly obvious. "He is very much looking forward to meeting you again."

"It never ceases to amaze me, just how many of you creeps are willing to serve that crusty old goat scrotum, and for what? A smidgen of his tainted aether?" I laughed, with every intention to infuriate him. From the look on his face, it was clearly working. "Your knees must have epic calluses from constantly slurping down his putrid seed!" It was juvenile, I know, but from the look of unbridled rage on his face, it was worth it.

"How dare you profane his Divine Lordship? He wields power like you cannot begin to fathom."

"Yeah, yeah, like the last time when he tried to use his 'power'." I chuckled, accentuating the word. "Yet here I stand, and his little statue and temple crumbled from his failed effort."

He was fuming, but I could also tell I had rattled him.

"Spouting lies will get you nowhere," he spat.

"There are far more powerful beings in this universe than your beloved goat scrotum but believe what you will. So, are we going to do this?" I asked, drawing my sword.

The inquisitor smiled and pulled the mace from his hip, no, not a mace, it was a fucking sceptre, with the imperial crest atop it. Mace or not, I still didn't want to be hit by it.

"Hannah, lead them away with Master, I will hold him here," I shouted and launched myself at him as fast as I could.

The man's aura was unbelievably heavy, and I feared he was a Saint, so I knew I couldn't hold anything back.

Wind-steps, focused strikes, I threw as much Qi as my body could bear into my techniques, as well as calling upon sword intent, augmenting my already frankly ridiculous physical strength as much as I could as I slashed at him. But the inquisitor blocked the strongest strike I could manage with casual ease and gave me a contemptuous smile. I was stunned and about to dis-engage, to try and use skill where surprise and strength had failed. But the next thing I knew, I was flying, and barely conscious as I tumbled end-over-end through the dirt. When I finally came to a halt, I wanted to rise, but I couldn't think straight, my head was spinning, my vision blurred. I could tell I had a concussion and bits of me were broken. I coughed and pain ripped through me, sending frothy blood all over myself, fuck, punctured lungs again then. I tried to move and realised it wasn't just bits, rather most of me that was broken, and I knew I was dying. It was a shit way to find out where I fitted on the totem pole, my natural gifts had allowed me to fight above my level before, so perhaps it had made me a little conceited, I mused. I struggled fighting Reynard after all, who'd been a Sage, at least until the buffs were cast upon me. But that was before I reached spirit knight, I just hadn't realised how far outmatched I would still be by a Saint, it was humbling, but it was too late for regrets.

I was starting to struggle to breathe as I watched the inquisitor slowly approach, fuck me, he had launched me at least a hundred metres and I had carved a pretty decent furrow into the forest floor, no wonder I was so banged up. There was nothing I could do, except watch and he didn't even seem to care about the others, his eyes focused solely on me, his shit-eating grin a testament to how much he was enjoying seeing me in such a state. I refused to struggle, I wouldn't give the wanker the satisfaction, especially as I was largely incapable of much more than squirming.

I was suddenly felt a large flux of aether to my left and it took a monumental effort to turn enough to look, damn spinal injuries! Master was literally glowing, the surrounding aether flooding towards him as he finally succeeded in forming his core, Master was a sage! I was glad I got to see it before I died, Master deserved it. At least they now had a chance of escape. The inquisitor stopped his stroll towards me and turned to face him.

"Oi, Goat-sucker," I choked out, "It's me you want." The blood-spitting effort leaving me even more short of breath.

"Yes, but as much fun it is watching you suffer, it will be even sweeter to see the look of anguish on your face as your fr…"

His spiel was interrupted by Master hitting him like a fucking freight train, however my moment of joy at the sight was tempered almost immediately by the stark realisation that even as a freshly risen Sage, he would have little chance against the inquisitor. The two of them impacted into one of the giant trees with such force, that they left a crater in the monstrously hard bark. Even with the pain I was in, I found myself wincing, that had to hurt! Master was using all his strength to bearhug the stunned inquisitor and keep him trapped in the crater.

"Make me proud, son," he yelled, and I was filled with dread, he had never intended to fight the man. The inquisitor realised too and struggled ferociously to try and get away, but being partially embedded in the tree, Master had him held tight. He forced his fingers into Master's flesh, desperately attempting to free himself, but Master just roared and held on until there was suddenly a monumental bang and flash of light. The concussive wave came towards me, and I knew I wouldn't survive. I closed my eyes to welcome death's embrace, hopefully it would be quick.

I felt the blast wash past me, but it didn't hit me, I briefly wondered why, but the rushing wind sounded so pleasant, and it was getting hard to think, so I just let the sound carry me away. I was vaguely aware of someone holding my mouth, maybe I was drinking? Choking? Then, I was somewhere else.

Disembodied, my consciousness floated in an infinite void, my only company the distant stars. Suddenly, the stars began to grow larger and brighter until they were so bright, I had to close my eyes. I had eyelids! No, not just eyelids, I could feel my body was back, but there was no pain. What the fuck was going on? The light slowly began to dim, and I risked opening my eyes, squinting as the light resolved into a wood panelled wall with a small window to the star filled void outside. I looked down and inspected my standing body, pleasantly surprised that there was no sign of injury. Definitely not in Kansas anymore, Toto!

I was interrupted from my self-inspection, by a cough from behind me, instinctively I grabbed my sword hilt before turning around, which was weird as I was sure I wasn't wearing a sword a second ago. As I spun around, I was confronted by a large fireplace with two armchairs beside it, the left hand one held a man I didn't recognise, but who looked oddly familiar.

He was holding a wineglass and gently placed it down upon a small coffee-table, one that I swear wasn't there when I first turned around. "You won't need that, my son." He smiled.

"Where did the table come from?" I asked.

"What table?" He winked at me.

I looked down to his side and saw that both the table and wineglass were gone.

I felt like I was losing my mind and took a few steadying breaths.

"It does take a little getting used to," he said.

"What's going on?" I asked, keen to understand why everything was so weird.

"Other than your consciousness and this sliver of mine, nothing in this place truly exists, well, at least outside of our will or awareness. There is no intrinsic object permanence."

Well at least that sort of made sense. "But I was still aware of the table? Shouldn't it have stayed?"

The man slapped his leg. "Excellent, you got me, I willed it away to illustrate the strangeness of this place."

I made to sit in the other armchair and took a sip of the ice-cold can of coke. It was delicious.

"You catch on quick, and that leads me rather nicely me to another point, you must keep control of your thoughts in this place, it can quickly go wrong."

He was right, imagine if I'd been thinking about a seventy foot—

"School your thoughts, son!" he said, thankfully interrupting my chain of thought.

"So how come all of this." I gestured to the room around us. "Is permanent?"

"It's not," he replied. "All of this is held in place by my will, to give us somewhere to speak in person, so to speak."

"Seems a bit risky, a stray thought and it will turn into a right shit-show."

"Shit-show," he slowly repeated. "Quite a colourful turn of phrase, but yes, you're correct. I originally had no intention of communing with you until you cultivated your own stable soul space. Except then you went and died, and so I was forced to improvise. Hence, we find ourselves in a temporary construct inside your soul."

"I died then?" I asked, strangely at ease about the idea.

"Well, technically." He smiled. "But no son of mine will be killed quite so easily. Although next time, you won't be so lucky."

"Can't have you bailing me out all the time, I guess." I chuckled mirthlessly.

"You misunderstand, it wouldn't be that I am unwilling, rather that I am unable, this is but a tiny sliver of my consciousness that I placed inside you to assist with unlocking your bloodline, unfortunately, even with assistance, reviving you took most of the power with which I was imbued."

"Why couldn't you come and get me? I was alone for so long, I had no-one." I knew I was whingeing, but I wanted to know why I was abandoned.

"For me to come down to your plane would cause catastrophic damage, I'm sorry, but know that you are loved, and both your mother and I hoped you would be able to reach me someday," he said wearily.

At first, I thought my eyes were playing tricks on me, but as it got progressively worse, I noticed that my father was starting to grow translucent.

"I don't have long left, son, be quick if there is anything you need to ask."

"Is my mother with you?"

"I don't know, she left to bring you back to the lower realms. If she is not with you, I have no idea where she is."

"How do I fully unlock my bloodline?"

He was getting fainter and fainter.

"Become more powerful, the journal will help."

"What are you? Who are you?"

"Pr...Sec...ord, Jer..."

The sound was intermittent, like a poorly tuned radio, soon no more sound was coming from his lips, gods damn it!

He smiled as he faded away, and I was overwhelmed with emotions, happiness that I got to meet my father, but frustration too as there was so much more I could have asked, and I wish I would have thought to hug him. The room faded as he did, and I was briefly back in the void, before my thoughts grew sluggish and unconsciousness took me.

Chapter 40

When I awoke, I was disoriented for several seconds as my brain reconciled where I had been with where I was. Looking around, I realised that I was back in my own bed, in my suite at White Manor. How did I get here? I noticed a warm lump next to me and looked over, it was Ellie! Her arm was draped across my stomach, and I gently stroked the hair from her face, trying not to wake her. I thought about Master, and I was sure he was gone, the only explanation for what happened was that he detonated his core. After such a long time trying to form it, he immediately used it to sacrifice himself and save us all, I began to weep for my mentor and friend. I was no stranger to grief, but he would be sorely missed, so I let the tears flow. Despite my best efforts, my quiet sobbing had woken Eleanor.

"I'm sorry," I said, wiping my eyes. "I didn't mean to wake you."

"Don't be," she said, gently kissing me. "Hannah told us what happened, I'm so sorry."

"Hannah's here?" I asked, "and the others?"

"Yep, she carried you all the way back, you were in pretty bad shape."

I thought about Hannah's betrayal, I'd be lying if I said I didn't harbour any resentment. Master would still be alive if. No. I refused to get caught up in that toxic spiral. She was just trying to save her mum, it was a shitty situation and she'd lost her mum anyway, besides, she'd apparently saved my life, or at least helped to. I decided to make sure I would be there for her, grief and guilt were an awful combination, I would know.

I smiled at Ellie. "I missed you," I said, kissing her. "I love you, Eleanor Harris."

"I love you too, Josh."

Then we were in each other's arms, and it was all a blur, both of our first times, a little awkward, and driven by a bittersweet combination of love, reunion, and grief. It was completely spontaneous, but I wouldn't have changed it for the world.

Afterwards, as we lay in each other's embrace, Ellie filled me in on what had happened since I returned. I had been asleep for three days and Ellie had been by my side for most of it, caring for me. Apparently, she had developed a good level of finesse with her water magic, enough to keep me clean. Mikey had been in nearly as often, eager to make sure I was okay and so had Tilly and Stelman. I was thankful to have such good friends and a girlfriend like Ellie. Despite my pain, I was blessed, and it was good to remind myself of that.

"We should probably get dressed and go see everyone, they'd want to know you're okay," Ellie said.

"Maybe we could..." I started and kissed her.

Despite how much we'd enjoyed ourselves, eventually we realised just staying in bed any longer would be plain mean and so we headed to the shower to get cleaned up, which proved to be a bad idea as the sight of Ellie's beautiful body in the shower, just delayed us even further. God damn, I was like a dog in heat, and I needed to exercise some self-control. Eventually, after the 'vigorous' shower, we dressed and made our way downstairs.

Everyone was in the dining room eating lunch when we walked in, apart from Hannah, who after handing me over to Felix had apparently refused to leave her room. Upon seeing us, Mikey was on his feet immediately and bowled me into a fierce hug.

"I missed you too bruv." I chuckled.

Still gripping my shoulders in his arms, he stepped back a little. "Don't take the piss." He scowled. "You were in a right state, we were all worried about you."

"Sorry. You're right," I said sheepishly.

"I did come up to check on you earlier, but from the sounds in your room, I could tell you were busy!" He winked conspiratorially.

I could tell my cheeks were flushing and I saw Ellie's were the same, I don't know why he winked, it was clear to the entire room what he was fucking talking about. Luckily, we were saved from our embarrassment by Felix clearing his throat as he approached.

"It's good to see you back on your feet, Master Josh," he said stoically, pointedly ignoring Mikey's comment, what a legend!

I wasn't willing to settle for that though, he was more than just a butler to me. He was my friend and I swept him into a hug. Letting him go, I gave him a second to re-compose himself, which he did the same way he did just about everything else, with quiet understated dignity.

Even Stelman and Tilly wanted hugs too, which was cute, whilst everyone else gave me friendly nods and we settled into lunch, everything back to normal. Well, almost, I still had Hannah to deal with. Everyone regaled each other with tales of our exploits in our time apart, and when I filled them in about the demon and my other fights, I spent the following five minutes receiving lectures on taking unnecessary risks, which I took on the chin, it was only because they cared.

Ever the consummate professional, Felix had already begun to organise places for those old enough, giving his tacit approval for my network of 'eyes' to start being seeded around the country. Some of us could feel the Master Bronstad shaped hole at the table, but such is life, and we all just had to carry on, he was gone but not forgotten.

After the excitement calmed down, I asked where Hannah's room was, and excused myself from the table to go and speak with her. Ellie offered to come too, for which I was grateful, but giving her hand a gentle squeeze, I told her it was something I needed to do on my own.

I knocked on Hannah's door. "Come in," she said quietly from inside.

Hannah was sat on her bed looking out across the grounds, it was a lovely view of the gardens, and she didn't even look over as I took a seat beside her. I saw her tense up as I sat, and I knew she was dreading what I'd say, so I didn't say anything, just put an arm around her shoulder and pulled her into me. Her initial stiffness quickly sagging as she began to sob.

"I'm so sorry Josh, I...I was so scared, I didn't know what to do, I..." she rambled, trying to explain herself.

Letting go of her, I knelt in front of her and grasped her by the shoulders. "Stop, just stop," I said firmly.

Her chest heaving, she looked at me with a face full of shame and grief awaiting me to berate her. I could also tell she wanted me too and was feeling like she deserved it. But that wasn't going to happen.

"What was she like?" I asked.

Ignoring my question she continued, "Master Bronstad, it's all my fault, if I hadn't..."

"Stop," I said, slightly louder, squeezing her shoulders more firmly.

There was a brief instant of panic on her face, before she took control of herself, awaiting what was to come.

"What was she like?" I gently asked again.

I could tell she was getting angry, she wanted me to scream at her, blame her for what she did. The guilt was eating her up and she wanted to be punished, but I was her friend, and was determined to give her what she needed, not what she wanted.

"You should hate me, I got him killed, I got my mother killed," she started ranting, but when she saw I gave no reaction, she changed tactics. "You're why my mother was killed, I hate you," she screamed and slapped my face.

I'm not going to lie, it stung, not the slap, but her words. Whether true or not, I was a big part of what happened to her mother, and I guess I was also carrying some guilt around for that. I clenched my teeth to stop myself reacting from my own pain.

"Stop this Hannah, it's not going to work, the whole thing's awful but I'm not to blame and you're not to blame. It was a bunch of pricks, who were willing to do anything for the promise of power from an even bigger prick, and we were just caught up in it. Could we have done some things differently? Maybe? Maybe not? Sometimes shit happens and we just have to do the best we can. I refuse to have a victim mentality about it, what about you?"

"I want them to pay," she said, the rage evident on her voice as she clenched her fists. Which was good, I just needed to channel her anger in the right direction and without her losing herself to it.

"As well you should, I want them too as well, but a wise man once told me that even if you want revenge, you shouldn't let it define who you are, it's just another task of many in your life. So, as much as I want them to pay, I want to ensure the safety of our friends in that realm even more," I said, "It's just nice that the two coincide," I added with a smile, which Hannah begrudgingly returned.

We sat there in companionable silence as I let her process what I'd said, and several minutes passed before she found her voice again. "It was Ingmar, wasn't it? Who said that?"

I could feel a tear roll down my cheek, as I nodded in affirmation.

"He was a good man, I'm sorry," she whispered.

"I know, I'm sorry too, thank you for saving me," I said.

"What are friends for?" She nudged me with her shoulder.

"So…what was your mum like?"

And so, Hannah told me all about her mother, and we laughed and cried together, healing a little more in the process.

Epilogue

Everyone allowed me a day or so of normality to decompress before letting me know what was happening with Earth, for which I was grateful, as it was not great. Aether levels had kept rising at an ever-increasing rate and although it still hadn't reached critical mass, more and more strange occurrences had begun to be reported.

Many were relatively benign, such as houses mysteriously tidied overnight, gardens beautified and in full bloom, and some were positive, such as the numerous tales from hospitals of people mysteriously healed, often from terminal afflictions.

Others were more malevolent, mass disappearances had started to become regular occurrences, in one particularly extreme case, the population of an entire town. Reports of terrifying creatures were also becoming more common, often with video footage of the event. Some had even made the evening news, such as the sinking of a cruise ship in the Atlantic, the few survivors and eyewitnesses swearing it was the work of a huge tentacled creature. Which meant some sort of Kraken had already awoken, and I knew if that was the case, then it was only a matter of time before more creatures from myth and legend appeared, and Earth definitely not prepared for it.

A few people had already started to develop 'abilities', with YouTube videos and TikToks popping up of them in action. As usual most of the comments were decrying the videos as fake, and some were, but not all, not by a longshot. People had started awakening

Religious nuts were loudly exclaiming it to be the start of the end times, an opinion that was gaining more traction than it should have, largely due to how woefully uninformed people were about the real cause. If something wasn't done soon, it wouldn't be long before society collapsed into mass panic and hysteria, which would only compound the situation. The whole thing was quickly devolving into a complete clusterfuck, and I had no idea where to start to help. Plus, as if Earth wasn't complicated enough, I still needed to help stomp out the Demon's influence from Antanel, an influence that had spread to the very highest echelons of the empire. It was…overwhelming!

I suddenly heard footsteps rapidly approaching down the hall before Mikey burst through the door without even bothering to knock.

"Josh, we need to get to town now!"

Mikey wasn't one to panic easily, so I knew it was something important. "Calm down bruv, what's going on?" I asked.

"Your sister, Josh, your fucking sister, she's been seen in town!"

The End
Josh and friends will return in Book 2 – Resurgence

Printed in Great Britain
by Amazon

26161196R00185